A girl's

Five-year-old Rosie Carter had never known
her real father. But when she and her mother
went to visit the Double O Ranch, Rosie
couldn't help wishing for a dad like rancher
Adam Garrick. Little did she guess that some
wishes *could* come true....

Bernadette "Bennie" Grant loved
ranch life...until her blue-blooded
grandmother came for a visit, insisting
Bennie be taught the social graces.
Trouble was, Bennie's nanny, Lucky Myers,
was even less of a lady than Bennie!
But Bennie's dad sure seemed to like her....

Daddy's Little Cowgirl

A chip off the old block...

Relive the romance
By Request
Two complete novels by your favorite authors

JUDITH BOWEN

was born in Edmonton, Alberta, and grew up in a logging camp in the Rocky Mountain foothills. She had many friends who lived on farms and ranches, a fact to which she attributes her love of the outdoors, not to mention her fascination with cowboys. Judith currently lives in British Columbia with her own hero and their three children.

KIMBERLY RAYE

has always been an incurable romantic, so writing romance novels is the perfect job! At the moment, she's hard at work on her next, hot love story for Harlequin's ultrasexy Blaze series, featuring her favorite type of hero—a rough-and-tough cowboy with tight jeans and a killer smile! Born and bred in the Lone Star State, Kim still lives deep in the heart of Texas with her very own real-life cowboy, Curt, and her young son, Joshua.

Daddy's Little Cowgirl

Judith Bowen
Kimberly Raye

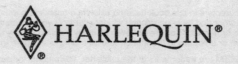

HARLEQUIN®

TORONTO • NEW YORK • LONDON
AMSTERDAM • PARIS • SYDNEY • HAMBURG
STOCKHOLM • ATHENS • TOKYO • MILAN • MADRID
PRAGUE • WARSAW • BUDAPEST • AUCKLAND

HARLEQUIN BOOKS

by Request—DADDY'S LITTLE COWGIRL

Copyright © 2001 by Harlequin Books S.A.

ISBN 0-373-21719-6

The publisher acknowledges the copyright holders of the individual works as follows:

LIKE FATHER, LIKE DAUGHTER
Copyright © 1998 by Judith Bowen
GETTIN' LUCKY
Copyright © 1998 by Kimberly Raye Rangel

This edition published by arrangement with Harlequin Books S.A.

Visit us at www.eHarlequin.com

Printed in U.S.A.

CONTENTS

He was always a father.
Now he had to learn how to be a dad....

LIKE FATHER, LIKE DAUGHTER
Judith Bowen

CHAPTER ONE

THE FINE JUNE MORNING Dot Wolinski came all the way up the lane with the letter from Beau's widow was a morning Adam Garrick knew he'd never forget.

Still, how different could that day have been from half a dozen hot dusty ones both sides of it? As soon as he signed for the envelope, as soon as he saw the Washington State postmark, he felt the bottom sink right out of his gut.

It was the same feeling he used to get when—too sore and too tired and maybe even too old—he'd climb on the last bull in the last event of the day in some no-name stampede. This might even be worse. The handwriting was spiky, as though the writer had been in a hurry. Definitely a woman.

He knew what woman. He'd seen her exactly once, the day she'd married his best friend eleven years ago.

Dot hung over his arm, busting with a curiosity he had no intention of satisfying. "Hot enough for ya?" She wiped her broad flushed face with the tail of her pale blue Canada Post-issue shirt.

"Gettin' there," Adam replied automatically slipping the letter into his shirt pocket. So far, June had been hotter than usual. Should he offer Dot a drink—iced tea, a can of pop, maybe? It was only neighborly.

Letter or no letter, he decided there was no way out of it. "Cold drink, Dot?"

He could see powerful forces of indecision on her face.

On the one hand, he knew, she yearned for the chance to pump him about the mysterious letter; on the other hand, coming up his lane must have set her back this morning. She had the rest of her route to cover. Many ranchers and farmers in the area rented post office boxes for their mail these days, but the Garrick ranch still enjoyed rural route delivery. Dot Wolinski was a stickler; she liked to think folks on her route could set their clocks by the red flag going up on their mailboxes every morning.

"Sounds awful good, Adam, but I'd best be on my way," she finally said. Then, a long shot—after all, registered generally meant *some* kind of trouble, woman or otherwise. "Hear anything from Helen lately?"

"Nope. Not a word." Hell, Dot would know. She brought the mail. She'd know before he did if his ex-wife wrote him. But Helen never did. After all, it had been six years since the divorce. Why would she?

Adam stifled the urge to snatch the letter from his pocket and rip it open as he watched Dot climb into her aging half-size Toyota pickup. He nodded casually in response to her departing wave.

Then he turned and walked into the dark cool interior of the ranch house, feeling blindly for the envelope. He was alone. It was the housekeeper's day off and she'd taken her daughter with her.

This wasn't supposed to happen. Ever. Beau's widow wasn't supposed to know who—or where—he was. She wasn't supposed to know *anything*.

Beau had promised him, dammit, that night the two of them had put back the better part of a bottle of rye whisky. He thought of the first time he'd seen Beau Carter, blond and skinny and not quite sixteen, clinging to a Kananaskis rock face way beyond his experience. He thought of Beau's big friendly grin as the rescuers arrived. Adam and a couple of the other park wardens had had to pick him off and take him to his campsite. Adam was older than Beau, by six or seven years, but they'd become friends. True friends.

Adam shook his head. He'd worked for the parks service for two years—could it be fifteen years ago already? Damn, some days he felt like thirty-seven going on a hundred. Still, big grin or no big grin, Beau Carter knew how to keep a promise.

But Beau was dead. Had been for nearly two years.

Adam tore open the letter and scanned it. Stunned, he let it drop onto the kitchen table.

Beau's widow was coming to Glory, and she was bringing her daughter with her.

Adam's daughter. The child he thought he'd never see....

"OPEN UP!"

Caroline froze at the thunder of fists on the outer door. *Please*...not again. Couldn't he leave them alone, even for one night? Hadn't he already made their life hell? How much more did Phil Carter require of his cousin's widow?

She grabbed the remote control and turned the sound off, illogically leaving the television to flicker silently in the corner. Then she held her breath, praying that Rose wouldn't awaken. She glanced at her watch. Nearly midnight. If she stayed quiet, perhaps he'd be fooled into thinking she wasn't home.

"Look, Caroline, I know you're in there. Maybe I can offer you some kind of a deal. *C'mon, open up!*" The door chimes clanged wildly in the near-empty room. Most of what she cared about was in storage. These sticks and bits of furniture still left—the armchair and sofa bed from a discount furniture outlet, the elderly television set, the boring table lamps one of Beau's distant relatives had sent as a wedding present—she didn't care what happened to them.

Tomorrow, come hell or high water, she and Rose were out of there.

Angry shouts. Then a few solid kicks on the heavy oak door that chilled her blood. So far he hadn't hurt her, not physically. But she didn't trust Phil Carter. She didn't trust any of the Carters.

Deal? Ha! What kind of deal could he possibly offer her? After everything he'd done to them these past few months? Maybe she shouldn't wait until tomorrow. Maybe she should leave right now, tonight, as soon as he gave up and left.

Just the thought of being free of Philip Carter—of all of them—the instant she got behind the wheel of the aging station wagon she'd hidden in a neighbor's garage made Caroline's heart race with crazy anticipation. To be free, finally free! She intended to leave the Jeep where it was— let Philip wonder what had happened to her. Let them all wonder. Her plan was simply to disappear. To take Rose and the cash she'd managed to scrape out of some forgotten accounts and head for Canada. She'd go see Sharon La-Salle, her old college roommate.

And Beau had a cabin he'd built years ago on land owned by that rancher Beau had always thought so much of, near some little town called Glory. Hadn't Beau always told her that regardless of what happened in his own life— and lots had, maybe too much—he could depend on Adam Garrick, no questions asked? She'd only met the man once, had a vague recollection of six feet plus of tough-looking cowboy. Hard face, hard eyes, a hard mouth. But his wife had been nice, as she recalled, although she couldn't re-member exactly what the woman had looked like. Why would she? That day she'd had eyes only for Beau...their wedding day.

She'd written to both Sharon and the rancher when she'd

made up her mind to go to Canada—registered, so she'd know the letters got there. She hadn't heard back from either of them yet. On the other hand, she hadn't expected to be leaving so soon.

It didn't matter. She could manage financially for at least a couple of months, if she found somewhere fairly cheap to stay. Maybe she could even live in Beau's old cabin for a while, if it was anywhere near habitable. It might even be fun. By then...well, maybe by then she'd have some answers about what had gone so wrong.

Poor Beau. He'd never been a businessman. He trusted people too much. He believed in everyone's dreams. He'd never have guessed that his own flesh and blood, his cousin, would be capable of such treachery to his widow and child.

Caroline felt a tiny shiver of panic, all too familiar these days. To think that less than two years ago she and Beau had been deliriously happy, still in love after a decade of marriage, overjoyed with the unexpected blessing of the child they'd never thought they'd have, living a more than comfortable life in one of Seattle's tonier suburbs. She'd been a Lake Washington mama, married to a man from one of King County's most prominent families. She'd had a housekeeper, money to travel, a car of her own.

The Carters. Sleek, prosperous, unquestionably civil—or so she'd thought. Had it all been a cruel joke? Or had she just been naive? Garden parties, a box at the symphony and home-plate tickets at the King Dome. A welcome—if not especially warm, still a welcome—for the girl their son had met on a Sun Valley ski holiday and married after a whirlwind three-week courtship. It was the kind of crazy romance that only happened in novels. The handsome prince marries the penniless college student he meets working in the ski-rental shop.

Now, at thirty-one, she was a widow. Beau was dead and

the Carters had turned their backs not just on her but on their only grandchild. Beau's cousin had done his best to ruin her and run her out of town. Well, Philip Carter had succeeded—for now. And as for the mammoth sorting-out task she'd left her lawyer, she wouldn't even have bothered if it hadn't been for Rose. She was fighting the Carters for Rose's sake, and she was running away for Rose's sake, too. No child of barely five should have to ask the kinds of questions her daughter was beginning to ask.

Questions Caroline was too miserable and too worn-out and too dispirited to even try to answer.

"*Goddammit, open this door, bitch!* If you don't talk to me now you'll be talking to the sheriff tomorrow. *I'm warning you.*"

Caroline held her breath and said nothing. Threats, Beau's cousin was full of them. And there'd be no sheriff. The house was still legally hers, on paper, anyway, until the end of the month. Even if Philip did plan to sell it then to repay what Beau apparently owed the family company.

Finally, after a few vicious oaths that she was pretty sure her mother-in-law had never heard from her buttoned-down Ivy League favorite nephew, she heard him stomp off the porch and slam into his car. Seconds later came the roar of a powerful engine and the squeal of tires on wet pavement.

She sat where she was for a few more minutes listening to the silence descend on her nearly empty house. She realized her hands were shaking. Her knuckles were white and her heart slammed painfully in her chest. What had they done to her these past few months? Hounded her and harassed her at every turn, blaming her for Beau's death and holding her hostage to Beau's debts. Succeeded in turning her from a happy trusting independent person to someone who practically jumped at her own shadow. Someone who, thank heaven, had had the sense to have all the locks changed a week ago. Just in case.

Caroline shut off the television and got to her feet. She walked quietly to the door of the bedroom where her daughter slept.

Her gift from God.

The window was open and the rain-soaked breeze off the lake gently lifted the violet-sprigged muslin curtains. Caroline drew a long shaky breath.

How she loved this little girl! How she prayed that she'd be strong enough and steady enough and calm enough to wage this battle for Rose. Caroline didn't want her child ever to know that so many of the people she loved had deserted her. Her grandmother. Nell. Uncle Phil and Auntie Jean.

"It's a question of blood," Beau's mother had said vaguely, fretfully, the one time Caroline had confronted her and demanded an explanation for what the family was doing to her and to Beau's daughter. A question of blood.

But it wasn't, whispered something deep and still in Caroline's heart as she gazed at her sleeping child. It was a question of love.

Love.

Couldn't they see that, any of them? She closed her eyes and clung to the door frame and let the tears flow unchecked. What she was doing—taking her daughter away from all she knew and loved—was exactly what she must do.

She'd held back too much for too long. Ever since Beau had died. She had to leave this place. There was no other way.

THEY COULDN'T HAVE PICKED a better time to travel. The late June orchards and vineyards east of the Cascades were thick with buds and blossoms. The ranchlands of northern Idaho were still soft and green with early-summer bunch-grass and sage, and wherever they looked white-faced calves galloped stiffly in twos and threes, tails high. Montana was wide open and glorious under big blue skies. Caroline had studied the map closely to make sure they went through Kalispell.

It was crazy, but she'd wanted to see Kalispell, Montana, ever since she'd read a Louis L'Amour Western that featured a hero who went by the name of the town. An orphan, no doubt; she'd forgotten the details. Kalispell. The very name whispered romance and the Old West.

They had lunch there, at a diner that had old-fashioned jukeboxes at each booth and served the biggest banana splits Caroline had ever seen. The fresh rough scent of sun-baked pines and chill mountain air took them into Glacier National Park, which bordered Canada's Waterton Lakes Park. Every hour behind them, every mile away from Seattle, eased Caroline's pain. Every giggle from the little girl beside her told Caroline she was headed in the right direction.

Even her decision to tackle Going-to-the-Sun Road through Logan Pass, the amazing road built in the thirties and seemingly pasted onto the side of the mountain with chewing gum and pebbles, was the right one. She fought her panic, terrified every inch of the way, sure that the brakes of the motor home in front of her would fail and they'd all roll back and plunge into the abyss below. *End over end over end. As Beau had done....*

But at the rest stop at the summit, where Rose chased butterflies among the mountain bluebells and gentians and buttercups and where Caroline sat and clasped her trembling knees and closed her eyes to the thin rays of the mountain sun, she knew that this decision, too, had been the right one. They needed to cross this mountain divide, she and Rosie. They needed to do something difficult. Something important. They needed to leave Seattle behind them, and Washington and the endless rain and all the Carters. They needed to breathe fresh new air and glimpse the faces of the mountain gods and remind themselves of simple pleasures.

Beau had loved the mountains. He said the mountains were where his spirit felt safest. Caroline had wondered at his choice of words. *Safest.* He'd loved climbing. And in the mountains he had died, broken and half-buried by the rock slide that had claimed him. It had been a miracle that his body was ever found. In some ways Caroline wished it hadn't been. Secretly she knew Beau would have preferred it that way. The ache of a funeral so long after he'd disappeared—seven months—and the publicity that surrounded it had been almost too much to bear.

And she believed that they had blamed her, somehow. That they felt marriage should have changed him. That if he'd loved her more, he wouldn't have taken off as he had done so often, disappearing into the mountains on long solitary treks with only the barest of plans.

Well, perhaps they'd been right....

Caroline squelched the thought. It was disloyal and it was untrue. Absolutely untrue. Yes, Beau loved the mountains, but so, too, did he love her and their daughter. She stood, brushing the fine grit from the backside of her jeans. "Rosie!"

"Oh, Mommy!" Rose was chasing what had to be the hundredth butterfly.

"Time to go, Rosie Red," Caroline said firmly.

For a moment Rose faced her, head down, hands on childish hips, in a characteristic pose that made Caroline smile. From this distance, she could get away with that smile. Then her daughter gave in and trudged toward her. Before she'd gone half the distance, her mood had swung from truculence to joy, and she ran the last twenty feet and jumped into Caroline's outstretched arms with a shriek.

Rose was small for her age and fine-boned, and Caroline was glad she didn't mind being picked up and carried by her mother. Sometimes. Once in a while—not often—Caroline allowed herself to wonder about Rose's biological parents, the strangers to whom they owed so much.

"Popsicle?" Rose wore her most winning, most hopeful smile. It was easy to forget that this wasn't Beau's child. She was so like Beau, in so many beloved ways.

"You bet. Soon as we get to the park gates." Caroline laughed and swung her daughter around and around until her head swam. Gray, blue, green, Going-to-the-Sun Mountain's stern visage on the other side of the abyss alternated with the summer green of the mountain meadow at the roadside pull-off and the impossible blue of the Montana sky. A sky like that...well, there just *had* to be a heaven.

They began the long smooth descent to St. Mary's Lake, nestled on the eastern slopes of the Rockies, the lake revered in ancient times by the Blackfeet and the Piegan. Most sacred of waters. Shining, mysterious, serene, unchanging.

Rose slept most of the way to the international border. And as Caroline drove through the foothills and into the prairies, mile after lonely mile, she counted her blessings.

CHAPTER TWO

"I DON'T GET IT, Adam." Balancing awkwardly, Lucas Yellowfly kicked the chair away from his desk with one foot and glanced at his friend. "Is this a legal problem?"

Lucas had a paper bag in his left hand and a hot covered cup in his right. That new coffee place wasn't going to last, he reflected—not in a town of two thousand souls, as the town fathers liked to put it. No way. But until it went belly-up, he was going to make sure he got his daily share of decent caffeine.

He sank into the leather swivel seat, which he'd managed to maneuever into its new position, and glanced at Adam again. Then, after a quick look to make sure the door between him and Mrs. Rutgers was firmly closed, he put both feet up on the glass-topped coffee table and unwrapped the Swiss-cheese-and-turkey-on-rye he'd picked up on the way back from the courthouse.

Mrs. Rutgers, bless her interfering little heart, was retiring this fall and Lucas couldn't really say he was dreading the event. He'd inherited her, along with the worn carpet and the chipped melamine bookshelves, when he'd bought into the practice a year ago. Mrs. Rutgers would be the first of the fixtures to go.

Lucas looked up. "I have to be honest with you. I'm not clear on what your problem is."

"Why in hell not?" Adam whirled.

"Whoa..." Lucas whistled softly. He could count on one hand the times he'd seen Adam Garrick lose his temper.

"Who's the goddamn lawyer here—you or me?"

"Me." Lucas took a bite of his sandwich and chewed thoughtfully, watching the tall man who'd turned again and begun to pace in front of the long window that faced the street. Work boots—some of the barn still on the heels, Lucas noted with his usual attention to detail—faded jeans, an ordinary plaid work shirt. Still, when had Adam Garrick ever cared about how he looked?

But, hey, was this any way to treat a buddy who'd managed to work him into his lunch hour as a special favor? Lucas had even slipped out of court early. But for Adam Garrick, his old hell-raising rodeo partner, he'd do it. If the problem couldn't wait. Whatever the problem was. It couldn't wait, Adam had snapped. Lucas had wondered at the urgency. Now he saw that Adam hadn't even bothered to change his clothes before he drove into town. Folks generally weren't in that much of a hurry in Glory, Alberta.

Lucas took another big bite of the sandwich, then frowned. Damn. He'd told the girl at the deli to hold the mayo. Somebody new. "So...*is* it a legal problem? You're going to have to fill me in."

"Could be. I don't really know." Adam turned to face him. He patted his shirt pocket absently, as he'd already done several times. Earlier he'd taken a piece of paper, a letter, well creased, out of that pocket and waved it at Lucas, then folded it up and stuffed it back in. "The kid's mine. That's what I'm trying to tell you. I want to know where I stand. What kind of claim she might have."

"Uh-huh." Lucas carefully pried the cover off his coffee. "The mother, you mean." Lucas had known Adam for nearly twenty years and, in that time, he'd seen him face a lot of scary stuff. Rodeo bulls. Ornery broncs. Do-or-die mountain rescues in the park service. Being flat broke, busted leg in a cast, and watching his wife walk out on him, that time for good. Right now, he was about as rattled as Lucas had ever seen him. About as rattled as Adam Garrick ever got. Not a muscle moved on his face. *That* was the giveaway.

"Yeah, the mother," Adam said heavily.

"Old flame?" Lucas ventured.

Adam shook his head. "No."

"You'd better tell me about it. From the beginning."

"It's a long story."

"So tell me."

"You recall Beau Carter?"

"Carter?" Lucas frowned. "Name's kind of familiar—"

"He wasn't from around here," Adam broke in. "He was from the States. I helped get him out of some trouble in the Kananaskis once, years ago. He was rock climbing, just a kid, sixteen or so. We ended up pretty good friends even though I was a fair bit older." Adam frowned. "A few years after that, I guess he might have been eighteen or nineteen, he looked me up. I was rodeoing at the time."

Adam paused and Lucas knew he was thinking of Helen. Helen had hated his rodeoing; she'd nagged at him to quit, to settle down, to give her the babies she wanted, to build up the Double O Ranch and turn it into a paying proposition. "And?"

"Well, anyway, damned if it didn't turn out Beau wanted to try rodeoing, too. He broke his arm that first summer and I packed him off home to Seattle. The next year he was back. Couple of good sprains early in the season, and then in July he broke his collarbone at the Pincher Creek Stampede." Adam shook his head and gave Lucas a crooked grin. "Old Scar. Remember him? He was one helluva horse. Weren't too many could stay on that old hay burner, and Beau Carter wasn't one of them.''

Lucas had the weirdest feeling that this wasn't just Beau Carter's story, this was Adam's own story. From what Lucas knew of him, Adam Garrick could have been that hell-raising kid himself.

''So, before I sent him back to Seattle that second summer I asked him just what he was trying to prove. He was no ranch kid brought up tough the way you or I were. He came from some rich family down there in Seattle. City boy. Money no object.''

Adam continued after a sharp glance at Lucas. ''What he told me was, well, he figured it was like he was already dead already or soon would be. He'd try anything, take chances—''

''Hold on. Dead? What's that supposed to mean?'' Lucas finished the last bite of his sandwich.

''He said he had something wrong with him—I forget exactly what. His dad had died of it when he was forty. His granddad, too. I don't know—'' Adam shrugged ''—guess the kid thought it'd get him eventually.''

He took a deep breath. ''To tell the truth, Lucas, I never paid much attention. How could a guy take something like that seriously? Beau was young, he seemed healthy enough, he had women hanging on him all the time. Hell, it was hard to see that he was suffering.''

Lucas smiled.

Adam's face clouded. ''But I guess it was true, considering what happened.''

''What happened?''

''I didn't see him for a while and then one day we got an invite to his wedding. Some hurry-up affair. I didn't want to go, but Helen did.'' Lucas knew what that meant—

Adam's ex-wife generally got what she wanted, except when it came to Adam's way of life.

"We went. I hardly remember it. Beau seemed happy. I don't recall anything about the girl he married except she seemed awful young to me. But then, they both did.

"Well, that was that. He showed up in Alberta maybe once or twice a year to ski some glaciers or do a little rock climbing. He was always alone. Sometimes he called, sometimes he didn't. Helen and I were beginning to have our problems and I had other things on my mind."

Adam stared out the window that overlooked Glory's dusty main street and didn't say anything for a few minutes. "Then about six months or so after Helen left for good, I got a call. Beau was at the airport and he was driving down from Calgary that night. Said he had a proposition to put to me."

Lucas realized Adam was finally getting to what had brought him into town this morning.

"Dammit, Lucas. I don't know how to tell you this. He wanted me to—to get his wife pregnant."

"He wanted you to *sleep with his wife?*"

"No. He wanted me to agree to, uh, provide the male side of it and they'd have it done properly by a doctor down there in the States."

"Properly?" Lucas wanted to grin, but he knew his friend wouldn't stand for it. "You mean artificial insemination?"

Adam said nothing.

Lucas put down his coffee. It was cold, anyway. "So, why didn't he get his own wife pregnant?"

"Because of whatever the hell he had that was wrong with him. He'd told me he had no intention of passing it on to some kid of his. When he came out to the ranch that night, he told me he'd fixed it years ago so he couldn't have any kids, not even by accident.''

"He had a vasectomy.''

"I guess so. Anyway, we got drunk and talked about all the good times we'd had and all the good times we were going to have and he did his best to talk me into it. He said he wasn't going to settle for some anonymous donor, some pimply-faced medical student getting his wife pregnant. He wanted me, figured I was healthy—or whatever. Damned if I know.''

Adam squared his shoulders and gave Lucas a hard look. "Well, the long and the short of it is I said no. It just seemed too far-fetched and crazy to me. I still don't know if what I did was right or not.''

Lucas could see the pain in Adam's eyes. There was more to this story, a lot more.

"So?''

"Yeah, well. So a few months later I went down to Seattle to pick up that Luger stud horse I bought—''

Lucas nodded. Adam had come back with a top-notch quarter horse stallion, which he'd bred to his own champion cutting horse mares.

"You're not going to believe this." Adam made an abrupt sound, an attempt, Lucas knew, at humor. "To make a long story short, while I was down there I screwed around with this woman, somebody who had a cabin next door to the Carters' on Puget Sound. She ended up pregnant. Beau knew. It's the goddamn stupidest business I ever got myself into, Lucas, I swear. The divorce had come through by then, so I did what I figured I should and offered to marry her. She wasn't interested. Said she wanted to finish college and had plenty of plans for the rest of her life and they didn't include me.''

Adam's voice was gruff. Lucas could tell he was forcing

himself to finish the story. "Anyway, she had the kid and—" He stopped abruptly.

Lucas had a pretty good idea what was coming next. "And your friend and his wife adopted the baby?"

"Yeah. Can you believe it?" Adam faced him fully, eyes anguished. "A private adoption. The...uh, the mother wrote and told me. She knew Beau and his wife wanted kids. She thought I'd be pleased the way it all worked out. That's the last I heard from her."

"And Beau? Is he still part of the picture?"

"He's dead. Over a year ago."

"Uh-huh." Lucas's mind was spinning. "The hereditary disease."

Adam laughed, a short bitter sound. "Hell, no. Beau never changed. Got himself killed rock climbing in the Cascades without a partner. No plan filed, no emergency supplies, nothing. The rangers found him after the snow melted in the spring."

"I see." Lucas stared at his friend. "And now his widow's coming here?"

Adam nodded and patted his shirt pocket again. "And her daughter," he said grimly. "*My* daughter."

"And you're wondering what your status is with regard to this kid? Your obligations?"

Adam said nothing for a moment or so. "I guess so," he said finally. "Beau promised he'd never tell her I was the one he'd asked about the AI business. His wife, that is. I don't think she knows about the...the other thing, either. Beau knew I was the father. He thought it was funnier than hell, considering."

Lucas was silent for a moment. "I'll look into this, Adam," he finally said. "But my first thought is that none of this is your concern. Beau was legally married, right? He and his wife went through all the hoops and adopted the baby legally, with the natural mother's full consent. She ever name you as father?''

Adam shook his head. ''I don't know.''

''It doesn't matter. Adoption records down there are sealed pretty tight, from what I've heard. So the mother really has no way of finding out even if she wanted to. In the eyes of the law, dead or alive, your buddy is the father, period. That's good. It's got nothing to do with you.''

''It's not *good* for me, dammit. *It's my kid!*''

''Yeah, yeah. You know that. The biological mother knows that. Technically, sure, it's your kid. But not legally. Besides, you don't think *she* suspects any of this, right? The widow?''

''I hope not,'' Adam said grimly.

''So? My advice is—'' Lucas balled up the wax paper he'd taken off his sandwich and, with a perfect arc, tossed it into the wastepaper basket on the other side of the room ''—don't tell her.''

DON'T TELL HER.

Adam gripped the steering wheel so hard his knuckles cracked. He was driving too fast. He glanced in the rearview mirror and eased off the gas pedal. He'd heard there was a new Mountie in town, a real apple polisher. That was all he needed, another speeding ticket, just when he was trying to get the summer season off the ground. The back of the pickup was loaded with supplies he needed to pack into the Tetlock cookshack before the first batch of dudes arrived on Saturday. He sighed. Rhonda Maclean, his office manager, was making the same noises she made every year about quitting. Damn, that woman got on his nerves.

And now Beau's widow coming to town. Couldn't be happening at a worse time. Adam recalled Lucas's big grin after he'd made that lucky toss back at his office.

Well, *of course* he wasn't going to tell her, was he? What did Yellowfly take him for—a *complete* idiot?

Fact was, he couldn't blame Lucas if he did. More than once over the past five years or so, Adam had cursed himself for being stupid enough to father a child accidentally. Completely irresponsible. Inexcusable. *At his age?* But the one time Beau had referred to it, in a letter a year or so after Adam's trip to Seattle, it hadn't seemed all that bad, the way things had worked out. Hadn't seemed all that terrible.

I can't tell you how much this means to me and the woman I love. I know you don't want to hear about it and I won't mention it again, I promise, but I want you to know Beau Carter's one helluva happy camper these days. I never dreamed family life could be so fine. Maybe you ought to give it another try, buddy.

Family life. Yeah, sure. Adam felt a pang. Sometimes it still hurt that Helen had walked out like she did. Not that he blamed her. And it wasn't that he missed her. Some days he had to think a couple of minutes before he could even recall what she looked like, and there were parts of her he remembered a lot better than her face. At least there hadn't been any kids involved, just Helen and him and a lot of hot sex between rodeos and no money most of the time. He knew he'd been hard to live with. He supposed it could have been worse; at least he didn't drink much or smoke or do drugs. And Helen for sure was no saint. Still, now when it was far too late to put the pieces back together again, he wished he'd made a little more effort.

The house always seemed so empty and he didn't know what he would've done if Mrs. T hadn't agreed to live in during the week. And Janie. Full-grown and a woman in years, but his housekeeper's youngest daughter would never be older than the eight or nine years she'd reached inside her head. He'd even gotten used to Janie and felt a kind of softness when he thought of her and her fat little face and her pudgy arms and her big gap-toothed grin.

Hell, didn't we all have our troubles?

Adam slowed down for the turnoff from the highway. Another eight miles and he'd reach the familiar gray-bleached pole sign, pointing the way to the Double O, home of champion Simmentals and cutting horses—and gateway to the Tetlocks. Adam had to admit Helen's idea of running trail rides into the Tetlock Mountain backcountry had paid off. But it wasn't his style. He was not a patient man. He hated the aggravation of dealing with overenthusiastic city folk who fancied themselves cowpunchers—"eco dudes" his foreman called them. There were summer schools now for roping, riding broncs, trailing cows... It was enough to make a real cowboy weep.

Most days he was torn between closing down the trail-riding operation altogether and keeping it going for the welcome shot of cash it brought into the Double O each year. Every fall he decided to close down and then every spring, when the phone calls started coming from the big Eastern cities—even Europe sometimes—he changed his mind.

He hadn't yet finished paying off the mortgage he'd raised on the place when Helen left. It was only fair: half for him, half for her. She took her half in cash. Next year he'd be clear—and free to do what he wanted again.

Next year. Wasn't that always the way? He'd been living in next-year country most of his life.

Adam's eyes narrowed as he drove down the long approach to the ranch yard. Was that a strange car in the driveway next to the house? Mrs. T usually parked her old sedan in the garage. Besides, it looked more like a station wagon than a sedan from this distance. Maybe Rhonda had dropped by to see what else she could extort from him before the season started. He had no idea what Rhonda drove these days. And damned if she was going to get any more money out of him, either. Or anything else.

It couldn't be Beau's widow yet. He'd received the letter just over a week ago; she'd said she'd be coming through toward the end of the month.

But it wasn't Rhonda's car. The minute he drove into the yard he saw that the overloaded middle-aged station wagon bore Washington State plates. Which meant the blond woman talking to Mrs. T on the veranda must be Beau Carter's widow.

Which meant... Adam felt his heart jam in his chest.

Which meant the kid with shiny black curls rocking madly on the lawn swing beside a gleeful Janie, a flip-flopping rag doll tucked companionably between them... that little girl must be his daughter.

CHAPTER THREE

HE COULDN'T TAKE his eyes off the kid.

Get a grip, Garrick, he thought grimly as he drove toward the gravel patch by the garage. *Get a grip.*

He sucked in a deep breath and reached for the door handle. Then, with his other hand, he settled his hat more firmly on his head and climbed out. *Paste a smile on your goddamn face,* he told himself as he walked toward the house.

"Hi!" The shrill appeal forced him to glance jerkily toward the lawn swing. Janie's short arm was raised in greeting, her round face wreathed in smiles. "Hey, Ad'm! C'mere."

He raised one hand in a casual gesture, ignoring the invitation. The little girl beside Janie eyed him curiously and pulled the rag doll securely onto her lap, wrapping both her arms around it. Dark curls, a sweet face... Adam started to sweat. *Did she look like him?* The swing was a good twenty yards away; he couldn't see her all that clearly.

Look like him? What the hell kind of notion was that? Adam forced his eyes straight ahead, to where Mrs. T and the girl's mother were talking on the porch. The blond woman had turned to him. He felt exposed, as though he didn't have a stitch of clothing on. Again he forced a smile and prayed that Mrs. T wouldn't notice anything out of the ordinary.

He wouldn't have recognized Caroline Carter if he'd

passed her that afternoon on Glory's main street. He'd rec-
ollected that she was blond, but not the way her hair shimmered and moved in the sunshine, like something alive. It
was just past shoulder length and she'd pushed tortoiseshell
sunglasses up onto her head, so that they framed her face
and exposed her eyes—warm, brown, a surprising contrast
to the pale honey color of her hair. She was medium height,
slim, with hints of womanly curves in all the right places—
Adam cursed himself for noticing—beneath the loose
T-shirt she wore over jeans.

Still, she had *that* look. Class. Money. Those sunglasses
were no throwaway drugstore model; those jeans didn't
look the way jeans did on other women. Well, that was to
be expected, wasn't it? Beau Carter was from a wealthy
family, and his widow certainly wouldn't be suffering in
that department. He frowned slightly, catching sight again
of the aging station wagon parked in front of the house.
He'd have thought she'd be driving something a little trend-
ier, a fancy new Suburban maybe....

"Well, look who's here!" Mrs. T beamed. "I was just
saying how you tore out of here before lunch and never
told me a thing. I had no idea when you'd be back—"

"Adam Garrick," Adam interrupted with a nod at the
visitor and Mrs. T. He held out his hand. "You must be
Beau's, uh—"

"I'm Caroline Carter," she said easily, and took his
hand. Her hand felt small and light in his. And warm. She
smiled and glanced at Mrs. T, then back at him. "I'm sorry
to drop in out of the blue like this," she said a little breathlessly. "We ended up leaving Seattle earlier than we'd
planned. We spent last night in Cardston and...well, I just
thought we'd stop by and say hello this afternoon."

Her voice was clear and quiet. For some insane reason
he thought of the way a perfectly shaped flat stone skipped

across a trout pool on the Horsethief on a summer day. Damn. He was wound up tighter than a two-bit pocket watch. Was it any wonder, considering?

"Good to see you," he said, taking a deep breath. *Did God keep track of these kinds of lies?* "We've been expecting you anytime now. Haven't we, Mrs. T?" He looked at his housekeeper. "I could use a glass of something cold and I'm sure Mrs. Carter could, too. What about..." He turned stiffly. "What about your, uh..."

"Please. Call me Caroline." Her quick smile did something dangerous to his spine, and he wished he knew what it meant. "A cup of tea might be nice. Thank you." She turned. "Rosie! Rose, darling. Come over here. There's someone I want you to meet."

Adam watched as the little girl climbed down from the swing and came slowly toward them, dragging her doll by one arm. Janie skipped heavily at her side, obviously delighted with the little visitor—for the time being. Janie's moods could swing from sunshine to thunder in seconds. Just now she was all smiles.

Ten feet away, the girl stopped and stared at him. *This child was his. His daughter.* One crazy weekend with a stranger, he'd made her. He'd always regretted that; how could he regret it now? She was real, flesh and blood. Her name was Rose. She belonged to him in a way that no one else on earth belonged to him.

"Come here, Rose," her mother ordered quietly, and the girl obediently trudged forward, then rushed the last few steps and buried her face against her mother's waist.

Caroline Carter laughed. "She's shy, I guess," she said with an apologetic look. She ruffled the child's dark curls and smiled. Adam couldn't tear his eyes away. If one of his Simmental bulls broke out of the back pasture and charged across the lawn right now, he still didn't think he'd be able to take his eyes from this woman and child.

"Rosie?" The child peered up at them, still clinging to her mother. "This is Mr. Garrick. Adam Garrick. He was one of Daddy's best friends. Remember me telling you about him?" The girl nodded solemnly. "Say hello, sweetie."

The girl whispered something Adam couldn't quite make out.

It was like a bucket of ice water dumped on Adam's head. *This was Beau's daughter. Not his.* He couldn't forget that. He didn't know what to say. He didn't know anything about kids. He'd never spent any time around kids and he'd never particularly wanted to, either. The child smiled a secret smile and hid her face again.

"Let's go in, shall we, girls? Let's get some lemonade." Mrs. T broke what Adam felt was a horrible silence. No one but him seemed affected, though. "I'll put the kettle on."

"Me, too! Me, too!" Janie crowed, and clambered laboriously up the steps. "C'mon, Rosie. C'mon!" Janie weighed in at close to 160 pounds on her four-foot-eleven frame, suffering from the obesity common to many Down's Syndrome children—for children they were, no matter their age. Rosie pulled away from her mother and dashed up the steps, reaching for Janie's hand, and the two of them followed Mrs. T into the cool dim interior of the house, giggling.

Which left him standing there alone with Caroline Carter.

"Look. I've got a few things I have to take off my truck before I join you." Another forced smile. "Is there, uh, anything you'd like me to bring in from your car?"

"Oh, no. I don't think so." Her eyes looked stricken.

"Don't let us interrupt anything you had planned for today, Mr. Garrick—"

"Adam."

"Adam. Okay. We'll just drive on. I have a friend in Calgary I'm hoping to see. I—I wouldn't dream of imposing on you, now that—" She stopped abruptly, abandoning whatever she'd been about to add. Blood had risen under her pale skin—was she uncomfortable, too, in this odd situation?

Had his reluctance been as plain as that? Adam felt ashamed of himself. What a jerk. He cleared his throat. "We're counting on you staying for a while, ma'am. You're more than welcome to bunk here at the Double O. As long as you like. It's a big house, plenty of room. We'd be happy to have you and—" he had to get this over with, had to *say* it "—your daughter. Mrs. T's got a couple of the spare rooms all fixed up for you."

"We-ell…"

Adam pressed his point. "Why don't you just go in and have that cup of tea or whatever, and you can make up your mind later."

She looked relieved. "If that's all right with you—"

"It's fine," he said roughly. "Whatever you decide is fine with me."

He walked with her to the door. As they made their way up the broad wooden steps of the veranda, she said softly, her eyes catching his, "I…uh, I had no idea that you and your wife were divorced. Beau never said anything. Your housekeeper told me just now."

Adam stared. Her blond hair had turned dark, caught in the shadow of the screen door as he held it for her to enter the kitchen. *She was a beautiful woman; his friend had been a lucky man.*

"I'm sorry—"

"Don't be," he said, and shut the door firmly behind her. "It's been six years. That's a long time ago."

SIX YEARS SINCE the divorce had come through.

Nearly seven years since Helen had given him the news: she'd had enough. Enough of his promises to quit the rodeo circuit, enough of being broke most of the time, enough of trying to run the ranch by herself. She'd had enough of everything—including, and maybe mostly, him.

He'd been home from the hospital just a day, after one of Swanipool's prize Brahmans had pitched him into a fence at the Strathmore Rodeo. He'd had his right leg in a cast, three ribs taped and a dozen stitches on his left shoulder where he'd caught a nail or something on the way down. He wasn't feeling good and it wasn't the kind of pain liquor could take away, either. When Helen walked out—she'd had her bags packed and sitting by the door for a week, she told him—he couldn't tell if he was glad or not.

In a way he was. He was sick of arguing and fighting with her. In a way he wasn't. She'd been the best thing that had happened to him for about as long as he could remember. Bad as their marriage had turned out, Helen and the Double O had given his life a center. Even on the road, chasing rodeos, he hadn't felt that big empty hole when he thought of home, like he had before. What was home, back in those days? The run-down foothills ranch he'd inherited from a bachelor uncle he barely knew.

His parents were dead; he hadn't seen his brother, who was in the army, for years. No, the number-one mistake he'd made was getting married in the first place.

Still, it had seemed like a good idea at the time, and Adam hadn't given matrimony a whole lot more consideration than he gave most things. It wasn't that you'd call him impulsive—more that he didn't give much of a damn about anything and was always primed for something new. Something unknown…even better, something dangerous. Rodeoing, rock climbing, chuck-wagon racing, white-water canoeing. That was why he and Beau Carter had gotten along so well.

Nobody'd told him marriage was the biggest risk of all.

Had he learned anything? Not much. The ink on the divorce was barely dry and there he was making an offer to marry someone else. Practically a stranger.

But a stranger who was pregnant with his child.

The weekend that had happened was just a blur in his mind. He'd driven down to Washington to see Beau and do some business. Helen had been gone awhile and he was just getting used to being alone again. He bought the horse he'd come down for and was celebrating with Beau at his summer place in Puget Sound when this woman who was staying in the cabin next door came over and…well, it was pretty hard to mistake what she had on her mind.

Cabin—hell! Cabin to him was that shack the other side of the back field he and Beau had knocked it together in a week during their spare time. The Carter place was more like a mansion. Nine rooms and a gatehouse. Housekeeper. Big launch moored out front.

He recalled Beau's neighbor vaguely from maybe a dozen years before, the gawky kid sister of someone he'd dated from time to time on other visits to see Beau, way before he married Helen. Gawky kid had turned into a knockout grown-up woman and Adam didn't need an engraved invitation. They'd had a hot three days, just the two of them, at her place next door after Beau had returned to his wife in Seattle.

His daughter had been conceived there. Rose.

An accident, pure and simple. But accidents happened,

and Adam was willing to take responsibility. He'd never run from consequences, not ever. It had been a blow to his pride when she laughed and turned him down flat and told him what a silly old-fashioned man he was and that she wasn't wrecking her life by marrying some Alberta cowboy just because she'd been dumb enough to get pregnant. He couldn't deny he'd been relieved. She wouldn't consider an abortion, and when the baby came, Beau and his wife had adopted her. Adam didn't want to know details. He didn't want to know anything. All he wanted was to shut the whole thing out of his mind.

And for nearly six years he'd had his wish.

ADAM FINISHED unloading his truck and headed back to the house. Janie met him at the door. Her eyes were wide and her small feet, amazingly nimble for someone her size, were practically tap-dancing on the kitchen linoleum.

"Rosie's stayin', Ad'm," she blurted, nodding and clapping her hands. "Little Rosie. She's my fren', Ad'm." She blinked her jet-black eyes several times, then opened them wide, as though to gauge his reaction. "They're gonna *stay!*"

"That's great, Janie," he said with a smile, and ruffled her hair.

She squealed and slapped at his hand playfully. "Stop it, Ad'm! Stop it right now!"

Great. Wasn't it? He'd had a change of heart while he was hauling his supplies off the truck. He owed it to Beau to do whatever he could for his widow, no question. As for the kid...she was his secret and would remain his secret. *Don't tell her,* Yellowfly had said. Caroline obviously didn't know anything about his connection to Rose, and she'd never find out. The best thing for everyone involved would be for him to forget it. Caroline had said she was on her way to Calgary; she probably wouldn't stay at the Double O more than a few days at the most.

Surely he could drum up a little enthusiasm for the sake of the buddy who'd shared so many good times with him.

He opened the refrigerator and pulled out a can of root beer, popping the tab as he walked to the living room. He heard Janie humming and skipping behind him. Yes. He was feeling better about this whole thing already.

Mrs. T had dug out some real china cups for their tea. She must have gotten the message that their visitor was used to the finer things in life. There was a lace cloth on the coffee table, which held a plate of cookies. Mrs. T had seen the Queen once, on a visit to the Calgary Stampede in 1958, and had never entirely recovered from the exposure to royalty.

The girl sat on the floor, cross-legged, and watched the cat wash herself. She didn't look up when he came into the room.

"So." Adam smiled broadly and Mrs. T gave him a narrowed glance. "Mrs. T looking taking care of you? Janie tells me you've decided to stay after all."

The woman sat perched on the edge of what Adam knew to be a very uncomfortable sofa. She nodded and set down her teacup. "If you're absolutely sure it's all right..."

"I'm absolutely sure. I'll go bring in your bags." He took a long swallow of his soft drink, aware that she was watching him. His voice sounded unnaturally hearty, even to his own ears. "Car open?"

"Yes. I've got the keys here for the rear door. It's very kind of you. It'd be lovely to stay here for...well, for a little while. A day or two. Thank you," she said quietly, and stood. She fished the car keys out of her jeans pocket and held them out to him. He jangled them lightly in his hand, aware of how warm the keys were—from her body.

From where they'd lain deep in her pocket, at the sweet warm juncture of thigh and belly....

Adam stepped back as though he'd been stung. What was he—nuts? He left the room, ignoring Janie's chatter and her demand to "look at her, see Rosie, see the kitty."

He shoved the screen door so hard it slammed back against the building, its spring protesting, and stepped out into the afternoon sun. Nuts? That wasn't the word for it. What was he doing even *thinking* those kinds of thoughts about Beau Carter's widow?

Hadn't he had enough trouble in his life?

CHAPTER FOUR

"Now, THEN." Mrs. T set a plate of bacon beside the platter of scrambled eggs on the table and drew up her chair opposite Caroline. "How long is your little holiday here in Alberta?"

Adam glanced up, feigning casual interest. Yes. He'd like to know that, too.

Since yesterday afternoon he'd been trying to piece things together. Nothing fit the way it should. The old car packed to the wheel wells, too many suitcases for a summer vacation, the pictures...

"Actually we don't have any deadlines, Mary," she said. "I'll have to see how long Rose puts up with me." She smiled. "And with traveling of course."

"Well, that must be nice!" Mrs. T beamed. "Not having anything to get back for, I mean."

Caroline nodded and reached for her coffee mug. Adam thought her cheeks seemed a little flushed this morning, her eyes bright. "It is."

She took a sip of her coffee, long lashes shadowing dark eyes. "We're looking forward to it. I—I haven't spent much fun time with Rose since...well, since my husband died," she finished quietly.

"My Lord, what a sad sad business that is. Losing a young husband like that." Mrs. T shook her head vigorously. "All those things you see on the television these days. What do they call 'em—adventure sports? It makes

my blood run cold, it does. I don't know what gets into
grown men who ought to know better—not to say nothing
bad about the dead, you understand, my dear.'' She patted
Caroline's arm reassuringly.

"Thank goodness Adam's given up all that craziness. I
always tell him, if he'd given it all up when he should've,
years ago, he'd still have a wife around here, someone to
take care of him. Maybe even a couple of little kiddies by
now, and he wouldn't have to keep fending off the likes of
that Rhonda Maclean, neither. And there's others, I know,''
she added darkly.

Adam remained silent, figuring it wasn't worth the protest. He'd heard it all before, many times.

"Some women plain can't resist the dangerous type,''
she added confidentially to Caroline. "D'you understand
my meaning? Can't seem to help themselves. Now take me.
Give me a clean-living, down-to-earth man like Mr. Tump
any day of the week. A *reliable* man.''

Mrs. T delivered another of her haven't-I-told-you-so?
looks, which Adam also ignored. He got up and poured
himself a second cup of coffee at the stove.

Down-to-earth and reliable? Mary Tump's small wiry
wind-burned husband spent eight months up on his trapline
in the hills behind Bragg Creek and the rest of the year
sitting silently whittling useless items out of diamond wil-
low on the porch of the Tumps's ramshackle homestead
over near Cayley, an area known as Tumpville to the locals.
If it wasn't for Mrs. T's steady work... He supposed you
could call Angus Tump reliable, all right. At least you knew
where the man was at all times.

His housekeeper squeezed Caroline's arm and smiled
warmly as he took his place again at the end of the table.
"Don't you worry, my dear. We'll make sure you and Ro-

sie have some real good times while you're here—won'
we, Adam?''

''Sure we will.'' Adam gave their guest a careful smile
Friendly. Helpful.

Caroline had on a blue skirt this morning and a white
blouse that buttoned down the front. It had short sleeves
and her arms were smooth and lightly tanned. She wore a
simple watch with a leather strap and no other jewelry but
a plain wedding band. Adam couldn't stop sneaking
glances at her when he was pretty sure she wasn't looking
He was fascinated. He kept thinking of her and Beau. A
quiet little creature like this? She seemed just about the las
woman he'd ever thought bold brash Beau would fall for
And, man, had he fallen. Adam recalled some of the letter:
he'd received back when Beau and Caroline were first mar
ried. He'd had a difficult time relating his friend's rapture:
to his own somewhat grimmer experience with the marita
state.

To each his own.

Adam reached for another slice of toast. Out of the cor
ner of his eye, he caught a glimpse of the child. *He had to
stop thinking of her as his daughter.* She happened to
glance up at him just then and giggled, hiding her face
behind her hand. The other hand was no doubt clutching
the rag doll that went everywhere with her.

Adam looked away. She was playing a game with him
but he wasn't sure how he should respond. He wasn't used
to kids. If he had his preference, he'd keep as much dis
tance as possible, both emotional and physical, between
himself and Caroline's daughter during the short time
they'd be at the Double O. No way was he going to star
playing peekaboo.

''Ad'm!''

"Janie?" He raised his head in response to Janie's shout from the other end of the table.

"You like Rosie, Ad'm? You like my new fren'?" she demanded.

Trust Janie. He'd seen it before: Janie Tump had an uncanny ability to pick up on what was going on around her—what was *really* going on.

"Of course I do, Janie," he answered evenly. "Rose is a fine girl. Good company for you."

Janie crowed with delight and immediately scrambled off her chair and trotted around to Rose's chair to smother the girl with a big hug. Rose giggled again. Adam was glad to see Janie diverted from that particular line of inquiry.

Watching them, he felt the odd sensation he often felt around Janie, that he'd do anything to shield her from those who could hurt her. Over the years since Mrs. T had come to work for him, Adam had slowly and reluctantly come around to regarding Janie the way her mother did—as one of God's innocent creatures set on this earth to be accepted and loved for who and what she was. No more, no less.

Like the magpies. Like the coyote pups, playing in the sun-warm sand in front of a hillside den.

He glanced away to see that Caroline was staring at him, a vulnerable look on her face, her mouth twisted in a small smile.

Damn. Adam pushed back his chair abruptly and stood. "I've got a lot to do this morning, Mrs. T. I need to get the rest of that Tetlock stuff organized and track down Rhonda if I can. If she calls here, take a message or send her out to the barn if she shows up. I'll try and be back for lunch." He strode to the kitchen door and reached for his hat, which hung on a rack beside the door. "Caroline?"

He swung to meet her inquiring gaze. "Feel free to do what you want while you're here. Any of the boys will saddle a horse for you if you want to ride. Maybe I could show you around this afternoon.'' He shrugged. ''Is there anything in particular you'd like to do?''

''Oh, no. I wouldn't want to interrupt your work.''

''I've always got time for visitors,'' he said gallantly, ignoring Mrs. T's skeptical expression. ''Anything you'd like, just ask. I'd be pleased to show you what I could.''

''There is one thing,'' Caroline said slowly. He saw the appeal in those brown eyes, the flash of pain, and braced himself for whatever was coming next.

''What's that?''

''Beau told me he built a cabin somewhere nearby. If it's not too much trouble, I'd like to see it while I'm here.''

The cabin. Adam faltered for only a split second. ''Sure. No problem.'' He opened the screen door and nodded. ''I'll take you there this afternoon.''

Adam frowned as he walked toward the barn, determined to put his guests out of his mind. He could have wished for better timing with this visit. He had a million things to do. Where in hell was young Ben, the new wrangler, for starters? He was supposed to be bringing some saddle horses down from the Winslow place this morning. Rhonda. He had to get hold of her. Nail down terms. Then he had to call the co-op, finalize a big food order that had to be airlifted into the Tetlock camp. Normally Rhonda would have handled that, but where was she when he needed her?

Women. Trouble. Maybe not for other men, but they'd mostly meant trouble for him. No question, life dealt some damn strange hands from time to time. For a man who generally went out of his way to stay clear of women— well, most of the time, anyway—he'd sure ended up stuck with a houseful.

Beau's widow here, sleeping under his roof, in the bed-

room down the hall. He still couldn't believe it. Mrs. T
with her gossip's eye, alert to anything—he'd have to
watch out he didn't let anything slip. She knew him better
than Caroline did; she might see something Beau's widow
would miss. Then there was that damn Rhonda Maclean
keeping him dangling as usual, and the first Tetlock guests
due to arrive in just over a week. Well, he already had the
bookings for the first two weeks confirmed. No leverage
for Rhonda there. He'd have to see what happened after
that if it turned out she wasn't bluffing this time.

Even the small fry around the place were female—Janie
and Rose. Sure, he knew Janie was no kid at nineteen, but
she was a kid inside her head, where it mattered.

Adam pulled back the big sliding doors to the barn and
stepped inside. For a few seconds he stood still, allowing
his eyes to adjust to the dimness after the bright morning
sunshine.

Beau's widow. What was going on with her? Yesterday
afternoon he'd carried in four suitcases. There were still
half a dozen piled in the station wagon. Who took a vacation with that kind of luggage? And then, last night, when
Caroline had come and rapped on his office door at ten
o'clock and asked him if he'd mind, please, going out to
the car and getting Rose's whale. It was her bed toy, Caroline explained, all earnest and polite and tired-looking in
her long robe and slippers, her hair freshly brushed. Rose
wouldn't settle down without it.

Adam had wanted to reach out and touch that pale
smooth hair. He'd restrained himself of course, blaming the
impulse on too many months without a woman, and agreed
to go fetch the toy. Then, when he'd managed to find it,
just where she'd said it was in a box with other things, he'd
inadvertently dropped some of those things on the ground.
Photographs. Pictures of Caroline and Rose and Beau. A

young handsome Beau—Adam felt his gut clench in grief, an ache that never really left him. A smiling baby. *Rose.* A beautiful blond woman with merry eyes.

Cursing, Adam stuffed the pictures back in the box. Something about this business stunk to high heaven. Something was definitely not right.

Who in hell went on a trip and took along all their family photographs?

ADAM DIDN'T SHOW UP at lunch. Caroline spent part of the morning playing Go Fish with Janie and Rose in the sunny veranda that ran along one side of the house. Before that, Mrs. T had set a batch of bread to rise and then, as Caroline and the girls became involved in their card game, had started pies. Four of them. Two lemon and two rhubarb.

Caroline had watched her knead the big dishpan full of bread dough and smiled when she gave the two girls each a piece of dough. Rose was delighted with the new experience and had poked and prodded and squeezed, ignoring Janie's patient instructions. Now several very misshapen, rather grayish lumps of dough rested in a greased muffin pan, awaiting the oven.

Mrs. T fielded phone calls between her various kitchen duties, and once, after they'd gone to play cards, she called to Caroline to please get the door because she had her baking pans in the sink and soapsuds to her elbows.

There'd been a slim, gum-chewing, boot-wearing, black-haired young woman on the porch.

"Hi! Where's Adam?" she'd asked cheerfully, and when Caroline asked to whom she was speaking, a little taken aback at the brash question, the girl had thrust out a slender tanned hand. "Rhonda Maclean. Pleased-ta-meetcha. Who're you?"

"Caroline Carter," Caroline had said, amazed to find herself replying.

"Uh-huh. Just visitin'?" The question seemed casual, but the blue eyes were alert.

"Yes. Just visiting for a day or two."

"Fine. Great. Where's Adam?" she repeated, shifting her gum to the other side of her mouth and raising one hand to shade her eyes and glance toward the barn. "He down at the barn?"

"Who is it, dear?"

Caroline was about to answer when Mrs. T appeared beside her, wiping her hands on a kitchen towel.

"Oh, Rhonda. Adam figured you'd show up one of these days," the housekeeper said with an edge to her voice. "He's over at the barn, in the storeroom. Said to go straight down there when you got here."

Mrs. T shook her head as the young woman clattered down the porch steps and strode jauntily off, waving at one of the young cowboys Caroline could see working with some horses in a corral a short distance away.

"That's Rhonda, all right," she muttered. "Two days late on the job and giving Adam nightmares about quittin' before she even gets started. She puts him through this every summer," she added enigmatically with an apologetic glance at Caroline. "Never mind me. You go on back to the girls. We'll have a cup of tea in a few minutes when the kettle boils."

After lunch Caroline settled Rose on the crazy quilt that covered the child's narrow painted-iron bed. Rose drifted off to sleep almost immediately. Caroline lay for a while beside her and watched the shadows the leaves made on the wall, feeling the gentle, peculiarly maternal kind of happiness she'd almost forgotten was possible. Her sleeping child nestled against her. The quiet. It was so quiet here at

Adam Garrick's ranch, she heard only the occasional sound of a calf bawling or a dog barking in the distance. And some strange noise a bird made outside the screened open window.

Rose didn't nap anymore, not regularly, but when she was tired, as she'd been since they'd started traveling, she seemed to welcome her afternoon rest again. Because Rose was napping, Janie insisted on having a nap, too. Mrs. T laughed and said she'd never sleep, then urged Caroline to take the opportunity to go for a walk by herself.

"The girls will be fine, my dear," Mrs. T said, seated in her rocking chair with one eye on her knitting and the other on her favorite soap opera. "Take your time. I'll look out for Rose if she wakes up."

The dust was hot under the soles of her sandals and squirted up in tiny puffs as she walked. Behind the house was a pole-fenced meadow with a small stand of trees on the far side. She'd seen the trees earlier from the window of the room she'd slept in. Poplars and willows and mountain ash.

Caroline made her way slowly toward the trees, plucking at the long grasses as she went. Daisies bloomed in clumps and she caught the sweet scent of wild roses and clover on the wind. When she reached the trees, she sank down beside a big cottonwood, leaned against the gnarled trunk and clasped her knees. She nibbled on the end of a stem of bromegrass.

From this angle, she could see the room Rose occupied on the second floor. Her own room was beside it. Flies and grasshoppers buzzed intermittently, hidden in the grass. The sun shimmered on the green of the meadow and the red asphalt tiles of the roof.

Caroline felt tension seep from her body into the sun-warmed ground. It was as though she'd been wound up for so long that she'd forgotten what it was like to feel such peace. And safety.

Yes, and safety. It was a feeling she hadn't had since Philip Carter started to make her life miserable, back before Beau's body had even been found. She'd felt so alone all these months. She'd ached that she couldn't shelter her daughter from things a girl of five shouldn't have to think about.

Now. How very strange to be here where Beau had spent so many weeks and months long before she'd met him. Where, still a teenager, he'd built the cabin he'd been so proud of and where he'd grown to know the man he'd admired so much.

Caroline shivered. She couldn't help it. Somehow, despite all the times Beau had talked of the Double O, she'd never quite pictured it this way. Then she smiled and reached for a fresh stalk of grass.

Adam Garrick.

Her memory had served her well. Beau's friend was one tough-looking man. When she'd seen him arrive in the pickup truck yesterday afternoon, she'd actually felt something like fear. She laughed nervously now, remembering. Imagine—*fear!*

He was easily six feet tall, perhaps an inch or two more. He looked lean, mean...merciless. She'd made an instant decision that she wouldn't want to be on the wrong side of a dispute with him. On the other hand, hadn't Beau had always said there wasn't a better man to back you up if you were in trouble? Hadn't he said Adam Garrick was a man to depend on?

Inexplicably Caroline had felt some of that, too, as she'd watched him walk toward them. He carried himself with a smooth easy grace that had none of the awkwardness she'd sometimes observed in a horseman temporarily separated from his horse. This man was fit, able, very physical. An athlete in his prime.

How old? She knew he was older than Beau; she didn't know how much. He couldn't be more than forty. He was deeply tanned and wore his hair unfashionably long. His hat was creased and dusty and looked as though it had been sat on or stepped on more than once and punched back into shape. She remembered Beau talking about old rodeo days, way before he'd met her. About how his buddy Adam Garrick had no equal for sheer male willingness to step up to any cross-this-line-if-you-dare situation, involving man or beast. Beau had admired that; it was the sort of thing that made Caroline shudder. She'd seen a little too much of it in her own husband to admire it in another man.

Maybe that accounted for her odd response to Adam Garrick, one she could only term an instinctive fear. Her first impulse, immediately stifled, was to call her daughter to her. To protect her child from whatever ancient terror a fierce unknown adult male such as this might bring from the darkness to the fireside. A stranger. Who was he? Friend or foe?

As though he would hurt her—or her daughter! Beau had said he'd trust this man with his life. Caroline knew some of her reaction could be attributed to the state of nerves she'd been in the past few months. The mess with the Carter family. That, and the long drive. Nearly a thousand miles. She was ready to jump at a cloud passing over the moon.

He'd had a grim expression when he met them, too, as though he'd just as soon throw them off the place as say hello. But that had changed—she wasn't sure when—and this morning he'd been as polite and hospitable as anyone could ask.

It had been a shock to learn he was divorced. She recalled his wife as fairly tall and a redhead, but there were no pictures around the place, or none she'd seen. That wasn't surprising. Divorced people probably didn't keep reminders of their ex-spouses around.

The housekeeper had shown her to a well-furnished bedroom on the second floor of the old frame house. It had a connecting door to Rose's small room, which might have been a dressing room at one time before the ranch house was modernized. Caroline had slept well for the first time in weeks.

Well, one thing she *wasn't* going to do on this trip was spend all her time thinking about her problems. This was supposed to be a vacation. Caroline got to her feet and glanced around. Mrs. T had said there was an old cabin in back of these trees somewhere. Would that be Beau's? Most likely.

Well, if Adam didn't have time to show it to her, maybe she'd just explore a little herself. She glanced at her watch. Rosie would probably sleep another hour or so.

The cabin was about fifty yards into the trees. It was gray and weathered and looked as though it had stood there a long time, yet it couldn't be more than twelve or fourteen years old. Beau had built it of logs, but they were short lengths that fitted into uprights spaced at intervals along the outside walls. It wasn't big, perhaps twenty feet by twenty-four.

The windows were boarded up, but she could just peek between the weathered planks. Cobwebs, a dusty wooden floor where the sunlight stabbed through the shadow. It was too dark inside to see anything more.

Caroline stood at one end of the cabin and shaded her eyes, examining the chimney. It seemed solid enough, built of river rock mortared into place. A ramshackle mess of twigs and sticks sat atop the chimney. The nest of some kind of bird. Or maybe a squirrel.

Caroline felt her interest growing. Was it habitable? Somehow she'd never associated something this rustic with her husband. She thought of the Carter summer place on Puget Sound. Not a cottage or cabin by any stretch of the imagination. That he'd built this rough cabin, and why, was a part of her husband she didn't really know. Just as she'd never understood why, even after they were married, even after Rosie had come into their lives, Beau had clung to his long solitary treks in the mountains.

Caroline walked around to the front of the cabin again, determined to try the door. There was no way she could get in; a hefty padlock secured it. Suddenly annoyed that she couldn't do anything more without asking for help, she grabbed the door handle and rattled it vigorously. Then she stepped back and rubbed her hands on her skirt and, balancing awkwardly, gave the wooden door a halfhearted kick.

A sound behind her—the scrape of a boot heel? the snap of a twig?—made her whirl around.

"For heaven's sake! You scared me!" she said, putting one hand to her thudding heart. Adam stood at the edge of the trees—how long had he been there?—watching her, a slight smile on his face. Her eyes were drawn to the shape of his mouth. Firm, straight, only the tiniest hint of humor. He must have seen her kick the door. Wearing sandals. She felt ridiculous.

"Looks like you found the place," was all he said, then walked toward her. She watched his approach—jeans, plaid shirt with the sleeves rolled back, scuffed leather boots. The hat.

"Yes. I didn't want to disturb you from whatever you were doing...." That didn't sound right—she'd had a sudden flash of the jaunty Rhonda Maclean heading down to the barn a few hours before. She took a deep breath. "Mary suggested I explore a little on my own."

"Sure. Good idea." A few yards away from her, he changed the direction of his approach and bent down at one corner of the cabin, feeling around under the lowest log. The key. He tossed it gently in his hand. "I take it you'd like to go inside."

She nodded. He came to stand beside her on the sagging step and touched her arm lightly. "Careful. Boards are rotten."

"Mmm." He fitted the key into the lock and after wiggling it a little, this way and that, twisted it and the padlock sprang open.

He hooked the open lock into the hasp screwed to the frame and reached down to grip the door handle. He gave it an initial shake and then, before he opened the door, he turned toward her. She suddenly realized how close they were. "Sure you're ready for this?" he said enigmatically, still with that half smile.

She nodded again. What could he mean? It was just an old cabin. But her heart pounded as he shoved open the door and pushed it back on squeaky hinges.

He stepped aside and nodded. "After you, ma'am."

CHAPTER FIVE

HER FIRST IMPRESSION was of dust and neglect and an odd sort of ancient disorder. A table stood in the middle of the room, with two plain wooden chairs, pulled back, as though the occupants had just stood up from a meal, although there was nothing on the table but a long-silenced windup alarm clock. The chair seats were dull with dust.

Caroline's footsteps echoed on the plank floor. The air was cold and heavy, after the warmth of the summer breeze outside. *The chill of the grave.* A brown-painted iron bedstead at one end of the cabin held a battered old-style mattress, the stuffing spilling out in several places. If there weren't mice still in residence—Caroline wrinkled her nose, unable to detect the smell of mice—they had once made themselves comfortable here. Or perhaps squirrels had pirated the mattress stuffing for their nests.

The sound of Adam's tread behind her startled her. She hadn't forgotten he was there, just felt a little lost in amazement to find herself in Beau's cabin after all these years. It was so different from anything she'd imagined, so plain and spare.

Adam came farther into the room and paused at a simple nailed-up shelf that held an irregular line of paperback books. She watched as he ran his thumb along the spines and saw puffs of dust erupt and hang in the few light shafts that penetrated from the open door.

He swung to meet her gaze. For a few tense seconds

Caroline felt the full force of his personality as he seemed to probe her with his eyes. By contrast, his face held no expression. At least none she could make out. *What did he want from her?*

"I'll try and pull a few boards off the windows," he muttered, turning as he spoke. "Then you'll be able to see better in here."

His footsteps faded as he stepped back onto the grass outside. A minute later Caroline heard him wrench at the boards on the window nearest the door and there was a squeal as rusty nails gave way. He pried at another with the board he'd removed. The interior grew a little lighter.

To one side, not attached to the stone chimney, which had a sort of rough hearthstone and fireplace at its base, was a small woodstove, its pipe running straight up through the roof. The stove's chrome trim still glinted but the iron plates on the cooking surface were fuzzy and red with rust. Beau cooked in here? It looked as though he had. On an open shelf lined with stick-on shelf paper were half a dozen plates, some upside-down glasses and mugs, two cheap tin pans with lids and a cast-iron frying pan, the entire lot festooned with cobwebs. A glass jar, its lid obviously rusted in its threads, held something lumpy and white that was probably sugar. If there'd been anything else edible in here that the mice could get at, they'd no doubt carried it off by now.

Caroline reached out—as Adam had—and ran one finger along the chrome of the warming oven above the stove. Her finger came away gray with dust. On the wall was a faded calendar, turned to the month of August. Caroline walked closer. She read, in Beau's careless hand, "Three Hills Rodeo, saddle bronc, 2 p.m." penciled in on the tenth, a Saturday. The calendar dated from thirteen years ago, when Beau was nineteen.

Caroline stepped back, suddenly cold in her thin cotton shirt. She crossed her arms, hugging herself.

"How's that?" Adam reentered the cabin, breathing hard. He'd managed to tear off several boards from two of the windows. "Brighter?"

"A lot better. Thanks."

He looked around, made a halfhearted gesture toward the center of the room. "Not much to see."

"No."

He said nothing more and she was glad he didn't. She held her breath and walked closer to one of the windows. It, too, was festooned with cobwebs, and a corner had broken away, a small glowing triangle that let in the summer air. She put her finger to the opening, stopping it up, then jerked back when she felt the still-sharp edge of the glass.

"I miss him," she said, then raised both hands to her face, horrified. She wiped hurriedly at the hot wetness on her cheeks. "I wonder how I'll live my life without him. How I'll survive. I worry that I won't be able to raise my daughter properly on my own."

She tried to hold back, pressing her trembling lips with her fingers. Finally she gave up and gazed out the window at the blurred green and blue beyond the dirty glass. The words sounded—to her—hoarse and strange, not her voice at all.

"I'm not strong, by myself," she whispered, agonized. "Beau wasn't strong, either, but together we were. Do you know what I mean?" She didn't dare risk a look at Adam. "We were too young when we got married, that's all. Twenty, both of us. Is that too young? I don't know. People said so. But we were in love. I don't regret a minute of the time I had with Beau.

"I still can't believe what happened. Some nights I wake up and I'm scared. I'm alone. That's when I know it's true.

He's gone. I'll never see him again." She paused, tried to catch back the horrible broken words. "He's dead. *Dead!* Rose won't remember him when she grows up. She's too young. She won't remember her daddy. Maybe it's better that way. I don't know. Is it?"

She covered her face with her hands and wept. Thank goodness he made no move to comfort her. Thank goodness he had the decency to say nothing. What must he think?

"I'm sorry," she managed, making another desperate effort to contain herself. She bent and scrubbed at her tears with the hem of her shirt. "You'll have to excuse me. I just...I just kind of cracked when I saw that calendar and saw Beau's writing there and realized when he wrote that I didn't even know him. It was the summer before we met. This cabin..." Her voice failed her and she turned. She could barely make out Adam's features, standing as he was well in the shadows of the room.

"I realize there's a whole part of my husband that I didn't know," she went on. "I didn't know that young man who rode saddle broncos in the rodeo with you. The man who needed so much time by himself in the mountains. That was a stranger to me. He was someone *you* knew, not me. He read—" she made a wild gesture toward the shelf Adam had touched "—he read *these* books. He cooked here. Made meals. I never even saw my husband warm up a can of beans for himself...."

Caroline turned back to the window, shocked at the passion she heard in her own voice. The anger. She heard a heavy step behind her.

"Look, Caroline—" he made no attempt to touch her, and for that she was grateful "—maybe I should go back now. Will you be all right here alone?"

She nodded, unable to trust her voice. Then she thought

of what her display must seem to him. She whirled. "Adam…"

"Yes?"

"I'm so sorry. He was your friend. I haven't forgotten that."

He paused at the open door. "He was more than a brother to me," he said, then walked through the open door into the brilliant sunshine.

SUPPER THAT EVENING was a noisy affair. Rose and Janie chattered a mile a minute. Caroline was pleased to see how easily her daughter had adjusted to their surroundings and loved to hear her prattle about calves and kittens and a robin's nest she'd seen in the company of her new friend, Janie Tump. Janie smiled steadily, nodding vigorously at some of Rose's comments and chiming in with noisy supportive sounds. She seemed flattered and completely happy to have a friend who looked up to her as Rose so plainly did.

There were two more at the table this evening, both men sitting near Adam at the far end of the table. Curley, Adam's foreman, had been introduced to her earlier and the new wrangler sat with them, Ben Longquist, the young man Caroline had seen Rhonda Maclean wave at earlier in the day. Ben was nineteen and handsome in a boyish sleepy-lidded way. Mary Tump had already told her Ben was a local boy and had hired on with Adam for the summer to save money for college. He was in charge of looking after the horses for the paying guests during the Sunday-to-Friday excursions into the Tetlock Valley.

Caroline welcome the extra company. She didn't know what had come over her that afternoon. In all the months since Beau had died, she'd never done anything like that—

weep in front of a stranger. And not just any stranger, but this tough-looking man!

She noticed that Adam avoided speaking to her. From time to time she'd glance up and catch him giving her a brief impassive look. He'd immediately turn away and say something to one of the men beside him. Other times, more often, she'd notice him studying Rose. His face then held an expression she couldn't begin to fathom—somewhere between wariness and perplexity. He never said a word to her daughter and Caroline was beginning to wonder why. Maybe he just didn't like kids. Some men didn't.

"Ben, how's your aunt Sylvie? She's got a new little one, hasn't she?" Mary Tump called out down the table, interrupting the men. "Just last week, didn't I hear?"

"Yes, ma'am. Tuesday morning early. Fine, healthy boy."

"Well, isn't that nice. A baby brother for little Ellie. What a sweetheart that Ellie is." Mary turned to Caroline and explained, "Ben's auntie lives in town. Her man's not around much. Away most of the time with his job, and one thing and another."

Caroline nodded. None of this meant anything to her, but she enjoyed the homeyness of being included in Mary's conversation.

"And how's your uncle Joe gettin' on?" she inquired, with a big wink for Caroline's benefit. "Hasn't he got married yet? What's the matter with that man? For heaven's sake, tell him I can fix him up with someone if he's desperate!"

"I'll be sure and tell him that, ma'am," Ben said amiably.

"Tell you the truth, I'm surprised Joe Gallant let you off the place," growled Curley. He was a tall, spare, leathernecked man who could have been anywhere from fifty to seventy. "Don't he need you over there? Drive tractor or somethin' for the summer?"

Ben glanced at Adam. "Uncle Joe says Adam can teach me some stuff about horses."

Adam gave him a pained look and resumed buttering a slice of bread.

"Uncle Joe told my ma Adam was just the fellow to make a man out of me—not that I need any help, you understand," Ben went on, with a sly glance at Curley and a wink down the table to where Caroline and Mrs. T sat. Caroline watched the exchange, fascinated.

"Ha! If that means learnin' a fella to rassle b'ars and bust bad broncs, it ain't worth much as a job description these days," Curley muttered. "Eh, Ben? Don't suppose it'd cut any mustard with that fancy course you're fixin' to take at the university, now, would it?"

Ben shook his head and grinned. "Suppose not, Curley."

"Mr. Curley?"

All three men looked at Rosie, who sat beside Adam's foreman and was now staring up at him with her most winsome smile.

Curley frowned. "Say—you talkin' to me?"

"I sure am!" She nodded vigorously, causing her black curls to dance.

The dour foreman actually cracked a smile. Caroline held her breath—she had no idea what Rosie might say.

"How come they call you Curley when you don't hardly have any hair at all? Only a little bit around the ears."

Caroline cringed. But she needn't have worried. The foreman's wintry smile broadened a fraction.

"Why, I suppose that's just the reason they call me Curley, li'l lady," he said enigmatically, with a wink at the other two men. "That's cowboy humor for ya. Contrarylike. I guess you know what they always call the biggest fella on the outfit?''

"Fatty?" Rosie asked hopefully. Janie covered her mouth and crowed with delight.

"Nope. Slim."

Caroline wanted to giggle herself, but managed to contain it. She glanced up and happened to meet Adam's gaze. For a moment they shared the humor of the situation across the table, the way old friends do, and then the moment was gone. Caroline was stunned; when he wanted to, this man could see right inside her soul. Thank goodness, he showed little sign of wanting to. Then she changed her mind. It was only that they'd both known Beau so well, she told herself. That gave them something in common.

After the meal she called Sharon again. It was a little worrisome that she hadn't heard from her, although Caroline had left Seattle before Sharon had a chance to write back. No one answered the phone.

But it was Friday. Perhaps Sharon had gone away for the weekend. Caroline's plan was to leave the Double O on Sunday afternoon, possibly connect with Sharon that evening, or spend the night in a motel and get in touch with her the next day. She'd counted on spending some time with her old college roommate, both to catch up on their friendship, which had been put on a back burner since Rose's arrival, and to get some help help finding somewhere to live. Caroline had enough cash to rent a small place for a couple of months. By then, she hoped she'd have found some prospects for work, either back in Seattle or in Idaho, in her hometown of Twin Falls, or maybe even some seasonal work here in Canada. She hadn't given that possibility too much thought, other than to recall that it was probably illegal to work in a country you'd entered as a visitor. She'd worry about that when the time came. When the money ran out.

The best solution of all would be to learn that Maddie Reinholdt, her lawyer in Seattle and an old friend of Beau's, had been able to make sense of his affairs and had not only settled with the Carters but had discovered money in the bank for her and Rosie to live on. Yes, that would be best of all. But she'd stopped being a dreamer a long time ago, long before Beau disappeared.

Caroline didn't see much of Adam for the rest of the weekend. He seemed to be preoccupied with preparations for the trail-riding business he ran in the summer. He offered, once, to take her and Rosie out riding, but Caroline couldn't help noticing how halfhearted the offer was, and she politely refused. She took Rose and Janie to Beau's cabin on Saturday afternoon, and the girls played house and had a wonderful time sweeping out the dust and rearranging the pots and pans. When they were finished, it didn't look a whole lot cleaner, but most of the dust had been moved from one place to another.

Mary Tump and her daughter didn't leave for their days off until Sunday, a fact Caroline welcomed. She wasn't sure why, but she didn't want to spend a night alone in that big house with Adam Garrick. She didn't think she'd ever met anyone less approachable. What a contrast to the sociable outgoing man she'd married! Yet Caroline knew how much Beau had thought of his friend. And Adam had said Beau had been more than a brother to him....

Late Sunday morning Adam came up to her on the veranda, where she was sitting with her feet up, enjoying a second cup of coffee. The distant mountains, bathed in the fresh clear air, seemed close enough to reach out and touch. Janie and Rose were rocking on the lawn swing, singing at the tops of their lungs, Rose's Raggedy Ann doll flopping between them. Caroline's bags were packed, and she and Rose were ready to leave after the light lunch that Mrs. T had insisted on preparing.

"Caroline?"

She sat up straight, startled for a moment as Adam's shadow fell across her chair. "Yes?"

"Uh, I'd like to see you for a few minutes, if I could. Before you go."

She stared at him. Was something wrong? "Why, certainly."

"Alone," he added, with a frown and a quick glance down the veranda. It was deserted.

Caroline set down her coffee cup and got to her feet. She hadn't realized how close Adam was, and when she stood, she was no more than a foot or two away from him. His height and his serious expression were daunting. Caroline took a quick breath. "Sure." She looked around. "Here?"

"I thought we could step into my office for a few minutes." He glanced toward the lawn swing. "If you think the girls will be okay."

"They'll be fine." She tried a casual smile, but nothing she did felt casual around this man. She followed him into the house and down the hall to the small office he kept on the main floor. The window in the office overlooked the lawn and barn and corrals in the distance.

"Sit down."

Caroline took the chair he indicated, then stood up again. "I...I think I'll stand," she said. "I'll keep one eye out for Rose and Janie," she added, not quite truthfully, and moved to the window.

The instant she'd sat down she'd realized that sitting put her at a disadvantage. Adam was pacing the room, frowning, looking almost as though he'd forgotten he'd invited her in.

"Adam, I want to tell how much I appreciate these last few days at your ranch," she said somewhat stiffly. "I have enjoyed—"

"Never mind that," he broke in bluntly with an impatient movement of one hand. "Forget that. It's the least I could do, isn't it?" His gray-blue gaze froze on her. He sounded almost angry. "Considering?"

Well. These weren't the most gracious of reasons for inviting her and Rose to stay...*considering.*

"What I brought you in here for is this," he began again, still frowning, "and there's no easy way to say it. Have you got money?"

Caroline stared at him in utter shock. She felt her cheeks warm and knew it had nothing to do with the temperature of the room.

"It's none of my damn business and I know that," he said. "Go ahead and say so. But I want to know if Beau provided for you properly, that's all." Adam paused. "He married you. It was his responsibility to do the right thing by you and your—" was there the slightest hesitation? "—daughter. I want to know if he took care of it."

Caroline felt her spine stiffen. *You're too right,* she wanted to scream, *it's none of your damn business.* Pride didn't allow it. She hesitated a few more seconds, to be sure her emotions were firmly in check, then ventured, "Why do you ask?"

"You'd like to tell me to go straight to hell, don't you?" He swung to stare at her and then, to Caroline's amazement, smiled. "You want to tell me to mind my own goddamn business. Am I right?"

The transformation nearly took away her breath. His features, normally so hard-edged and uncompromising, assumed an easier, gentler...handsomer look. The devilment she'd seen so often in her husband's eyes was echoed in

Adam's. Something inside her ached. *Perhaps there really were a few things in common between these two men who at first glance couldn't have been more different.*

"The thought had crossed my mind," she admitted quietly. "But I know you must have your reasons. So I won't."

"Good." The smile stayed near his eyes, but his jaw firmed. "Believe me, I don't want details. I have no interest in your personal affairs. I only ask because I couldn't let you drive away from here this afternoon if I thought you were short of money."

"I—I wouldn't *dream* of asking you for money."

"I know you wouldn't. That's why I'm offering. I saw that car you drove up in. Beau had money, plenty of money. I knew his family. I know how he lived. I figure his widow ought to be driving something a little better than a beat-up ten-year-old station wagon."

Caroline stood a moment, quietly considering. Not one detail had escaped this man. Should she be surprised? No man who'd made a life of high-risk adventure, as Adam apparently had, would have survived this long if he hadn't trained himself to pay attention to every detail. Every time. And his offer, though unthinkable, was generous.

"Thank you for your interest in our welfare." She drew in a deep breath and managed a smile. "I know you mean well by it. I've got money. As much as I need. The car is in good condition. I have no worries on that account. It'll get us back to Seattle safely."

"Promise me you'll let me know if you run into trouble?"

She met his gaze for a long tortured moment, then she took another deep breath. "No. No, I won't promise that, Adam. Thank you for asking. I appreciate your generosity and…and everything you've done for us. But you probably won't hear from me again. I—I just wanted to come up here and see this place that Beau talked about so much. I wanted to see his cabin—''

''It's yours.''

She smiled. ''That's preposterous. Maybe he built it, but it's on your land.''

''It's not. Beau bought the five acres the cabin's on from me. I'll buy it back from you, whenever you say.''

Caroline swallowed. Her throat felt dry, and yet at the same time she was close to tears. *Beau, Beau, what have you done?*

''Well...'' She glanced out the window. Rose was just climbing down from the swing. It was time to leave. ''I don't know what to say. Maybe we can talk about that some other time. I'll write to you. Right now—'' she looked at him ''—I don't even want to think about that cabin,'' she said softly. ''I just want to think about the future, not the past. The past is over.''

He nodded but his grim smile told her the truth: the past was *never* over.

ADAM stood at the window. It was pitch-black outside. It had to be midnight, or close to it. The sight of his own face reflected in the dark glass irritated him and he turned away with a curse.

That wasn't what he wanted to see. He wanted to see what she'd looked like when she'd waved goodbye. Her eyes were dark with feeling—she was a feeling kind of woman. Everything about her was soft and feminine and yet, deep down, a streak of steel ran through her. She'd wanted to tell him to go to hell—and he wished she had—but she was too damn ladylike to do it.

And Rose. *His daughter.* Tears streaking down her face as she waved goodbye to Janie. Janie blubbering and bawling her eyes out. Mrs. T blowing her nose ten times in five minutes. Women!

Rose's tears had *hurt,* like a long-ago bone injury that aches in stormy weather. His daughter—crying. And there was nothing he could do about it.

He saw Caroline weeping in the cabin all over again. The dust, the gloom, the broken pane of glass. The mess everywhere. She looked so small in the light from the window, her shoulders so narrow, her hands so slender and fine. He'd wanted to step over and pull her into his arms. He couldn't stand to see a woman cry. But how could he do that? There was too much else this woman made him feel. Scary stuff. Stuff he never wanted to find out.

Well, they were gone. Both of them. The visit he'd dreaded was over. Mrs. T and Janie wouldn't be back until Tuesday evening. He was alone. And he still had a hell of a lot of work to get through.

Adam walked into the kitchen, opened a cabinet and poured some whiskey, straight up, into a thick glass mug that had once held peanut butter. Good old Canadian rye. He wasn't much of a boozer, but he figured nobody'd blame him for taking a drink tonight. He'd put his feet up, maybe try to find a baseball game on the TV.

A man alone. In his natural state.

But when Adam sank into his favorite chair in front of the television, he frowned and thrust his hand down beside the cushion. What the hell...?

He pulled out a Raggedy Ann doll. The kid's doll. Idly he studied the red yarn braids, the sewn-on feet at the end of the floppy legs. Then he pushed the doll's vest aside and saw the heart embroidered where a heart should be: "I love you."

He settled the rag doll on the seat beside him and pointed its face toward the television set. Then he turned up the volume and picked up his drink.

They'd be back. It was just a question of when.

CHAPTER SIX

AT LEAST SHE HAD the address right.

Caroline quickly scanned the directory and found the name she was looking for: S. J. LaSalle. Sharon's name was right above another for the same apartment: Gregory Baxter.

Hmm. Was she married? Caroline was ashamed to admit she hadn't exchanged much more than Christmas cards with her college roommate for several years. She glanced at Rose, who was grumpy at being roused from the sound sleep she'd fallen into during the drive to Calgary. She'd left her beloved Raggy at Adam Garrick's ranch and been inconsolable. Then there'd been the extra delay of two stops at service stations to ask for directions. Sharon taught at the University of Calgary, but her apartment was on a tree-lined boulevard along the Bow River.

Caroline pushed the intercom button.

"Yes?" The disembodied voice was definitely male.

"Hello? This is Caroline Carter. I'm looking for Sharon LaSalle. Is she there?"

"Oh, shoot." There was a short pause, then, "I guess you'd better come up."

"Is Sharon there?"

But the door buzzer had already gone off to admit her. Caroline grabbed for the door with one hand and for Rose's hand with the other. She'd parked on the street—would the car be okay there for a few moments? It had to be. The days at the ranch should have left her rested and full of energy. Oddly, although she'd slept well, she felt drained, emotionally and physically. She'd be glad to settle down somewhere with Rose and stay in one spot for a while.

Hey—was this such a good idea, going up to the twelfth floor of an apartment building to meet an unknown male? He must be all right, she decided. Would a serial killer say, "Oh, shoot"?

Gregory Baxter was a sandy-haired bearded man with a pleasant smile. He said he was Sharon's partner—whatever that meant—and that Sharon, unfortunately, was currently away.

"She's doing a summer fellowship in Boston," he explained, adding that he had just that afternoon returned from a two-week visit with her.

"I took her your letter and she was delighted to hear from you. She said to pass on her regards if I saw you and to say how sorry she was to miss you. She probably wrote back, but I guess you'd already left. Is this your little girl?"

Caroline nodded. "This is Rose."

"Hiya, Rose," Baxter said, with the kind of too-wide grin people reserved for children they didn't know. "How old are you?" He didn't wait for Rose's answer. "Say—" he frowned "—is there anything I can do for you while you're here? Where're you staying? Did you fly in? Maybe you'd like to borrow my car...." He looked from her to Rose and back again. "How about coffee or something? There's not much in the fridge right now, but I could pop out to the grocery store and be back in a few minutes."

"Oh, thank you, but no thanks," Caroline said, somehow finding the energy to smile. This was a disaster. She hadn't realized until now how much she'd been counting on Sharon's advice and aid. Now she'd have to...well, she'd just have to change her plans.

"We have our own car." She noticed that Rose was glaring at Gregory Baxter. Obviously her daughter was not impressed. "But we're not staying anywhere just at the moment. We're going to look around for a weekly rental near Calgary, maybe on a lake somewhere."

Gregory smiled. In relief? "That's a great idea. There are some cabins toward Banff, out that way. Bragg Creek, too. But they might be pretty expensive this time of year, I don't know...." His voice trailed off.

"We'll find something," Caroline said cheerfully, tightening her hand around Rose's. "Say hello to Sharon when you talk to her. Tell her I'll be sure to keep in touch. Nice meeting you, Gregory."

He waved; she waved back and half dragged Rose around the corner to the elevator. Once there, she lifted Rose to punch the button—one of her daughter's favorite tasks—and dredged deep into the reserves that motherhood had shown her she had, that every woman had, and said, "How about a stop at McDonald's, Rosie?"

"Yesss!" Rosie immediately brightened. "Then I want Raggy. I wanna go back and get Raggy." She thrust out her bottom lip. Caroline knew that stubborn look very well.

Inspiration struck. "Raggy's having a holiday, just like you are, Rose. Think of that! She's visiting Janie and Mary and everybody at the ranch." Why hadn't she included Adam?

"And Curley?" Rose looked intrigued.

"Curley, too." The elevator arrived, coming down, and they got on with two well-dressed elderly ladies, both wearing gloves and hats, one of whom had an empty grocery cart.

Rose immediately gave both women and the cart a sober appraisal. Then, as the elevator doors closed, she turned to one. "Did you guys steal that from Safeway?"

THEY SPENT the night in a very ordinary motel on Sixteenth Avenue. Long after Rose fell asleep in her own double bed—she'd been thrilled and had begged her mother to let her bounce on it, just once or twice—Caroline lay awake. The traffic was heavy and sirens punctuated the night. Pools of light from passing cars swirled and flowed and vanished on the white tile ceiling.

What am I doing here? Caroline's mind raced over the events of the past week or so, lingering longer than she would have liked on those three days at the Double O. *Why have I come here? Why have I taken Rose away like this? Why didn't I stick it out, force Beau's family to provide an explanation for what happened? Demand justice?*

Was she a coward? Was she doing the right thing? Who could say? Nothing had gone right since she'd come to Canada, but that wasn't to say that, starting tomorrow, everything wouldn't suddenly fall into place. All the plans and ideas she'd had in rainy Seattle could still come to pass. She'd had a setback or two. That happened. So Sharon wasn't here. Big deal. She could check the morning paper over breakfast and spot a wonderful little cottage for rent, not too far away, not too expensive. She and Rosie would drive out there and Rose would fall in love with the place, and there'd be a little girl just her age staying right next door. The family would invite Caroline over to play cards in the evening and they'd barbecue hamburgers and listen to music as they sat on the lawn chairs, watching the two girls play at the side of the lake. And, of course, the lake would have a firm sandy bottom and clear water and be shallow for miles....

More like muck and weeds and swimmer's itch. Caroline turned over onto her stomach and hugged the pillow to her hot cheek. She would not cry. *She would not...*

EVERY MORNING when Adam put on his hat, he saw the rag doll staring at him with her goofy little stitched-on smile and starry eyes. He'd hung the doll on the hat rack just inside the kitchen door, so that when they turned up— as he knew they would—if he didn't happen to be around, Mrs. T would be able to find it.

It had been almost a week since they'd left. He was surprised they hadn't shown up yet. But maybe the girl had outgrown the doll. Maybe he'd just imagined her attachment. After all, what was it—cloth and thread and yarn? Tattered and worn, at that. It could easily be replaced at any toy store.

Adam jammed his hat on his head and stepped out onto the porch. He'd been sticking close to home this week. Was that why?

Nope. He'd been trying to catch up with Rhonda Maclean. For the first time in the three summers she'd worked for him, he was beginning to suspect his annual bluff might not pay off. He hadn't seen Rhonda for four days, and he'd had her on the payroll for more than a week. The payroll *she* was supposed to be keeping track of. Damn her fickle woman's hide.

And one of his most dependable horses had come down with a hoof infection. The vet had said he'd have to put Duke on pasture for a couple of weeks, no riding, no work, which meant he needed another horse, pronto. The trouble with this guest-ranch business was that most of the people who signed up and paid big money for a week in the mountains had never been on a horse before. Every animal in his string had to be dead quiet and reliable. He'd see if Ben could put his hands on another horse, maybe borrow one. The Winslow boys might have a horse they could spare.

Adam frowned. Making arrangements. Not his favorite part of running a business. He'd rather be trailing cows or working a green horse or...hell, he'd rather be pulling calves in a March nor'easter. You had to be a people person, as Mrs. T said, to be in this business. And a people person was one thing he was not.

"Adam!"

Ben had just climbed into one of the dark green Double O pickups. Adam walked over to the vehicle and put a foot on the running board. "Going after a horse, Ben?"

"Yeah. Thought I'd check over at Cal's place. He says he's got a nice mare that might suit us. Part Morgan."

"Good." Adam pulled down his hat to shade his eyes a little more. He glanced sharply at the youthful wrangler, then gazed toward the mountains. "Anything else, Ben?"

"Well, yeah." The boy looked a little red around the ears. "Rhonda called."

"Uh-huh." Adam removed his foot from the running board and stepped back.

"She ain't coming over this morning, after all," Ben got out in a rush. "Says she might make it after lunch."

"Uh-huh. Well, thanks for passing on the news, Ben."

The wrangler nodded and put the pickup into gear. Adam thought Ben's color was a little high. Trust Rhonda Maclean—she'd chase anything with a belt buckle. He ought to know. She'd chased him long enough, though to no avail. He hadn't always been as particular as he was these past few years, but any way you called it, Rhonda Maclean wasn't his type. He didn't doubt for a moment that she'd been smooth-talking Longquist. Well, hell. Ben was old enough to take care of himself.

So—just what *was* his type? Did he even know anymore? Silky swinging blond hair, big brown eyes, a tender smile flashed through his brain and he cursed himself out loud. What in God's name could he be thinking of? Hadn't he been in and out of enough woman trouble to last him the rest of his days? Look where that one crazy weekend down in Seattle had gotten him, for starters.

Rose's sweet face and bouncy black curls were before him as though the girl herself stood there. Rose. His daughter. His flesh and blood. He couldn't get it out of his head. And Caroline Carter worshiped the ground the child walked on. So had Beau, from all accounts. How could he— Adam—say Rose should never have been born? That she was a mistake?

Adam shook his head. This was too deep for him. Personal regrets were one thing. But hell. *If wishes were horses...we'd all be riding in style, wouldn't we?* Adam had never spent more than a minute in his life wishing he could turn back the clock. He wasn't going to start now.

"Say, Boss, how we gonna handle the haying this year? You goin' to town, hire a crew?" Curley lifted his stained and greasy ball cap, with the words "Glory Co-op" stitched across the front. He leisurely scratched his fuzzy bald crown. "Or you want me to?"

"You better see what you can scare up yourself," Adam said tersely. "I got my hands full just now." Haying was the last thing he wanted to think about. He had half a dozen tourists arriving day after tomorrow, and no Rhonda Maclean to take care of the hundred and one details she generally took care of. Ordering supplies, taking reservations and deposits, scheduling, making sure the dudes were happy, general office coordination, paying bills, filing mail, readying the Double O guest quarters.

Then he frowned. *Hay?* "What's the rush? You can't be thinking of taking hay off just yet, Curley."

The older man settled his cap again and glanced at the sun, high in the morning sky. "Everything's comin' early this year. I figure we can cut that first crop inside of ten days."

"Hire any crew you can." Adam turned to walk toward his office. He didn't know what he'd do without his dour foreman. Ed "Curley" Splint kept the ranch on track during the summer while Adam was preoccupied with the Tetlock Valley part of the business. "Just don't bother me about it until I get this first bunch set up. I'll probably have to go out with them Sunday, make sure everything's working okay all the way down the line. See how they're making out up at the camp. First thing I'm going to do, and I'm going to do it right now, is track down Rhonda."

"Good luck, Boss," his foreman drawled. He shut one eye and sent a stream of evil-looking tobacco juice to the base of an immature Russian thistle struggling to get a hold in the damp ground near the harness shed. It was Curley's firm belief that enough tobacco juice and there'd be no need for herbicides. "You're gonna need it."

Rhonda wasn't home. She wasn't at her brother's place over at Nanton. She wasn't with her aunt, Gwendolyn Miller, who ran the hair salon in town. She wasn't in the bar, either. Adam was sure, because he called the newest watering hole in Glory, a place he'd never been in—way too much greenery and bamboo for him—but the kind of place he figured Rhonda Maclean might check out. Mind you, it was only midafternoon. Even for a girl who enjoyed bar life, that was early.

It was after supper before he finally reached her. She was home. And she had bad news.

"I made up my mind, Adam." He could hear her chewing gum at the other end of the phone.

"Uh-huh. About what, Rhonda?" Damned if there was anything to decide. She was working for him, wasn't she?

"Something's come up."

"Yeah, and what's that?" It started down in his boots and crept right up his legs. The feeling was the rubbery feeling he'd always gotten just before he climbed on a bull or a wicked bronc in some rodeo. *Fear.*

"I got on at the Bar U for the summer. I'm gonna run the office there. They're paying more than you are, Adam, government wages. And you get to dress up a little." Rhonda's gum chewing picked up in tempo. "Besides, it's so dang boring around your place." The Bar U was a Pekisko Creek historic ranch run by Parks Canada and open to tourists in the summer. The staff dressed in period costume. "All those corny jokes Curley comes up with every time he sees me? Huh!" She snorted. "And it's lonely, too. Just Mary around, mostly, and that old gimp of a daughter of hers."

Adam gripped the phone and managed to hold his temper. He'd ripped into Rhonda more than once over her attitude toward Mary's daughter.

"I'm tired of it. I told you you'd have to pay me better'n you did last year."

"You sure took your time telling me, Rhonda." Now what? Put in an emergency call to the employment center? Hire a student?

"I guess so. Sorry." But he could tell she wasn't. "Just heard this afternoon about the Bar U." She laughed, that bright breezy laugh that made him want to swear out loud. "Maybe next year, eh?"

"Sure. Maybe." He hung up and let his breath out slowly. He couldn't afford to burn his bridges. He couldn't afford to cuss her out the way she deserved. Rhonda knew the job and he might end up hiring her next year if she wore out her welcome at the Bar U, which was a distinct possibility.

His bluff hadn't worked. He'd drawn the line at a ten percent raise. She hadn't taken the bait. Day after tomorrow he had four German tourists and a couple of Americans coming in, a retired dentist and his teenage son. They'd be tired, hungry, with the same dumb questions he heard every year.

What in tarnation was *he* going to do with them?

ADAM WASN'T HOME when the call came that Caroline and Rose planned to drop by the ranch to pick up Rose's doll on their way to the U.S. border. They were cutting their holiday short and heading back to Seattle, Caroline said. Mary Tump took the message, and in the chaos that ensued after Adam returned from Calgary with the first batch of clients for Tetlock Tours, was it any wonder she forgot to mention it right away?

Adam had gone to Calgary with Marty Gardipee, owner and driver of a fifteen-passenger van that he contracted to Adam for the summer. They'd picked up six jet-lagged Germans—two more than Adam had expected—and then had to wait an hour before the Americans' flight came in. On the trip to the ranch, Marty fussed incessantly about his passengers slamming the doors too hard or getting finger-marks on the windows; by the time they arrived at the Double O, Adam was about ready to call it a day. And the afternoon had just begun.

At the ranch he had to assign the tourists to their cabins—he put the Germans in the three cabins he'd built two years before, two each, and the Americans, father and son, into the bunkhouse. They seemed pleased. Adam hoped they'd still be pleased in the morning. The bunkhouse crew weren't as particular about their housekeeping as some might have liked.

Luckily Mary and her temporary help had managed to get the cabins ready for occupancy the day before, a job that normally Rhonda Maclean would have overseen. Sheets, towels, soap, firewood. Janie had helped. Adam had seen her walk slowly and laboriously from the house to the cabins, carrying towels and sheets, piece by piece. The repetitive task had kept her busy all morning.

Adam knew he was under major obligation to his housekeeper for going the extra mile for him. The cabins were pretty basic—a set of bunk beds on one wall, double bed, cold-water faucet, rolled-steel airtight stove, tiny bathroom, no shower, no kitchen, no hot water. The tourists were expected to shower in the washhouse, an outbuilding near the bunkhouse, and to eat in the cookshack, which Adam opened for the summer. It was an old frame building that dated from the earliest ranch days, back in the twenties. The ranch-style facilities fit right in with most tourists' expectations of cowboy life, and Adam had never had any complaints.

Yet, he reminded himself grimly.

Luckily the Germans appeared to be satisfied despite their jet lag, thrilled to find themselves in what they probably considered real frontier territory. The Americans seemed easygoing enough. Father and son wandered off for a hike shortly after they arrived, which left Adam to cope with the Germans, all of whom wanted to know details about the trail ride next day. Also, what was on the menu for the week, how to call Dusseldorf and from which phone, what the UV index was at this time of year, if there were laundry facilities at the Tetlock camp and whether it was permitted to pick wildflowers.

When he spotted the familiar overloaded station wagon slowly making its way up the drive, he felt a rush of nerves that he could only attribute to the day he'd had so far. He'd expected them—yes—but not like this. He'd rehearsed how he'd handle it from beginning to end. A casual greeting, handing over the doll, a farewell, a friendly smile, a few words wishing them a safe drive home—or wherever.

Not this. Not this heart-stopping crazy rush where his eyes sought hers—not his child's eyes, *Caroline's*. Where a grin he didn't even know he had in him plastered itself all over his damn-fool face. He knew it did. He just couldn't seem to stop smiling.

"Hi!" She pushed up her sunglasses and squinted as she looked up, smiling, too. The window was down and he leaned forward so he could peer into the car. Rose was in the rear seat, one hand on the stuffed whale and the other on the seat-belt release. *His child.* He felt a pain, deep, deep in his side, like he had a broken rib.

"Hi, yourself," he said, still smiling, turning to Caroline again. His gaze locked on hers. Her eyes weren't more than ten inches from his. He could feel the soft movement of her breath on his face.

Her eyes clouded slightly. "We...uh, did Mary mention we'd be stopping in?"

"No." Adam felt his smile fade. "She didn't. I guess you're after that doll Rose left behind." *Jeez...what had gotten into him for a minute there?* He straightened his arms, putting some distance between him and the woman behind the wheel.

"Yeah." She glanced at Rose, then up at him. "What I've been through over that Raggy! I was really hoping she'd forget all about it." She shook her head, smiling, adult to adult, *parent to parent.*

Adam stood back from the vehicle. A strange feeling had come over him. "I'll get it. It's in the house. Are you, uh..." He waved one hand toward the house. "Are you in a hurry?" He knew his voice didn't sound right. He sounded stiff. And formal.

"We-ell..." She glanced around. Three of the Germans milled around the yard, talking and gesticulating; a fourth sat on the porch steps. Adam had no idea where the other two had gone. "It looks like you're kind of busy."

"You could say that," Adam said briefly. He caught her gaze again. Her eyes weren't as dark as he'd remembered, more a sort of tawny brown. The color of buckwheat. "My office manager pulled out on me. I'm going nuts here trying to settle these dudes in and sort out all the details."

Lightning struck. "Say—you wouldn't want a job, would you?" Then he grinned quickly, to show he was only kidding. *What kind of fool are you, offering Beau's widow a job?*

For a few seconds she looked shocked—as he'd expected she would. After all, he wasn't even serious. Was he? She was rich, or next best to it, despite the vehicle she drove. And even if she was looking for work, why would she consider working for him?

"Thank you." Adam had to lean forward again to catch her reply. Her answer was so soft he barely made it out. "Thank you very much. I—I believe I would...."

CHAPTER SEVEN

THE TROUBLE WAS, Caroline thought, everything had gone wrong with her life at once.

Beau had disappeared. In spite of enormous odds that he'd never be found alive, Caroline had prayed desperately for a miracle. Yet she'd had to face the fact that her prayers would not be answered; Beau would not walk out of the mountains, not after so many long weeks and months.

She had to shoulder her own grief and her daughter's bewilderment, and she also had to deal with her mother-in-law, who called Caroline several times a day, alternately raging and weeping uncontrollably. Eunice's husband had died in his forties and now her only son had disappeared and was presumed dead. Caroline had begun to have serious fears for Eunice Carter's health.

Philip Carter, Beau's cousin, had assured Caroline that, financially, there would be no problem. As Beau's widow—if, in fact, Beau was dead—Caroline and Rose would inherit everything. As Beau's cousin and partner in Carter Investments, Philip Carter was in a position to know. But his assurances soon began to ring false.

Within a month of Beau's disappearance, Caroline had discovered there was very little money in the household account she drew upon to buy groceries and pay bills. Then, when she visited her banker, she was told there was almost no money remaining in a joint account, money set aside for a family trip to Europe before Rose started school. Only a few months previously they'd had over eight thousand dollars in that account. There had been two withdrawals, both in the month before Beau disappeared, both cash, and both to Beau Carter. Where had that money gone? What had Beau needed it for? And why hadn't he told her?

Then she'd discovered that their house was mortgaged to the hilt. Yet Beau had paid cash when they'd bought the house five years before, shortly after they adopted Rose. Where was the money he'd raised on the mortgage? Over $250,000.

By this time Caroline was scared. What was happening to her? To Rose? Her husband had disappeared. Her mother-in-law was becoming more difficult and had begun to blame Caroline for ruining Beau's life and making him unhappy enough to walk into the wilderness and never come back.

Then Philip Carter stopped returning her phone calls, and the next time he spoke to her, he'd told her that there was nothing. No money. No investments. No shares in the family company. Nothing. And no expectations, either. The family had not approved of his marriage to her, he informed Caroline. It was no secret that Rose was not Beau's natural daughter, and as a result, the family was washing their hands of them both.

Philip said Beau had been a secret gambler. He'd racked up enormous gambling debts and raided every source of money he could access to pay those debts. He'd robbed Caroline and Rose, and he'd robbed the family company. Philip did not want the Carter-family laundry aired and did not plan to investigate further, except to say that if Caroline had even one dollar from Beau, he, Philip, would make sure it went to pay Beau's debts to Carter Investments. Caroline had only Philip's word about all this, and she no longer believed much that Beau's cousin told her.

Still, facts were facts. She had very little money and she had a child to support. She had no husband. She had no help from Beau's family—even Eunice had stopped calling and had refused to see her granddaughter any longer. Caroline was sure it had been at Philip's urging, but nevertheless, there it was. Rose had been hurt by her grandmother's withdrawal, and Caroline had been hard-pressed to explain to the little girl just what was happening to them both.

So far, she'd been reluctant to ask for help from her own family. Her parents, she knew, would jeopardize their modest retirement to help her any way they could, and Caroline didn't want that. She'd sold much of the jewelry and art Beau had given her to pay the mortgage and buy groceries. In the end all she really had was Beau's broken body coming back in the spring to grieve over and to bury in the family plot overlooking Puget Sound. After the funeral there had been nowhere to turn. She'd stuck it out for another year, hoping that Philip would be proved wrong and that her lawyer would make some sense of Beau's affairs. That had not happened.

Not yet, anyway, Caroline reminded herself, settling into Adam's chair in his office and switching on his computer. It was going to happen; it *had* to happen. Or what was there to go back for? She might as well start over somewhere else, a single mom. Get a job, put her daughter in day care. Make new friends. Lots of women with less going for them than Caroline Carter had done it. She could do it, too.

Maybe not in Canada. There were immigration rules about that. But this temporary job working for Adam Garrick was a bolt from heaven, she thought as she scanned the screen, trying to understand his filing system. Showing up just when Rhonda had quit—pure dumb luck. She was grateful. She hadn't had much of that lately.

The summer-cottage idea, for instance. Two cabins she'd gone to see were very nice but beyond her budget; the three affordable ones had been so infested with ants and silverfish and plain old mildew that she hadn't had the heart to try to fix them up. She'd taken Rose to Drumheller to visit the dinosaur museum and they'd stayed in a motel by a man-made lake near Lethbridge for a couple of nights. They'd swum and sunbathed, and then, despite her reluctance, Caroline had decided to go back to Seattle. Surely the worst was already behind them. Surely Beau's family would change their minds about her and Rose eventually. Surely, by now Maddie Reinholdt, Beau's friend and her lawyer, would have sorted out the details of Beau's financial mess. Caroline hoped so—or where would she come up with the money to pay her? If it wasn't so painful, it'd be funny. Really.

As she'd told herself so many times, it was only because of Rose that she hadn't walked away from the whole nightmare. Occasionally she imagined meeting another man someday. She was still young, just thirty-one. She could have a family again, maybe even a baby. Caroline frowned at the blinking cursor and bit her lip, recollecting the heartache she'd experienced knowing she could never have a child with the man she'd married. She'd always known; Beau had told her early on in their relationship. But still... She felt vaguely disloyal now, even thinking about that.

And then, for no good reason at all, her new employer's image swam into her mind. She remembered the remote way he'd frowned as he moved her bags and Rose's back into the bedrooms they'd occupied only ten days before. She thought of how she'd had to look up into his face. And how the fabric of his shirt had stretched across the breadth of his shoulders when he reached up to straighten his hat.

With his brooding dark look—almost angry—he was so very different from her golden-haired Beau.

Adam had barely taken time to show her around his office before he'd headed out on the trail with the tourists Sunday morning. He'd told her he'd be back in a day or so, and if she couldn't figure things out on her own, she should just forget it until he returned.

She wasn't going to forget it. She was going to figure this filing mess out. She was going to show him that she was worth every single penny he paid her this summer.

Caroline shook her head and put Adam firmly from her mind. Had it come to this...this cliché? The lonely love-starved widow fantasizing about the first man she'd spent any time with since her husband's death?

Good grief.

ADAM PULLED into the ranch yard about five o'clock, an empty four-horse trailer rattling behind him. He'd left his mount up at the small wrangle pasture at the trailhead. The dudes had packed in yesterday with Ben and old Farley, Ben's helper, a man who wanted no responsibility but who was a wonder with a horse, and reliable—if you could just keep him sober. Farley looked forward to a summer in the bush; he liked to know that the devil hiding in a bottle of cheap sherry was more than forty miles away over rough country.

Jim Hillerman, the guide Adam hired for the summer, along with Ben and sometimes Farley, accompanied the paying guests on the six-hour cross-country ride from the Double O ranch to the Tetlock Valley camp. The day before, Adam had gone with them on the first trip of the season, just to make sure things went the way they were supposed to. No sense telling the guests the trip could be done in an hour's hard riding and half an hour in a pickup;

what they didn't know wasn't likely to spoil their fun, as Curley liked to put it.

"Mary?" He walked into the ranch house, then stopped, immediately struck by the silence. Still, somebody was around—he could smell the good smell of one of Mrs. T's famous beef stews simmering in the kitchen. And if he wasn't mistaken, she'd baked bread today, too. He could use a decent meal after the traditional bannock and bacon and beans served up to the guests their first night at the Tetlock camp. They'd been thrilled with the cowboy fare, but Adam had spent too many years in the saddle to have much appreciation left for campfire cuisine. Give him a mess of fresh buttered garden peas and fried spuds and a nice big sirloin, well-done, any day.

Adam hesitated. He could use a shower in the worst way. But even more, he wanted to know where everyone was. He went back onto the porch. Even the dogs had disappeared.

Just then he heard excited barking in the direction of Beau's cabin, and he headed around the house toward the disturbance.

What met his gaze when he stepped out of the trees at the edge of the clearing was something he'd never thought he'd see.

Ed "Curley" Splint was up a tree, straddling a big branch and attempting to tie a rope swing to it. "How's this? High enough for ya?"

"A little higher, Mr. Curley!" Rose called up to him, her voice sounding strange and bright—and so welcome Adam stopped in his tracks.

"How about here?"

"No! A little lower!" She jumped up and down, giggling as she ordered Curley to do her bidding. Adam heard Janie's familiar loud crowing noises that he knew meant happiness, clapping her pudgy hands at the same time and making awkward hopping movements to mimic Rose's. Caroline, he saw at once, stood to one side next to Mrs. T in the shade of the cottonwoods. Both women wore aprons and were smiling. The dogs barked madly, no doubt as astonished as he was to see his foreman up a tree.

No one had noticed him yet. Adam drew a slow breath. He realized his heart was thumping, and he didn't think it was because of the short walk from the house. He didn't want to examine the thought too closely. He wanted to stand there for a minute or so and let himself forget about everything—the new batch of guests, Rhonda, the business, Duke's sore foot, the unexpected appearance in his life of the child he'd fathered...Beau's widow. Beau. The cabin the two of them had built. The grief that had never really left him.

Then Bozo, one of the cow dogs, a collie mix, spotted him and ran over, tail wagging and tongue lolling. He bent to scratch the dog's ears.

"Say, boss!" Curley sat straight on the branch and Adam could see that his face was brick red clear up to his hat brim and no doubt beyond. "What you doin' back early?"

"Heard you were up a tree. Figured I better hurry home before the show was over," Adam replied, unable to keep from smiling. Damn! He never thought he'd see the day—

"Tie it good, Mr. Curley!" Rose chirped. "Don't forget to tie it!" She had her hands on her hips as she called out instructions.

"Yes, *ma'am!*" Curley bent to his task again and Adam walked toward the two women. Caroline smiled and he nodded to them both.

"When'd you get back?" Mrs. T demanded.

"Just now." Adam kept his attention on his foreman's efforts in the tree. "Ten minutes ago."

"I wasn't expecting you until after supper sometime," Mrs. T said. "Oh, darn—my stew! I plumb forgot it." She clapped a hand over her mouth. "I'd better get back."

"Thought I could smell one of your stews cooking in the kitchen, Mrs. T," Adam said. He couldn't think of anything else to contribute to the conversation.

"Well, did you give it a stir?"

"No."

"Men!" She nudged Caroline with an elbow. "You stay here with the children, dear. I'll just go back and see to that stew." She hurried off, muttering to herself.

Adam stood awkwardly beside Caroline for a moment. He didn't want to look at her again, now that the two of them were alone. Well, hardly alone, with Curley and Janie and Rose making a racket just a few feet away.

Adam moved toward the tree. "Need a hand?"

"Nope." His foreman released the knotted ends of the rope and inched his way back along the branch toward the tree trunk. "I can get down same as I got up," he said. "Just give me room, Boss."

Rose pushed the swing, which wobbled drunkenly from side to side, then turned to Adam and put her arms up in a natural gesture. Alarmed, Adam met her gaze, childish and blue and trusting. "Lift me," she said simply.

How could he refuse? His heart hammered in his throat as he took her under the arms and lifted her onto the seat of the swing. She was lighter than he'd thought she'd be. *A small feather of a girl.* A tiny fragrant wisp of her hair blew across his cheek as he lifted her, and he shook his head softly to dislodge it. His palms were sweating; the fear was as bad as any he'd experienced when he'd climbed aboard the wickedest bull on the ticket, back in his damn-fool rodeo days. *She's just a kid*, he insisted to himself. *Just a five-year-old kid.*

But she wasn't. She was *his* daughter. And no one knew, only Lucas, and he'd never tell. Now he'd touched her...lifted her in his arms, released her, smelled the kid-sweet scent of her hair. Felt the warmth and heft of her body. Felt the wiry, wriggling, living strength of her.

Adam put his hands on her small back and gave her a gentle push to start the swing, then walked away, trying to ignore the big smile she aimed at him.

"Thank you," Caroline said quietly. Adam met her eyes in a swift glance and looked back toward the swing. Janie clapped and sang tunelessly. Rose pumped her legs back and forth, back and forth.

"She misses her father so much," Caroline continued in a low voice. "She's usually so shy with men. Most men. I've been delighted to see how she's taken to Curley. They've become a real pair these last two days. And now you."

Adam couldn't prevent himself from looking at her. The warmth in her eyes stopped his breath. *And now you.* He turned toward Beau's cabin and jammed his hands in the pockets of his jeans. "Well, uh, guess I'll head back now," he said.

"Adam?"

"Yes?"

"I've been thinking..." She smoothed her apron, then looked up at him again. A slight flush dusted her cheeks and brightened her eyes. "I've been thinking maybe it would be a good idea to move out here to Beau's cabin."

"What—out to this shack?" There was no plumbing, it was a mess, the roof probably leaked—there were a million reasons she shouldn't move out here.

"Sure. Why not?" She smiled. "You said it's mine now,

that you sold it to Beau way back when. I could clean it up and it'd be perfect for Rosie and me. All we need.''

"There's no water, no plumbing! You'd be crazy to move out here.''

She colored. "Maybe." Then she shrugged. "I suppose you're right. I just...well, I just thought it might be a good idea for us to have our own place if we'll be here all summer.''

There was that. It was early July. They'd likely be here until the season was over, Labor Day. Adam gazed toward the cabin again. It was sturdy enough. And if she was really determined, he could bring in water. Fix the roof.... No, dammit! Was he out of his mind?

"You're welcome to stay in the house," he said gruffly. "You know that.''

"I know. And I'm very grateful to you. And to Mrs. T.'' She was silent a moment. "Well, maybe we can discuss it later.''

She was serious. But there was no damn way he was letting her move out here, into this...this shack. What would people think? Then it struck him—what would they think of her living in the house? Mrs. T and Janie were there only part of the week. Did people care about things like that where she came from? They still did around Glory. Not that he gave a tinker's damn; people could believe what they liked about him and were welcome to it. But he didn't want them tarring her with the same brush—or his child.

And she could hardly move into the bunkhouse. He'd never hired a woman before who didn't have a place of her own in the district. Only Mary Tump, and that was a special arrangement.

"How'd you get on with the books?'' he asked. They'd talk about the cabin another time. He needed to think.

Caroline laughed. "Well, I have to say you're obviously not a bookkeeper by trade—"

"You're damn right there," Adam broke in, relieved to have changed the topic. "You get anywhere?"

She nodded. "There's still a ways to go. But last year's records were clear enough, so I modeled some of the stuff I found on those." She stopped, and against his will he looked at her again. She was smiling slightly, that soft womanly smile she had. Not mocking like Rhonda's. Not bursting with goodwill like Mrs. T's. Not a come-on, like the smiles of half a dozen women he could name. Just simple and sweet and open. Trusting. Vulnerable.

"Good," he said absently, then started toward the house. How in hell had Beau left her in the kind of straits she must be in to have taken a job with him? He wanted to know, but damned if he was going to ask her again.

"Adam?"

"Yes?" He lowered the brim of his hat against the late-afternoon sun.

"We can talk about this after supper?"

"What's that?"

"The books. I'm going to need a little help setting things up."

Adam paused and reached down to pluck an overripe stem of bromegrass. "Sure. After supper. Shouldn't take more than an hour or so."

CHAPTER EIGHT

HE WOULDN'T SOON FORGET the look on her face when he plunked his records for Tetlock Valley Tours on the desk—a Tony Lama boot box over a third full of receipts and scribbled phone messages and cryptic notes to himself that he had to admit he couldn't always figure out. His handwriting wasn't great at the best of times.

Amazement first. Then, to his chagrin, outright amusement.

"You're *joking!*"

"What do you mean, joking?" He pawed through the box, certain he'd spotted a hay receipt he'd been looking for—that belonged with his Double O books. The ranch books he didn't have too many problems with—straight entries for sensible things like feed, gas, equipment parts, harness repair and taxes, sales and purchases of stock from time to time.

"This...*box!* Is this how you've been keeping track of records? Your Tetlock Valley trail-ride business?"

He pulled out the hay receipt. Aha! "Seems like an okay method to me. At least you know where everything's at." He tucked the receipt in his shirt pocket and allowed himself to meet her eyes. "Right?"

"Uh-huh." Her eyes danced and her cheeks were pink. A delicious pink. He frowned and reexamined the contents of the box. "I'd hate to be your accountant," she added.

"My accountant hates to be my accountant," Adam returned. "But he's hard up and he needs the work."

Caroline laughed. "Well, we'd better get at it." She dragged the box toward her and began riffling through the pieces of paper. "We'll start by separating out all the phone calls and reservations, okay? See where we are."

"Fine by me." Adam pulled up a chair and, at her direction, sorted phone messages on the desktop. She turned back to the computer screen and after some frowning and rapid keystroking wheeled her chair toward him.

"I'm setting up a spreadsheet here. I figured this out earlier. Guests each week, how many, language spoken, special diets, paid in full or not, personal data and so on. That sound all right to you?"

"Caroline."

"Yes?"

"I'm telling you straight—anything you do is fine by me. I'm not fussy. My only interest is getting this box of papers into that computer in some form that you or I can work with. Is that clear?"

She nodded. "Very clear."

"Okay. So quit asking me if it's all right by me. This is not exactly my area of competence. When you keep asking me—well, you make me think I *should* know. I don't." He paused, suddenly realizing what he must sound like—the grumpy boss.

"Mmm." She didn't seem to have noticed. She scrutinized Adam's phone memos, then transferred the information to the computer, ignoring him. He sat back and watched her.

She had on a plain blue top, sleeveless, and a skirt and sandals. Bare legs. Adam could see neat toes, the nails unpainted, peeping out from the ends of her sandals, and he tore his gaze away. The sweater that she'd loosely thrown over her shoulders, kept slipping off, revealing the tantalizing smoothness of lightly tanned upper arms. As she worked, she constantly hitched it up. The movement fascinated him.

Was it her? Or was it just that she was a woman, and it had been so long since he'd spent any time with a woman? That had to be it, Adam decided, annoyed with himself. He supposed that was what happened when a man's ways set in with him, bachelor ways. And certainly there was no question that this particular woman was strictly off limits.

She was his best friend's widow, although he supposed that wasn't such a big deal. More importantly she was the mother of his child. Adopted or otherwise, there was no doubt in Adam's mind that Caroline and his daughter were made for each other. The woman who'd given birth to Rose wasn't much more than a blur in his memory. According to word he'd had from Beau a couple of years after they adopted Rose, she'd married, moved to Europe somewhere and started a family of her own. She was history. He was sure he'd never see or hear from her again. He was sure he wasn't much more than a blur in her mind, either. An unexpected encounter that had yielded unexpected consequences. *All's well that ends well.* Maybe so...but *had* it ended?

A small sound drew his attention. Rose stood just behind the partly open door. *All's well...* Had she read his mind? She had on a pink nightie and a fuzzy little bathrobe with one pocket turned inside out, and sure enough, she had her Raggy clutched in one hand. Her eyes, as she regarded him somberly through the door opening, were huge and curious.

Adam got to his feet. He didn't know what to do. He shoved his hands in his pockets and took a step back. "Er, Caroline...I think there's someone here to see you."

"Rosie!" Caroline wheeled her chair around and held

her arms out. A smile lit her face. Adam felt the old ache he'd felt before. "Look at you! Did you have a bath already?" Rose came into the room and proceeded toward her mother. Caroline wrapped her arms around the girl and slid off her chair until she was crouched down beside her. She smoothed back Rose's hair, which was damp. Curly, black, shining. She kissed her on the forehead, then straightened her robe and turned her pocket back inside, patting the fabric.

"Janie's mommy gave me my bath," Rose said, looking pleased with herself. "I said she could."

"You did? Well, I guess you're all ready for bed now. What a big girl you are these days! Have you brushed your teeth?"

"Uh-huh. See?" The child bared pearly white baby teeth for her mother to inspect and puffed her cheeks out importantly.

"All clean. Are you ready for a story?"

Rose nodded solemnly and raised her eyes to Adam's in limpid appeal.

Hell. He strode over to the window overlooking the side yard and leaned against the wall. He wasn't reading any story to any kid.

He glanced at his watch. It was still light at almost eight-thirty. He hadn't realized he'd been holed up in the office with Caroline for the past two hours. This was taking longer than he'd expected. He should have thought of that. The kid needed her mother. He couldn't work Caroline the way he'd expect Rhonda to work. Not when she had other things on her mind besides his lousy business records.

"Adam?"

He realized she'd spoken to him and whirled away from the window. "Yes?" His voice sounded forbidding. He cleared his throat.

"I—I'm just going to go up and read Rose a little story and put her to bed. I won't be more than twenty minutes..."

"Fine." He waved his hand. "Take as much time as you need. I'll sort the rest of these receipts. We can finish in the morning."

"No. I'll be back. Rose?"

The girl looked up at her mother.

"Say good-night to Mr. Garrick," Caroline said softly.

Adam froze. Rose took a step toward him, then another. Dear Lord—what did she expect him to do? Adam stared. Rose tilted her face toward him for a second or two, waiting, eyes half-closed. Then when Adam did nothing—*what did she want him to do?*—she opened her eyes wide and scowled at him. "G'night, Mister," she said, hitching Raggy close to her side.

"Good night, Rose," Adam said quietly. Clearly she had expected more. A hug? A good night kiss? Adam had no idea. "Sweet dreams."

She smiled then, a shy smile, and slipped her hand into her mother's. They left, and after they'd been gone a few moments, Adam went to the door and closed it.

What was wrong with him? This was just a kid, for Pete's sake. He had to get used to her being in the house, that was all. He'd brought the whole damn thing on himself by hiring her mother, and now he had to deal with it.

"SAY, I HEARD RHONDA got on with the Bar U for the summer."

Adam frowned and ran his pencil down the list Caroline had sent with him. "You heard right, Ted."

Ted Eberly, the co-op's warehouseman, fortyish, balding and single, tossed another box of canned peaches in the back of the pickup. *Peaches.* Adam checked the list and crossed off Caroline's entry for two cases of canned peaches.

"So? I hear you got somebody else out there at the Double O now doing your office work. Real looker, they say."

Adam put the list back in his shirt pocket and leaned against the side of the pickup. He adjusted his hat brim, lowering it over his eyes. "Where you hearing all this, Ted?"

"Oh, I don't know." The warehouseman colored. "Here and there." He removed his broad-brimmed straw hat with the curled up sides and wiped a sleeve across his brow. Then he shrugged. "You know. Heck. People talk."

Adam stepped on the running board of the pickup and climbed over the side. He started rearranging the load. He needed more room. He still had an order to pick up at the vet's, and Caroline had a list of stuff for him to get from the drugstore, too. Since he'd hired her nearly two weeks ago, she'd already made improvements. She had everything listed and entered in one of her databases in the computer, and she provided him with facts and figures at the end of each week. Prices, amounts, menus. Cost per guest. Adam couldn't complain. Things had never run so smoothly this early in the season before.

"Say, wasn't there a sack of rolled oats in that order, Ted?"

"Rolled oats? Lemme check." The warehouseman went back into the cavernous gloom of the co-op building. He appeared a few minutes later with a sack, which he tossed to Adam. "Here." Then he stood back on the loading dock, hands on his hips, still grinning.

"So? Is she a Yankee or what?"

"She's an American."

"Jeez. Is that legal? Working for you like that? I heard she had a kid with her, too."

Adam gave the warehouseman a level look. "Anybody ever tell you that you talk too much, Ted?"

"All the time," Ted returned cheerfully, then let out a hoarse laugh. "One of the bonuses of the job, man. Ya hear things. This and that. News. You know. Before it hits the papers."

"Well, I've got some news for you, Ted." Adam hopped off the truck and came close to the warehouseman. He dropped his arm over the other man's shoulders, buddylike, and lowered his head confidentially. "Listen real careful, Ted. Now, first off, you heard right. She's gorgeous."

"She is?" Ted's eyes lit up and Adam had a sudden notion to jam the guy's straw hat right down over his ears. A notion he resisted. With difficulty.

"Uh-huh. And, yes, she's got a kid. A real nice little girl. And, yes, she's from the States. And you know what else, Ted?"

"What's that, Adam?" Ted looked a little alarmed. Adam wasn't sure if it was his lowered tone or his tight grip that was having the effect.

"She's mine." He released the warehouseman and slapped him lightly on one shoulder as a no-hard-feelings parting gesture. "Got that, Ted? Mine. You pass the word on. I don't want you or any of your lowlife buddies sniffing around the Double O or you'll have me to deal with. She's strictly off limits. Got that?"

He opened the door to his pickup and waited for Ted's answer.

"You bet. Gotcha, Adam!" Ted waved, his neck as red as the feather in his hat band.

Adam couldn't wipe the grin off his face as he drove away, leaving the warehouseman staring after him on the loading platform. He had no doubt Ted would spread the message he wanted spread, which was that Caroline and her daughter were under *his* protection. Last thing she needed to deal with was a bunch of Glory good old boys coming around.

She's mine. Ha. Well, she'd never have to know he'd lied about that one. But it definitely wouldn't hurt Ted Eberly and his buddies to think it was true. Besides, he was doing her a favor, steering off any interest, wasn't he?

At the vet's Adam picked up some more of the solution that Curley was using on Duke. Whatever was bothering the gelding's foot seemed to be getting better, but it would still be several weeks before they could put the animal back to work.

Then he headed down Purcell Avenue toward the drugstore. One of the guests coming in Saturday had requested a supply of a particular herbal tea that Caroline had discovered was only available at the druggist's. Now *this,* Adam thought with a grimace, was exactly why he needed somebody like Caroline or Rhonda. Herbal tea, for crying out loud!

He spotted a parking space half a block from the drugstore and backed into it. Just as he opened the door, someone hailed him from across the street.

Cal Blake. And his new wife, Nina—well, hardly new. They'd been married over a year already. And their brandnew kid, too, judging by that fancy wheeled buggy Nina was pushing. Adam waved and crossed over to their side of the street.

"How's that little mare working out?" Cal looked terrific—tanned, relaxed, healthy. There definitely were some men that marriage and family life suited.

"She's great. I appreciate you sending her over, Cal. Don't know where I'd have been without a replacement on such short notice." So far, Adam had been doing his best to ignore the baby carriage, which Nina jiggled gently as they talked.

"Adam!" Nina gave him one of her big beautiful smiles. "Don't tell me you haven't seen our Anna yet. Look!" She bent over and drew down a light blanket. Adam had to stoop a little to peer inside the carriage. It was a baby, all right.

"Isn't she adorable?"

"Sure is," he said noncommittally. Did all parents think they had the best-looking children who'd ever been born? What had Rose looked like as a baby? The thought flashed into his mind and the familiar ache struck him again. There was so much he didn't know about her. So much he'd never know, had no right to know.

"That's what you called her? Anna?" he asked, for lack of inspiration.

"Anna Marigold Blake," Nina said triumphantly with a tender glance at her husband. Cal couldn't have been prouder. He reached for his wife's hand. All of a sudden Adam felt completely superfluous.

"Well, I'd best be on my way. Got something to pick up at Foster's for one of the guests coming in day after tomorrow."

"How's the trail business going this summer?" Cal asked, still holding his wife's hand.

"Fine. Fine." He'd just leave it at that. "The usual."

"Rhonda Maclean pulled out on you last minute, huh?"

"She did," Adam admitted. "No surprise there. We'll see how the Bar U treats her."

Cal laughed. "Yeah."

"So who's helping you out for the summer?" Nina asked, frowning.

"I, uh, hired on somebody else. Nobody you'd know," he added hastily.

"Young Longquist tells me she's a widow," Cal said softly, eyes cautious. Cal knew damn well it was none of his business—but they'd been friends a long time.

"You remember Beau Carter?"

Cal nodded.

"His widow. She's up for the summer and was looking for some work." Adam glanced back at his truck. "Well, hate to run, but I've got a few more stops to make. See you later, Cal." He tipped his hat and nodded. "Nina."

"Take care of yourself, Adam," Nina said, and smiled.

Adam pushed into the welcome coolness of the air-conditioned drugstore. Damn. Now Ben. Didn't anyone in this town know how to keep his mouth shut?

"EASY, FELLA. That's it. Easy, now." Adam leaned against Duke's near front leg, and the gelding raised and lowered it several times, then lifted it again. Adam frowned. Obviously the leg remained fairly sensitive, although the swelling above the hoof had gone down. Adam still wasn't entirely convinced the animal hadn't picked up a splinter or something.

He picked up the horse's leg twice more, then let him set it down. The gelding turned his big head and blew fragrant hay-scented breath into Adam's face, making him smile. He'd had Duke since he was a frisky three-year-old. The gelding was going on fourteen now and was still one of Adam's most valuable animals.

Suddenly Duke threw up his head and whickered. That meant company. Adam slipped the halter he carried over the gelding's head. Maybe Curley'd come back early.

"Adam?"

"Over here." *Caroline.* He hadn't seen her since yesterday, when he got in with the new batch of guests. He'd gone to town with Curley after supper to see if they could round up extra hands for the haying crew. They'd brought two men back to the Double O.

"Hi. I wasn't sure you were here."

He glanced at her. She wore jeans and a T-shirt and had tied her hair back with a scarf. She looked about eighteen. "What's up?"

"I guess you're busy," she began.

"So-so."

"Remember that tea I had you pick up from the drugstore?"

Adam frowned. "Yeah?"

"Well, it's entirely my fault, but in all the rush of breakfast and getting the guests off this morning and then getting Rose and Mrs. T and Janie off and—"

"Hold on. Rose has gone somewhere?"

"With Mrs. T and Janie. They're going to bring her back tomorrow around suppertime. She really wanted to go and I..." Caroline bit her lip. Her voice was a little shaky when she continued. "I decided I should let her. It's hard, but I know she's not a baby anymore. I don't want to be overprotective—"

"Could you open that stall door there?"

Adam waited while Caroline lifted the latch and pulled open the door to the box stall. He led Duke out. The big gelding limped slightly. Adam stopped and waited for Caroline to shut the door and join him. When she did, Duke stretched over his big bony nose and sniffed her hair.

"Friendly, isn't he?" she said.

"He likes the ladies, all right." Adam led the gelding slowly to the door of the barn, then took him to one of the small corrals and opened the gate. He slipped off the halter and smacked the animal lightly on the rump. "Away you go, big fella." The gelding limped into the enclosure, lowering his head to the short grass there. Adam kept Duke in a small corral during the day so he didn't overwork his sore leg.

He looped the lead rope up and slung it and the halter over his shoulder. "What's on your mind, Caroline?" Obviously she hadn't come down to the barn to tell him that Rose was having a sleepover with Mrs. T and Janie.

"The tea. I was wondering if someone was going up to the Tetlock camp later today or tomorrow." Caroline squinted at him from under the hand she used to shade her eyes. "If someone was, he could take up the tea that German wanted so badly. Otto Schroeder."

Adam stopped. So...they were alone, the two of them. Curley planned to start his first hay cut tomorrow, Monday. Mrs. T and Janie and Rose wouldn't be back until Monday evening. Duke was on the mend. His foreman wasn't counting on his help with the hay, at least not with cutting.

"Maybe you'd like to go up there yourself?" he suggested. "Take a look at the camp setup. The job would make more sense to you once you've seen it and..." Adam couldn't stop the feeling that was welling up inside him. Damn it, he wanted to show this woman Tetlock Lake. He wanted to spend a day with her, riding, showing her the sights of the high country in July. There was no better place on earth.

"...I'd like to take you if you're interested."

"You mean, ride a horse?" She looked worried, but she was smiling.

"Yeah. Ride a horse. We've got a few that make sitting on a rocking chair seem pretty adventurous." He grinned.

"What about...what if Rose needed me?"

"We'll have a radiophone. And besides, we'll take the shortcut. The guests don't know about it. We'd be able to get back here in under two hours if we needed to. What do you say?"

"Yes," she said. "Yes, I'd love to go." Her eyes were alive. Excited.

"How soon can you be ready?"

"That depends. What do I need to take?"

"Personal stuff. A toothbrush, maybe. Everything else is up at the camp."

CHAPTER NINE

THE TRAILHEAD CAMP, which consisted of a shack for old Farley to live in, a horse shelter and feed shed, and a pasture for grazing spare horses, marked the beginning of the real mountain trail through the Horsethief Pass. Farley's camp, seventeen miles from the Double O, through the hills and over a winding gravel road was mainly a provisioning point for the higher-country Tetlock Valley camp. Adam or one of his hands trucked in groceries and supplies on a weekly basis, which the old wrangler packed up to the mountain camp.

Once in the Tetlock Valley mountain camp, after a day-long horseback ride from the ranch, the guests stayed in one place for the week, taking short day trips if they wanted to explore the high country.

If Adam had to go up to the camp for any reason, he generally used the shortcut to shave saddle-weary hours off the trip.

Today he took his time driving to the camp. It was just past noon, and Adam wanted this trip to last. Even taking it easy, it wouldn't be more than two or three hours from Farley's to the Tetlock Valley camp. They'd get there in plenty of time for supper, then tomorrow they'd head back around lunchtime. Twenty-four hours, that was all the time he had with Caroline.

"You think Barbara will mind us showing up like this

for supper?'' Barbara Hillerman, Jim's wife, was in charge of the cookhouse at the Tetlock Valley camp.

Adam glanced at Caroline. She'd untied the scarf from her hair and it blew wildly in the breeze from the open window. Sunglasses hid her eyes.

"Barbara's pretty easygoing. I don't think two extra people showing up for supper is likely to bother her."

Caroline braced her back against the door of the pickup and kept her gaze on him. Adam ran one hand over his jaw, conscious that he hadn't shaved this morning. "Tell me about Barbara and Jim," she said simply.

Adam thought for a moment. "Well, you've met Jim." Each week, Jim Hillerman, a bearded, bespectacled, serious-looking man, brought returning guests down to the Double O on Friday and went out with the next batch on Sunday.

"Uh-huh."

"The Hillermans used to have a small spread of their own east of Glory. More a farm, really, although I don't think they put in any crops. Maybe cut a little hay, that's about it. A few geese, some dairy goats. Barbara had a big garden and she used to sell some of the stuff she grew at the farmers' markets."

"How long have they worked for you?"

"Four years," Adam said.

"They still have their farm?"

"Nope. Bank took it over." Adam sent Caroline a quick look. "Foreclosed. Jim wasn't cut out for farming. Barbara, either. Too interested in things that didn't pay. They bought a place in town and now they spend their summers up at the Tetlock. Jim's a naturalist. That's what he really likes. I don't think there's a man alive who knows more about fossils and rocks and wildflowers. He's crazy about getting into the backcountry every year."

"Barbara, too?"

"Anywhere Jim goes is fine with Barbara."

Caroline turned to gaze out the windshield. She didn't say anything for a few miles, and Adam had the distinct impression she was thinking of Beau. He was sorry he'd mentioned what he had about Jim and Barbara and the kind of marriage they had.

But he never expected her next question.

"Do you miss your wife, Adam?"

Adam shot her a glance. Did he miss Helen? He hadn't really thought about Helen in months. They'd been divorced more than six years, and the marriage had been bad for a lot longer than that. Sometimes it felt like he'd never been married. "No. Can't say that I do. Why do you ask?"

"How long were you married?"

Now, this was personal. Adam wasn't sure he wanted to answer questions like this. Still, it seemed to matter to Caroline, as though she was sorting something out in her own mind more than trying to understand what went on in his.

"We were married for eight years."

"That's quite a long time."

"Long enough."

"What's that supposed to mean?" She laughed. "Don't tell me you weren't happy at least part of that time. You must have loved her. I can't imagine you marrying someone you didn't love."

Adam shot her another hard glance. What the hell was she getting at? And as for knowing him—she didn't know him at all. No more than he knew her.

"I never thought much about it to tell the truth," Adam admitted. "Just seemed like the thing to do at the time. I suppose we were in love. Some people might call it that."

Caroline said nothing for a few moments as though expecting him to go on. "And?"

"It didn't work out," Adam said brusquely. "Turned out I didn't do relationships all that well. I never should've gotten married in the first place. I'm not the marrying kind. I don't blame Helen, not a bit. She put up with plenty and tried her best to work things out."

"What happened?"

"I was stubborn. I never saw things her way. She was right about a lot, this trail business for one thing," Adam said, looking over at Caroline. She was listening intently, which disconcerted him. He frowned and turned his attention back to the road. "It was Helen's idea to build up the ranch with cash from the tourists. She wanted me to spend more time ranching. She wanted kids. But I was stuck on the rodeo life. I couldn't give it up—well, not then, at least. And there's no money in it. Not for guys like me."

He smiled at the irony of it. When *had* he given it up? After his wife walked out on him for good. After it was too late.

"What about you?"

"Me?" He frowned. They were almost at the trailhead. He couldn't believe it—he'd never talked like this in his life before. Not about personal things.

"Did you want kids?"

Adam felt the old ache again just under his ribs. "I never thought much about it." Which was the gospel truth.

"And what about the other?"

"What other?"

"Marriage. Do you think you're the marrying kind now?"

"Damned if I know," he said shortly. What was she getting at? "I suppose a man can change. Some men."

He was grateful she left it at that. She sat in silence as he negotiated the last hairpin curve before the long climb to the trailhead camp.

Old Farley was there. His dog, a huge husky cross, came bounding across the meadow to meet them. When Farley ambled out of his tiny cabin, he was pulling his suspenders up over his shoulders.

"Well, well. Visitors. How ya doin', Adam, you old son of a—" Farley clamped one hand over his mouth, eyes wide. "Oops. This here's the missus, eh? Come on in, both of youse. I'll pour a coffee. Got a fresh pot on."

"No time to stop, Farley," Adam said with a glance at Caroline. He wasn't going to correct the "missus" comment. There were one or two things old Farley had never figured out, such as what Helen looked like and the fact that she'd left more than six years ago. "We're going to ride up, come back down tomorrow. You got some gear here we can use? Couple horses?"

"There's Miss Minnie over here—" Farley pointed to a large brown mare grazing in the pasture "—just a-layin' about, gettin' fat. She'd make a nice quiet mount for the missus. Very peaceable, she is." He beamed at Caroline, displaying an interesting assortment of tobacco-stained teeth.

"And I don't suppose you'd mind takin' that green-broke gelding young Ben brought up last week, boss. That black? I've been workin' him a little, but so far he don't seem that interested in learnin' and he's durn hard on the pots and pans. I'd 'preciate you taking some snort outa him. These bones ain't as young as they used to be." He grinned again at Caroline and bobbed his head a few times and tipped a nonexistent hat.

"I suppose I could do that, Farley." Adam didn't feel like his bones were quite as young as they used to be, either, but he didn't want to mention it to the old bronc buster. After all, Farley had at least thirty years on Adam. He just hoped the gelding didn't have *that* much snort in him. He didn't appreciate the challenge quite the way he might have ten years ago.

"Caroline. Why don't you get your bag out of the truck and go sit in the shade over there and we'll get the horses ready. Or go pour yourself a cup of Farley's coffee."

"I'll watch."

Adam hesitated. He'd have preferred Caroline to be somewhere else when he got on that green horse. If there was going to be any kind of rodeo, he'd just as soon she wasn't around.

The horses were easy enough to catch and, beyond switching their tails at the summer flies, neither one moved a muscle as he and Farley put on saddles and bridles. But Adam didn't miss the tiny flick of the black's ears as he tightened the cinch, or the half-closed eyes that only simulated boredom. Damn, he thought with a quick glance at Caroline, who had climbed the corral fence and was perched on the highest pole. *This horse is going to blow up.*

And he did. Adam mounted smoothly and had barely found his right stirrup when the gelding went straight up. Then he came straight down and twisted to the right and went straight up again. Adam felt the adrenaline surge through his body and he gave the gelding a good kick. Without spurs, the gelding didn't even notice it. "Atta boy!" Adam yelled and through the dust thrown up by the gelding's hooves, glimpsed old Farley hanging on to the fence, grinning his damn-fool face off and Caroline white as a sheet.

A couple more jumps and the gelding changed his mind. He streaked out across the pasture, full tilt. About halfway, he tried to quit, but Adam kept him at a fast gallop all the way around the field before coming back to Farley and Caroline. He eased the gelding to a lope, then a walk. The gelding stopped and shook his head up and down and flicked his ears back and forth and gave a big moist horsey sigh.

"That's the stuff, boss!" yelled Farley. "By gar, that there took a little jam out of 'im. You see now why I can't keep the dints out of the pots and pans when I put a pack saddle on 'im?"

Adam nodded and swung out of the saddle and stood for a moment talking quietly to the animal and patting his sweat-darkened neck. He felt good. He felt damn good. There was nothing like a few minutes on a frisky horse. It reminded him of what he'd always liked best about cow-boying.

"Are...are you all right, Adam?"

Caroline's horrified voice sobered him immediately. "Of course I'm all right. Me and the black here were just getting to know each other a little better, weren't we, big fella?" He scratched the gelding's nose and the animal tossed his head, jingling the bridle buckles.

"You ready, Caroline?" He peered up at the sun. It must be after two o'clock already.

"Is...is *my* horse going to do that?"

Adam laughed. She looked so worried. "Miss Minnie won't even burp. Matter of fact, you might fall asleep on her if you aren't careful. Come here." Caroline climbed down from the fence. She didn't seem convinced.

"Now. Have you ever ridden a horse before?"

She nodded. "A few times. Quite a while ago."

"Well, it's like riding a bike," Adam advised, ignoring old Farley's guffaw. "You don't forget."

Caroline stood close to him and he positioned her so that she faced Miss Minnie's left side. The crown of Caroline's head was just below his chin. He swore he could smell the faint flowery scent of her hair or her perfume...or whatever.

"Now, grab the reins in this hand." Caroline reached up obediently and grasped the reins in her left hand. "Now, put your other hand here." Adam guided her hand to the cantle. "Left foot in the stirrup."

Caroline lifted her foot and inserted it into the big wooden stirrup. "Ready?" She turned slightly and nodded, her eyes alight, and Adam had the craziest impulse to just lean forward a couple of inches and...

What was he thinking of? "All right. Leg up and over and into the saddle." He raised her slightly as she swung her leg up.

Then she was looking down at him and smiling, absolutely delighted with herself. He grinned. "Nothing to it."

"Nope," she mimicked, drawling. "Nothing to it."

Old Farley cackled and slapped his hand on the fence rail. The dog barked. All Miss Minnie did was flick one ear to dislodge a fly. Adam couldn't stop grinning. "Okay. How about you try that a couple more times? Maybe walk around a bit. I'll get our gear from the truck."

THE HIGH COUNTRY was at its best. The alpine flowers were in bloom, the air hummed with the sound of a thousand insects, and the leaves were the full dark green of July. All the summer scents lay in the wind: the thick leaf mold under the trees, the fireweed and the last of the wild roses, the thin sharp smell of snow blowing down from the glaciers. An hour or so from the trailhead they came to Lace Falls, a narrow wavering stream of water that dropped from high up on a cliff to fall nearly three hundred feet, looking like a white froth of lace.

They stopped there to eat the lunch Caroline had packed. That had been a surprise. Adam hadn't even considered taking a lunch, knowing they'd be at the Tetlock camp in plenty of time for supper. But Caroline pulled apples, date

squares, thickly-sliced-ham sandwiches on Mrs. T's homemade bread, pickles and a vacuum flask of sweet milky tea
out of her bag. They spent half an hour eating their lunch—
him leaning against a sun-warmed pine trunk, her leaning
against a big granite boulder—relaxing and listening to the
falls while the horses cropped at the sparse mountain grass.
Adam was glad the falls made conversation difficult. Conversation didn't always improve a situation, in his opinion.
They'd talked enough in the truck to last him a while.

Besides, he needed time to think. He was coming to the
unwelcome conclusion that there were a quite a few things
he liked about Caroline Carter. Too many things. Woman
things.

He thought about his impulse back there when she got
on the mare. He'd wanted to lean forward and kiss her.
Right in front of old Farley! That was crazy. He hadn't had
any serious relationships since Helen left and had no interest in one now.

Still, as they made their way slowly along the trail, he
couldn't help allowing his gaze to linger on her when he
was sure she didn't see him. He felt like a kid, someone
who'd never noticed a grown-up woman before.

They got up to the camp just before five. The lake, small
and green and absolutely perfect in its high mountain-valley
setting, was always unexpected. You came over a bare
rocky ridge after a good climb of about fifteen minutes, and
there it was, spread out before you. The glacier at the far
end of the lake dipped right into the jewel-green waters,
and the snowy peaks rose to nearly eight thousand feet on
all sides.

At the base of the lake was the Tetlock Valley camp,
with its cookshack, its five canvas-topped, log-bottomed
wall tents—one for the staff, four for the guests, doubled
up—and its small corral and fly shelter for the horses. An-

other shed stored baled hay and grain, which Adam had airlifted, along with the initial foodstuffs, early in the season.

There was a small floating dock with two runabouts tied to it for guests who liked to spend the day out on the lake, either fishing or just enjoying the scenery. During their week here, guests set their own agendas. Many of them hiked and took a lot of pictures. Others went out with Jim Hillerman or Ben Longquist on day-long horseback explorations, into the nearby mountains. Others hung around the camp and read. Adam had discovered from experience that most guests preferred to do what they wanted, as long as the necessities were taken care of. That meant a big breakfast and evening meal together, a packed lunch and an evening campfire with storytelling under the stars.

It was a simple recipe for success. The guests paid plenty for it and went home happy, pleased with their Rocky Mountain wilderness experience. And, whether Adam liked this part of his business or not, these tourists helped keep the Double O solvent, regardless of the price of beef.

Adam left the Caroline at the cookshack with Barbara and turned the horses loose for the rest of the afternoon. Ben was out with three of the week's guests, including the Austrian who had ordered the herbal tea, and Jim was down at the dock tinkering with one of the outboards. Adam went to help him. Jim was no talker and Adam had some thinking to do.

There was no question about it—he was attracted to his best friend's widow. *Very* attracted.

Just recognizing the feeling helped. Ever since she'd first arrived, back in the middle of June, he'd realized he wasn't reacting to her the way he did to most women. Until now, until he'd recognized the feeling as plain old-fashioned garden-variety lust, he'd been thinking it was something to do with Rose. He couldn't deny that he was uneasy around Rose. But now at least he knew that what made him uncomfortable with Caroline had no connection to his daughter.

What kind of excuse for a man harbored lustful feelings toward his buddy's widow? As a family friend, so to speak, didn't that put him in a position of trust? Sure, Beau had been dead for nearly two years, but his widow definitely had *not* come up to Alberta looking for a new relationship. She'd come because she was on the run from something—Adam sure wished he knew what. And because she was broke—he wished he knew why. And because she wanted to see where her husband had spent a few summers before they'd met. That was all.

There was only one thing to do, from his point of view—only one thing a man of honor *could* do. Nip the whole thing in the bud.

CHAPTER TEN

BARBARA HILLERMAN had a pleasant open expression and thick graying fair hair pulled back into a loose knot. She wore faded jeans and an apron and had the wide smile of a woman determined to look on the bright side of everything, generally successfully.

Adam had led Caroline right up to the door of the combination cookshack and Hillerman sleeping quarters. He'd dismounted, then helped her dismount; Caroline was thankful for the support when her knees promptly gave way the instant her feet touched the ground. Adam hadn't said a word, simply handed her over to Barbara before remounting the black and leading Miss Minnie toward the horse corral. After the camaraderie of the afternoon, Caroline was a little taken aback at his curt dismissal now. Still, the man was a mass of contradictions; she was sure she'd never understand him.

"What a nice surprise! Where's your little girl? Jim told me what a darling she is. My heavens, you look like you could use a cup of tea," Barbara said, smiling merrily and not waiting for an answer before leading Caroline inside.

One end of the large long room was set up with four wooden tables and chairs. A freestanding metal fireplace, shiny red, was tucked into one corner, and two shabby but comfortable-looking overstuffed sofas were drawn up on each side of the fireplace, with a braided rug between them. A bookshelf between the windows held tattered copies of paperback books and old *National Geographic*s. With the exception of the deer antlers on each side of the door—which she could have done without—Caroline liked the feeling of the room very much. Checked curtains at the windows completed the rustic look.

At the other end, behind a self-serve counter, was Barbara's kitchen. Caroline could smell good cooking smells from somewhere, probably the oven. She hadn't realized until now how much of an appetite she'd worked up. Barbara immediately went to the six-burner propane range and turned on a flame under an industrial-size stainless-steel kettle.

"Sit down," she invited, waving a hand toward one of several stools pulled up to the long Formica-topped counter. "Make yourself at home. Tea'll be ready in no time. You didn't say where your little girl was."

"She's gone off with Mrs. Tump and Janie to stay overnight at their place," Caroline said, helping herself from the plate of chocolate-chip cookies the other woman had pushed toward her. "It's a first for me, too. The anxious mommy." She smiled wryly and shrugged. "I'm sure I'm more worried about it than Rosie is."

"Kids are tough." Barbara retrieved a brown-Betty teapot from a shelf over the sink, then opened a covered tin on the counter and extracted two teabags. "Jim and I only had the one. Matt." She glanced at Caroline. "He's fifteen, nearly sixteen, and working here for the summer. Nuts about horses. Adam hired him as a helper to bring in wood and clean fish for the guests, that sort of thing. I don't think he's worth what Adam's paying him." Barbara laughed. "That's Adam. He'd like everyone to think he's tough as old barn boots, but inside he's nothing but a big softie."

"I wouldn't have described him quite like that," Caroline murmured, suddenly wondering if that was why he'd hired *her*. Had he felt sorry for her? Was that it? Her dismay as quickly dissolved. Of course he hadn't—that was nonsense. He needed her to replace Rhonda. And she was doing her best to make sure she was worth every penny he paid her.

"How long have you known Adam?" Barbara raised one eyebrow and poured a pale stream of tea into one cup.

"Not long. I really only met him in June, when Rose and I stopped in on our way to Calgary." Caroline reached for her mug of tea. "Actually I guess you could say longer than that," she corrected herself. "He and his wife were at our wedding." Caroline stared for a few seconds into the golden tawny bottom of her tea. "My husband and Adam were the best of friends," she finished softly.

"Were?" Barbara queried, just as softly.

"My husband's dead," Caroline said firmly, setting down her cup and meeting Barbara's pale blue gaze. "Nearly two years ago. He was hiking in the mountains and he...he was killed in a rock slide."

"Oh, I'm so sorry to hear that. I didn't mean to bring up bad memories."

"Oh, they're not bad memories," Caroline said, and smiled. She covered the other woman's hand briefly with hers. "They're good memories. We were married nine years. We had a wonderful marriage. I just...I just wish Beau had lived to see our little girl grow up."

"Mountain climbing." Barbara gave a disdainful shrug and blew on her tea. "Sounds like something Adam would've gotten up to in the old days. Or my Jim. I suppose that's why your husband and Adam were such good friends?" She raised one eyebrow and, when Caroline said nothing, continued, "Adam was a regular terror once. I suppose you know that. I must admit, he's improved quite a bit with age. Most men do." She laughed.

Caroline shook her head. "I don't know anything abou
Adam. Mary Tump mentioned the adventure stuff, though
She seems to think as little of it as you do!" She tried a
laugh, but suddenly tears choked her. Quickly she forcec
them back, aghast. What brought *this* on? Talking abou
Beau? So easily, to another woman? A woman who jus
might understand some of what she'd gone through wher
her husband would disappear, sometimes for weeks, inte
the mountains?

She stood and walked to the window, then took a deep
breath, determined to change the subject. The lake, severa
hundred yards away, was a luminous green in the afternoor
sun. "When do the guests have supper?"

"Half-past six," Barbara said. "I've got a big roast ir
the oven and some coleslaw in the refrigerator. Fresh rolls
Carrots. Pickles. Mashed potatoes. Gravy. Canned peache:
and sponge cake with whipped cream for dessert. Plain anc
plenty of it. They work up big appetites in this fresh air.'

"Well." Caroline felt steady enough to turn. "Just give
me something to do and I'll do it," she said, managing
another smile. "That's what I'm here for—to give you a
hand and see how everything works."

Barbara gave her potatoes to peel. Apparently it was a
job that sometimes fell to her son, Matt, who showed up
at the door half an hour after Caroline's arrival. The relie
on the boy's face when he discovered someone else peeling
vegetables nearly made her laugh.

The two women worked companionably together. Car
oline felt comfortable enough to venture a few questions o
her own. "Whatever happened to Adam's wife? Does she
live around here?"

"Don't ever call Helen his 'wife' or he'll take your head
off," Barbara advised with a smile. "No, she took off—
somewheres in B.C., I heard. I don't believe he'll eve

marry again, not that lots of women haven't tried their darnedest to change his mind.''

Caroline tossed a peeled potato into the huge aluminum pot of cold water Barbara had ready. *Not the marrying kind.* Hadn't he said that himself? And why did the thought send an odd little shiver down her spine? He certainly wasn't a type she fancied.... A sudden image of the sexy flirtatious Rhonda floated into her brain. *Adam and Rhonda?* Or some other woman?

''Well,'' she began, smiling to show Barbara it didn't matter either way to her, ''Adam's an attractive hardworking man. He seems to be reasonably successful at ranching and this Tetlock business. I suppose he'd be considered a fairly good catch around here.''

Barbara laughed. ''Oh, he's that, all right! Just not all that eager to take the hook again.''

Caroline dropped another potato into the pot. ''He must have been in love with his wife to be so dead against marriage now,'' she mused. No matter what he'd said about Helen. She herself had been in love with Beau. Did that mean she wouldn't consider marrying again? She frowned—she'd never thought about it quite that way before. The old ache struck her. *No family. No baby of her own.*

''I wouldn't know,'' Barbara said, opening the oven door to check the roast. ''I didn't know Adam and Helen all that well back then. Jim did. I think they had an okay marriage. I never heard otherwise. Who can say what goes on behind closed doors? I know Adam's rodeoing was hard on her, but that's pretty much true for anyone married to a rodeo cowboy. It's no life for a family man.''

''But they never had any children.''

''No. To tell the truth, though, I wouldn't be surprised to find out that Adam has a few sprinkled here and there.

There's a lot of very willing young ladies who follow the rodeos around.''

Barbara gave her a knowing look, and Caroline was amazed to find herself bristling at the implication that Adam had been unfaithful to his wife. That he might even have fathered children indiscriminately. She was no prude, but Adam had struck her as a man of honor through and through. Of course Barbara had known him for years and she'd just met him a few weeks ago. Barbara must know what she was talking about.

This was another reason she and Rose should move out of the ranch house the minute she got her first paycheck and could buy a few furnishings. Adam was a normal red-blooded man. No doubt he'd like his privacy back so he could conduct his love life however he wanted—at least when the Tumps were away.

That thought rankled, too.

"Well, I'm done," Caroline said, gathering up the potato peelings. "Anything else?"

"Not just now. Thanks for the help. Why don't you have a look around the camp?"

Caroline walked around the perimeter of the camp, saw the neat line of outhouses behind the guest tents and the rail pasture where the horses were kept during the week. She walked a few hundred yards along the lake, then returned and climbed to a small knoll above the camp and watched Adam, Jim and Matt bent over the outboard in the distance, occasionally revving it up. A couple of riders entered the camp from the far side, led by Ben Longquist, the young wrangler. The day-trippers were back.

She stood, thinking she'd wander down to the dock, not wanting to seem too unsociable, just as a third runabout headed in. A fisherman guest. She glanced at her watch and smiled. Just six o'clock. Looked like everything at Tetlock Valley Tours was running according to plan.

AFTER SUPPER Adam patched through a call so Caroline could talk to Rose. The radiophone was in the tiny office at the back of the cookshack, between the kitchen and the Hillermans' sleeping quarters. While she waited for Mary to answer, she studied her employer, standing as he was with his back to her at the small-paned window that over-looked the lake. Adam was tall, dark and handsome—not classic—in a rugged beatup kind of way. Character. Integrity. A certain blunt charm. There was grace, definitely, and a solid sense of physical strength and competence that tended to inspire feelings of safety just being near him— perhaps the qualities Beau had admired and relied on in their adventures together.

He had an undeniable male appeal; she could understand the local interest in his love life. How many really eligible men lived in this isolated part of the country? But she also got the impression that he was a man who didn't change his mind easily.

Suddenly he turned and handed her the phone. "Here."

"Caroline? Is that you, honey?" Mary's voice came through, erratic and high-pitched.

Then Rose was on the line, talking a mile a minute. Caroline caught her breath, partly sheer relief, silly as she knew that was. *Of course* she knew that Rose was just fine, *of course* she knew that Mary was perfectly capable of taking care of her. It was just that until she heard her daughter's dear little voice, her heart couldn't be entirely easy. Rose had never spent a night apart from her before.

Was she imagining it or had Adam tensed when she'd started talking to Rose? She saw him grip the window frame and his shoulders looked stiff. He hadn't glanced at her once since he'd patched through the call. Maybe he was in a hurry to leave. He could go anytime; there was no reason for him to stay and keep her company.

"—and I had my favorite supper and Janie's mommy read me a story and they've got two kittens under the porch and—"

They chatted for a few more minutes, then, to Caroline's surprise, Rose asked if "the mister" was there.

"Do you mean Adam, Rosie?" she asked, glancing at Adam, who'd turned his head when she spoke his name. She shrugged slightly in response to his questioning look. "You want to speak to Mr. Garrick, sweetie?"

Silently she held out the phone to Adam, who paused for a split second, then stepped forward and took it from her.

"Adam Garrick here," he said gruffly.

He frowned as he listened to Rose. "Uh-huh." He glanced at Caroline and his expression gradually changed to something quite different. "Yes, I see what you mean." There was a gleam of devilment in his eyes. "You want me to kiss your mommy good-night because you're not here to do it and you always kiss your mommy good-night, is that it?"

He actually smiled as he listened to Rose's response. "Uh-huh. Got it. All right, I'll say good-night to her. You bet."

He hung up the phone. Caroline's cheeks were burning. Adam grinned. "I guess you got the message."

"I did." She wanted to protest that it wasn't necessary, but of course she knew there was no reason to protest. He wasn't going to kiss her good-night because he'd been told to do so by a child. All that mattered was that Rose's worries had been addressed.

"She wants me to kiss you good-night."

"Thank you for passing on the message," Caroline said awkwardly, preparing to leave the office. "I appreciate you going along with her. She's just turned five, you know."

"She seemed worried that you'd miss her."

Caroline smiled. "I *do* miss her. It's funny, though. I never dreamed she'd be worried about *me*——"

Adam stared, one hand on the doorknob, a very odd expression on his face. Vulnerable. Pained. Baffled. "You seem to have a very good relationship with her," he said slowly.

"Yes. I do." Caroline felt her heart flood with love for her child. Her gift from God. She'd been so blessed—in so many ways. "I...I'm not sure if you know, if Beau ever told you—I didn't give birth to her. We adopted her. I've always..." She swallowed back the thickness in her throat, then rushed on. "I've always been so grateful to her natural parents—whoever they are—for giving her to us. Beau knew who her mother was, somebody his family knew, but I didn't. I always wanted to believe she was mine. Deep down, I—I never wanted to know anything about it..." Her voice ended in a whisper, her eyes rising to his in an appeal, one human being to another, for understanding. *"Not anything!"*

Adam stared at her for another long moment, then opened the door and left without saying a word.

"Then you forget about the message," Caroline said with a wry expression in spite of herself. "I appreciate your going along with her. She's just rabid that you know."

She almost worried that she'd said too much.

Caroline smiled. "I do hope she'll be all right, though."

"She'll be fine."

Adam stood and studied the dark blush spreading over Caroline's face. Vulnerable, tamed. Damned if you...

CHAPTER ELEVEN

CAROLINE FOUND Adam's behavior hard to fathom. Until now, he'd been somewhat remote, yes, but still polite and considerate. Walking out on her when she was speaking so frankly—which she realized, too late, she should never have done—was something else. It was plain rude.

They spent the evening around the campfire where, to Caroline's surprise, the seemingly shy Matt revealed himself to be a virtuoso on the harmonica, accompanied by the more affable Ben Longquist on guitar. Some of the Germans sang folk songs; some told stories. Other adventures, the granddaddy bull trout that got away, the trophy bighorn sheep that vanished into the mist, the wasps' nest stirred up by a lead horse on the trail... It was a pleasant end to a long day.

Adam showed her to her tent. There'd been no reference to their earlier conversations. He lit the Coleman lamp with careful expert movements and pumped it up to a white-hot glow, then demonstrated how to turn it off. Caroline watched, fascinated.

"There's fresh water there." He indicated the pail on a wooden stand just inside the door, water that Matt had carried to each tent earlier. "You'll have to excuse the rough facilities. This isn't the Ritz, you know," he said with a slow grin.

"I'm aware of that," she said, adding, "I've never been to the Ritz, if you must know."

"No?" He hunkered down to examine the freshly split wood laid carefully inside the stove on a bed of twisted paper. "I'll light this." He tossed in a match, and smoke spilled out the open door before Adam firmly closed it. "Don't bother throwing more wood on it." He gestured at the box of split firewood by the tent door, then adjusted a knob on the chimney. "It'll go out in a couple of hours. You should be warm enough with that down quilt, but this'll take the chill off for now."

"Where are you sleeping?" She blurted it out, not thinking.

He seemed surprised by her question. "Oh, I'll roll out under the stars."

"Outside?"

"Yeah. Old cowboy custom." He grinned, then winked. "Besides somebody's got to keep the bears out of the compost pile."

She swallowed. Bears? Surely that was another tall tale. "You don't mean it," she said flatly.

He just grinned. Still, it was cold outside now. How cold would it be before morning?

"This is crazy," she said, with a quick glance at the two bunks in the tent. "It seems ridiculous for you to have to sleep outside on the ground when there's a spare bed right here." She swallowed again. Would he think she wanted company? "Why don't you sleep here and I...I'll go up and sleep on one of the sofas at the cookshack. I'm sure Barbara and Jim won't mind."

Adam gave her a hard look in the light of the hissing lamp before stepping out the door. "Go to bed. Like I said, I'll sleep under the stars. If you need anything, just yell."

Caroline was glad she'd brought a flannel nightgown. She decided to wear woolly socks under the quilt and blankets, too. It was quite a lot colder at this elevation than down at the ranch. And, despite the thin canvas shroud overhead, she was basically sleeping outdoors.

She brushed her teeth at the basin, rinsing with water from the bucket, then sluiced her face, gasping at the icy chill of the water. She brushed her hair and swung her feet up onto the narrow cot. She heard nothing from outside, beyond the crackle of the dying fire and a few murmurs from distant tents. The Tetlock Valley guests had all retired for the evening. Breakfast came early.

Caroline yawned and pulled the covers up, wriggling around until she felt comfortable and warm. Then she began to think. She thought of Rose asleep—she hoped—in her bed at the Tump house. Would Mary's husband be home? Mary had said he was home most of the summer. What kind of man had married Mary and fathered Janie and her five older siblings, all grown-up and in homes of their own? She supposed she'd meet him one day.

She thought of her mother-in-law back in Seattle and wondered how she was doing. She'd always been fond of the woman, although Eunice Carter was not an easy woman to know. She was cool and distant—according to Beau, she'd always been that way—but she'd been very civil to Caroline. At least until Beau died. And she'd been so happy when they adopted Rose and had showered the baby with expensive trinkets from the exclusive jeweler she patronized and had given her handsome stock certificates at every birthday. Caroline reflected that Eunice had gotten it all wrong; the little girl would have preferred hugs and kisses and teddy bears and puppies, not sterling silver and blue-chip investments. Still, she knew Eunice meant well.

Was Eunice wondering what had happened to them both? Caroline felt a twinge of guilt at the sneaky way she and Rose had left Seattle. At the time she'd been so stressed out she couldn't imagine escaping Philip Carter's threats

any other way. Now? Now, she wished she'd at least let
Eunice know they were safe and sound. Caroline turned
over on the thin mattress and snuggled into the quilt. The
crackling of the wood fire and the faint smell of wood
smoke were soothing. She closed her eyes. She'd write to
Eunice; tell her they were all right and that they'd be back
at the end of the summer.

Vaguely Caroline thought of Adam, stretched out somewhere in his bedroll under the open sky. She supposed he
must be used to it; it was something cowboys did. Still, it
was silly of him not to take the other bunk or agree to her
suggestion about sleeping at the cookshack. He was a stubborn man.

She must have dozed off. Because the next thing she
realized, her eyelids had snapped open and it was pitch-
black in the tent. And cold. The stove had gone out, and
the fire outside had long since died down.

What was *that?*

Caroline heard it again, the lonely drawn-out howl of a
wolf somewhere. It was the sound that had penetrated her
dreams and awakened her. Was there any sound quite so
mournful, quite so chilling?

The wolf had to be quite a distance away. But still…
Caroline shivered again and held the quilt tightly to her
shoulders. *There it was again.* Only this time it was a lot
closer. Or maybe there were two, answering each other. Or
a whole pack on the hunt.

And bears. What had Adam said about bears? In the
muzziness of half sleep every scary children's story from
Little Red Riding Hood to *Where the Wild Things Are*
sprang into Caroline's mind in living, breathing, pulsing—
horrifying—color. And the newspapers. Hadn't she read
about bear attacks on sleeping hikers? In Yellowstone and
other parks?

She sat up in bed, wrapping a blanket around her, and cautiously put her feet over the side. Spiders? Mice? She was glad she'd worn the woolly socks to bed. She knew she was only half-awake, probably not thinking clearly, but she also knew she wasn't going to get a wink of sleep with Adam out there alone. It gave her the creeps. He could just accompany her up to the cookshack where there were solid wooden walls and she'd sleep there, and then he could come back and sleep here.

She made her way to the door, feeling along the canvas wall. It was cold and damp. She opened the door carefully and stepped outside. It wasn't as dark as it had seemed. There were some clouds, but half the sky was brilliant with stars. The fire had died to a dull red glow, and she could see that Adam had stretched out his bedroll on the other side. Not faraway, thank goodness.

She walked slowly around the fire, still clutching the blanket. "Adam?" she whispered. "Pssst, Adam—are you awake?"

There was no answer. Caroline's eyes had adjusted somewhat and she saw that he lay on his back, the covers pulled up to his shoulders. She hadn't thought about actually waking him up. She'd hoped he wouldn't be asleep. She bent near him, trying to see his face. Was he asleep?

"Adam? *Omigod!*" Suddenly he grabbed her arm and pulled her close.

"Caroline?" His voice was hoarse. She *had* woken him up. Then, in less than an instant, he was wide awake. She felt his grip tighten on her arm until she almost cried out. "What's wrong? What's going on? Why aren't you in bed?"

"I'm fine," she whispered, tugging her arm away. "I'm okay." He seemed to realize then that he had grabbed her and, as quickly, let go. She nearly fell back.

"What the *hell* are you doing out here?"

He sounded angry, and she felt indescribably foolish. Bears? Wolves? Things that went bump in the night? "I— I thought you must be cold out here. I really think it's so stupid that you won't use that bunk in there. You'd be much more comfortable."

"And?"

She could barely make out his features. He put his head back down so that she had to lean over him to see him at all. Her brain wasn't functioning at full speed. What was he talking about? "And what?"

"What about you?"

"Me?"

"Would you be more comfortable?"

"What do you mean?" She was confused. She wished she'd never left her bed. "Well, of course I'd be more comfortable. I can't sleep. And I don't think it's right that you should have to sleep outside like this—"

"Caroline?"

"What?"

"Shut up and go back to bed."

She stared at him.

"Listen. If I wanted a bed, I'd go and bunk in with Ben and Matt. I'm not going to sleep in there with you. In that tent. Is that clear?"

With her? Caroline was glad of the darkness. She knew her cheeks must be red; they felt as hot as that little steel stove had been earlier when Adam lit it. "You're worried about your, er, my reputation?" she managed, not entirely sure where the conversation was going, or why.

"I don't particularly care. And maybe you don't, either. But a lot of people are going to notice me coming out of your tent tomorrow morning, and they are going to jump to a certain conclusion. And they're going to tell other peo-

ple. Don't you care what they're going to tell other people?''

"No! I mean, yes! That's ridiculous. Why would anybody think something like that?'' Caroline realized she was
still whispering and so was he. She could see his point.
Why hadn't she thought of all this before she'd come out
here? Why hadn't she stopped to think how unlikely it was
that wolves or bears would venture into the camp? And if
they did, Adam Garrick would certainly know how to take
care of himself....

She frowned. Had she mentioned her plan yet, that he
take her up to the cookshack? "Anyway, never mind that.
I was going to suggest—''

"Unless...'' he interrupted her, then paused.

Caroline tried to read his expression, but with no success.
"Unless what?''

"Unless you're inviting me to share your bed, Mrs. Carter.''

Caroline sat back on her heels as though struck. *"No!''*
Oh, God, *now* what did he think of her? She felt like a
complete and utter idiot. "Of course not!''

"Or...'' His hand snaked out again, and this time his
fingers slipped behind her neck. He pulled her closer to
him and, off balance, she put one hand down to steady
herself. She touched his bare warm shoulder, then instantly
removed her hand and fell awkwardly against him, morti-
fied. He held her tight. "Or maybe it's just as Rose said,
and you really can't go to sleep without your good-night
kiss.''

And his mouth was on hers then, hard, warm and—God
forgive her, *so thrilling*—she was responding to him as
though she'd been parched and desperate, dying of thirst,
and someone had turned on the shower. His fingers
clenched her nape and suddenly his other arm was around

her shoulders and he'd brought her even closer. The blanket she'd wrapped around her fell open. Their mouths joined, fused, moved hotly, gasping, touching, pursuing...tasting. She heard his breathing, harsh—and hers. Caroline felt a pit open under her in the earth. A huge black pit that scared her and yet invited her—seductive, warm, enveloping. *It would be so easy to lose herself in this man's arms. So very easy.*

"Omigod, *omigod!* What are you doing?" She tried to pull back, and Adam held her for a few seconds longer, then released her abruptly. "I'm sorry. I'm so sorry, Adam. I had no idea... I—I never should have come out here."

She stood up, hand over her mouth, and with a small scream that she mostly succeeded in swallowing, raced back to the tent.

THE TRIP BACK was uneventful. If you could call something that resulted in wobbly knees, aching thighs and a bottom that felt as though she'd been sitting on rocks uneventful. Adam seemed to be in more of a hurry than he had been on the trip up. So was she; she missed Rose. And she'd made up her mind she was definitely moving to Beau's cabin just as soon as she could get it ready.

As for last night's events, he hadn't said a word. Other than the carefully folded blanket she'd found outside her tent door in the morning, there was no indication that anything had happened.

There was no companionable lunch by the side of the falls this time, either. Just as the waterfall came into view, Adam turned and rode back to her.

"Hungry?" he asked with a quick glance at her and the mare. Miss Minnie hadn't even worked up a sweat, despite the faster pace Adam had set. Caroline was becoming quite fond of her.

"Not really," she said, sitting straight to stretch her back. "That was a big lunch we had." Barbara had cooked up some rainbow trout before they left.

Caroline groaned. How could she say something so mundane? So pedestrian? How could she—and he—pretend that everything was the same as it had always been? How could they both ignore her midnight visit?

"Here." Adam took a plastic bag out of one of the pockets in his windbreaker and tossed it to her. It was a package of high-energy trail mix. Raisins, cashews, chocolate bits, pumpkin seeds....

"I've got more if you want it," he said, and reined the black around to take the lead again. The swish of the gelding's tail was the last thing Caroline saw as they disappeared around a bend in the trail.

Well, she thought. That pair deserved each other. She kicked Miss Minnie's side and swiped at a mosquito that buzzed around her nose. The brown mare flicked her ears a few times in what seemed like sympathy to Caroline, then obediently plodded forward.

They could trot all they wanted, those two; she and Miss Minnie were walking.

Just as they reached the crest of the last hill before the descent to the ranch, Adam stopped. He waited, arms crossed, leaning forward on the pommel. The gelding shook his head up and down impatiently, but didn't take a step. Caroline had the distinct impression that the gelding was getting an education this trip, and that he'd already learned it didn't pay to do something the man on his back didn't want him to do.

"How you making out?" There was concern in Adam's eyes—fleeting, but there all the same. Caroline felt slightly heartened. "You okay?"

"I'm fine." She gingerly moved a little in the saddle.

"I'm going to be sore, I think. But that's to be expected, considering I'm no rider."

"You've done well." He cracked a smile. "For a tenderfoot."

His compliment, brief and qualified as it was, warmed her. "I suppose a person could get used to this. I've certainly enjoyed the opportunity to get up into this country. I appreciate you asking me." There she went again. Whenever she felt nervous or self-conscious around Adam, she started sounding like some book on etiquette.

He frowned. "Listen. I'm sorry about what happened last night. I was way out of line." He held up his hand to stop her from speaking. "That's it. That's what I wanted to say. You've got my complete apology. There was no excuse for my behavior. None at all."

Excuse? Caroline glanced over at the trees beside the trail. Damn him, anyway! An apology was one thing, but wasn't he going on a bit? Surely it hadn't been *that* much of a hardship.

"Okay?" He held up his hand again in a version of Scout's honor. "It won't happen again."

"I apologize, as well," she said stiffly. "If I hadn't been foolish enough to come out to warn you about the wolves or—" Too late, she realized what she'd said. She snapped her mouth shut.

"Wolves?"

"Wolves. And bears," she added firmly. In for a penny... "I heard a wolf howling. I couldn't sleep. I thought it would be better if I went up to the cookshack, if you took over my tent. I thought it might be dangerous out there. I meant what I said—I thought it was stupid that you were sleeping outside when there was a perfectly good shelter—"

"And *bears?*" He was doing his best not to smile; she could tell. "You heard a *bear?*"

"I heard *wolves.*" She wanted to smack him. "Laugh all you like, but—"

"I'm not laughing. Am I laughing?" He addressed his mount's ears. As if on cue, the gelding blew a big bored horsey snort and shook his head, jangling his bridle. Caroline flushed. That horse should be in the movies.

"I suppose it's all pretty ordinary to you. You and Ben and Jim and everybody. But it's not to me," she finished, head up, eyes straight ahead.

"Listen, Caroline." Adam nudged his horse right up to the mare. The two animals nibbled each other's necks affectionately. Caroline's knee was pressed hard against Adam's. "I appreciate your concern." His voice was low; he wasn't laughing.

"I think it's real sweet of you to worry about me out there all alone." He paused and she sneaked a glance at him. "But I still shouldn't have kissed you. I shouldn't have done it, no matter what. You're a damned attractive woman, and I won't deny that once in a while I've felt the kind of thing a man feels when he's around an attractive woman. But you're my employee, you're my best friend's wife—"

"Widow," she snapped. *Once in a while...*

"Widow," he said, and this time she did see the glimmer of a smile. "Right, widow. I guess that's different. Still, I had no business doing what I did, and while I can't say I'm genuinely sorry I kissed you, I shouldn't have done it. And that's the end of it I hope."

"Fine. I accept your apology," she said, feeling that if her back was any straighter, she'd pitch right out of the saddle. "I apologize, too. And since you're being completely honest with me, I'd like to tell you that I've made up my mind about something, too.''

"What's that?'' He looked skeptical.

"Rose and I are going to move out to Beau's cabin.''

"No way.''

"Yes,'' she said, meeting his gaze. "We are.'' The black shook his head just then and Adam pulled him up with a curse. "My decision has nothing to do with what happened last night. I'd already made up my mind. I intend to use my first paycheck to buy a few things, and then we're going to move in. Probably next weekend.''

She slapped the reins on Miss Minnie's neck, and to her amazement, the mare stepped forward smartly, leaving Adam and the gelding to bring up the rear.

High time, she thought, mentally promising Miss Minnie an extra sugar cube. High time for them both.

CHAPTER TWELVE

"SHE THOUGHT there were *wolves?*"

"Yeah, well, it's true, there were a couple," Adam said irritably. "Somewhere." He wasn't crazy about the way his friend and legal adviser was reacting to the story he'd just told him about the trip he and Caroline had made up to the Tetlock Valley camp. He hadn't mentioned kissing her. Naturally.

"And she was going to *rescue* you? How?" Lucas laughed. "Hey, I'm dying to meet this woman. When can I meet her?"

Adam scowled. Lucas Yellowfly was a well-known Glory lady-killer. The poor Indian kid from across the tracks had come back to town a year ago all grown-up and loaded for bear. He had a top-drawer law degree, a fancy city haircut and custom-made suits from some back-East haberdashery. Lucas was handsome, his law practice was hopping and he was very noticeably—in a town this size—unattached.

Adam wasn't sure he wanted Lucas to meet Caroline any more than he wanted Ted Eberly and his cronies to meet her. What was going on with him these days? Where did all this protectiveness come from? Caroline. Rose. He didn't like it. He checked his watch. Still half an hour before he'd promised to meet them at the Glory co-op.

"Soon enough," he answered vaguely. "So, you hear anything from Seattle?" Adam hooked a chair from where it stood against the wall in Lucas's office. Lucas was playing lawyer, sitting behind the desk today. Adam sat down, stretched out and eased his feet onto the coffee table.

"You better not let Mrs. Rutgers catch you doing that," Lucas warned, with a fake worried glance at the door, which stood ajar. Adam got up and closed it. Anything that went on in this room was between him and Lucas.

"Haven't you got rid of her yet?"

"October." Lucas ran an index finger across the base of his throat. The gesture didn't really fit with the big grin on his face.

Adam sat back down.

Lucas pulled some files toward him on the desk. "All right. This is the story. I have a buddy down there in one of the big firms. He was able to get his hands on a few facts." Lucas looked up. "Unfortunately, very few. She still not say anything?"

Adam drew a hand over his face and shook his head. "Not much. I asked her once or twice, but, hell, according to her, she's got money, she's got a home, she's doing just fine. 'Thank you very much and mind your own damn business, Garrick'—that's the impression I get." He frowned, thinking of how insistent she'd been to move into Beau's cabin this week. That was why they were in town—to buy her some supplies.

"Well, from what I can figure," Lucas went on, glancing at his notes, "she's not doing so fine. Beau Carter's will was probated ten months ago, and there's nothing in it for her or the kid."

"The hell you say!" Adam stared at his friend. "That's crazy! The guy was rich. I was down there. I saw the way he lived. Fancy cars, big house, the works."

"When was that? Five, six years ago? He's broke now," Lucas said, "or at least according to what my friend turned up. Beau left her everything in his will, just the way you'd expect, only there was a big mortgage on the house, no insurance and no property left. No joint property, anyway. Apparently he'd sold everything sometime in the year or so before he died.''

"I don't understand," Adam said slowly. None of this made any sense at all.

"You ever see any signs of gambling? Drugs?"

"Gambling? Well, sure. A few cards here and there. Poker, the usual stuff the cowboys get up to in the bunkhouse on a Saturday night. A few bets on the horses. No drugs. I never saw any *real* gambling, if that's what you mean," Adam said.

"Apparently he got the bug bad. According to what my contact was able to find, he cashed in everything to pay off some big debts. Gambling debts is all anybody can figure. He may have had people after him.''

"What do you mean, people?" Adam's first impulse, the instant he recognized what Lucas was saying, was to get in his pickup and take Caroline and Rose back to the ranch where they'd be safe. *People?*

"You know. Crooks. The mob. Loan sharks." Lucas shrugged and flipped the file shut. "Whoever he owed money. Bad guys, good guys. I have no idea. I was hoping you might.''

"I don't know anything about it." Adam thought for a moment. "Beau was definitely wild. No question. But that was a long time ago, before he got married. Wine, women, the usual stuff, you know what I mean. I figured he'd settled down. Any man would have, in his place." He met Lucas's gaze. "She's a fine woman, Lucas. She's good-looking and she's smart and she's a terrific mother to the kid.''

"What's this about, Adam?" his friend asked softly.

"The little girl? Are you having second thoughts? Maybe thinking you should hook up with the mother and get a chance to play daddy to your own kid?"

"Hell, no!" Adam scraped back the chair and stood. He walked back and forth in Lucas's office, aware of his friend's scrutiny. "I just feel sorry for her, that's all. Having to pick up work with an outfit like mine for the summer. A woman shouldn't have to do that. Not if her man provided for her properly. I got the feeling she's not getting along too great with Beau's family, either. *That bastard!*"

He swung to face Lucas. "How could he do it? How could he leave her like that? No money, no home, nothing for the kid, then just…just walk out into the bush and not come back!"

"I understand it was an accident," Lucas said quietly. "A rock slide. He intended to come back, Adam. He just got hurt and never made it, that's all. His luck ran out. He must have planned to make things right—"

"Planned? Ha!" Adam paused, collecting his anger. And sadness, too—Beau Carter had been the best friend he'd ever had. "No. Remember? I've been there, Lucas. I know what it's like. There's no damn way he should have gone out alone. No emergency support. No supplies. No radio. No plan filed with anyone. It's just asking for trouble. It's goddamned irresponsible, that's what it is!"

"So what are you going to do about it, Adam? The guy's dead."

"Nothing. There's nothing I can do. I'll keep her on for the summer if she wants to stay. Pay her what I can. Then hope like hell it works out for her. The rest of her life, whatever."

"Maybe she'll meet some guy and get married again," Lucas said. "That might be for the best."

"Yeah. Maybe." Adam scowled. He had to restrain himself from telling Yellowfly exactly where he could put that and the rest of his good ideas. He grabbed up the jacket he'd tossed down on Lucas's bookshelf when he'd come in. "I'll buy the cabin off her. That'll mean some money for her and the kid for a while."

"Cabin?"

"That cabin out behind my place that Beau built. I, uh..." Adam wasn't sure he wanted to meet his friend's gaze. "I told her Beau owned it, that he'd bought the land off me fair and square."

"That's bullshit."

"I know that. But she doesn't. I'm not sure why I said it, except that she seemed so desperate, so...scared. Alone. I just wanted her to feel, I don't know, that she wasn't with a bunch of strangers up here, that the place Beau had built was hers. That he'd left it to her and the kid." Adam shrugged on the jacket. "That he'd done *something* right, the bastard."

"You know what, buddy?" Lucas stood and came around to the front of his desk. He held out his hand and Adam shook it. "You're the sappiest, most soft-hearted old stove-up son-of-a-gun bull rider that ever lived."

"Ah, hell. It's just a shack. She plans to move into it, too," he added, reaching for the door.

"No kidding."

"Uh-huh. And she's being damn stubborn about it. She's over at the co-op buying sheets and towels right now."

STUBBORN WASN'T the word. More like ornery. Pigheaded. She wouldn't listen to reason. Adam had pointed out that there was no electricity, nothing but a hand pump for water—*if* there still was water in the well. The roof no doubt leaked, the chimney needed repair, there was no phone. He even went as low as to mention that there were probably quite a few mice settled in there, spiders for sure. Maybe even a rat or two.

She said she'd set out traps and spiders didn't bother her. She pointed out to him that all the tourist brochures said there were no rats in Alberta; he had to admit it was true. He finally gave up and decided to help her. That was partly why he was in town. He was picking up some shingles and a reel of half-inch PVC hose to run a water line out from the house; it couldn't be more than eighty, ninety yards through the trees. He hadn't cleared his plans with her, but how could she object? An outhouse was one thing, but she needed a clean safe water supply. There were health reasons to consider. He hoped she'd realize he wasn't trying to take over; he just wanted her to have a few comforts. Her and Rose.

Rose.

As usual Adam tried his best to block Rose out of the equation. But it was impossible. He hadn't understood just how impossible until she and her mother had been under his roof for a few weeks. The fact was, he was getting used to the kid. Worse, he kind of liked her. He had to admit that he'd been deeply affected when Rose arrived at the Double O with Mrs. T and Janie, about an hour and a half after he and Caroline had returned from the Tetlock camp. She'd leaped out of the car and run into her mother's outstretched arms. Caroline hugged and kissed her daughter half a dozen times and Adam could see just how hard this separation had been. Then, to his shock, the little girl had run up onto the porch where he was sitting and thrown her arms around his neck and squeezed hard and kissed him loudly on the cheek.

"Thanks for taking care of my mommy, Mister," she said sweetly, her smile full of delight. "I had a lot of fun and Janie's mommy says I can sleep over again sometime.

And they've got kittens!'' She'd nodded solemnly, eyes
wide, as though daring him to believe her. Then she'd raced
back down the steps to her mother again. Caroline and Rose
had walked hand in hand to Mrs. T's car to help her unload.

Adam had sat in the rocker, stunned. There was no going
back. Maybe it wasn't such a bad idea that the two of them
were moving out to Beau's shack. Much as he pretended
he didn't care, he knew something had already happened
to him this summer; he'd never be the same Adam Garrick
he was before. Even after they got in that jalopy of theirs
and drove away, back to Seattle. Out of his life. His daughter might never know and her mother might never know,
but *he knew*. She was his flesh and blood, the daughter he
never dreamed he'd ever see—and he'd spent time with
her. *A little piece of his life.* Touched her, held her—he
thought of lifting her onto the swing seat that time, the way
her hair had grazed his face—and now she'd put her arms
around his neck and kissed him.

And he'd kissed her mother, too. Caroline. What had he
been thinking of? Well, he knew the answer to that one—
he'd wanted to kiss her from the day he'd met her. Sheer
male-female stuff. He'd felt it often enough over the past
thirty-seven years to know exactly what it was. But what
had started out as a dumb joke, as something the kid had
said on the phone, maybe something he'd planned, just a
kiss to scare her off a little—in case she was getting ideas,
which he knew *he* was—had turned, in the snap of a twig,
into something else altogether.

The instant his mouth had touched hers, he knew what
he really wanted was to haul her into the bedroll with him
and love her properly. Now, right now. He'd wanted to kiss
her and kiss her again and touch her everywhere until they
were both drunk with the wanting. And then he'd hike up
her nightgown and take her with a heavenful of stars as

witness. He'd never felt so hot so fast. And it'd scared him. It still scared him.

She'd wanted it, too. That scared him more. She'd kissed him back. She'd moaned and clung to him and forgotten all about hanging on to that dumb blanket she had around her.

Then, suddenly, her brain had started working again, and so had his. He'd never forget how she stood up and screamed a crazy little strangled scream and ran back to her tent, while he lay there, his blood pounding, wondering if there were *two* such fools in the world as himself.

So, maybe this cabin idea was for the best. The more distance between them, in every way, the better. He'd hate it if Caroline felt she had to quit over something like that, and it wasn't just because he needed her in the office. But he *was* her boss. He wasn't supposed to do stuff like that. Yet even as he promised himself that it wouldn't happen again, he knew he couldn't swear he'd be able to keep that promise. One thing he did know—there was no place in her life or his for a summer affair.

Adam parked in front of the co-op and got out. They were there, waiting for him on the sidewalk outside. Rose clutched her rag doll in one hand and a bright plastic bag from the toy store in the other.

"Guess what? Guess what?" She didn't wait for him to answer. "We bought a new doll kinda like Raggy for Janie. We're gonna play dolls. Janie's big," she said confidentially, leaning toward him and nodding, "but she likes to play with dolls, just like me."

Adam often wondered if Rose had any idea that Janie was different from other playmates she'd had, or did she think she was the same, except that she was "big"? It didn't seem so.

"That's great. You about ready?" Adam addressed his inquiry to Caroline.

"Yes," she said happily. "We got everything on our list. The cashier said they could load it on your truck somewhere out back. She said you'd know where."

"I do." Looked like Eberly was going to get his chance to meet the mystery lady, after all.

Rose waited in the truck, busily inspecting Janie's new rag doll. Caroline got out and, to Adam's dismay, climbed up on the loading dock to check her packages, piled on a pallet that Eberly wheeled out of the dim interior.

Adam was forced to introduce them. Caroline smiled and said hello. Eberly practically slobbered. Adam felt like kicking him.

"This everything?" he asked sourly, trying to nudge Eberly's attention back to the job at hand.

"Yep. That's about it—" Eberly nodded, then gazed helpfully at Caroline "—isn't it, ma'am? Would that be all? Is there something else I could get you?"

"Let's see." Leaning on the pallet, Caroline went over each package. "Towels, sheets, cutlery, soap and cleaning supplies, two pots, a frying pan, four bags of groceries, dishes, the teakettle..."

"You could have gotten some of this stuff from home," Adam complained. He still wasn't happy about word getting around Glory that Caroline Carter had moved out of his house and into that damn shack. "I'm sure Mrs. T could've set you up."

"Oh, she offered," Caroline said with a smile. "But we wanted our own things."

"What's this?" Adam picked up one side of a heavy flat carton. "Grab on to that end," he directed the warehouseman, who quickly complied.

"It's a fold-up cot for Rose," Caroline said. "I thought

you'd be able to use it at the Double O after we left. For extra guests or something.''

Left. Adam's felt a chill run down his spine. He hated the thought. He should be looking forward to the day they left. He was getting his priorities thoroughly mixed up. And it was only July.

Caroline climbed back into the pickup, and Adam jumped down from the loading dock to fasten the tailgate. Eberly sidled up. "Say," he began out of the corner of his mouth, "how come she's movin' out? Something happen? I thought maybe she'd be bunking in with you—"

"Listen here, Ted."

"Uh-huh?"

"She's a lady. You got that? And that cabin belonged to her husband, who is dead. It's hers now. You understand?''

Ted nodded, his face red with more than his annual sunburn.

"She wants to play house, that's fine with me. Anything she decides to do, anything at all, is just fine with me. You got that, too?"

Ted nodded again.

"Good." Adam smiled. But he knew damn well that Ted Eberly understood exactly what that smile meant. It meant he'd break every bone in Ted's miserable body if he started spreading rumors about Caroline Carter.

"Sometimes it doesn't pay to be the first to get the news, Ted," he added softly with another smile. "Sometimes it does."

"Jeez, I know just what you mean, Adam." Ted wiped his moist upper lip with his sleeve. Then he grinned conspiratorially. "Just *exactly* what you mean."

Rose wanted to stop for ice cream. When Caroline met his glance over Rose's small dark head—she sat between them on the bench seat of the truck—Adam felt something inside him crumble. Was it the appeal in her eyes? The tiny smile? The one-adult-to-another look? The heat? The exasperation of the long day? The motherly pride? Whatever it was, Adam knew he would've driven to Calgary to get ice cream for the kid.

He wheeled up to a window at the Glory institution, the Grizzly Drive-in. Adam had brought girls here for banana splits and malts in his '65 Chevy; he'd been here with yelling pickup-loads of high-school boys for Grizzly double cheeseburgers, loaded. Nothing had changed since then, not even the faded sign advertising a co-op dairy pool that had been out of business for years.

He passed a maple-walnut cone, single, to Caroline and a double-chocolate to Rose.

"Oh, look, Mommy! Look how *big* it is. Thanks, Mister. Aren't you having one?" She took a big lick of her ice cream. "They're really good!" She smiled up at him and Adam couldn't help but shake his head and smile back.

Could it be possible for a little kid to get that much enjoyment out of an ice-cream cone? Was it possible that *he* could feel so good, having his own daughter say, "Thanks, Mister?" Was this what kids were like?

He turned the radio on low so he'd feel less of an obligation to talk on the drive home. He needn't have worried. Rose finished most of her ice cream—Caroline tossed the last melting bit out the window—and then, before they'd made it halfway to the ranch turnoff, she leaned over and put her head on her mother's lap. Within minutes, she'd fallen asleep.

"She's tired." Caroline stroked her daughter's black curls, apparently not minding the chocolate smudges on her skirt. She glanced at Adam and smiled. "It's been a big day for her and she missed her nap."

Adam couldn't think of anything to say, so he returned his attention to the road.

Just as he shifted down for the turnoff to the ranch a few miles later, he cleared his throat. "Look, Caroline..."

"Yes?" Her hair was blowing in the wind from the open window, whipping across her face.

"You're sure about this. I mean, you're sure about wanting to move into that beatup old cabin?"

"I am."

"It's nothing to do with..." He took a deep breath. He had to say it, had to know. "Well, it's nothing to do with what happened up at the camp. Me kissing you and all."

She didn't answer right away. She looked out the window for a few seconds, then down at her sleeping daughter. She cradled Rose's face gently in both hands.

Finally she met his gaze again. "No, Adam. It's not because of that," she said softly. "I...I've accepted your apology and besides—"

Adam had to strain to hear.

"—it wasn't all your fault, anyway. It's not just you. It takes two, that sort of thing." She swallowed, holding his gaze for a few long incredible seconds before he had to glance quickly back at the road or he would have driven right into the ditch. "Doesn't it?"

CHAPTER THIRTEEN

ADAM ASSIGNED two men from the haying crew—they were between cuts—to hammer some new shingles on the cabin roof. Then he found fault with the way they did the job.

He could easily have put in the water line himself, but Curley said he'd do it. After his foreman unrolled PVC pipe and snaked it through the trees and got the faucet inside the cabin roughed in, so that Caroline could have at least the luxury of a cold-water sink, Adam tore into him for the way he'd run in the line.

No one could do anything right on Caroline's cabin, yet Adam kept telling himself he wanted to stay out of it—because that meant keeping his distance from Rose and Caroline.

Except it never seemed to work out like that. Every evening at the supper table he heard an update from Rose and Janie, who chimed in with her comments, difficult as they sometimes were to understand. And he had to look down the long dining table at Caroline, who smiled more often as each day went by. He seemed to get wound up tighter and tighter while she got happier and more relaxed.

Caroline had told him she was moving over their personal things on Thursday afternoon, ten days exactly after the two of them had returned from the Tetlock Valley. In between readying the cabin she kept up her work, entering figures, keeping tabs on food and equipment orders, taking new reservations. The summer was almost fully booked. The Tetlock Valley trail business would definitely turn a good profit this year.

It always surprised him to come into the house in the middle of the afternoon to find her hunched over the computer in his office, curtains drawn against the sun. She'd have half a cup of cold tea by her side, neat piles of files on the desk. Sometimes she'd be frowning, perhaps chewing on the end of a pencil. He didn't know why it surprised him. Perhaps it was the simple fact of finding a woman in his house, a young woman—something he never really got used to. Or the fact that she seemed to fit in so quietly and so well. Mrs. T adored her, his foreman had admitted that he got quite the kick out of the ''little pot-licker,'' as he called Rose, who followed him around asking questions whenever he was in the yard, and Janie...well, Janie was in raptures.

Rhonda had worked in his office the past couple of summers, and he'd never had that same quiet feeling of surprise and anticipation when he walked in on her. No, it was something about Caroline Carter. Something that fascinated him, and yet at the same time something he didn't want to think about too much.

He had to admit the cabin was looking almost livable. Caroline and Mrs. T had swept out all the cobwebs, washed the windows and floors and hearth and even managed to scour most of the rust from the small cookstove. They'd cleaned the shelves and put up fresh shelf paper. Then they'd tacked curtains over the open shelves, which held glasses, plates and cutlery for four.

''This way,'' she said, eyes shining as she lifted a corner and showed him, ''we'll be able to have company for dinner.''

He'd looked at her, wondering if she'd meant anyone other than perhaps Janie or Mrs. T once in a while.

He'd driven over to Mrs. T's oldest daughter's place to pick up a sofa bed and chair the Dempseys were replacing. The furniture was worn but clean and serviceable, and Caroline had said she'd be happy to use it for the summer. She'd gotten Curley to build a rickety partition across one corner of the cabin to make a little bedroom for Rose. The child was delighted and showed him her new folding bed and the shelves for her books and the few toys she'd brought, and the rack Curley had put up with hooks for her clothes. Her mother, she told him, was going to sleep on the sofa bed. Adam had wondered. He hadn't wanted to ask.

Adam cleaned the chimney himself, the pioneer way, by tying a small spruce tree to some rope and running it up and down inside the stone chimney, dislodging soot and creosote. He warned that the fireplace, built by a couple of amateurs, would in all likelihood spew smoke into the room. Caroline assured him she had no intention of using it.

It seemed she had an answer to every question, a solution for every problem. Even the mice deserted him; at his request Curley checked, and it turned out there were no rodents in residence at all.

The first week Rose and Caroline lived in the cabin, Adam was stunned at the change. For one thing, his house was much quieter without Rose's chatter and the laughter from her and Janie. Mrs. T was quiet, "ruminating" she said. Janie fell into one of her cranky melancholy states, what her mother called a "time," but on this occasion, at least, it was a quiet sulk, not the tears and foot-stomping tantrums that Adam had sometimes seen.

He often wondered how his housekeeper managed with

her large difficult daughter. Yet Adam was well aware that Mrs. T didn't wish Janie to be anything other than she was. "A joy," she always said. "She's a wonderful joy to me and her father." And Adam knew she meant it.

Her father? What did Angus Tump have to do with the raising of his youngest? What had he ever had to do with raising *any* of the six Tump children? Still, who could say what kind of relationship Angus had with his daughter or any of the rest of his brood? And what kind of man was Adam to pass judgement?

The following week Adam joined the haying crew. It was hot dusty labor and Adam reveled in it. He was up at dawn, driving a tractor all day or loading bales into the big hay sheds, and often didn't get back to the house until dark. If he didn't fall into bed exhausted, it seemed, he didn't sleep at all.

There was no reason for him to see Caroline or Rose. He left notes for Caroline in his office, on the desk, notes to do with the Tetlock Valley operation. She left him notes back, usually on the kitchen table, answering his questions or detailing new reservations or changes to schedules. He began to believe that this new distant arrangement suited him just fine.

Then, late one Sunday evening, he realized that if he thought he'd reined in his feelings for Caroline, he was only fooling himself.

After seeing the latest batch of guests off on the trip up to the camp with Jim and Ben, he'd packed a lunch for himself and joined the haying crew working some leased land on the river flats a few miles away. The temperatures hit the high nineties by midafternoon, and Curley threatened and begged and harangued the crew to get the crop in, swearing the weather was changing. He could tell, he said, by the way the poplars fluttered. A southeasterly always brought rain.

ADAM GOT BACK to the ranch house absolutely beat. He was too tired to even bother with the Sunday casserole supper Mrs. T had left in the fridge for him to warm up. He was almost too tired to take a shower, but he knew it'd be impossible to fall asleep itching from the hay dust that got in his hair and down his throat and under his shirt.

The lights were on in the kitchen and he naturally assumed that Mrs. T had forgotten to turn them off when she and Janie went home. It was still dusk at ten o'clock; midsummer in the northern latitudes made for long summer days.

Upstairs Adam headed for the bathroom, yawning, unbuttoning his shirt as he walked down the hall in his bare feet. Just as he put his hand on the doorknob, the door swung open from the inside and Caroline emerged.

"Oh!" She put one hand to her throat, the other still reaching out toward the light switch on the bathroom wall. "Heavens! You scared me, Adam."

"Sorry. I didn't know you were here." He knew that Caroline and Rose continued to use the house facilities such as shower and bath, as well as stowing some of their groceries in the second fridge and the storeroom freezer. But he'd forgotten. Amazingly, for the first time in a very long time, Caroline and Rose were not on his mind.

But now, there she stood before him, pink and flushed from her bath. He could smell a million feminine scents wafting out on the humid air—roses, jasmine, mint, a subtle underlay he could only liken to green tea, the kind served in Lee's Café in Glory. The bathroom gilded the edges of her hair, carelessly tied in a knot atop her head, innumerable wisps escaping to frame her face in a fuzzy glow. The robe she wore—he'd have sworn she had nothing on underneath, but somehow curbed his strong desire to look more closely—was pale pink, with a little design on it.

"I, uh, just took a bath," she said, too quickly, pulling her hand away from the light switch and cinching her belt even more tightly around her waist.

"I see." Adam did not step aside. He couldn't move. He was intensely aware of her soft, sweet, clean femininity and his filthy, sweaty, hay-flecked appearance, his shirt hanging open, his feet bare. His fingers itched either to reach out and touch her, which he would never allow himself to do, or to somehow, unobtrusively, fasten a couple of the buttons on his shirt. He noticed that she'd glanced at his bare chest and her cheeks had turned a dull red. He felt his blood slow and thicken.

He cleared his throat. "H-how is Rose?"

"Oh, she's fine," Caroline said, still breathlessly. "She's very well, thank you."

"Where is she?" Adam frowned and made an effort to get control of the emotions richocheting through him.

"She's at the cabin. Asleep. She's..." Caroline laughed softly, but he could hear the nerves in it. Was she as rattled as he was? Was that *possible?* "She's sound asleep. Big day today."

"Oh?"

"We went to town and she had a swim in the Glory Memorial Pool. They've got a nice shallow end, and water toys, and there were a lot of kids her age in the—"

She stopped herself and gave him a stricken look. He wanted to bend down and silence her with his mouth—oh, foolish, foolish man. "I guess you aren't interested in hearing about our day," she whispered, her eyes locked on his.

"Yes," he said, amazed that his voice was so steady.

"Yes, I am. I like to hear what you and Rose are doing. I haven't seen you in a while."

"Four days," she said in a voice he could barely hear.

"What's that?" He somehow forced himself to take a small step backward into the darkened hallway, to give her some room. He noticed the yellow patch of light that spilled from the door at the end of the hall, his bedroom, a beacon inviting them in…lighting the way.

"Four days."

He nodded and frowned. "Four days. That's right."

"Well, I'm glad I saw you. Rose wanted me to ask if…" Her voice trailed off.

"What did Rose want?"

"She wanted to invite you to have dinner with us tomorrow," Caroline said, too quickly again. "You'd be our first guest. Except for Janie of course." She smiled. "Will you come?"

Adam stared at her, his breath caught in his throat. "And you?"

"Me?" She held his gaze.

"Do *you* want me to come?" He couldn't believe he'd said that.

"Oh, yes! Of course I do," she said. "I'm sorry. I should've said we both wanted you to be our guest." She seemed to have recovered from whatever had thrown her off. Probably just the surprise of finding him right outside the door when she thought she was alone in the house.

He nodded and swallowed. "Okay. Tell her I'll be there." He frowned, aware of how ungracious he sounded. "Look, you finished in here? I could come back later."

"No, no. I'm finished. I'll just get my stuff," she said, and stepped back into the small room. She scooped up a zippered bag, then gathered shorts and a T-shirt and whatever else she'd taken off, some white lacy bits—Adam resolutely looked away, down the hall to the light that mocked him. Mocked him and his miserable mixed-up life.

This woman is raising your daughter—the child you threw away. This is your second chance. She wants you, the way a woman wants a man, and you know it. You can feel it. She's waiting, right here in front of you. She's yours for the taking. She needs a man in her life, she needs you— and you need her.

He knew he wouldn't do it; he knew it was impossible. He took a cold shower, all the while reminding himself that she'd been standing here before him, naked and willing. *And he didn't have the guts to do a damn thing about it.* He'd never fallen into bed so bone tired, knowing he wouldn't sleep.

Supper with the two of them was a chance to prove to himself that things still *were* the same, dammit. That none of what he was feeling mattered one way or the other.

He went into town in the morning and bought a blowup beach ball for the kid. He couldn't arrive there empty-handed. He paused, thinking maybe he should bring something for the mother, but decided against it. He wasn't going courting. This was just a simple supper invite from a couple of females who were playing house. On the way to the cabin, though, through the woods, he stopped and plucked a few of the buttercups that grew along the path. They were foul-smelling but looked nice and bright.

Caroline was touched, which made him feel silly. ''Oh, thank you, Adam. Look, Rosie!'' Caroline put the buttercups in an enameled tin mug, filled it at the newly installed sink, then set it in the center of the table, which was laid for three. Cutlery, napkins, wineglasses for two, a small tumbler at the third setting.

Adam looked around. He felt very large and in the way. There was wood smoke in the air, a pleasant pungent fa-

miliar scent. He noticed the wood range was going, which
made the room too warm, but the windows were all open
wide, curtains fluttering in the breeze. Curley had been
right; the weather had changed.

"Thanks, Mister!" Rose took the beach ball from him
and immediately carried it outside where she kicked it up
and down the grass in front of the cabin, sending the dogs
into a frenzy of excited barking. They chased it madly,
unable to do anything but bat it with their heads and paws.

Caroline went to the door. "Rosie?" she called. "Stay
away from the grill with that ball, okay?"

Adam heard a muffled shout in return. He'd noticed a
small grill, a hibachi, on a couple of cement blocks set up
outside.

"Have you settled in all right?" Why in hell had he ever
thought *this* was a good idea? What was he *doing* here?
He could be home eating a plate of microwaved tuna casserole in front of a baseball game, or he could drive into
town and have a few beers and a burger at the café in the
Glory Hotel. He was bound to meet up with people he knew
there. Glory folk. Shoot the breeze, chat up the waitress,
pretend he had a social life.

"How does it look?" Caroline waved one hand to take
in the small cabin and its contents.

"It looks fine. Are you comfortable?" *Can you sleep
nights?*

"Oh, perfectly. I'm so glad we moved out here. I really
appreciate all the help you and Mrs. T gave us. And Curley," she murmured, nodding. "Curley has been a real
gem."

A gem. That was good.

"Actually, we invited Curley, too. Rose wanted Mister
Curley to come—that's what she calls him. She's very fond
of him and I really think he likes her, too, although he'd

never admit it to me or Rose. His bark's a lot worse than his bite, isn't it?"

"Oh, I wouldn't mention that to Curley, if I were you." So he wasn't the first choice for a supper invitation.

"He said he was too busy, anyway. I'm glad you could join us," she went on with a sideways glance at him. She bent down to take something out of the cooler. "Rose has been looking forward to having visitors." Caroline lifted the cover off the dish. "I hope you like chicken."

She smiled and Adam knew he'd eat anything this woman had prepared with her own hands. She looked beautiful and young and competent, in her calf-length skirt, simple T-shirt and checked apron. She'd tied her hair back, but curls had escaped the ribbon, reminding Adam of last night when he'd surprised her in the bathroom. He had to stop thinking of that.

"Can I help you with anything?" he asked awkwardly.

"No. Why don't you just sit down here and I'll toss these on the grill. We can eat in ten minutes." She disappeared through the door. Adam felt vague relief. He'd been afraid she'd ask him to do the honors at the barbecue. He wasn't big on charring meat outdoors, but he knew a lot of people thought men were born with a barbecue gene. If they were, he'd missed it.

He sat down gingerly in the old upholstered chair he'd brought over from the Dempseys and leaned back. The springs bore slightly to the left, but it was comfortable enough. He studied the matching sofa. Did she stretch out on the cushions, or did she fold it out and make it up each night?

He'd never know. He turned his attention to the rest of the cabin. Hard to believe this was the same shack he and Beau had thrown together in a couple of weeks one summer. Beau had wanted a place of his own when he visited, he'd said. Of course Helen had been around in those days. Maybe Beau hadn't liked Helen all that well; he, Adam, had never known. They'd had a good time building the cabin. For a city slicker Beau was surprisingly handy with an ax.

He heard the door slam. Rose came in, and he felt himself tense. It didn't matter how often he saw the girl, he never seemed able to relax around her. He couldn't stop remembering that she was his daughter. He kept trying to find traces of himself in her. She was dark-haired, like he was, and had blue eyes, also like him. But so did a million kids. He honestly couldn't recall much about the woman who'd given birth to her. He'd never dreamed he'd ever be in this situation. Now he couldn't imagine going back, couldn't imagine what it would be like when Caroline and Rose left.

Rose smiled shyly at him and went to the sink to wash under the cold running water. She wiped her hands on her shirtfront.

"All ready!" Caroline came in the door with the platter of meat. "Adam? If you'd like to pour the wine, we can eat. There's a corkscrew on the table."

Adam opened the wine and poured a glass for each of them. He didn't drink wine all that often; he preferred beer or plain water. Caroline put a plastic jug of milk on the table and the platter of golden grilled chicken. Then she retrieved a plate of something else from the cooler, something brown and green and mixed-up-looking, and set it down. A salad appeared, as well, and then the three of them sat down.

"Cheers!" Caroline said, raising her glass. "Here's to a great haying season and more good summer weather."

Adam raised his glass and drank, catching her eye over

her glass. Something burned deep in his gut—and it wasn't the chardonnay.

"Me, too!" Rose raised her glass of milk and insisted he and her mother clink glasses with hers. They did, then smiled. Adam felt very strange, as though he'd dropped in on Caroline and her daughter from another planet. They looked like a family, the three of them. This was family life, this ordinary domestic peace and pleasure, and he wasn't a family man.

"Have some. Rose helped make it." Caroline handed him the platter piled high with brown and green and, now that he had a closer look, tomato pieces and various vegetable things.

"What is it?"

"Taboulleh. We bought the bulgur in town at the health-food store and robbed Mrs. T's garden for the rest of the ingredients. Parsley and mint and tomatoes and onions. We eat this a lot in the summer when it's hot," she said, smiling. "It's very nutritious."

Adam ladled some onto his plate next to the chicken. Bulgur? What in hell was bulgur?

By the time he left, not much past eight o'clock, he was feeling quite pleased with himself. He'd made some flimsy excuse about getting home—not wanting to spend the evening with Caroline, especially after Rose went to bed—but he'd handled it. He'd managed to get through dinner. They were two adults, two grown-up sensible adults. Sure, there'd been that hot kiss back at the camp three weeks ago, but hell, that sort of thing happened.

It wasn't going to happen again. Spending a couple of hours alone with the two of them was the big test. He'd passed. With flying colors. He'd even eaten some weird Middle Eastern dish. And he'd drunk white wine.

Bulgur. He had to admit—it had tasted pretty good.

THREE DAYS LATER, Adam knew he hadn't passed the test, after all.

He'd been to town again and on his way home stopped at the mailbox and pulled out a letter addressed to Caroline. Spidery elegant writing. The American stamp and the thickness of the letter, on cream-colored expensive-looking stationery, had chilled him to the marrow. He'd been living in a kind of dreamland. She didn't belong here; she belonged *there*. At and the end of the summer, she was going back. And taking his daughter with her.

By the time he got home it was dark. He thought about waiting until morning. But then he thought maybe the letter was important. As far as he knew, it was the only one she'd received since she'd come to the Double O. Maybe it was about money or Beau's affairs.

Adam made his way along the path by starlight. The grass had been tramped down over the past several weeks, and he could have walked each twist and turn blindfolded. He had no notion whatsoever of sneaking up on the cabin. Usually one of the dogs that stayed there overnight barked a welcome or a warning. It was sheer odds that this time none of them did.

He stepped on the little wooden stoop and raised his hand to rap on the door.

And froze.

Between the two curtain panels that didn't quite meet over the window in the door, he saw Caroline in the soft light from the lantern. There was a candle stuck in a holder on the table and she was bathed in the glow of the candle and the lamp, her shoulders bare, her skin golden. A basin stood on the table, and from time to time she dipped a sponge into it and dreamily ran it over her arms, her face, her chest. She had a tiny scrap of an upper garment on, a piece of silky material no bigger than a handkerchief.

Adam felt like a peeper. He stepped back. To hell with playing postman. His heart hammered. Although he no longer stood on the little stoop, he could still see her.

She crossed her arms and slowly lifted the garment over her head and tossed it onto the table. Her back was toward the door. Throat dry, he watched as she took the sponge, dripping, and ran it over her arms again, this time sponging her breasts, as well. He couldn't see her breasts, but he could imagine them. The imagining was maybe even worse than the seeing.

Adam heard a great roaring in his ears. He felt his own breath rise up and choke him. He turned and walked away blindly, careful not to stumble or to move too fast or to frighten the cabin dogs into barking now. The last thing he wanted was for Caroline to know that he'd seen her. That he'd spied on her. That he'd invaded her privacy.

Invaded her privacy? He'd stared, for God's sake! Gaped like a bloody sex-starved teenager.

What was wrong with him?

In the five-minute walk from the cabin to the house, Adam realized what was wrong with him.

He was lost. He was utterly lost.

CHAPTER FOURTEEN

CAROLINE HAD NOT expected Eunice Carter to reply to her note so quickly, if at all. When she saw the envelope lying on her desk in Adam's office, she wondered that he hadn't mentioned it, then recalled that he'd been in town most of the day before and she hadn't seen him.

She studied the postmark. Eight days from Seattle. *Eight days!* Probably faster in the Pony Express era.

Caroline slit the end of the envelope with her thumbnail and pulled out three closely written pages covered with Eunice's thin copperplate. Her mother-in-law had received an education at a time when penmanship mattered.

She sank down in the faded chintz-covered armchair by the window to read her letter.

When she'd finished, she sat quietly for a few more minutes, trying to absorb what she'd just read. She saw Curley heading for the barn with Rose right behind him, carrying a small pail. Janie brought up the rear, struggling to keep up. It was a beautiful summer morning. Where was Adam? His truck wasn't where he usually parked it. She heard the distant sounds of Mrs. T clanging pots and pans in the kitchen.

The small sights and sounds of the Double O were so familiar now that the ranch, which had once seemed strange to her, felt almost like home. She'd been here well over a month already, and somehow couldn't imagine gathering up the energy and the enthusiasm to make her way back to Seattle and sort out her life there. As she must do soon.

At least, she thought, holding the letter up to the light and glancing at the first page, there was some hope now. Hope that something might change.

Eunice Carter was receiving counseling, she wrote, apparently had been since before Caroline left. She'd been relieved to receive Caroline's note and to learn that she and Rose were safe. She also mentioned recalling Adam Garrick as a man she didn't particularly care for, but to whom she'd always be grateful because he'd once saved Beau's life.

Caroline didn't know what *that* was all about.

Eunice offered her apologies—"heartfelt" was the word she used—for the way she'd treated her and Rose lately, and Caroline knew how much that had cost her. Her mother-in-law was not a woman who apologized often or easily. She went on to write that she'd been so confused, but that now things were beginning to clear; Caroline wasn't at all sure what that meant. She said she'd spoken to Philip and her lawyer and added some muddled comments about the outcome of those conversations. Caroline wasn't convinced that Eunice was completely healthy yet. Still, she'd taken the first step by seeking help.

That was important. And Eunice had said that she missed Rose terribly—Caroline noted wryly that *she* was not included in the sentiment—and that she wanted Rose to forgive her for not being a part of her life in the past few months. Then there was a long rambling paragraph about how difficult it had been to come to grips with Beau's death, which Caroline skimmed. She'd learned to live with her own grief and, whether or not it seemed selfish to others, did not want to relive the events of the past two years through her mother-in-law's eyes.

All in all Caroline felt enormously relieved. She was glad she'd decided to write to Eunice. She'd reply this week and give her more news of Rose and their summer at the Double O. Maybe even have Rose draw a picture to enclose. Then, when they went back to Seattle after Labor Day—which was her original agreement with Adam—they might be able to start repairing their relationship.

Now, if only she'd hear from her lawyer soon. If only Maddie Reinholdt would write to say she'd pieced together Beau's affairs and found there were some resources, after all, for her and Rose. An insurance policy. Perhaps a modest trust account that had been overlooked. Some property that hadn't been sold to pay…whom? Caroline still couldn't believe that Beau had stolen money from the Carter family company and gambled it away. That just wasn't the Beau Carter she knew. But who was he? Had she known the man who'd lived in the rough cabin out behind Adam's place? Had she known the youth who'd ridden in rodeos and skied glaciers—just for the fun of it?

How well did you ever know *anyone?*

Adam had admitted he hadn't known his ex-wife well; how well had Helen known *him* after eight years of marriage? Enough to walk out on him when she realized he'd never change, which showed she had some sense of self-preservation, at least. She couldn't really have loved him, though, or understood him—

"Ready for a cup of tea?" Mrs. T interrupted Caroline's train of thought by poking her head through the half-open office door. "Oh, I see you've got a letter."

"From Rose's grandmother." Caroline smiled. "In Seattle. I wrote a couple of weeks ago to let her know how we were."

"Isn't that nice! Well, whenever you're ready, the kettle's on.'' And with that, the housekeeper continued down the hall toward the kitchen.

Caroline got up and carefully refolded the letter, replaced it in the envelope and slipped it into her skirt pocket. She had tons of work to do today and she really ought to get started, but it would be pleasant to sit in the kitchen with Mrs. T for a few minutes and have that cup of tea first. Rose and Janie would be fine with Curley for a while. Caroline had gradually relaxed about Rose's expeditions on the ranch. There were strict rules about where Rose and Janie could go and where they were not allowed. The bunkhouse, the corrals, the Horsethief River that ran a few hundred yards from the house, behind the cabin—fairly high at this time of year with snowmelt from the mountains: these were all off-limits. Mrs. T had assured Caroline that her daughter understood these long-standing rules very well and would not lead Rose astray.

''Where's Adam?'' As she entered the kitchen, Caroline voiced the question she'd had at the back of her mind all morning. She hadn't seen much of him since he'd had dinner with her and Rose three days ago. *That* had been an experience....

''Didn't he tell you? He's gone up to the camp.'' Mrs. T poured out two mugs of tea and Caroline sat at the scrubbed wooden table, tucking one foot underneath her. ''Left early this morning and said he'd be back in a few days. I thought for sure he'd have mentioned it to you.'' Mrs. T frowned.

''No.'' Caroline reached for a freshly made date square. ''You're going to send me back to Seattle a butterball! I'll miss your baking, that's for sure.''

''We're going to miss you, dear.'' To Caroline's amazement the housekeeper blinked rapidly, as though holding back tears. ''And Janie! My goodness, Janie's going to be so sad when Rosie leaves. 'Course she'll have her school again come September and she loves that.''

Janie took the school bus to a special sheltered-workshop program in Glory where she had the daily job of stirring muffin mixes and helping behind the counter of the little lunch room and bakery the facility operated ten months of the year.

School. Next year Rose would be starting first grade. Next month, when they got settled back in Seattle, Caroline planned to enroll her in kindergarten. She wondered where the years had gone since she and Beau first set eyes on the tiny black-haired yawning infant. She'd been three days old when she'd come into their lives.

Caroline suddenly realized that while she was daydreaming, Mrs. T had been speaking.

''...and I'm going to set out lunch early, if you don't mind, Caroline. Just a plate of sandwiches and some ice cream for the girls, if they want it, and why wouldn't they on a hot day like this?'' She raised her eyebrows in amusement.

''I want to get into that garden for an hour or two, since it's going to be such a scorcher,'' she went on. ''The weeds just *melt* when I pull 'em and lay 'em out in the hot sun. 'Specially that quack grass. Otherwise there's no getting ahead of the darned stuff. Supposed to hit thirty degrees today, according to the radio. What's that in Fahrenheit? Hardly remember anymore since we switched. Must be well over ninety. 'Nother cup of tea?''

Caroline refused; she drained her cup and ten minutes later was lost in her figures and lists and didn't hear a thing until Mrs. T called her to lunch. The girls were already at the table when Caroline arrived. They were in very high spirits.

''No nap! No nap!'' Rose chanted, tapping her spoon on

the table. Janie joined in, half coordinating her "No nap!" with Rose's.

"Hush, girls! I told them they didn't have to go upstairs for a lie-down after lunch if they didn't want to," Mrs. T explained, setting a plate of tuna-salad sandwiches and a jar of pickles on the table. "I hope that's all right with you? It'll be hotter'n Hades upstairs."

"Rose can do without a nap for one day," Caroline agreed. "So, what'll you do this afternoon, girls?"

The two of them looked significantly at each other and giggled. Janie covered her mouth with one hand and made waving gestures with the other. "Go 'way," she mumbled. "Go 'way, Car'line."

"Now, Janie," her mother said mildly. "Is that any way to talk to Rosie's mommy? She just wants to know what you two are getting up to this afternoon while we're working."

The girls burst into giggles again, and Caroline smiled at the housekeeper and shrugged one shoulder. There was no dealing with them in this mood! Secretly she was pleased. Rose seemed so happy here at the Double O. Having friends like Janie and "Mr. Curley" was part of that happiness. She'd never seen her daughter so confident and outgoing. It revealed another side to the girl's character, and again, fleetingly, Caroline wondered about the parents who'd given her life.

She poured them each a glass of milk, then reached for a sandwich herself. She glanced at Adam's empty chair. Not that he always joined them for the noon meal, which Caroline and Rose ate several times a week with Mrs. T and Janie, but why hadn't he mentioned plans to go up to the Tetlock camp? She was doing the payroll today and tomorrow; he was usually around then so he could answer questions and sign the checks.

Adam. Her employer was on her mind a lot these days. And not in the role of employer, either. She'd made it seem that Rose had particularly wanted to invite guests the other evening, but she'd been pleased that he had come. In many ways it surprised her that he'd accepted; she had the definite impression he wasn't crazy about kids, Rose included. Nor was he a particularly social, hey-come-to-dinner kind of guy. Sure, he had friends, she knew that. Glory folk, neighbors, other ranchers. But there was an intensity and a directness about him, a sense that he had no time for fools of any kind—and that made her think he wasn't an especially good choice for a Glory matron short of amiable men for a dinner party.

The loss was theirs. Caroline recognized the breathlessness she so often felt around him. She knew what had caused her to double-knot her bathrobe after she'd cinched it so tight she could scarcely breathe when they'd met outside the bathroom in the ranch house. She was horribly, desperately, *pathetically* attracted to him. There was something so compelling about his sheer maleness. Nothing could have brought it home to her more than the shock of seeing him standing there outside the door, literally reeking of a sweaty male muskiness, his shirt hanging open to reveal a hard-muscled chest. She could still see the short white scar that crossed his lower ribs diagonally, perhaps some old rodeo injury. Dust and short wisps of hay had been stuck to his shirt and in his hair.

He'd challenged her. He hadn't stepped back immediately, as she would have expected him to do. His first response had not been to let her pass, but to hold his ground. Perhaps even to move forward, *to take her in his arms*...

This was more than foolishness. These were sophomoric silly fantasies. Ridiculous! No wonder there were so many jokes about widows. Here she was, mooning over a man who had no interest in her. Clearly he could control himself—as he'd promised her at the camp. Why couldn't she? Of course she wasn't entirely sure it took much effort on his part. He'd given her no hint that he felt anything similar to what *she* was feeling. And thank goodness for that.

For all she knew, he had an ongoing relationship with some local woman. Caroline groaned in disgust. She couldn't believe herself! As if he'd need a *reason* to be immune to her.

She couldn't win. The only solution was to bury herself in work. Think payroll data. Think grocery orders. Get everything done before Adam got back, so all he'd have to do was sign a bunch of checks. She could leave them on his desk with a note.

Later Caroline couldn't recall exactly when she began to feel uneasy about Rose and Janie. At some point the background noise of them playing outside her window in the lawn swing ebbed. Then there was silence. At first it didn't register, but when she hadn't heard a shout or the bark of a dog or anything at all for a while, she got up and went to the window.

The heat lay on the grass and the trees outside, heavy and still. The sky was a deep, dense, hard-boiled blue with just a few wispy clouds on the horizon. She saw a distant plume of dust along the road that led to the ranch and paused, waiting to see who it was.

An unfamiliar late-model car came into the yard, slowed, then pulled up in front of the house. For a moment or two, nothing happened, then the driver's door opened and a man wearing a rumpled summer suit got out and walked slowly toward the house, as though unsure he was at the right place.

It turned out he was not. He was a salesman for a veterinary-supply company and he was looking for a neighboring ranch. Caroline didn't feel confident giving him directions, so she walked around to where Mrs. T was bent over in the garden, wearing a huge floppy pink hat and sunglasses. The housekeeper gave him detailed directions, and the two women stood for a few moments and watched as he made his way back to his car and drove off.

Something about talking to a stranger in the ranch yard sent shivers down Caroline's spine.

"Have you seen the girls?" she asked Mrs. T.

"Girls?" The housekeeper glanced around. "No. Not for a while now. They were on the yard swing earlier..."

"Yes, I saw them. But they're not there now and I just wondered if they'd been here in the garden."

"I didn't see them." Mrs. T took off her hat and wiped her glistening brow with the sleeve of the cotton shirt she wore. She was well prepared for the sun. "Darn it." She frowned. "Janie knows she's not to go anywhere without letting us know where she is."

Mrs. T joined Caroline as she began to walk back to the house. "They'll likely be with Curley. Or maybe gone upstairs to take that nap, after all."

But they weren't with Curley. Curley, in fact, was nowhere to be found, and when Caroline checked, she couldn't see his pickup in the yard. Maybe he'd driven to town. Or out to the fields. He'd naturally assume the girls had gone up to the house. It wasn't the foreman's responsibility to look after her child.

Fear grabbed at Caroline's pulse and pricked along her arms and back. *Where were they?*

Still, there was no point in panicking. They were no doubt just playing quietly somewhere. She'd only frighten them—and Mrs. T—if she flipped out and started yelling and dashing around looking for them.

She went back to the house and climbed the stairs to the

second floor. Rose wasn't in her little bed, where she some-times still napped. She checked the bedroom she'd slept in herself before they'd moved to the cabin—not there, either. Heart hammering and with no one to observe, she yanked open all the doors to the rooms upstairs, including Adam's.

"Rose?" she said cautiously. "Janie?" Surely to good-ness the girls weren't hiding, thinking it was a tremendous joke to play on their mothers. She walked into Adam's room and opened the closet door. No children giggling and yelling, "Surprise!" Several pairs of dress boots stood on the floor, shirts hung neatly on hangers, conservative stripes and plaids and chambrays, several Stetsons on the top shelf, brown, gray, tan. Three leather belts, buckles hooked over a peg inside the door. She caught the faintest scent of Adam—his clothes, his skin...

She felt like a voyeur, especially considering what she'd been fantasizing lately, and quickly left the room to do a thorough search of the upper floor, every closet, every bed-room, the bathroom, every place a couple of girls could possibly be hiding.

They weren't there.

As she came down the stairs she heard Mrs. T clattering in the kitchen.

"You find 'em, Caroline?" she called out.

Caroline went to the kitchen, taking a deep breath before she stepped in, schooling her features to appear calm, at least as calm as she could manage. "They're not upstairs. I'll go to the cabin. Maybe they're playing there."

"They sneaked in here, all right. I think they had some-thing planned." Mrs. T gestured to a half-open cupboard door. "Half a jar of cookies missing and some juice. Who knows what else? I'll bet they decided to have a picnic under the trees somewhere." She shut the cupboard door and restored a chair, which had been dragged to the counter, to the table.

That was it. Surely. They'd just packed up a little lunch and were eating it under the trees in the shade nearby. Caroline hurried to the cabin, keeping a sharp eye out for the girls under the swaying poplars and cottonwoods along the way.

"Janie? Rose?" she called out regularly as she walked. No response.

They weren't at the cabin, and from what she could tell, no one had been there since Caroline and Rose had left this morning after breakfast. Sun glinted off the dishes, dry now, stacked on the wooden drainboard in front of the window. The cabin was warm and quiet, and yet the very silence pulsed horror. The braided rug on the wood floor, the faded floral sofa and chair, the children's storybook she'd been reading to Rose every night, turned over on the arm of the sofa. Raggy sprawled facedown, forgotten on the floor.

Caroline put both hands to her mouth. *Rose. Rose!* Somehow she made it back to the house. Mrs. T was alarmed by now, too. She waved plump hands and kept muttering, "My goodness, my goodness," and offering homilies until Caroline wanted to scream.

Someone had to take charge. Where was Curley, for God's sake? Where was *anyone?* She needed help. How could she and Mary search for the girls? She certainly didn't know the area, didn't know where to look, other than the obvious places, which she'd already searched.

She saw the dust of a vehicle approaching and felt tremendous relief when she saw that it was Curley's truck. She ran out the door and down to the corral where he'd stopped. He was just lifting a roll of wire out of the back.

"Curley!"

"What is it, missus? You okay?" Curley jumped down from the truck and pulled the bill of his hat lower. His blue eyes were razor sharp.

"It's Rose—"

"Rose!"

"—and Janie." Caroline gasped, holding her side after her run down the hill. "We can't find them anywhere. Oh, Curley—" The tears that she'd held back until now spilled over. *My baby. You've got to help me find my baby.*

Curley frowned and headed toward the house, leaving the tailgate down and the door of his pickup hanging open. He asked where she'd looked and then went to speak to Mrs. T, who by now was wiping her eyes with the corner of her apron.

Adam. Caroline ducked into the office and dialed the Tetlock Camp radiophone number with trembling fingers. While she waited for the connection, she prayed that, miracle of miracles, Adam would actually be nearby, maybe even in the cookshack.

"Barbara Hillerman speaking."

"Barbara. It's Caroline. Is Adam there? I need to speak to him."

"Well, that's lucky! He just came up for coffee with Jim. Anything wrong? Hang on a sec. I'll get him for you."

Caroline waited another interminable minute.

"Adam Garrick here." The sound of his stern voice undid her completely.

"A-Adam—" Her voice broke and she tried desperately to swallow, to get hold of herself. How could she? Her world was cracking into a million pieces.

"Caroline! For God's sake, what's the matter?"

"It's Rose and Janie. They're lost. We can't find them anywhere!"

"Where's Curley?" Adam cut her off. His voice was

iron-hard and seething with tension. She felt as though he'd take her head off, right through the airwaves.

"He was in town or something. He just got here. He's looking for them, too, and so is Mrs. T and—"

"Never mind that. I'll get there as soon as I can. Keep looking. Don't panic."

Caroline started to say she wouldn't, then realized the connection was gone. Adam had hung up. He was already on his way.

CHAPTER FIFTEEN

DON'T PANIC, he'd told her.

What about *him?*

He'd never saddled up so fast. Ten minutes after Caroline's call had come in, he jammed his heels into the gelding's side. The animal responded with the heart Adam had always known he had. Gimp was what the old-timers called it. A horse that never gave up. The black had it in spades.

The trip he and Caroline had made in an easy two hours, the gelding cut to under one—leaping dry creek beds, jumping windfalls on little shortcuts Adam knew, scrambling on the uphills—forty-seven minutes to be exact.

He left the gelding snorting and blowing and flecked with lather at the trailhead corral and yelled for Farley to come out and take care of him.

The old horse handler emerged from his shack, scratching his grizzled head. "Problems, Boss?"

"Maybe," Adam said, tossing him the reins. "I'm heading down to the ranch pronto to find out. Cool this fella off and give him a good feed of oats tonight. He's earned it."

Belatedly he dug deep in his pocket; thank God he had the keys to his truck. He hadn't even thought to check at the camp before he left. Adam gunned the engine and drove off in a spray of gravel. He glanced once in the rearview mirror to see old Farley staring after him, snapping his suspenders thoughtfully.

Slow down, Garrick. He forced himself to release his

pressure on the accelerator after the pickup's back end skid-
ded around a corner. *Lot of good you'll do Caroline and
Rose if you go off the road up here.*

Rose.

Leaving the camp without checking for his keys was not
like him. He wasn't a man who got rattled in a tight situation. It didn't pay to get rattled; he'd learned that long
ago. He'd faced death more than once, either in the bull
chutes or on the mountains or running whitewater, and he'd
never felt what he felt now. Pure, paralyzing fear. It was
dangerous, that kind of feeling. It could cause a man to
make mistakes.

Mistakes. The mistake he'd made was allowing Rose and
her mother into his life at all. His life had been going along
just fine before they arrived. He should've bit the bullet
and sent them on their way when they showed up at the
ranch that second time, looking for the kid's doll. He could
have hired somebody in Glory, even part-time, to take care
of his office work when Rhonda pulled out. One of Mrs.
T's daughters—anybody. He'd told himself he was doing
it for Beau; he told himself he owed it to his buddy to do
what he could for his widow. To show some hospitality.
To act like a goddamned human being, for a change.

*What he wanted was to get to know his daughter. What
he wanted was a second chance.* Now what? Was this the
second chance? Or was this no chance at all? Not if anything happened to Rose—or Janie. He tramped on the gas
pedal again. *Or Caroline.*

He couldn't bear the thought.

ADAM GLANCED UP. The clouds were building rapidly, but
it looked like the rain would hold off for a while. Not long,
but maybe until they'd found the girls. Wherever in hell
they'd gotten to.

"Have you looked down by the granary?" he asked his foreman. He'd never seen Curley Splint move as quickly as he had in the past half hour.

"Angus checked there. Say—" Curley squinted at Adam "—you figure maybe we should call the cops?"

"Maybe," Adam replied grimly. "But not just yet. They've only been missing for a few hours. Where could they go?" He waved his hand impatiently toward the corrals. His bulls were all out with the cows on summer range, another relief. The sale bulls were in a secure pasture some distance from the house. Of course there were other dangers—horses, old well shafts he didn't know about. The river. "There's only so many places. They've got to be here. Where're the women?"

"They're checking the cellar up at the house. Nobody thought to look down there yet."

Adam knew he'd see Caroline's pale face and huge eyes for the rest of his life. He knew how close she was to a complete breakdown the minute he'd arrived, yet she was trying her best not to let it show. Mrs. T was carrying on enough for the lot of them, although she'd apparently quieted down some since her husband got there. Curley had insisted she call Angus Tump right away. He'd been hunting for the girls for the past hour, as had two men Curley had called in from the haying crew.

So far they'd covered the barn, the house, the equipment shed, the bunkhouse, the three tourist cabins, the cookhouse, Caroline's place again and the woods between the house and the cabin. Curley had gone down to the river but seen no sign of them at all, no footprints in the mud at the water's edge—nothing. Adam was pretty sure they wouldn't travel that far, but something in his gut wouldn't let him rule it out entirely. Sure it was off-limits, but what did that mean? Just how responsible was Janie Tump, no matter what her mother said? *If they'd gone to the river, there was no telling where they'd be found.*

He'd even looked inside all the ranch vehicles, remembering how, as a boy, he'd sometimes crawl into the back of the family car on quiet boring summer days and fall asleep on the hot vinyl seat. All the vehicles were empty.

Adam even checked the dogs. They were accounted for—which was unusual, for he'd have thought one or two would have stayed with the girls, which was their habit since Rose had arrived and the two girls spent so much time outdoors. But no, the dogs were all hanging around the house, getting in the way.

That didn't leave much. Unless they'd wandered off somewhere into the trees behind the cabin and just kept wandering and by now were good and lost. Adam felt a chill run down his spine, despite the heat and humidity— the clouds were about to burst any minute. The girls would be safe enough overnight somewhere, under a tree; he wasn't worried about wild animals or anything like that, but it would be a horrible experience for them.

He heard a wail and looked up. Mrs. T and Caroline were emerging from the house. From the sound of things, there'd been no sign of the girls. Caroline had her arms wrapped around her and was following Mrs. T, head down. Was she feeling cold, too? Adam didn't think he'd ever seen anyone look so frightened and miserable in his life. He walked toward her.

"Caroline." He could see the tracks of tears on her dust-streaked cheeks. Her lower lip trembled. "They'll turn up soon. You'll see. Curley or Angus or one of us is bound to find them and—"

"Do you think that salesman who came here took off with them?" Her voice was hoarse from calling the children.

He frowned and put one hand on her shoulder. She bowed her head slightly. "The fellow you told me about who came here looking for the Oarlock Seven? The salesman?"

"Yes."

"What kind of a guy was he?"

She stared up at him. "I don't know. An ordinary kind of guy, I guess. A salesman."

"Do *you* think he took off with Rose and Janie?"

He got a shadow of a smile and gave her shoulder a slight squeeze. She shook her head. "No."

"Well, okay—"

"Adam! Mother!"

Adam turned, still with his arm on Caroline's shoulder. It was Angus Tump, coming toward them across the field. He wasn't hurrying, but then Adam had never seen Angus move fast.

"What happened?" Curley yelled.

Angus waved his arms a couple of times. "Found 'em!" came the faint message.

"My God." Caroline collapsed against Adam and he tightened his arm around her. He felt her shoulders shake as the tears came. *"Oh, Adam!"*

He wanted to comfort her, but if he'd been free he would have walked over and given Angus Tump a good shake for being his usual communicative self. Then he reminded himself that Janie was Angus's daughter; he'd been just as worried as the rest of them. He was a father, too.

Mrs. T screamed and flew toward her husband and threw her plump arms around his neck. He patted her back awkwardly, not removing the filthy-looking black stump of a pipe he always had in his mouth.

"For cryin' out loud, man, where *are* they?" Curley

sputtered, slapping his cap against his thigh. Curley looked furious now that the worry was relieved.

"Down at the hay shed," Angus waved one hand in the direction of an old hay shed that stood several hundred yards off in the field behind the barn. Weathered and gray and a good twenty-five feet tall, it was a big open wooden structure with a roof. It held mainly overflow from the second cutting in years when they had a good crop. They hadn't been near it yet this summer, although there were several tons of last year's hay sitting in there. Why hadn't he thought to check it earlier?

He felt Caroline wipe her eyes on his shirt and raise her head. He still held her close; for support, he told himself. "They okay, Angus?" he asked.

"Fine." Angus went on patting Mrs. T's broad back. "There, there, Mother. Don't carry on so. Our Janie's right as rain. T'other girl, too."

"Why didn't you bring them back with you?" Adam demanded. He'd still like to give Angus Tump a good shake, if for nothing else than being such an aggravating man.

"What, wake 'em up? Why, they're sound asleep, the both of 'em!" Angus said around his pipe stem. Big smile. "Plenty of half-eat stuff layin' about, too. Chocolate chips and p'tatie chips and jelly powder 'n' whatnot."

"Jelly powder!?" That got Mrs. T's attention. She raised her head from where she'd rested it on her husband's shoulder. "That darn Janie! She's always trying to get into my jelly powder. Takes it into the bathroom and locks the door and licks up as much as she can. I can always tell when she's got a green tongue or a purple tongue or..."

Suddenly Mrs. T started to laugh, then she wiped her eyes with her apron, and when she took it away from her face, she was crying again. "Wait'll I get a hold of her. I'll give her such a talkin' to—"

"Here they come!" Caroline called out. Her voice was tight with emotion. Adam ached for her. His own throat hurt. She hadn't moved from the shelter of his arm, which suited him just fine. She still had his shirt firmly clenched in her hands. He felt her anxiety as they all turned as one toward the hay shed to see the two girls ambling toward the house, each dragging a bag behind her. They didn't seem aware of their audience.

The adults stared, seemingly paralyzed by the events of the past several hours. Suddenly the girls stopped, too, and gazed at the knot of grown-ups facing them.

"Whassamatter?" Janie said. She waved one pudgy arm and smiled when she saw her father. Her face was smudged with chocolate and jelly powder. "Whassamatter, Dad?"

Mrs. T burst into tears again and ran toward her daughter, who instantly burst into tears, too. The two plump women wrapped their arms around each other and wailed in unison.

"Well, for cryin' out loud," he heard Curley mutter to no one in particular, resetting his cap on his fuzzy pate. "*Women!* Would ya look at that."

Adam stepped aside as he felt Caroline move away. He took a deep breath, willing back the wave upon wave of raw emotion that roiled through him. *Thank God! Thank God they were safe.*

Just then there was a mighty crack in the sky above and a flash of lightning. Huge fat pods of rain hit the grass and blew into Adam's face.

"Rosie!" Caroline cried and swept up her daughter, who dropped her bag and threw her arms around her mother's neck.

"Mommy!"

Caroline buried her face in Rose's hair and hugged her tight. "Oh, Rosie, darling!"

Caroline stumbled blindly toward him, carrying Rose, and Adam put his arms around them both. The girl wrapped one arm around his neck, which felt good, so very good. He gathered them close, wanting to shelter them from more than the storm. "Mr. Adam...Mommy," Rose said in a small shaky voice.

The heavens opened with another thunderous crack and within a minute they were soaked to the skin. Adam didn't care. The rain was warm; all he wanted was to stay just where he was, savoring the feeling of Rose and Caroline in his arms. *A family.*

Thunder rumbled again, and sheet lightning swept across the sky to the northwest. This definitely was not a great place to wait out a summer storm. Rose lifted her head from where she'd tucked it tightly between his and Caroline's. Adam didn't think he'd ever been this close to the girl, close enough to see each tiny freckle.

"Mister?" Her little wet face shone. She licked the corners of her lips and wrinkled her nose. "Why are we getting wet out here in the rain, you and me and my mommy?"

Rose went to sleep surprisingly early, about half-past eight, considering her long afternoon nap in the hay shed. Mrs. T and Adam had insisted they have supper at the ranch house and get Rose bathed and into warm dry clothes. Over the meal the adults heard bits and pieces from the girls, which allowed them to cobble together the tale.

"We ate junk food," Rose solemnly told everyone at the table, eyes wide. "A *lot!*"

It seemed they'd planned it in the morning—thus the giggles at lunch—and had made their kitchen heist early in the afternoon when Caroline was busy in the office and

Mrs. T was pulling weeds in the garden. They'd climbed up into the cupboards and loaded two plastic grocery bags with all the delicious things they could find—shredded coconut, chocolate chips, ladyfingers, potato chips, soup mixes, crackers—just about anything they could either stuff in their mouths or mix up in an old bucket they'd found for their pretend cooking.

They'd had a wonderful time and had eventually fallen asleep in the afternoon heat under the shelter of the hayshed roof.

Caroline made a point of reminding Rose several times during the meal that, in the future, she had to let someone know where she was at all times.

"Who will you tell if Mommy's not there?" she asked again.

"Janie's mommy or Mr. Curley or Mr. Adam or—" Rose screwed up her face. "Who else?"

"Or Ben. Or any other adult you know who lives here, remember?"

Rose nodded vigorously. "Okeydoke!"

Everyone laughed at hearing one of Curley's common expressions in the girlish voice. Adam's foreman hauled out his pocket handkerchief, a big red polka-dotted affair, and blew his nose loudly several times. Curley, Caroline believed, had been truly affected by their scare that afternoon. Adam couldn't seem to keep his eyes off the girls, although he didn't say much. Had he changed his opinion about Rose?

Thank goodness for Adam Garrick, Caroline thought again and glanced at her watch. She didn't know what she'd have done if he hadn't been there. It was almost ten o'clock.

In all the excitement she hadn't had a chance to thank

Adam. She didn't know if he planned to return to the Tet-lock camp early in the morning or not.

She went to Rose's tiny room. Her daughter was sleeping soundly, half-covered by blankets and sheets, one arm around her whale, the other around Raggy. Caroline tiptoed closer and pulled the covers higher. In the low light that spilled from the cabin's main room, Rose looked so tanned and healthy. *And happy.* It seemed a shame to take her away from all this and bring her back to the city. They might even have to rent an apartment now that their house was gone. That meant a far different life than she was living now. No grass, no trees, no pets. A goldfish, maybe.

She bent down and kissed her daughter softly on the cheek. The girl didn't stir.

Caroline carefully doused the gas lantern. She picked up a flashlight she kept near the door. It was only three or four minutes' walk to the house; she could be back in fifteen minutes and get ready for bed herself. She wouldn't be able to sleep if she didn't thank Adam properly. She had to tell him how much his presence had meant to her today. The way he'd come down from the camp, no questions asked. The comfort he'd offered, too, before Rose was found, one human being to another. It had been so long since she'd felt the solace of a man's arms around her.

Solace, Caroline? Is that what you really felt? Caroline determinedly thrust the thought to the back of her mind.

The path was sodden. The rain had let up just after supper. A typical summer shower—big buildup, lots of thunder and lightning, then, in an hour or two, it was all over. By the time she got to the ranch house, she was wet from the knees down. Her skirt clung to her legs.

Surprisingly the house was dark. Everyone must have gone to bed early. She stopped and was about to turn and go back to the cabin when she smelled the sweet pungent odor of tobacco and saw the glowing end of a cigar or cigarette on the darkened porch.

"Come on up." It was Adam. Relieved, Caroline made her way up the steps. The half-moon didn't throw much light under the roof of the veranda.

"I didn't know you smoked," she said, at a loss. His presence there surprised her.

"You come to see Mrs. T?"

"No." He was standing, leaning against the wall of the house. She couldn't see his face, except when he drew on what she now saw was a thin cheroot-type of cigar, half-smoked. "Looks like they've all gone to bed, anyway."

"They left. Went home with Angus an hour ago."

"Oh."

There was a minute or so of silence, which felt like a very long time to Caroline's overstretched nerves.

"I—I didn't know you smoked," she repeated, just to say something. She wished she hadn't come.

"I don't." He spoke through his teeth, without removing the cheroot, and sent another puff of smoke into the damp night air.

"I see." *That* made a lot of sense. Adam seemed testy. As though she'd disturbed him by coming along just now. As though he resented the intrusion. All of which made her even more nervous. Might as well get it over with. "Actually, I wanted to see you."

"Me?"

"Yes. I wanted to thank you for coming to my rescue this afternoon." She managed a weak laugh, which sounded utterly foolish in the thick silence that lay between them. She wished she could see his face; on the other hand, she was glad she couldn't. "I realize I was panicking...."

"You had your reasons."

"I know. But I—" Caroline stopped, twisting the hem

of her shirt between her fingers. "I didn't know what to do. Mrs. T was...well, she was pretty upset herself. Luckily Curley came back from town when he did. But—" She paused, then rushed on. "You were the one I thought of. I felt I had to tell you...."

Adam drew on his cheroot again and the tiny flare showed his features all angles, dark and light. His eyes appeared tormented, but Caroline was sure it was just the odd light.

"Well. That's about it, I guess," she said, and shrugged slightly. "Thank you for helping out the way you did. I know it was a lot to ask, leaving the camp on such short notice when you had work to do. It's a long trip. I just want you to know that I do appreciate it—"

"Caroline." His voice, low as it was, cut through her words.

"Yes?"

"Why do you talk to me like that?"

"Like what?" Was that *her* voice, so reedy and thin?

"Like a retired schoolteacher." One last flare of the cheroot and Caroline saw it arc through the darkness onto the gravel path beside the house. "From the last century."

Caroline didn't know what to say. So she said nothing. Did she really sound as ridiculous as that? Perhaps she did. She felt vaguely hurt.

He took a step toward her, then another. Suddenly he was looming over her in the darkness and she could smell the tobacco on him and the rain, damp hair, wet denim....

"Why don't you say what you mean?"

He raised one hand and laced it through her hair, so that his fingers gripped the nape of her neck and his thumb rested lightly on her cheek. She swallowed. "Wh-what do I mean...?"

That hadn't come out right. She swallowed again. He

stepped even closer and slipped his other hand under her hair, gripping her head tightly, turning her face up to his. *Oh, God...Adam...*

"Why was I the one you thought of, the one you had to tell? *Think about it.*" He paused, then went on in a deep intimate voice, "*This* is what you mean, Caroline, *this* is what you should say. 'I ache for you, Adam'—*say my name,*" he ordered softly.

"Adam," she whispered.

"You walking up here tonight in the dark is like tossing a match into a powder keg," he continued in the same low voice. "I've been trying my damnedest to ignore what's been building between us for weeks, but I just can't pretend anymore. I've been ready to go up in flames for so long I can't remember what it was like before you came here. Do you know what I'm talking about?"

She nodded.

"'I ache for you the way I know you ache for me'—that's what I hear behind all that crazy stuff you tell me. That's what I want you to say. Straight out. And I want you to say it—" he moved his thumbs lightly down her cheek again and she breathed in sharply "—because it's *the truth.*"

Caroline felt her knees go soft. She raised her hands to steady herself and involuntarily put one hand on his shoulder.

"*Isn't it?*" He'd pinned her completely with his eyes. What could she say? He'd demanded the truth. She swallowed again; her throat hurt. Infinitesimally she nodded. God help her—it *was* the truth.

He bent quickly and touched his mouth to hers. His mouth was hard and cold and warm, all at the same time. *And unutterably welcome.*

His kiss was feather soft, his mouth tantalizing hers as

he held her head perfectly still in his hands. Then he looked at her intently. She could just make out his features in the pale light. "This is what you want, isn't it? You know how much I want you. You've known it for a long, long time. You can feel it...."

"Yes," she managed, her voice thick and foreign to her ears. She was trembling; her nerves were screaming, every last one of them. *"Oh, yes."*

"Open your eyes." Her eyes flew open; she hadn't realized she'd closed them. "Look at me." He held her gaze. Her knees, her eyelids, all her joints melted. Her stomach felt like she'd just gone over the summit in the roller coaster at the fall fair. Then he kissed her again, and this time Caroline felt the fire flow freely through her veins, from him to her and back again. An electrical current cracked and flashed through her, just like the sheet lightning they'd seen earlier in the day. She clenched the fabric of his shirt in her fist, just as she'd done when he'd put his arm around her that afternoon.

Yes, yes, he was right: *this* was what it was all about. *This* was the way things were between a man and a woman. It wasn't about pleases and thank-yous and being friends. Or courtesy and cheerfulness and making a good impression. No, it was about heat and sex and the deep painful connection that could ignite—no one knew why—between a man and a woman. Spontaneous. A need to mate. To create. It had ignited between Adam and her weeks ago and burned steadily ever since. She'd denied it with every scrap of her being; still, she'd known.

He was a wonderful kisser. He took his time, feeding her pleasure, taking his own. She felt her arms creep up his shoulders until she was against him, every inch of her, their mouths joined, their bodies flesh to flesh, with only the thinnest fabric, his shirt and hers, between them. Caroline

felt Adam's heart thud against hers, her breasts flatten painfully against his chest.

It was as though an enormous barricade within her had
burst. She couldn't get enough of him. She raised herself
on her toes and locked her mouth on his, and he groaned
and slid his hands down, until he was holding her in his
arms. Then he slipped one hand under her shirt. She gasped
at the sudden bold contact of his hand, rough and warm,
on her bare skin.

He was breathing hard; so was she. Where was her brain?
She had a child sleeping alone a hundred yards away....
This was crazy!

Yet to pull away from him was a kind of torture she
couldn't bear either.

"Adam...*Adam.*" She shuddered as he trailed hot smoky
kisses along her jaw and down the side of her throat. With
enormous effort, she forced herself to go on. "We...we
can't do this."

"Do what?" he muttered. He hadn't stopped kissing her,
not for a second.

"Wh-whatever... *You* know."

"Make love?"

"Yes."

"But it's what you want, isn't it? And you know it's
what I want." He looked into her eyes.

"I don't know." *I wish I knew!*

"The house is empty. We're alone. We could go upstairs
and—"

"I know. But I...I've got to get back to Rose."

She might have tossed a bucket of cold water on him.
He swore softly and stepped back. "God, I'm sorry, Caroline. I didn't think." He ran his hands through his hair,
which was in wild disarray already. "I didn't forget about

Rose.'' He laughed softly, almost to himself. ''How could I forget about her? I couldn't. I just wasn't thinking.''

''Nor was I,'' she confessed in a whisper.

''But something has happened here. Between us.'' He held her gaze.

She nodded.

''There's no going back. No pretending.''

She shook her head. ''No. There's no going back, Adam.''

''This is ripping us apart, both of us. We've got to deal with it, one way or the other.''

''Yes.''

''Maybe not now. But soon. You think about it.'' He bent slightly and kissed her again, gently this time. *As though he cherished her.* ''It's up to you what happens next, Caroline. Yes or no, it's up to you.''

CHAPTER SIXTEEN

ADAM KISSED HER AGAIN at the door of the cabin. She'd kissed him back hungrily, her mind reeling from the events of the past ten minutes, her body aching for completion.

A completion that could not be. It made no sense, no matter which way she looked at it. And during a nearly sleepless night she had plenty of opportunity to turn Adam's challenge over and over in her mind. Yes, she was desperately attracted to him. Yes, she'd been denied the fulfillment of—*be honest, Caroline*—sex and the pleasure of a man's arms for a long, long time. And this *was* lowest-common-denominator stuff—raw physical attraction. Even Adam had nearly said as much. He wasn't asking for more. How could he? She and Rose were leaving Alberta in less than three weeks.

But what about her? What did *she* want from a relationship? Could she call a brief affair with Adam Garrick a *relationship?* Hardly. An encounter was more like it.

And then the horrible thought struck her. What would Beau have thought of her throwing herself into the arms of his best friend? She hadn't considered that. She'd stopped thinking of Adam in relation to her husband long ago, shortly after she'd accepted his offer of the job. It was just too difficult to keep the two men side by side in her head. Beau was Beau, the husband she'd loved with all her heart, and Adam was...well, Adam.

She could still picture in her mind's eye the first time

she'd seen him. She recalled the immediate shiver of what she'd thought was fear, but now knew was another emotion just as primeval.

Tossing and turning, punching her pillow into this lump and that, Caroline desperately sought sleep. Too many questions, too many considerations to weigh and balance, and her mind was a jumble from the day's events. She'd had the letter from her mother-in-law—was that only this morning? Rose and Janie had gone missing and been found, and now...now this.

She felt certain of at least one thing. Whatever happened between them—or didn't happen—Adam would not hold her decision against her. Rough edges, yes, but a gentleman. In fact, she wouldn't be surprised to find out in the morning that he'd gone back to the Tetlock camp. It would be his way of giving her time and space to make up her mind.

She was more and more certain she could never take up his challenge. Tempting as it was to fantasize about a night in Adam's arms, she had to live with herself. And, really, could she accept such a stark sexual adventure? What about feeling? What about love?

Hurt squeezed her breath. There so many things she barely dared to dream of anymore. Yes, she longed for love. She was strong and young and healthy—yes, she longed for a mate who would give her another child, the baby she so desperately wanted. Yes, she longed for someone who cared for her and Rose and who understood them both completely.

But this wasn't it. Adam wasn't offering that—he couldn't. He'd said earlier that he didn't "do" relationships well. All he offered was a brief exciting encounter.

Maybe in another life, maybe at another time—yes, she could easily imagine a short passionate fling with a man like Adam Garrick. Footloose, fancy-free…why not? But she was a mother now and she had a mother's cares to consider. A mother's responsibilities. She could not afford to risk her heart, not with any man, while her future and Rose's security were in such jeopardy.

Her heart? Had she really been as hopelessly foolish as to fall in love this way—with this man? A man like Adam? Did she dare admit it, even to herself?

She realized her pillow was damp with tears. *Perhaps it was already too late.*

THREE DAYS LATER, on his way back from town, Curley picked up the mail and brought Caroline another letter from her mother-in-law. He came to the door as she was getting Rose to bed late Saturday evening. Rose was tremendously excited about the events of the next day. She was going with Janie and her mother to Janie's sister Katie's farm once the current lot of tourists had left for the Tetlock Valley camp after breakfast. Caroline wasn't certain which held the greatest attraction—Janie's young cousins, who were close to Rose's age, or the newborn litter of piglets Janie had told her about.

"We're gonna see baby pigs, Mr. Curley," she said, jumping up and down in her pajamas, foaming toothbrush in one hand.

"Pigs, huh?" snorted the foreman, but his eyes twinkled. "I hate pigs."

"Yep. Baby pigs. You wouldn't hate *them,* I betcha. And Janie's mommy says there's eleven piggies, all squealing to beat the band." Rose nodded, eyes round and serious. "That's just 'xactly what she said— 'squealing to beat the band.'"

"Is that a fact? Say, give this here letter to your ma," Curley said with a wink. "And you remember to say howdy

to them little piggies for Mr. Curley tomorrow, won't ya?"
Caroline knew he adored her daughter, which put him on
a very high plane with her.

"You betcha," Rose replied with a giggle, repeating her
current favorite word. "You *betcha*, Mr. Curley!"

Caroline thanked him for the letter, which she didn't
have a chance to read until Rose had gone to bed. Then
she sat down in the wonky overstuffed chair by the window, near the gas lantern, which hissed and sputtered, a
sound she found oddly comforting in the long evenings. It
was beginning to get noticeably darker earlier as the summer slipped by—another reminder that soon they'd have to
go back to Washington.

Saturday was always one of her busiest days. She'd seen
Adam briefly at breakfast in the cookhouse before Marty
Gardipee arrived to take the current lot of guests to the
Calgary airport. Then Adam had disappeared, and in the
afternoon she'd been busy readying the cabins for the in-
coming guests and organizing last-minute details for the
departure next morning to the Tetlock Valley. She hadn't
spoken to him since the night he'd kissed her.

Was he still waiting for an answer? Surely not. Surely
the hard light of day had persuaded him how impossible
his proposition was.

She tore open Eunice's letter. This one was much shorter
than the one she'd received a few days before. Just a page
and a half, with a fairly brisk businesslike tone that had
been missing from the first letter. Eunice Carter wanted
Caroline to return to Seattle for a meeting with the family
lawyers. Some document had turned up apparently, which
required Caroline's presence. Something to do with Beau.
The meeting had been set for the twenty-third. Caroline
glanced at the calendar on the wall—ten days away.

She felt her heart speed up. What had been found? Something that Beau had left for her? A letter? She glanced at the page again. It didn't say a letter. A *document*.

Horrible thoughts crowded in. What if the rock slide that killed Beau hadn't been accidental? What if certain people wanted Beau dead—had wanted her handsome devil-may-care husband dead? What if he owed money, big money, to people who could arrange these kinds of things?

Caroline told herself she was being crazy. None of this was important now. Beau had been dead for nearly two years; there had never been even a whisper of suspicion from the authorities that his death was anything but an accident. Then why had Eunice written? She must have some information she felt she should share with Caroline.

She glanced at the calendar again. Ten days. She supposed she could leave for a day or two and then come back to finish out Adam's season. She'd promised him she'd stay until Labor Day. What about Rose? Could she take her? She'd have to make arrangements. Luckily she had the cash for airline tickets, thanks to working all summer with very few expenses. She wouldn't have to dip into the small stash she'd brought with her. Again, Adam Garrick to thank.

Today was Saturday. She'd call Maddie first thing Monday and see if she knew anything about this. Then she'd call a travel agent. Somehow she'd be at that meeting. Even if it was only for Eunice Carter's peace of mind.

AFTER THE GUESTS had left the next morning, and Rose and Mrs. T and Janie shortly after them, Caroline decided to visit the kitchen garden. She felt like making herself a huge salad for lunch. Lunch for one, for a change.

The place was very quiet. Curley and the haying crew were at work in the fields, on hot sunny days like this, Sunday or not. Adam's truck was nowhere to be seen. Caroline had to admit she felt a little relieved; she was not looking forward to their next meeting.

The raspberries hadn't been picked for a few days. She stood in the patch by the side of the garden and ate them by the plump warm handful, until the juice dripped down her arm. Nothing could have been more pleasant. Then she gathered an armful of lettuce and parsley and dill and popped two sun-warmed tomatoes and a cucumber in her skirt pocket. She deposited the vegetables in the cabin sink and, on impulse, decided to go down to the river to have a swim and a bath before fixing her salad. The raspberry juice had stained her face, as well as her hands.

Caroline felt almost light-headed as she took the grassy path to the river, wearing plastic flip-flops and her bathing suit and carrying a towel. Being alone was such an unusual pleasure. She would have loved to dispense with clothes altogether on such a peaceful summer afternoon. But as long as there was even a one-in-a-million chance that she'd be observed...well, she wouldn't do it. She was no free spirit. Still, even with a bathing suit, she looked forward to her solitary swim. Time alone, time to think her own thoughts, dream her own dreams....

And what did she think of when she finally found the courage to plunge, shrieking, right up to her neck in the cold waters of the Horsethief? What did she think of as she stood, shampooing her hair with bar soap in the leafy green shade, knee-deep at the side of the swimming hole? Or as she toweled herself dry on the grassy bank, flicking her towel at the occasional dive-bombing horsefly?

Adam Garrick.

She could not get him out of her mind. She could not stop thinking of what he'd said to her that night in the dark of the porch. What he'd felt like when she touched him, the way he'd kissed her. How he'd cut directly to the heart of the matter—the attraction that existed between them. He'd had the courage to face it; why hadn't she?

Back at the cabin, Caroline slipped into the loose-fitting plainly cut sundress that she'd bought the previous week in Glory. She tied on a checked apron, on loan from Mrs. T, and turned to the greens in the sink, still humming, the kind of aimless airy tune she produced when she was very happy. She wondered if Rose was enjoying the piglets. Since the day the two girls had gone missing, Caroline had to remind herself constantly not to be overprotective of her daughter. It was natural, she supposed, to overcompensate when she was the sole person responsible for Rose—

She hadn't heard anyone approach or a dog bark—arthritic old Stormy dozed in the shade on the north side of the cabin most days—but that was definitely the scrape of a boot heel on her outer porch.

Caroline dried her hands and went to the door. Before she could reach it, it opened and Adam stepped inside. He closed the door, then leaned against it.

Caroline stepped back. She wiped her hands on her apron again. He hadn't even knocked....

"H-hello." Her first thought was that her hair was a mess. She hadn't combed it since she'd been in the river and it hung in damp stiff ropes on her neck.

He wore his usual uniform—faded jeans, scuffed boots and a light chambray shirt with an unbuttoned vest over it. The sleeves of his shirt were rolled back, exposing tanned muscular forearms.

"Rose here?" He glanced toward the drawn curtain of Rose's little sleeping nook.

"No. She went with Mrs. T this morning to see some piglets at one of her daughter's farms."

"The Dempseys?" Adam seemed to relax slightly. He hadn't even noticed at her hair.

"No, one of the other daughters, Katie I forget the last name." Caroline took a step back and put her hands in the pockets of her apron. "Why? Did you want to see her?"

"No," he said quickly, his eyes locked on hers. "Not her."

Not her. She could barely breathe. Adam looked like a man tormented. His eyes held some of the same pain she'd seen on the porch four days before, a look she'd attributed to the faint light of the moon. It was broad daylight now. Then she saw his gaze shift to her hair and he frowned.

"What happened to your hair?"

"I had a bath in the river," she said. She raised one hand to her shoulder, feeling the end of a thick twisted strand. Still damp. She flushed, but she wasn't apologizing. She hadn't expected company.

He didn't say anything more, but Caroline felt her flush turn to near-scorch as his gaze lingered on her hair, then lowered in a slow appraisal of her body, to her bare feet, then back again, ending on her mouth. "So...we're alone?"

She nodded and tried to swallow. The lump in her throat swelled until she couldn't breathe.

His eyes burned into hers. She heard a faint roar in her ears, like traffic or rushing water a great distance away.

He reached into the pocket of his vest and tossed something on the table. Several things. Caroline tore her gaze from his to see what he'd brought. Pale foil packets. A half dozen at least. *Condoms!*

Shocked, she looked at him again. *"Adam!"*

"You'll recall the conversation we had a few days back."

"Yes, of course."

"You've had a chance to think things over."

She put her hands, both of them, to her hot cheeks. "Yes,

but…'' She glanced at the table, then back at him, stricken. ''Like this? Just like *this?*''

He took a step toward her and placed his hands on her shoulders. She had to turn her head to look up at him.

''Why not?'' he said. ''Why not like this? Rose is away, and there's nobody up at the house.'' He ran his thumb lightly over her bottom lip and she shuddered. ''Why *not* like this?'' he whispered, then bent his head to kiss her.

Caroline felt her blood start to pump again, as though it had stopped earlier. It rushed through her veins in a painful flood. His mouth was heaven; he kissed her gently, softly, still not really touching her beyond the weight of his hands on her shoulders. But that didn't last. He suddenly pulled her close, both arms around her, and ground his mouth down on hers, deepening the kiss until Caroline thought she might faint.

She really thought she would faint. One minute she'd been rinsing salad greens, daydreaming of this man. The next she was in his arms and he was causing her blood to erupt with his kisses. And he'd thrown down a handful of condoms on the kitchen table just to make sure she got the point.

She got it all right.

But…but this would never work. One of them had to be sensible, and it had to be her. ''Adam,'' she whispered when she got the chance. He had pushed down the strap of her sundress and was kissing her bare shoulder. ''We have to talk.'' He stopped kissing her shoulder, but didn't raise his head for a few seconds. Then he did, very slowly.

''You don't want this,'' he stated flatly, abandoning her shoulder and looking straight into her eyes. His face was no more than a few inches from hers, his eyes molten. The raw desire in his gaze made her insides jump.

"I...I think," she said, hitching up the strap of her dress, "we should talk. That's all."

"Talk," he repeated. He stepped back abruptly. "Sometimes talk gets in the way." His voice sounded different. Harder. "I thought you'd had plenty of time to think about this. You know how it stands with you and me. You know what happens between a man and a woman. It's a simple thing. I'm not coming here to seduce you like some young girl who needs romancing. I'm too old for that."

"I never expected..." Stunned, Caroline stepped back, too. *Oh, what was she doing wrong? Why couldn't she understand this man?*

"Good. Because I'm not prepared to talk you into anything you don't want. It's yes or no, that's all." He reached for his hat.

"Adam! Don't go." She moved forward and laid one hand on his arm.

"Why not?" He glanced at her hand, frowned.

"Please..."

"You want to talk." He sounded resigned.

"Yes. I do," she said. "I think we should."

Adam set his hat back on the table and ran one hand through his hair in an impatient gesture. "Okay. You'd better go ahead. I've done all the talking I plan to do."

"Sit down." Caroline first indicated a chair at the table. But then the presence of the foil-wrapped condoms leaped up and burned holes in her brain, and she quickly turned to the small sitting area. "Do you want to sit down?"

"No." Adam ran his hand through his hair again. "Sorry. I just don't think I can sit here and have a chat with you right now, like we're on some damn TV talk show."

"Okay. Fine." Caroline walked into the sitting area and paused by the window, the window that still had a tiny triangular hole in it, covered by transparent tape. She turned and took a deep breath. This wouldn't take long.

"I'm sorry I gave you the wrong impression—"

"Wrong impression!" Adam spun on his heel to face her. "What are you talking about? The impression I had was that you were just as hungry for me as I was for you," he said bluntly. "As I *am* for you. Is that the wrong impression?"

Caroline licked her lips. They felt dry. "All right. That's true," she admitted. "I have had, um..." She'd never had a conversation like this in her entire life! "I'll confess I have been very *conscious* of you lately. Aware of you as a man. And I admit I wanted to kiss you and—" she forced herself to continue "—even more, I guess you could say—"

"Caroline." He'd taken two steps toward her and suddenly felt overwhelmingly large and dangerous, right in front of her, not a foot away. "Look at me," he said.

She made herself look up at him, meet his gaze. She nearly cried out when she saw the fire in his eyes.

"Keep looking at me," he ordered. He raised one hand and cupped her burning cheek. Then, gaze locked on hers, he lowered his head slowly until their mouths touched. Slowly, expertly, he deepened the kiss until she heard her own soft moan and, despite herself, threw her arms around his neck and clung to him. *Oh, yes, Adam...oh, yes!*

His arms were hard around her, his hands touching, kneading, stroking her back. She felt tremors rack her body, right down to her bare toes. Then, shockingly, he drew back, breathing hard, the light of something more than desire in his dark gaze. *Triumph.*

"Now, tell me, Caroline, is that just being *conscious?* Is that just being *aware?*"

She closed her eyes and felt a fat tear squeeze out and

trail down her cheek. Her heart was racing. He was right—he was always right. But what did it matter? How could anything be different than it was?

"Why do you talk all that…that bullshit, if you'll pardon the coarse country expression, when *this* is what it's all about?"

He looked genuinely baffled. Caroline took another deep breath. "I have to go home in three weeks. For good."

"I know that."

"This is just sex, right?"

He hesitated, frowned. "Maybe."

"I…I've never thought of ever doing anything like this before. Don't you see? Just…just hopping in bed with some guy I'm attracted to…"

He didn't say anything. Was he asking himself what kind of modern woman didn't know or understand her own sexuality—at her age?

"And…I keep wondering, what would Beau think of—"

"Beau's dead." He set her slightly away from him so that they were no longer touching. "You got that? *Dead.* This is about you and me. Not Beau."

He moved away, back toward the door. "This might have happened even if Beau was alive. Who knows? I'm glad it didn't." He made a strange sound that she took to be a laugh. "Stranger things have happened, that's for damn sure."

She wrapped her arms around herself, feeling cold, although the cabin baked in the afternoon sun. She wanted to ask him not to go, but what was there to hold him?

He picked up his hat again then turned to her. "I accept your decision, Caroline. I wish things were different, but I know they're not. I won't bring it up again."

"Are you angry with me?" She had to know.

His expression softened, just a little. "No, I'm not angry. Not even with myself. I made a mistake, that's all. I'm just sorry I put you through this."

Then he left as quickly and as silently as he'd arrived.

CHAPTER SEVENTEEN

SO THAT WAS THAT.

He'd been a fool to think otherwise. Hadn't he told her he didn't *do* relationships? Hadn't his entire life been proof of that?

He plain didn't understand women. He'd never figured out why they had to make everything so complicated.

Well, that was fine. He could live with what she'd decided. And if she hadn't come walking up to the porch that night, smelling of rain and raising his blood with the prospect of all things soft and womanly, it never would have happened, anyway. Not that he was blaming her, not for a second.

What he'd told her had been the truth. It was his mistake. Two adults with no encumbrances—why not? A tumble in the sack might have done them both good. So when had a tumble in the sack *ever* proved anything? Face it, he told himself grimly. Some guys never learn.

Well, he'd learned. At least with this woman. If he could just keep his hands to himself for the rest of the month. She couldn't have made herself plainer about where she stood—although she'd admitted she was *attracted* to him— and now, she was going off to Seattle, anyway, for a couple of those days.

The fact was, she was still married to Beau Carter. He'd left her and the kid high and dry financially. He wasn't in her bed at night, giving her pleasure, keeping her warm.

But he was in her thoughts, and that was worse. The longer he was dead, the better he looked. Memory was like that; it depended on what you wanted to remember. And Caroline Carter had a pretty high opinion of her husband, dead or alive.

Funny, he still couldn't picture his best friend with her. Beau had been handsome and brash and ready for anything, the bolder, the better. He'd had a big laugh that made everyone around him smile, whether they knew him or not. He loved people and was never happier than when he was at a rodeo bar or a crazy poker game or a party of any kind. Yet at the same time, days had gone by when he was at the Double O, holed up in his cabin, when Adam never saw him. And if he did go to the cabin to see him, Beau would either be reading a book, in a complete other world, or he'd have headed off into the hills with a few cans of beans and a jackknife. Beau never did anything halfway.

But to hook himself up with a quiet little wife like Caroline? Adam couldn't quite see it. He'd have thought Beau would go for fire and sparks. Passion. Caroline was cautious, she was careful, she was ridiculously polite—look at the dumb speeches she gave him from time to time. She was modest, unassuming. *Loyal. A fiercely proud mother. Brave.*

And Adam was dead sure the passion was there, too. Just not for him.

Well, he wasn't going to spend the rest of his life moaning about missed opportunities. There were plenty of women around, local women, with a different opinion. And maybe it was time he looked up one or two of them.

But do they stir your blood? Do you care enough to bother?

Shit. It was a week since he'd gone down to her cabin, and he still couldn't stop thinking about her…them, what they'd talked about. Which pretty much indicated how well he was handling it.

Adam jumped off the binder to pick up a stick that was in his path. They had another field to go, and that would finish the hay for this year. If they were lucky, Curley might get that cut off the river flats before the weather turned. Two more batches of tourists lined up for the Tetlock Valley, then he could wind that down for the year, too. Pay off Ben and old Farley and the Hillermans, clear things out and lock up for the winter. This had been his best year yet. And most of that was thanks to Caroline. She'd run the office like clockwork. She actually seemed to enjoy working with that stuff, keeping track of all those details. And the tourists liked her. From what he could tell, she'd done a better job than Rhonda ever had. His accountant was going to be plenty surprised when Adam gave him the records for this year. Nice change from the boot box.

Adam paused, one foot on the running board of the machine. Looked like Curley's pickup coming across the field. He waited.

"Say, Boss! Just got a call from the ranch. The li'l lady wants to see you." Curley pushed back his cap and grinned at Adam.

"Caroline?"

His foreman looked at him oddly, then sent a stream of tobacco juice into the stubble beside the truck. "No, Rose."

Rose? What would Rose want with him?

"Hop in. I'll drive you to your truck." Adam had left his truck back at the lane that led to the field. "I'll handle the binder for the rest of the afternoon. Or Chuck will. No problem."

He grinned at Adam as he put the truck into gear and backed up. "Ain't she a regular sweetheart, that kid Rosie?

I wouldn't say this to just anybody, y'understand—'' he gave Adam a serious look from under the visor of his ball cap ''—but I'm gonna miss the li'l pot-licker when her and her ma head home.''

Adam drove into the Double O yard ten minutes later. He'd tried not to think about Rose and Caroline's upcoming trip to Seattle, but one thought had crossed his mind—what if they didn't come back? He'd told himself it wouldn't matter. The Tetlock Valley business was well under control and wouldn't fall apart if Caroline wasn't there for the last week.

And they'd be out of his hair, both of them. He could go back to things the way they used to be....

Of course they'd come back—they were leaving their beater of a station wagon here. And most of their gear, much of which Caroline had never bothered to unpack from the car. Adam couldn't get the idea out of his head that maybe she *hadn't* planned to go back. He still couldn't figure out why someone away for a few weeks in the summer—or even the whole summer, as it had turned out—would pack all her family photos. It made no sense.

Rose was waiting for him on the porch steps, her rag doll nestled on her lap. He parked and got out of the pickup.

''Mr. Adam! I was hoping you'd come.'' She stood as he approached. ''Mr. Curley said you would.''

Adam paused with one foot on the lowest step, looking down at her. Her little pixie grin went straight to his heart. ''Curley said you wanted to see me. What about?''

''Something.'' Rose shot a furtive glance toward the house. Adam could hear Mrs. T banging around in the kitchen. ''Something important. I wanted to ask you before my mommy came back.''

''Where's your mommy?''

''She's in town. She went to get our tickets for the airplane. 'Cept I don't wanna go on the airplane now. I want to stay *here!*''

Adam straightened and thrust his hands in his pockets. "What's this all about, Rose?"

"I'll miss the birthday party!" she said. "That's what. Only it's more like two birthday parties 'cause they're twins. I can't miss it. I just can't! And Janie's big sister said they 'specially wanted me to come and I already got a present picked out in my head and everything. Two presents.''

"Janie's cousins are having a birthday?"

"Yep. And I'm invited."

"When's the party?"

"Next week when we're supposed to be gone and I don't wanna go. I wanna stay with you!" A big tear that Adam could only suppose had been waiting patiently for his arrival popped out and slowly ran down her cheek. Rose's bottom lip trembled very convincingly.

Hell. "What does your mother say?" He sat down on the porch step beside the girl.

"She doesn't know yet. I just talked to Ryan and Barnaby's mommy on the phone and she 'vited me. I wanted to talk to you first. Private."

"Did you tell Janie's sister you wouldn't be here for the party?"

"No." Rose gave him a wicked smile. Adam couldn't help but smile back. *A conspiracy, father and daughter.* "I said I *might* be here. That's not lyin', is it, Mr. Adam?"

Adam was silent for a few moments. "No. I don't suppose it is. Not real serious lying."

"Good!" Rose beamed at him and bounced her doll on her knees. "So, can I? Can I stay here with you?"

"I'll have to talk to your mom first."

"Oh, that's okay. You'll be able to talk her into it. She

likes you, y'know. She told Janie's mommy that you were a very fine person. That's just what she said, 'He's a very fine person, Mrs. T.'"

"She did?" Adam grinned at the girl. He wanted to reach over and ruffle her hair, the way he did with Janie. He was pretty sure there was plenty of context that Rose hadn't picked up in the conversation she'd overheard, but it still made him feel good to know that Caroline thought he was all right. "And I've got to check it out with Mrs. T. She's the one who'll have to keep an eye on you most of the time."

"I could go with you?" Rose suggested, smiling up at him. "Wherever you go. I could ride in your truck with you and go to town and stuff. I'd be good, I promise."

"That might not be such a great idea. There's lots of places I go that are awful places for a girl." He glanced at her sideways to see the effect of his words. Damn, he was teasing her.

"Like where?" she demanded, lower lip thrust forward. Her eyes were bright, waiting for his answer, he knew, so she could pounce on it.

"Like barrooms. You've got to be grown-up to go in there—"

"That's easy—just don't go there when I'm with you!"

"And stinky old barns—"

"I love stinky barns! They're my favorite. Don't worry about that, Mr. Adam—" she put one small plump hand on his knee and looked up at him earnestly "—I *like* stinky barns. I saw a bunch of piggies in Janie's sister's stinky barn and they were real cute. Hey—there's my mommy!"

Rose was right. The station wagon rounded the corner by the barn and nosed its way slowly into the yard. Adam had told Caroline more times than he could count to drive one of the company vehicles, but unless she was going on Double O business, she always took that old wreck of hers.

He stood, feeling a little sheepish to be caught sitting on the porch steps in the middle of the afternoon. He had a fleeting image of Angus Tump on his porch, smoking and whittling the summer away. Rose had skipped down the steps and raced to meet her mother, and Adam could see her chattering earnestly as they approached. From the occasional look Caroline gave him as she came toward the house, carrying several packages, he had a pretty good idea that Rose had already filled her in—her own way.

"So, can I, Mommy? Can I? Mr. Adam says it's okay with him if it's okay with you."

"He does, does he?" Caroline's tone sounded somewhat ominous. Maybe, as another adult, he should step in here.

"I told Rose it was entirely up to you."

"Oh, Mister!" Rose wailed, as though he'd somehow betrayed her.

"She can stay if you want her to, Caroline, no problem. I'll talk to Mrs. T. Maybe it would make the trip a little easier for you," he suggested, thoroughly uncomfortable with the whole situation. One thing he knew—if Rose stayed here, Caroline would be back.

"I assure you, Rose is absolutely no inconvenience to me on this trip, brief as it is," Caroline said stiffly. "None whatsoever." He could see that she was still annoyed, but that didn't stop the sudden urge he had to go and put his arms around her, packages and all, and make her forget all about those goofy ten-dollar words she always threw at him when she got her back up.

"Fine. You decide. Makes no difference to me," he said, knowing it for a lie and hoping like hell she'd relent and let the kid stay. He wasn't going to say another word; this was between her and her daughter. *His daughter.*

Rose was jumping up and down, eyes squeezed shut, arms wrapped around her doll, hands clasped in a childish imitation of fervent prayer. Adam suppressed a smile.

"Oh, darn!" Caroline dropped one of the packages she was carrying and Adam stepped forward to pick it up.

"Thanks. Here," she said, indicating where he could place the package—on top of several others in her arms.

Instead, he reached out to grab another. "Why don't you let me carry some of those?"

"I can manage!" she said, angling forward to grip the package between her arm and the pile she was juggling. Adam easily removed it, then reached for another. "Stop it! What do you think you're doing?" she whispered fiercely, with a significant glance at Rose, who still had her eyes shut—only now her fingers were crossed, too.

"Giving you a hand, that's all," Adam replied, scooping up another package. "What did you do, buy out the store?"

"I said I can manage just fine!" she repeated in a low voice. "And no, I did not buy out the store."

"Caroline?"

"What?" She was so steamed she forgot her usual icy politeness. He had to admit he kind of liked it.

"Give it a rest," he said. "Okay?"

She glared at him for a minute, then her eyes softened. "Okay," she said, managing a small smile. She must have seen the humor in the situation, after all, as he'd hoped. "You're absolutely right. I'm being silly. Here." She handed him the rest of the packages—all of them. "*You* take them."

Somewhere on the short trip to the cabin, Rose proposed a swim in the river.

"You know back there when I had my fingers crossed?" she asked, skipping along the path with her doll in one hand.

"Ye-es," Caroline said, with a slight frown.

"Well, what I was *really* wishing for was to go for a swim. Down at the river. You, too, Mr. Adam—"

"Hold it, young lady," her mother began. He knew Caroline glanced at him over Rose's dark head, but he kept his eyes on the path. "It's one thing for you to try and plan our day, but you should leave Adam out of it. He's very busy, you know. Running a ranch is a lot of hard work."

"Is it?" Rose glazed up at him. "Is it a lot of work?"

"Sure it is," Adam admitted, then went on, unable to resist the opportunity. Why not? He rarely took any time off just to have fun. Maybe you needed a kid around to remind you of things like that. "But, hey, I'm never too busy to take a swim on a hot day."

"See!" Rose crowed, then raced ahead to the cabin.

"Well." Caroline didn't have to say anything else. But he could tell she was pleased under her facade of annoyance. "I guess that's what we're doing."

"I guess it is," he agreed with a grin.

TWENTY MINUTES LATER, they headed for the river. Adam had gone back to the house for his swimming gear and reappeared looking very different, very attractive, in plain navy trunks, a light cotton shirt, which he wore loose and unbuttoned, and incredibly beat-up canvas sneakers. She'd never seen him out of his working garb of boots, hat and jeans.

Caroline had decided she wouldn't swim. Somehow the thought of horsing around in the river with Adam and her daughter just seemed too...too personal. Regardless of what she'd told him, she was deeply, impossibly, *hopelessly* aware of him as a man and it was clear that wasn't going to change. Luckily she was leaving for good in less than two weeks.

Caroline ignored the cold sinking feeling that thought produced in the pit of her stomach. She'd jammed a large floppy straw hat on her head and stuffed a paperback novel, sunscreen and some snacks in her canvas bag. She'd changed into a sundress when she and Rose reached the cabin, not recalling it was the one she'd been wearing last Sunday until she saw the flash of recognition in Adam's eyes. He turned quickly and tossed the beach ball to Rose.

She felt like a fool for forgetting. The point was—and she might as well admit it to herself—she was flustered at Adam's unexpected decision to accompany them to the river. Somehow she'd thought that after what had happened last Sunday, he'd want to spend as little time with her as possible.

And Rose, too, although his attitude toward the girl had obviously changed. She'd noticed the difference since the day Rose and Janie had gone missing. Now Adam actually seemed to enjoy Rose's chatter. He seemed more relaxed with her. He patiently answered her endless questions and didn't go out of his way to ignore her, as Caroline felt he once had.

All of which pleased her. Sometimes all it took for a man who thought he didn't like children was to be around them for a while. Look how that old curmudgeon Curley Splint had softened up. Too bad Adam and his wife had never had kids. Caroline thought he'd make a fine father if he'd only give himself a chance. Still, she knew parenthood wasn't for everyone. Beau hadn't wanted children, not at first. She suppressed the pain that gripped her heart. *Would she ever have more children?* She'd known Beau couldn't father any children before she married him. She had thought she'd accepted that fact and that it didn't matter. But she'd been wrong. Thank goodness Rose had come into their lives.

Caroline spread the cotton blanket on the grass at the side of the river, well back from the tiny shingle of gravelly beach, and left her canvas bag there while she took her book with her to sit on a big rock at the water's edge. She could read there and at the same time watch Rose and Adam.

Adam plunged right into the icy water, swam a few powerful strokes across the swimming hole to the other side of the river and back again. He stood thigh-deep, hair slicked back from his dripping face, beckoning to Rose to join him. "Here—toss me the ball."

Rose tentatively threw him the ball and he returned it to her. They did this a few times until she was thoroughly wet from splashing, then he held out his arms and called out, "Come on. I'll catch you."

To Caroline's amazement, Rose accepted the challenge. She started up on the bank, yelled, "Here I come!", then ran screaming straight into the water, straight into Adam's arms. He caught her up with a grin and swung her high, round and round him, while she shrieked with joy. Caroline had the oddest feeling creep across her skin. *Adam cared.* He cared about Rose; he wanted her to have fun and enjoy the water. He was willing to take the time to make sure she did.

Then she thought of something else. This was father's play—rough and ready physical stuff that all children loved. This was what Rose had been missing. Caroline reminded herself to be grateful that Rose was having that kind of fun now and resolutely stared at the pages of her book.

When she'd read the same page for perhaps the sixth time, she gave up and closed the book. Just then Adam hauled himself out of the water onto the rock beside her. He radiated chill on her sun-warmed skin and she shivered.

"Don't touch me," she warned. "You're soaking."

Adam ducked his head toward her and shook it, sending droplets spraying on her shoulders.

"Don't!" she yelped, but couldn't help smiling at the same time. He'd never looked more attractive to her—all white teeth and smiling eyes and tanned wet skin. His body was lean and hard, and she was overwhelmingly aware of his near-nakedness. She was glad she'd decided not to swim; she couldn't imagine sitting here in a skimpy bathing suit next to this man, pretending she wasn't affected. Luckily he kept his attention on Rose, calling out encouragement as she splashed and played at swimming, kicking her feet wildly, while walking on the bottom on her hands.

When he finally glanced Caroline's way, she happened to be eyeing the scar she'd noticed before. "What's this?" To her dismay, she realized she'd actually reached out and touched the thin white line with her index finger. She snatched it back as though Adam's skin was red-hot, not river-cool.

His gaze met hers, and she read the flash of heat there before he glanced at the scar himself. "Old rodeo injury," he said simply.

She swallowed, desperate to continue the conversation. If they stopped talking, if he looked at her like that again… "From what?"

He frowned. "Caught a horn from a Brahman. Sonovabitch stomped on me a couple times, then turned around and came back and hooked me good." He smiled. "No manners, some of those bulls."

"I hope you learned your lesson," she said, horrified to think of him lying bruised and bleeding in a rodeo ring.

"Lesson?" He wasn't looking at her. He had his eyes on Rose. "What lesson is that?"

"To give up the rodeo business of course!"

He turned, suddenly serious. "Funny. That's exactly what my wife kept saying. I never gave it up then, and when I finally did, there was no one to give it up for. She'd had all she could take and walked out." He slipped off the rock and faced her so that his back was to Rose.

He took her two warm hands in his cold ones and bent forward to kiss her briefly—hard—on the lips. She felt her stomach clench, then slowly melt away into her toes.

"Funny, isn't it?" he murmured against her mouth. "How some guys just never seem to learn."

Then he was back in the water and Rose was shouting, trying to climb onto his back, begging him to play "horsey."

Caroline stood and walked to the blanket she'd spread out earlier, her cheeks burning, her knees shaky. Some guys just never learn, he'd said.

She could say the same thing about some women.

CHAPTER EIGHTEEN

THE PLAN WAS that Adam would drive them to the airport early Tuesday morning. Rose would say goodbye to her mother, who would then board her early-morning flight to Seattle. Caroline had relented and decided to let her daughter stay at the Double O, after all.

Adam's earlier doubts, some of which he'd mentioned to Lucas, seemed to stem from another life. Life before Rose. His resolve to keep his distance had made so much sense then, but summer was almost over and what did it matter now? He had four precious days to get to know his own daughter a little better.

Friday morning Caroline asked him if he'd mind taking Rose to Glory to shop for birthday gifts for the Webster twins, since she had a lot she wanted to get done before the Tetlock Valley crew came down from the camp that afternoon.

He suspected a test of some kind but was more than happy to oblige. Shopping with a child turned out to be a strange business. Rose confidently tucked her hand in his as they walked down the street, eliciting smiles from passersby. She dragged him into half-a-dozen stores before making up her mind on identical gifts—toy bows and arrows, complete with fake buckskin quivers.

"D'you think they'll like them, Mr. Adam?" she asked. He was certain she'd have been delighted with the gift herself.

"Sure they will," he answered. Would the thoroughly modern Sheila Webster approve, though? "I would have been real happy to get a set like this when I was a boy."

"You would? Well, let's get them then!" Rose decided, then added hopefully, "Maybe they'll let me play with them sometimes."

Adam was half tempted to add another set, then checked the impulse. He couldn't go buying war toys, not even fairly innocent ones like rubber-tipped plastic arrows, without consulting Caroline. It wasn't his place. Instead, he bought a basketball hoop that he could put up on the machine shed. Maybe they could toss her beach ball through it.... What did you *do* with kids?

Rose was delighted and thanked him repeatedly. She skipped merrily at his side as they walked back to the truck, hanging on to his hand and telling everyone who stopped to say hello about her new basketball hoop. Adam knew it was plain foolish, but he was bursting with satisfaction by the time they got to the pickup. Rose's joy was so simple, so genuine and abundant. How much of that joy had he missed in her life?

Adam couldn't imagine what might have happened if his marriage offer, put forward from a sense of obligation, had been accepted. He and Rose's natural mother had had nothing in common but physical need. No, with his track record that marriage would have been another bad scenario.

So how could he have regrets now about missing so much of his daughter's life? The best thing that could have happened was for his child to find parents like Beau and Caroline. And it *had* happened.

Getting to know her now, even though only Lucas knew the truth, was gravy.

When they got back to the ranch, Caroline came out onto the porch to meet them. Rose ran ahead, packages banging her knees, to report, no doubt, on all the details of their outing.

He hung back, watching that easy intimacy he'd so often observed between mother and daughter. He was an outsider here.

The quiet pleasure and look of softness in Caroline's eyes when she glanced up and met his gaze said it all. If there'd been a test, he'd passed it.

The afternoon, as expected, was chaotic. One of the returning guests, a very large pink Swede, had had a brush with poison ivy and was still itching and uncomfortable, even though he'd been liberally covered with calamine lotion and dosed with antihistamines by Barbara. Caroline soothed his injured feelings and made arrangements for his traveling companion to help him get ready to go to the airport the next day. Spirits much improved by the pampering and aided by his companion, the Swede hobbled off to their cabin for a nap before supper.

Then she took a French guest aside and gave him a bank draft—a refund due to a currency-exchange problem that he'd complained about on arrival—eliciting smiles and *mercis* and, Adam was sure, a recommendation of Tetlock Valley Tours to all his friends in Lyons.

Adam considered how he might have handled the situation. He'd probably have given the Swede a glass of whiskey and told him to grow up and quit whining. The Frenchman? He didn't know what he'd have done—maybe issued him a full refund and told him not to come back.

This was the first year Adam could remember when his immediate thought wasn't to close down the operation the minute the last guest got on the plane. And that was Caroline's doing, too.

After supper Adam called her into the office.

"Here," he said, and handed her a check. "This is for

the five acres the cabin's sitting on. I'm buying it back, like I told you. Maybe you could use the money for your trip to Seattle.''

Caroline glanced at the piece of paper and colored. ''I— I'm sure it's not worth that much,'' she said, then added, ''Besides, how do you know I want to sell it?''

Adam's heart stopped for a second. ''Don't you?'' Maybe he was wrong; maybe she meant to come back again, bring Rose with her. Maybe she'd use the cabin in the summers from time to time....

''I guess I should sell it,'' she said hesitantly. ''Whether I want to or not isn't really the issue, I'm afraid. I can use the money, that's for sure.''

There was a very long silence, during which Adam hoped she'd finally tell him what kind of financial straits she was in. Now that he'd grown to care for her and Rose, it mattered more than ever. But she said nothing.

''Deal?'' He extended his hand and she took it.

''Deal. What about...well, what about signing papers and stuff like that?'' She withdrew her hand.

''Papers?''

''Yes.'' She laughed nervously. ''Isn't there usually a deed or something when property changes hands? Lawyers?''

Adam shook his head. Papers? She'd given him a turn. ''Never mind that. This was strictly between Beau and me. We never had anything drawn up, just a couple signatures on a piece of paper.''

She looked doubtful, but Adam was glad she didn't pursue it. He didn't consider what he was doing much of a lie as it stood; still, he had no inclination to elaborate. His main concern was getting some cash into her hands.

Sunday afternoon was very quiet after the guests headed up to the valley. Adam drove over to Ben's uncle's ranch to shoot the breeze for a while. Joe Gallant had never married, but there was always plenty of activity around as his oldest sister and her husband and five kids occupied a house on the property and helped Joe with his hay operation.

He couldn't stop thinking about Rose and about Caroline leaving. Sure, she'd be back Friday afternoon, but that didn't stop him wishing he could spend every minute with her until she left—which was nothing but crazy. What was the matter with him? Last thing he wanted was to be a nuisance or in the way; that was why he'd driven over to Joe's place.

Finally he went home to a microwaved supper and a baseball game. He felt out of sorts and restless. He had all the next day to get through, just him and Caroline and Rose at the Double O. Of course Curley and the ranch hands were down in the bunkhouse, so it wasn't as though they were *really* alone.

Well, Mrs. T had been after him to replace some eavestroughing on the porch. That'd take him most of the day and give him something to keep his mind on. You had to pay attention when you were up a ladder.

After the game Adam went to bed, but he couldn't sleep. He replayed the summer over and over in his mind. Should he have done this? Maybe he shouldn't have done that. It reminded him of the state of mind he'd be in after a rodeo event—going over what he'd done right and what had gone wrong, trying to figure out how to do it better the next time. Finally, just before eleven o'clock, he decided to get up and find something to read when he noticed a reddish hue flickering on the wall opposite his bed.

He frowned. The sun had set well over an hour ago.... Then he leaped up and raced to the window, pulling on his jeans as he ran.

Beau's cabin was on fire.

CAROLINE SPENT the evening getting ready. She was taking one bag, which she packed carefully. She left out the robe she had on, intending to launder and pack it the next day. Since they were leaving so early Tuesday morning, she had arranged to put her suitcase in Adam's vehicle the night before. That way, she and Rose could just get up and dress and go straight out to the pickup. They'd have breakfast at the airport.

Tomorrow she wanted to have the entire day free to spend with her daughter. She knew she was being foolish; after all, she was only going away for four days. But she'd never left Rose with anyone before. If the girl hadn't been so determined not to miss the party, Caroline wouldn't have considered leaving her. She knew Eunice would be disappointed, but just now, Caroline felt it was more important that Rose go to the party with her little Glory friends, children she'd likely never see again after they went back to Seattle. Eunice would have plenty of time to spend with her granddaughter in the fall.

She trusted Adam. He was thoroughly responsible and reliable, she knew that. And, of course, Mary Tump and Janie would be around. Rose's clear affection for Adam surprised her, considering that he'd never gone out of his way to charm her or please her, as Curley had.

No, Rose would be just fine here in Glory.

Going back to Seattle meant she would see Philip Carter again. She'd heard nothing about her house; she supposed he'd sold it to pay the debts he'd said Beau owed the family company. Oddly Caroline realized she didn't dread seeing him. Something about her summer in Alberta had strengthened her resolve, had firmed up her purpose when it came to dealing with people like Philip. She'd worked for Adam for two months now. She'd done a creditable job of running the office operation of a small business, a skill she could bring to any number of jobs, and the experience had given her the confidence she badly needed if she was to support herself and Rose in the future.

Adam's money would help, too. Caroline thought of that brief sweet kiss at the river and put her needle down. She was ruining her eyes, anyway, trying to sew a button on Rose's cardigan in the flickering light from the lantern. So she sat back, closed her aching eyes and allowed her senses to flood with the sight and scent and feel of Adam Garrick. He wanted her, there was no doubt of that. Ardently. She was thrilled by his pursuit, thrilled to feel wanted by such a man. Yet he was a gentleman, too, and had accepted that she couldn't take what he offered. She wished she was free-spirited enough to respond to his challenge—as she knew so many women would. She was conservative; she couldn't help it, that was her nature. She'd had a fumbling sexual relationship in her first year of college, but other than that the only man she'd ever slept with was her husband. She was thirty-one and she was a bit of a prude.

She sighed and returned to her sewing. Another of life's offerings, passed by. She was grieving a little, she knew, for the lost opportunity. She supposed that was normal. But first things first. She had to get established somewhere, make a new home for herself and Rose and then…maybe then she'd be in a position to allow a new man into her life.

But she didn't want a new man—she wanted Adam Garrick.

Her task finished, she got up and went to the kitchen to poke at the fire in the stove. It was chilly tonight, and she could feel the cold seeping through the cracks in the log walls. She shivered. The cabin was unchinked; it was barely adequate summer shelter and she couldn't imagine anyone living here in the winter.

She went outside to grab an armload of wood. She threw back her head and gazed upward for a moment. There were a million stars in the sky tonight. Curley, bless him, kept her supplied with split firewood. She loaded the firebox, then poked several sheets of crumpled-up newspaper underneath the wood. It would take a few minutes, but the sticks would catch eventually. With the firebox jammed so full, the heat might last several hours. She hated waking up to a cold cabin, as happened on clear chilly nights like this.

Finally she made up her bed. She wouldn't miss this nightly task, or tossing and turning on a lumpy sofa-bed mattress. And it would be heaven to go to bed and read for a while, too. Still she hated comparing Beau's cabin to other accommodation she'd known. It wasn't the Hilton, but the cabin had served its purpose and served it well.

She checked on Rose with the flashlight. The girl was sleeping soundly, as she always did, one arm cradling her whale. Caroline smiled. She'd often thought a train could thunder by and Rose would not wake up.

Caroline climbed into the sofa bed and pulled the covers to her chin. She tried to sleep, lulled by the pleasant familiar sound of the fire crackling in the kitchen range.

She must have dozed off. Something—some unexpected sound, an acrid wisp of smoke—woke her. The starlight from the window didn't penetrate more than a foot or two into the room. The air was thick. *With smoke.* For a few seconds Caroline lay stunned, completely disoriented. Where was she? Was this her house on Lake Washington? Where was Beau?

She sat up. There was a horrible dull light flickering in the corner where the stove was. She leaped out of bed, glad she hadn't taken off her robe—although why she thought of that now, she had no idea. Desperately trying to hold her breath, she felt her way toward the fire.

This is crazy—you've got to get out of here. Never mind the fire. You can't possibly put it out, anyway.

She grabbed the bucket of water on the counter and dashed it at the red glow. A whoosh of steam and smoke billowed up and choked her. She stumbled away, fell over a chair, then got up and lurched blindly toward the corner of the cabin.

Rose. She had to get Rose. She had to get Rose and get out of here.

ADAM HAD NEVER raced down the stairs or out the door so fast. Someone at the bunkhouse must have noticed the flames, because he heard men shouting as he leaped off the veranda in the chill darkness.

Rose. Caroline…

Blood thundered in his ears as he tore down the path toward the cabin. *Goddamn cabin—why had he ever let her move in there?*

"Daddy! Daddy!" He heard Rose screaming to the left and he veered toward the sound. He couldn't see a thing; his eyes didn't seem to be adjusting to the darkness. *"Daddy!"*

Then, amazingly, Rose was in front of him and he'd scooped her up and she was sobbing against his neck. "Daddy, Mr. Adam—"

"Where's Caroline? Where's your mommy?" Adam jerked around, eyes desperately searching the darkness. "Caroline? Dammit, where are you?" His voice sounded hoarse. *Where was she?*

Rose was sobbing. "Sh-she goed back."

"Listen, honey." Adam set her down and peeled her arms from his neck. "You stay here. Right here. You stay by this tree…" He had a sudden idea. "Look. You put your hand on this tree and don't let go, do you understand? Hang on to the tree. *Don't let go.* I'll be back for you."

"Y-yes, Mr. Adam—" she hiccuped "—I won't let go."

Adam had already dashed away. He came around the corner of the clearing and his heart fell. The west side of the cabin roof was fully ablaze, and smoke poured out the windows. My God, if she was in there, she'd never come out alive....

Then he saw her, choking and coughing, leaning against a poplar not thirty feet from the burning cabin. "Caroline!" He strode toward her, anger flooding his heart. "What in hell are you doing here? For God's sake, don't you know you could have been killed?"

"Oh...Adam," she said weakly, and reached for him.

He crushed her in his arms, then held her away to have a good look at her. Her face was streaked with black and tears ran down her cheeks. "Are you all right?" He slid his hands quickly down her arms and back. "Are you hurt?"

"I—I'm fine. Adam, Rose is out here somewhere. I've got to find her—"

"I found her. Come with me, I know where she is. I left her at a tree down the path."

"Oh, thank God!"

"Boss? That you?" It was Curley. Adam didn't let go of Caroline. He could see the foreman's face glow ghastly white in the firelight. "Is the...the li'l lady all right?"

"She's okay, Curley. Get a couple men, see what you can do here. Try and stop it from spreading to the trees."

He turned and stumbled back to where he'd left Rose, his arm around Caroline's shoulders.

"Mommy!"

Caroline nearly fell—maybe she'd tripped over a stick or something, and Adam grabbed her. Rose ran toward them. He scooped her up again and held them both against his chest. Caroline was sobbing brokenly. He could feel the heat of her tears against his cold skin. He hadn't bothered to grab a shirt. Rose was whimpering. "I forgot my daddy wasn't here," she whispered, her arm tight around his neck. "I forgot he went to heaven...."

Adam's throat felt thick. He could see flames from the cabin roof shooting over the trees now. If they hadn't managed to get out... He didn't dare finish the thought.

"The cabin?" Caroline said finally, looking up at him.

"Gone." He squeezed her against him. "Why the *hell* did you go back in there?" He was angry, but not at her—angry at knowing how terrible the loss would have been if either of them had been hurt. Or worse.

"I didn't think it was that bad," she whispered. "It wasn't that bad then. I—I just thought I'd go back and grab my suitcase and Rose's Raggy. I knew exactly where they were—"

"Caroline." He interrupted her roughly and held her close to him, so that he could look deep into her eyes. "Promise me you'll never do anything so goddamn stupid again."

"I promise."

"Hey, you swore, Mr. Adam," came the little reproving voice. "You said a bad word."

"Goddamn right I did," he growled, not taking his eyes from Caroline's face. "Your mother made me do it."

TWO HOURS LATER Adam was back in bed, still staring at the ceiling. The cabin fire had died down considerably, but the reddish hue still flickered on his bedroom wall. There was nothing more that could be done. Curley's crew had the fire well under control and he knew his foreman would leave a man to keep an eye on it until it died out altogether.

He'd brought Caroline and Rose to the house to clean up and go to bed. *He wasn't letting them out of his sight after this....* He'd grabbed a shovel and gone back down to help to make sure the flames didn't get away from them and set a grass fire or get into the trees. At this time of year everything was tinder-dry.

Then, filthy and dog-tired, he'd come back up to the house and had a quick shower. The house was dark and quiet. Caroline had obviously gotten Rose settled down with no problem. Kids—they could sleep anywhere.

He didn't think he was going to get much sleep himself.

He heard the soft click as the door opened. He turned his head. Caroline stood there, in one of his old T-shirts he'd told her she could put on after her shower. His heart thudded painfully.

He watched as she padded silently into the room, her eyes seeking and holding his. He held his breath.

She tossed something onto his bedside table. Amazed, he recognized several small foil packets.

"They were in the pocket of my robe," she said, so softly he could barely make out her words. "I think that's a sign, don't you?"

Then she reached down and grabbed the hem of the T-shirt and pulled it over her head and dropped it on the floor. She stood there proudly, gilded by moonlight and firelight. He'd knew he'd never seen anything so beautiful in his life.

"I changed my mind," she said. "If you still want me."

He heard the painful shyness in her voice. He held out his arms and she slid into bed beside him. *So soft, so warm, so incredibly beautiful....*

He wrapped his arms around her and held her close to stop the trembling. He kissed her face gently, her eyes, her nose, her lips, the side of her throat. No, he definitely wasn't going to get a wink of sleep tonight.

"Caroline, honey," he whispered, between kisses. "I've *never* stopped wanting you. Ever."

CHAPTER NINETEEN

THE TREMBLING, which had begun with the shock of the fire and then the chill that penetrated her bones, soon turned to another kind of trembling.

Anticipation. Excitement. The shocking pleasure of Adam's kisses all over her body. He seemed determined to touch her everywhere, to lay claim to every nerve and muscle and bone, before he'd satisfy the aching deep within her, an ache that grew and grew until she was almost frantic with need.

Her breasts, her back, the smooth inner skin of her thighs—he touched her everywhere. Kissed her everywhere. Murmured words against her skin she couldn't hear but understood completely.

"Adam...oh..." This was heaven; this was a thousand times better than her fantasies.

He loomed suddenly above her, his weight pressing her deeper into the mattress. She gripped his shoulders, eager for their joining, but still he held back. Then he rolled to one side and she moaned in frustration. The condoms. She'd forgotten all about protection.

An instant later he was back, sheathed, positioned at the entrance to her body. "Yes...oh, yes!"

"Look at me." His voice was strained, harsh with emotion and maybe, just maybe, the strain of holding back. Her eyes fluttered open, fixed on his, not three inches above her. She hadn't realized she'd closed her eyes.

"I want you to look at me, to know it's me."

She felt him ease forward slightly and she gasped and arched against him.

"Dammit, Caroline—don't do that. I'm trying to go easy for you."

"Don't go easy...don't." She grabbed his head and pulled him down and kissed him with all the hunger and frustration she felt. Her groan melded with his, their mouths still joined.

In a few glorious mind-numbing moments it was over. She'd waited too long. She'd ached for him too long; he'd satisfied her quickly and completely and as perfectly as she could ever have dreamed. There could have been no other first time for them.

They lay together, face-to-face, breathing hard, in rhythm. His arms were around her, while her arms encircled his neck. Her right leg lay over his hip and she crooked it, bringing him closer; she never wanted to let him go. Not tonight. Tonight belonged to her. *To them.*

But a moment later he pulled away from her and reached down and dealt with the condom. Then he turned to her with a faint smile. "Don't want any accidents."

She thought of that, of the perfect union she'd just experienced with him. Their mating, their meshing. She thought of how much she'd wanted to have a baby one day, a sister or brother for Rosie. A baby that had been denied her in her marriage to Beau, but wouldn't be denied her with another man. *With this man.*

"I wouldn't care," she said softly, and he gave her a swift serious look.

Then he lay back and gathered her in his arms again and stroked her back and held her close. She felt his sudden distance, as though he was comforting her and she didn't want comfort. She regretted blurting out what was in her heart. That sort of talk was not part of the unspoken bargain between them. She heard the thunder in his chest—*that* part was real and true between them—and the steady rise and fall of his breathing. It seemed a long time before he spoke.

"I would," was all he said.

Then he turned to her and kissed her mouth and the peak of her breast and they began their loving all over again.

Caroline crept off to her own bed at dawn, leaving him with one last soft kiss on his shoulder. He was sound asleep. She peeked in at Rose, who was also sound asleep in her painted iron bed, warm and cozy under the old crazy-quilt cover. Caroline burrowed into the cold linen on her own bed and heaved a sigh from the bottoms of her feet. There wasn't an inch of her body that didn't feel well loved and well satisfied and…complete. Perfectly content.

She hoped Rose would sleep late. And Adam. At least he wasn't a dairy farmer; he didn't have to get up to milk cows. Caroline closed her eyes. What would tomorrow bring?

Tomorrow. Really, she meant *today*….

AFTER BREAKFAST, which Caroline cooked, feeling all thumbs in Mrs. T's kitchen—or perhaps it was because of Adam's intent and knowing gaze—they went down to the smoking ruins of the cabin.

Rose was very quiet, clutching her hand and keeping Raggy tucked under the other arm. "It's all gone, isn't it, Mommy?" she asked in a small voice. She was wearing some clothes Caroline had pulled out of the station wagon. Thank goodness they hadn't taken everything down to the cabin.

"Yes, darling. It's all gone." Caroline squeezed Rose's hand and glanced at Adam, who stood on the other side of the child. She had on jeans and a cotton sweater that had been in the bag she'd packed for Seattle. Curley had found her suitcase under the tree where she'd dragged it from the burning cabin and had brought it up to the house before breakfast. "We were just about finished living in it, anyway, weren't we? Now we can stay with Adam and Janie and her mommy while we're here."

"I guess so." Something in the grass caught Rose's interest and she dropped Caroline's hand to investigate. "Hey! Here's my beach ball. Remember I couldn't find it last night? Well, here it is! The fire didn't get it!"

The discovery of her ball cheered Rose considerably, and a few minutes later she was throwing a stick for the arthritic Stormy, waiting patiently while he limped to get it and bring it back to her. Then, when he dropped it at her feet, she'd pat the old dog extravagantly on the head. "Good dog. *Goooood* boy!"

Caroline stepped closer to Adam. The smoldering ruins gave her the creeps. There was something so horribly exposed about a place after a fire—a partly burned chair here, a blackened pot there. She saw a black knob on the ground, which she recognized as what remained of the old alarm clock. The kitchen range stood four-square and soot-black where it had always stood, its tin stovepipe fallen away. Was that what had caused the fire? The stovepipe coming away from the stove? Or had it been a too-hot fire, her fault for overloading the firebox? A chimney fire? They'd never know.

Adam took her hand, a natural gesture. "To think you and Rose might have been caught in this…" His voice was gruff.

"Yes." The enormity of what had happened was slowly sinking in.

He squeezed her hand and she returned the pressure. She didn't pull away. How could she, after last night? Still, no one knew of the change in their relationship, and she didn't want to have to explain to Curley or anyone else who might see them holding hands. This—whatever was between them, if anything—was too new, too fragile. She was going too many miles away tomorrow morning....

Adam kicked at a stone that had formed a base for the charred porch timbers. "Not much left. I'll put a crew on cleaning this up while you're gone."

Caroline didn't answer him. It had been Beau's cabin, all that remained of him in this place he'd loved so much. The simple furniture, the shelf of paperback books, the kerosene lanterns—all gone. She shivered and recalled an expression her great-aunt had used, something about a goose walking over her grave....

Adam put his arm around her shoulders and drew her close. "Cold?"

"No. Just thinking that this is kind of a sad end for Beau's cabin. Now there's nothing left of him here." Had she imagined it or had Adam tensed at her mention of Beau's name?

"No. Except what we remember," he said after a pause. He took his arm from her shoulders and didn't reach for her hand again. "Listen, what do you and Rose have planned for today? I've got some work I want to get done around the house...."

"You go ahead. Rose and I will be fine. I want to spend the day with her, since I'm leaving tomorrow." She felt inexplicably hurt, as though what had happened between them last night should have made a difference today. But that was silly—they'd had sex, that was all. Pretty incredible, but still just sex. They both had their own agendas; nothing had changed. "I thought we'd drive over and see the Dempseys this afternoon. Rose wants to play with the twins."

"Fine." Adam turned and began to walk back toward the path. "Coming, Rose?"

The girl tossed him the beach ball unexpectedly and laughed when he caught it with ease. Adam grinned and Caroline was struck by how comfortable the man and the girl now seemed with each other. With their similar coloring and gray-blue eyes, they could well be father and daughter. Rose had always seemed their little changeling girl, her dark coloring such a contrast to her own pale hair and Beau's blue-eyed-blond good looks. Of course their families and most of their friends knew that Rose was adopted. And even in the same families, strikingly different coloring and facial features were not unusual among siblings.

Caroline followed Adam back to the path. She couldn't shake the vague feeling of hurt that he seemed no different today than on any previous day, other than holding her hand for a few moments. She told herself she was being foolish. She had plenty to think about in the next few days. She had no time to waste mooning over a man who didn't *do* relationships.

But everything changed that evening when she came downstairs from putting Rose to bed.

Adam stood just inside the living room, and without a word he pulled her into his arms and kissed her. And then he kissed her again.

"I've been waiting for this," he whispered roughly. "This is the longest day I've ever lived through. Oh, Caroline, honey—" he pressed her hips against his "—I want you so much."

"You'd—" she began, then gasped as he gently bit the tender skin of her ear lobe. "You'd never know it the way you treated me today."

"Treated you?" He smiled into her eyes. "What did you

expect me to do—follow my brute male instincts and jump you every time you looked at me? Dammit, I've got work to do around here, a crew to boss around, eavestroughing to nail up...''

Caroline laughed. All the painful feelings she'd been nursing fell away, and she allowed herself to experience the joy of being with him again. She'd never felt so free in her life, and she liked the feeling.

''You all packed for tomorrow?'' he asked, nuzzling the juncture of her throat and shoulder. ''We're leaving early, don't forget.''

''Y-yes.'' Oh, that felt good! Her nerves and bones seemed to shudder in recognition of what he did to her, how he made her feel, just with his muttered words and his sweet kisses.

And his roving hands. ''Adam! Stop it.''

''You don't mean that,'' he said flatly, sounding remarkably unchastened. ''Rose asleep?''

''Yes. Maybe we should go to bed, too,'' she whispered, amazed at her boldness, ''considering how early we've got to get up.''

''No,'' he said in a low voice and with a look in his eyes that thrilled her to the core. ''Let's just take our clothes off and make love here.''

''Here?''

''Yeah,'' he said, his wicked fingers unbuttoning her jeans. ''I've already locked the doors.''

So they made love on the carpet in the living room, then Adam carried her upstairs and they made love again in his bed in the copper glow of the setting sun.

Caroline had never felt so desired and cherished. Adam's lovemaking centered entirely on her pleasure, which, he told her, was his pleasure. She lay against him, her head on his shoulder, enveloped in the comfort of his body next to hers. Reveling in the satiety of her own body and the sense of utter safety she had in his arms. *This man would never hurt her; this man would lay down his life for her and Rose. No wonder Beau had trusted him.*

Even the fleeting thought of her husband didn't change the feelings she had right now, right here, in Adam's arms, After all, as Adam had said, Beau was dead—and she was not. She had no husband to betray and how could she betray a memory? No, something had finally died last night with the fire that had consumed Beau's cabin. Somehow, in some mysterious way she couldn't begin to sort out or understand, she was free of Beau. Free to remember him in all his boldness and bravery.

Free to forget the pain.

Adam was so quiet. What was he thinking?

"Adam," she began, her cheek flat against his shoulder, her hand on his chest. "I have some things I want to tell you."

"Sure."

"It's a-about Beau and me." She could have sworn his heart changed rhythm, that his chest had tensed, ever so slightly.

"Go ahead."

"I haven't been completely honest with you—"

"Caroline." Adam interrupted. "Look. You don't have to tell me anything. Private things. Not at all. I don't expect you to."

"I know. I want to. I have to tell someone about how I feel inside or…or I'll just blow up and burst one of these days."

"Okay. Tell me."

She took a deep breath. "Beau was a wonderful man and I was very much in love with him, but in some ways, he hurt me terribly."

Adam swore. "*Hurt* you?"

"Not the way you think. He never hurt me physically. He wouldn't hurt a fly, you know that. But I could never understand how he could leave me and Rose and go off like he did. And before we got Rose, when it was just me."

Caroline raised herself on one arm and looked at Adam in the half-light of the rising moon. She pushed back her hair. "I used to go crazy with worry when he'd take off. *Crazy!* There I was, with a little baby, all alone—and he'd just up and leave. Sometimes for a week at a time, sometimes longer. He'd go off in the mountains and I wouldn't be able to sleep, wondering if this was the time he wouldn't come back."

"And one day he didn't."

"Yes." She realized she was weeping; she wasn't sure why. "One day he didn't." She didn't feel sad. She felt relieved to finally be telling someone what she'd hidden in her heart for so long. All those years she'd been ashamed even to think such thoughts, ashamed to feel such anger toward someone she'd truly loved. "And his family. I always felt they blamed me, Adam, that they thought it was my fault he'd go off. Of course then when he was killed…"

She couldn't go on. It was so unfair; the injustice had hurt her for so long. As though it wasn't enough to lose her husband like that, their child to lose her father, but to be *blamed* for it…

For a few minutes she was silent, letting the tears flow. Adam stroked her back. "It was nothing to do with you," he said softly. "It didn't mean he didn't love you."

"I know." She sniffed, trying to stem the tears. "In my head I know that. But in my heart—where it counts—I always felt I'd let him down. I felt there was something missing in me that he had to find somewhere else. In his damn old mountains!"

Adam peered at her in the semidark. She knew he was smiling by the sound of his voice. "His damn old mountains, huh?"

"Yes!"

"Some men are just made that way, Caroline. For me it was the rodeo. I tried plenty of other stuff, rock climbing, skiing glaciers, shooting white water, you name it. Nothing ever came near the thrill of the rodeo. There's no feeling in the world like climbing on a ton of ornery bull with just one red-hot idea in his cranky old head and that's to throw you off and stomp you into the ground."

"But that's so...so stupid!"

"Helen thought so, too. And now, these days, I have to admit I think it's pretty stupid myself. But I sure didn't when I was doing it. It's just some kink of nature, I guess. Some guys get their kicks from pushing around numbers in an office. Guys like me, we have to get our hands dirty. Could be it's the little-boy part that never quite grows up. Who knows? Hell, you can't blame yourself for the way Beau was put together."

She wiped her eyes on the sheet and managed a small laugh. "So you call yourself grown-up?"

"I do." He sounded more serious than she thought he would. "Took me long enough. And I was damn hard on a fine woman while I was doing it."

"Helen?"

"Yeah. The marriage likely would have fallen apart, anyway. It wasn't a match made in heaven, that's for sure. But that's no excuse for what I put her through. She deserved better."

"There's more, Adam. About me and Beau."

"More?"

"There was no money when he died. His cousin told me he'd been gambling, gambling heavily, and had stolen money from the company to pay off his losses. You know, borrowed it and never put it back? I—I just can't believe it, but I have to. We have no house to go back to. Beau's cousin sold it to pay back what Beau owed. And there was no insurance. Even the money in Rose's trust account was missing.''

Adam swore viciously. "Beau left you broke?''

"Pretty well.''

"That son of a bitch.''

"Adam!''

"Well, hell, it's one thing to live like an overgrown kid when you're single, but he should've been looking out for you and Rose. That's what a man does—he takes responsibility. I can't forgive him for that.''

"Anyway. That's what I'm going back to Seattle for. His mother wrote and said some papers of Beau's had been found and they wanted me there for a meeting. I guess I'll hunt for an apartment when I go back. And get Rose registered for school.''

"School?''

"She's five, Adam. She'll be going to kindergarten this year.''

"Five, huh?''

Caroline rested her cheek on Adam's shoulder again. She felt so good, so warm and happy now that she'd told him everything. He was Beau's friend; no one in the world could understand exactly what she'd gone through the way he could. "Yes. Five already, can you believe it? It seems just yesterday we got her.''

Adam said nothing for a long time. "So what you're telling me,'' he said finally, slowly, "is that you really have nothing to go back to.''

"Except this meeting,'' Caroline agreed sleepily.

She closed her eyes. Rest. She needed to get some rest; tomorrow was a very busy day.

ADAM FELT Caroline's body gradually relax. Then he heard the gentle sound of her snoring. He wanted to smile, but he just couldn't. He couldn't stop thinking about what she'd told him.

She had nothing to go back to.

And his suspicions were right. Beau had left her broke, the bastard. Just as Lucas had hinted. Adam meant what he'd said; he loved Beau like a brother, but he couldn't forgive him for not taking on a man's responsibilities when a woman and child were involved.

Because she's your daughter—is that why you care so much?

That wasn't it; he'd feel the same if Rose was Beau's flesh and blood. It made no difference.

Adam tightened his arm a little and Caroline moaned slightly, quit snoring and turned her face into his chest. The feelings he had for this woman scared him. He'd never felt anything like it before, not for Helen, not for any woman he'd ever bedded, and he'd bedded his share. Take this pillow talk of hers. Caroline talked all the time. He'd never talked with a woman in bed like this. Before, all he'd ever wanted was to get straight down to business—and then to sleep.

Maybe this was different. Maybe this meant something, something special.

It wasn't just sex. And it wasn't just Caroline, either. Rose was part of this picture, too. There was no going back now. This summer had changed his life. He wasn't the same Adam Garrick he'd been before Dot Wolinski brought him that letter in the middle of June.

But what about the lie he'd lived so long? No one knew

about Rose and him, only Lucas. How could he confess now? Maybe he didn't have to—maybe no one ever needed to know. Maybe it could stay his secret. Maybe that was the price he had to pay.

Adam heard the clock strike one downstairs in the living room. Five hours until they had to get up, eight hours until she was on that flight to Seattle. He watched her sleep, knowing she needed her rest, knowing he'd give anything to wake up beside her every morning for the rest of his life.

Just the thought of what he was considering put him in a cold sweat. He wasn't good at this; he'd *never* been good at this. Still, what had he told her? That a man could change, that *some* men could change.

"Caroline?" He nudged her gently. "Sweetheart? Wake up."

"Hmmm?" She turned sleepily and Adam quelled his sudden overwhelming desire to kiss her awake, to make love to her again. They'd made love enough times to know they were good together. Damn good. And, God willing, they'd have plenty more chances to find out.

"Are you awake, darlin'?"

"Hmm. Yes. I think so." She stretched luxuriously beside him. "Why? You have something in mind?"

"This is serious."

"What's serious?"

"Caroline, stay here. When you get back from Seattle, stay here with me, you and Rose. Don't go back."

"Stay?" She frowned and raised her head to meet his gaze. "For *good?*"

"Yes. You said you don't have anything to go back to there. Don't get me wrong, I know you can manage on your own at some nine-to-five job, but it's not your choice. You wouldn't be doing it if you hadn't been left high and dry. You need a home and a man. I'm that man. Rose needs a father. You want a baby. I can give you that baby."

"You mean, stay here and live with you?" She sounded shocked; Adam could have kicked himself for handling it the way he was handling it. Badly, as usual.

"Yes. I'm reasonably successful. I've got a home here I can share with you and Rose. I can give you what you want. We're good together, you and me. In lots of ways. You already know that."

"*Marry* you?"

"Yes." As soon as she said it, he knew that was what he wanted. "Marry me, Caroline." His voice was hoarse. *"Marry me."*

"Oh, Adam…" She stroked his face with blind fingers and lowered her head to give him a soft sleepy kiss. "Doesn't love come into it?" she whispered. "What about that, Adam? What about love?"

Love? The answer hit him like a freight train.

"That, too, Caroline," he whispered back, stricken. He looked deep into her eyes and felt every emotion in his body rise up and grab him around the heart. "That, too."

CHAPTER TWENTY

THE WOMAN behind the car-rental counter at Sea-Tac said it hadn't rained in the Seattle area for more than a month.

"Driest summer on record," she said cheerily, handing over the keys to a sporty coupe. "Here you go."

At the last minute Caroline had gone for the upgrade; she wanted to show up at her mother-in-law's house and at her meeting in style. She'd left the city like a whipped dog with its tail between its legs and she was returning head up, a woman with a future, a woman who'd gone a long way toward taking her happiness into her own hands. A woman who had just received a proposal of marriage from her dead husband's best friend.

She'd told Adam she'd consider his offer; in fact, she'd thought of little else. And really, whether or not Adam and Beau had been friends was of very little consequence. One of her aunts had married a neighbor who'd lost his wife to cancer. They'd grieved together and then found out how much more they had in common and married. It happened.

Her first impulse was to accept. No strings, no promises, no nothing. Just a simple heartfelt decision to put her faith in the future, in the life that she and Adam and Rose could have as a family at the Double O.

Her second reaction was more conservative and cautious. This turn of events had been so sudden; their relationship had escalated so recently and so quickly; what was Adam really thinking—was he just feeling sorry for them? Was this the tenderhearted Adam Barbara had hinted at?

And she needed to clarify her position with Beau's family. After all, despite how she felt about Philip Carter, he was Rose's second cousin. And Beau's mother, cold and brittle though she might be, was still Rose's grandmother. These were relationships that should be salvaged, no matter what she decided to do, or where she and Rose decided to live.

Her first stop, before she ventured to the hill to see Eunice Carter, was to have lunch with her lawyer. Maddie Reinholdt worked in an office on Hemingway Street, at the edge of the city's financial district. Maddie led her to the nondescript entrance of a restaurant off Spanner's Alley, near her office.

"Chinese okay?" Maddie paused with one hand on the brass door plate.

Caroline nodded. Maddie had greeted her with a big hug, which brought tears to Caroline's eyes. She was so lucky to have such a friend on her side, someone—like Adam—who had been Beau's friend first.

The restaurant was much nicer inside than Caroline would have guessed. "You mind if we sit in smoking?" Maddie whispered furtively.

"No. You don't smoke, though—" Caroline began.

"Started again a month ago. Nobody at the firm knows." Maddie slid into the booth they'd been shown. "I feel such a fool, magna cum laude at Brown, second in my class at Cornell, and I'm sneaking into the washroom a couple of times a day to cop a smoke. Pathetic, isn't it?"

Caroline laughed as Maddie made a wry face. "But don't they have a lounge in your office where you can smoke?"

"Yeah," Maddie said, and tapped out a cigarette from a mangled package she'd pulled from her skirt pocket. "But, like I said, nobody knows I started again. Never mind—let's talk about you. What are you doing, anyway, you and Rose? It was such a surprise to hear from you last week!''

"Rose and I went up to Alberta in June. I guess you know Philip Carter took over the house...."

"Yeah, and there's some funny business going on there, but we'll talk about that later. What happened in Canada?''

"I met a man, Maddie." Caroline felt her cheeks flush. Now why had she blurted *that* out? That wasn't what Maddie Reinholdt was interested in hearing.

"A man?" Maddie gave her a bright glance, her hand arrested as she held her lighter to her cigarette. "What kinda man, Caroline? A marrying man?''

"I...I think so. His name's Adam Garrick and he was a good friend of Beau's.''

"Adam Garrick?" Maddie said. "Oh, ye-es." She got a faraway look on her face and a dreamy smile that Caroline wasn't sure she liked. She blew out a cloud of smoke. "Tall? Kinda handsome in a rough outdoorsy way? Dark hair? Lean mean look to him?''

Caroline nodded and felt herself jumping to Adam's defence. "He's not a bit mean," she began stoutly.

"Oh, I don't mean he *is*—just looks that way. Like a guy who's suffered a little. Deadly to women." She smiled at Caroline, a friendly woman-to-woman smile.

"You know him?''

"Met him at your wedding. We danced a couple of times. I'd have been happy to visit the gazebo out back with him, but no dice. He wouldn't cooperate. Had a tall red-haired wife in tow, I believe. I don't think they were getting along that well. Lots of sniping back and forth, mostly her. Guess he dumped her, huh?''

"She dumped him," Caroline said. Oddly Maddie's off-hand summary of Adam and her recollection of him had fueled Caroline's sense of outrage. "He's a very fine person, you know, Maddie."

"Sure, very fine." She winked. "Sexy, too, huh?"

Caroline nodded reluctantly. "I suppose you could say that."

"You in love with him?"

"I...I don't know." That was the truth. In a way, Caroline thought she did love Adam; in another way, she didn't actually believe love could happen like that, or that it had happened to her. Still, how long had it taken her to meet, fall in love with and marry Beau? Less than a month.

Just then the waiter arrived and Maddie delivered a rapidfire order with a quick "You mind?" to Caroline. Caroline didn't; obviously Maddie was a regular and the staff knew her well.

Trust Maddie Reinholdt not to let go of an idea until she was finished with it. "Well, look. If you decide you *are* in love with him, grab him quick. Marrying guys aren't exactly thick on the ground. Not good-looking sexy ones, anyway. I should know."

"I just feel it's too soon," Caroline said unhappily. "And there's Rose to consider."

"Too soon?" Maddie stubbed out her cigarette and reached over and covered Caroline's hands with hers. Half-a-dozen silver and turquoise and topaz rings gleamed on her tanned manicured hand. Maddie Reinholdt wasn't everybody's idea of a Hemingway Street lawyer. "Too soon for what? It's been *two years*. You're young. Rose needs a father—hey, every kid does. This guy's in love with you. You deserve happiness. Figure it out, Caroline."

Caroline was grateful for the timely arrival of their meal. Of course Maddie didn't know Adam, not really; she couldn't possibly know if he was in love with her or not. Could be he was offering marriage for other reasons.

What reasons? He hadn't exactly presented himself as a man dying to get married again, had he? He'd said he didn't "do" relationships well. And no guy, no matter how tenderhearted, was going to ask someone to marry him just because he felt sorry for her. What had happened to change his mind? Could Maddie be right? Could it be that Adam Garrick really had fallen in love with her?

"How's your hot-and-sour soup?" Maddie deftly used her chopsticks to transfer some dry roasted chicken to her plate. "Great food, huh? Lucky I'm not in court this afternoon with all this garlic. Okay, let's talk about Beau and what's going on with that."

Typically Maddie's razor-sharp mind moved at lightning speed from one topic to the next. Before they left the restaurant, Caroline had discovered that, yes, Maddie had been able to ascertain that Beau had paid off some large mysterious debts the year before he died, but that the affairs of the Carter-family company were a lot more tangled than Philip Carter had let on. Maddie's requests for documentation had been ignored by the company lawyers, and she'd prepared a summary for Caroline that showed a few accounts with some cash that legally belonged to her as Beau's widow and beneficiary. Not much, but it would add to her small cache. Philip Carter, Maddie had told her with a dark look, had—as she put it—"dibs on exactly nothing, in spades."

She agreed to accompany Caroline as her legal adviser to the meeting scheduled with Eunice Carter and the Carter-family lawyers the next day. "If they don't like it, they can take a very long walk off a short pier, which around here isn't hard to find," she said in a satisfied tone. Caroline was pleased; she was less comfortable with the reason for Maddie's availability on such short notice. Maddie said she'd cancelled her long-standing Wednesday-afternoon tryst at the Grierson Hotel with her lover, an investment broker with a schedule as hectic as hers. Which, she assured Caroline, she wouldn't do for just *anybody*.

Eunice Carter's home was twenty minutes away, in the treed old-money neighborhood of Capital Hill. Caroline approached the address with trepidation. What would she find—a broken shell of a woman, still devastated by grief? The pulled-together icy woman Beau had remembered? A grandmother who simply wanted to stay in touch with her grandchild's mother? Someone Caroline could learn to get along with again, despite the hurt of the past year, for the sake of her child?

Nell, Eunice Carter's housekeeper, gave Caroline a big smile. "How's Rose, Miss Caroline? We've missed her so." She nodded significantly in the direction of the dark interior. "Her, too, though she'd never admit it."

"Rose is very well, enjoying her summer," Caroline replied noncommittally. "Is Eunice expecting me?

"Yes, ma'am, that she is." Nell led her to the morning room at the back of the house. Eunice rose from where she'd been sitting in a window seat, reading, and came toward her, hands extended.

"Caroline, darling." She offered her cheek, which Caroline dutifully kissed, recognizing the familiar scent of lavender and Chanel.

"It's wonderful to see you looking so well, Eunice. Thank you for inviting me to come to this meeting tomorrow." Caroline had decided to take the initiative with her mother-in-law. Her days of being intimidated by the matriarch of the Carter family were over.

"Oh, that." A frown crossed Eunice's carefully madeup face. Eunice Carter looked a great deal better now than the last time Caroline had seen her. That day, she'd burst into angry tears and accused Caroline of driving her son to what she felt amounted to suicide. "Lawyers, you know," she said vaguely. "Philip will be there, of course, and Freddie. Freddie asked me to get in touch with you." Frederick Blair was a senior partner in the prominent legal firm retained by the Carter family.

"And Maddie, too," Caroline murmured.

Eunice fixed Caroline with a pale blue stare. "The Reinholdt girl?"

"Well, she's hardly a girl anymore," Caroline said with a smile, wondering what Eunice would think if she told her exactly how Maddie had cleared her calendar for this meeting. "Beau always thought very highly of her, as you know. She'll be representing me."

"Representing *you?*" The icy stare had not wavered. Caroline returned her look bravely. *Think of Rose,* she thought desperately. *Think of Adam. Think of Janie and all she has to bear from strangers every day....* It helped.

A few seconds later, to Caroline's great relief, Eunice dropped her gaze and waved one hand dismissively, a familiar gesture. "Oh, well. Women are so modern these days. When my husband was alive...well, never mind. Would you care for some tea?"

Nell brought the tea and cakes, and Eunice inquired after Rose and smiled and even dabbed at a tear or two when Caroline showed her photographs she'd taken at the ranch. Caroline got the impression that Eunice truly missed her granddaughter. That knowledge alone made her feel the trip had been worthwhile.

Eunice frowned at the photos that included Janie of course, but Caroline didn't explain, knowing her mother-in-law was too well-bred to ask. The world of the Double O was so different from Eunice's world that it might as well have been on another planet.

They had their tea, talked civilly for thirty minutes, and

by the time Caroline got up to leave, she was actually feeling rather warm toward the woman she'd known as her mother-in-law all these years. She had high hopes now that the fracture in the family could be repaired and that she and Rose would find a welcome here in the future. Certainly Eunice would never change—she'd remain the distant glacial woman she'd always been—but at least Rose would grow up knowing her grandmother.

Before they left the morning room, Eunice went to her antique lady's desk and removed a sealed monogrammed envelope from a pigeonhole. "This," she said, putting the unaddressed envelope into Caroline's hand, "is a little something for Rose."

Caroline knew it was a check. She paused, wondering if it would do any good to tell her mother-in-law that a phone call would mean so much more to the child. Or a stuffed toy, or a trip to the zoo with her grandmother when they returned—even a picnic in the back garden. Then she tucked it into her handbag and smiled and thanked Eunice.

At the door she took a deep breath. She wanted no secrets. She wanted to put everything on the table, fair and square.

"I thought you should know, Eunice," she said evenly, "I'm thinking of marrying again."

A pin could have dropped anywhere in that great empty house, and Caroline would have heard it.

"Not that...that Garrick man?" Eunice laid one frail-looking hand, heavy with rings, on her green silk blouse just over her heart.

Caroline was surprised. She hadn't mentioned Adam Garrick, except to say that she'd worked for him for the summer and that they'd stayed in Beau's cabin, which was on Double O land. "Yes. Adam Garrick's asked me to marry him."

Eunice stared at her for a long moment, her pale gaze unwavering. "I never thought you'd forget my son so quickly," she said in a dull voice laced with bitterness. "And all he did for you."

"I haven't forgotten Beau," Caroline said. "I'll never forget him. I loved him with all my heart. But I'm thirty-one years old and I need to go on with my own life. Rose needs to go on, too...."

"I always felt that Garrick man was a bad influence on my son." Eunice nodded fretfully and Caroline knew with a sinking heart that she'd lost her, that Eunice Carter was back in some world of shadows, some world where grief would never end. "He made my son do dangerous things, you know. Rodeos and terrible things. Beau never would listen to me, although I warned him. He always looked up to that Garrick man. I couldn't understand what Beau saw in him." She shuddered delicately. "He seemed a dreadful man to me. Who were the Garricks? Nobody. Cowboys, travelers, farmers, every sort of rough element." She waved her hand disdainfully. "But what did I know? I was only his mother. Beau liked him. Just as he always liked that dreadful Reinholdt girl. And now you're—" she seemed to become aware of Caroline's presence again and leaned forward slightly to examine her face "—now you're going to marry him."

She reached out and gripped Caroline's hands with fingers that were cold and bony and very strong. "I hope you'll be happy, dear. I hope you'll bring Rose to see me sometimes. I do love her, you know. I love her so very much."

"I will, Eunice. I promise. Whatever I do and wherever we go, I'll always bring Rose to see you. You're her grandmother. She loves you, too." Impulsively Caroline put her arms around Eunice and kissed her cheek. Her mother-in-law suffered the embrace, even smiled a little, Caroline noted as she stepped back.

She squeezed Eunice's hands in hers. "I'll see you tomorrow."

"Tomorrow?" came the querulous response, a faint question in the pale eyes.

"At the lawyers'."

"Oh, yes. Goodbye." Eunice hesitated a second, then closed the big oak door firmly.

In the morning Caroline called her favorite hairdresser and booked a late-morning appointment. Ivan was delighted to see her, and she told him all about her adventures over the summer, including her unexpected proposal of marriage. He demanded to know who had cut her hair last and she said nobody he'd heard of and they laughed as always. He teased her and said she could have her cowboy. Him? He preferred loggers. Then he told her all the latest jokes and she left the salon feeling terrific. It had been a long time since she felt she could afford to spend fifty dollars on herself like that. For a haircut. Adam's money for Beau's cabin had made the difference. Think of it, she told herself gaily, as a gift from Beau. He'd always wanted her to look good. And for some reason she couldn't wholly fathom, she definitely wanted to look her best going into this meeting at the law firm.

She dressed carefully, in a pale green suit she'd owned for several years, and met Maddie at her office. They took a taxi to the meeting, which was in a conference room in the august chambers of Peters, Blair, McKenzie, McCullough. Maddie made a face when they walked out into the carpeted wood-paneled foyer, complete with original art on the walls, leather-bound library in the lounge area and politically correct receptionists—one young man, handsome but not *too* handsome, and one young woman, pretty but not *too* pretty.

Caroline and Maddie glanced at each other and laughed. It was the perfect icebreaker, although Caroline's palms were perspiring as the young man showed them into the meeting room. Frederick Blair was already there, as was Philip Carter, looking distinctly uncomfortable, and Philip's wife, Jeannie, a pale mousy little thing whom Caroline had always felt vaguely sorry for. A third woman, who turned out to be Philip's sister, Lorraine, was also present. After introductions and polite handshakes all around, Caroline sat down to await Eunice's arrival.

When she got there a few minutes later, greetings were exchanged again and then Frederick Blair invited everyone to sit.

Caroline sat. She was glad she'd brought Maddie.

"You are probably wondering why I have asked you to gather here today," began Frederick Blair. He was a tall bespectacled gray-haired man in navy suit and striped tie. "I must tell you that it has been on the instructions of one who is not among us, namely, Beau James Carter, deceased, formerly a principal in the family company in which you all have an interest, Carter Investments."

Caroline glanced at her mother-in-law, who had gasped slightly at the lawyer's description of Beau. Eunice was carefully madeup, freshly coiffed and a model of correct deportment for a woman of her class and station in life. She wore a beige linen suit with matching shoes and bag. Pearls at her throat and ears. Eminently suitable for a late-summer business meeting.

"To move directly to the matter at hand, I have in my possession—" here Blair lifted an envelope on his desk "—a recently discovered document written in the hand of

Mr. Beau Carter and addressed to me— Yes, Miss Reinholdt?''

''I'd like to know where the document was found and
why it's only been discovered now, not during probate.''

''An excellent question. I, too, would have preferred that
it be discovered during probate.'' He glared at each of them
in turn, as though they had perhaps been responsible for
the oversight. ''But the fact is, it was not. This document
was discovered earlier this month by staff cleaning the Carter summer house. The person who found the envelope—
in the back of a drawer in an unused desk on the second
floor—a Mrs. Pearl Williams, immediately contacted Mrs.
Eunice Carter, who had the document sent directly to me.
I opened the envelope in the presence of a witness here in
my office, whom I will call if any of you require it—a
precaution that will be familiar to those of us in the legal
business.'' At this point he sent a toothsome smile toward
Maddie, whom Caroline could almost hear groaning. ''This
precaution is taken,'' he went on, ''so there can be no question of the contents of the envelope that I received. Ahem.''

Mr. Blair now put his glasses on and began looking
through the document, which appeared to be several pages
in length. ''I will read the document now and I warn you
in advance that it contains very serious allegations, which
I have already taken up with the parties concerned.'' Blair
cleared his throat again and began to read. Caroline saw
Maddie make some quick notes on a steno pad she'd removed from her purse.

Caroline tried to follow the bewildering sequence of
dates quoted and amounts of money mentioned. She noticed that Philip Carter had gone a sickly shade of gray.
His wife had a wild frightened look on her pale face and
she clutched her husband's arm tightly.

''To sum up,'' Mr. Blair continued, refolding the document and setting it on the table beside him, "more than three years ago, Mr. Beau Carter noticed funds missing from several accounts at Carter Investments. He suspected that his cousin, Mr. Philip Carter, who is present here today, was using company money to pay gambling debts. Beau was aware of his cousin's propensity for gambling, although it is apparent that other members of Philip's family were not. Beau replaced the shortfall with money of his own, so that the missing funds would not be discovered by the other shareholders or by the comptroller. This action may have been morally commendable, to protect his cousin and childhood friend, but I want to make abundantly clear to all present that it was a very ill-considered move by Mr. Beau Carter and a course of action I would never have recommended if he had come to me. However, he did not seek advice from me."

Mr. Blair took off his glasses and cleaned them and put them back on. "Clearly Mr. Beau Carter had full intentions of being reimbursed by his cousin, Mr. Philip Carter, as soon as his cousin could make arrangements to do so. As you now know, when Beau died, his cousin had repaid very little of the money. Philip Carter subsequently saw the opportunity to place the entire blame on his cousin's shoulders, by telling his widow, Mrs. Caroline Carter, and his mother, Mrs. Eunice Carter, that Beau had defrauded the company.

"That is how the situation stands at present. We in this room will attempt to resolve it. Mrs. Eunice Carter prefers the police not be brought into this matter, although criminal charges could most certainly be laid if the documentation contained herein proves correct. However, as the company is privately held, the principals may decide among themselves what is to be done and what damages, if any, are to be sought."

Maddie cleared her throat. "So let me recap, if I may, Mr. Blair," she said pleasantly, glancing at her notes. "This man here, Mr. Philip Carter—" she nodded in the direction of Beau's cousin "—framed his cousin, who was trying to help him stay out of jail. Then he robbed his benefactor's widow and child of their rightful inheritance, even going so far as to lay false claim to the widow's house and property. In the course of covering his tracks and pursuing his greed, he humiliated her and her child, slandered her and her dead husband and, in effect, ended by running her out of town. Mr. Blair?"

There was an awkward pause, then Mr. Blair nodded. "That is substantially correct, Miss Reinholdt."

"And if Beau Carter had not had the good sense—or the benefit of second thought—to write down the details of these events, his cousin might have pulled off this fraud and gotten away with it," Maddie continued.

"Perhaps so," Mr. Blair conceded.

Caroline had never believed Beau was capable of what Philip had said, despite all the evidence. Now she was discovering the full extent of Philip Carter's treachery. If Beau's letter had not been found, Philip Carter *would* have gotten away with it.

She turned to face him. He refused to meet her eyes. His wife still clung to his arm like a frightened rat. Caroline felt an overwhelming surge of disgust for him and sympathy for Eunice, who, according to Beau, had always favored her clever nephew when the two boys were growing up. This was how the favorite nephew had repaid her.

Then she looked at Eunice, whose face was pinched and white. "I am so sorry, my dear Caroline." Eunice's voice sounded old. Defeated. "I am so sorry this has happened."

So sorry. Really, what else was there to say? Philip Carter would not apologize, she was sure, nor did she want apologies from the likes of him. Caroline stood up. Suddenly all she wanted was to get out of here. She wanted fresh air. *She wanted to go back to Alberta.*

"I will honor my mother-in-law's wishes on this, Mr. Blair. If Eunice does not wish to air the family laundry publicly, that is entirely up to her. Is that your decision, Eunice?"

Her mother-in-law looked at her. Caroline saw a trace of the fabled family matriarch in her clear blue gaze. "Yes, Caroline. Mr. Blair does not advise it, but it is my decision. I could not bear the names of the two young men I have always loved best to be dragged through the newspapers of this town. I am prepared to compensate you however you wish. Philip will no longer have a position of trust in this company. He will take out a mortgage on his own house and repay you what he took from the sale of yours. Your shares in the family company, and Rose's, will be restored to you—"

"Thank you," Caroline interrupted. She could not stomach one more minute of this talk. It sickened her. "My attorney will be in touch with Mr. Blair to take care of the details." She paused, shrugged. "It's only money, after all. Money is *not* everything. It's not love, is it? Or kindness, or anything else that really matters."

She took a deep breath. "I have only one thing to say to you, Philip." She looked directly at Beau's cousin and had the satisfaction of seeing fear mixed with the defiance on his face. He knew his aunt would support him, no matter what, her fear of scandal being greater than her fear of wrong. "In addition to a foul and despicable excuse for a man, you are a bully and a coward. Your cousin, my husband, was worth ten of you."

Then she looked at the rest of the assembled company. Neither Philip's sister nor his wife—nor Philip for that matter—had said a word so far. "I'd like to go now. I'm sure you will understand why."

Maddie took her arm. "You okay?" she whispered as Caroline reached for the door.

"Fine, Maddie," she whispered back. "I've never felt better, to tell you the truth." Only Adam could understand her joy now. Beau—her handsome, brave, generous, *loyal* husband—had *never* let her down.

"So," Maddie said when they got into the taxi. "Dinner tonight, you and me, to discuss all this. Okay?"

Caroline nodded.

"We'll figure out this mess, no problem," Maddie continued. "What did you have planned for tomorrow?"

"Well, I *had* planned to hunt for an apartment and register Rose in kindergarten and maybe even look for a job—"

"*Had*, huh? So what're you gonna do now?"

"I think I'll shop for some presents for Rose and everybody at the Double O, and then I'm going to buy a carry-on bag and stuff it with French lingerie and go back to Alberta and marry a cowboy."

Maddie's rich deep laugh filled the cab. "You're learning, Caroline! I *really* think you're learning."

CHAPTER TWENTY-ONE

ADAM GLANCED at his watch as he turned in at the Dempseys' lane. He was early. If necessary, he'd shoot the breeze for half an hour or so with Bill. Did kids' parties stick to a tight schedule? Maybe it had already run down and Rose was ready to be picked up.

He couldn't believe how quickly the time had passed since he'd taken Caroline to the airport. He'd returned to a message that Mrs. T wanted to stay home for an extra day because Janie had a fever and, as her mother put it, "wasn't fit to travel." Adam knew how his housekeeper worried about the health of her daughter, who suffered regular bouts of pneumonia every winter and spring. She just couldn't seem to shake off colds and other slight illnesses the way most people did.

That meant Adam had Rose to take care of on his own. By the second day he discovered he liked it. He tossed the ball with her; she followed him around like a puppy wherever he went; he even read to her before bed, what she called "funny stories"— they were short items he read out of his stock and outfitter magazines. He'd made her chicken-noodle soup three times already because she said it was her favorite.

Wednesday morning he'd taken Rose to a neighbor's to see a new foal. Cal Blake's prize quarter horse mare had just foaled, and Adam was as interested in seeing the newborn as Rose was. She was delighted with the Blakes' baby and the way Cal's wife, Nina, fussed over her. She chattered all the way home in the truck about how she loved dolls and babies and she wished she'd get a brother or sister someday. Then she mentioned, as she had several times since the fire, that her daddy was in heaven, but if she ever got a new daddy, her mommy would get a baby and then she'd have a sister or brother.

Adam had grinned to himself, wondering if she knew much about how babies came about. Obviously she understood part of the concept, that you needed a daddy, as well as a mommy.

Which made him think of Caroline. He wasn't quite ready to face how much he wanted her to accept his badly phrased proposal. He tried not to dwell on it, but it was impossible not to think of her almost constantly, especially at night when he got into the bed they'd shared. Would she come to his bed when she returned? It would be harder to keep their relationship discreet with Mrs. T and Janie in the house. He hoped there'd no longer be any need for secrecy, that she'd agree to marry him and they could announce it to the world.

More than once it had crossed Adam's mind that it was too much to hope for, him and Caroline. Too easy. He'd never trusted anything that came too easy.

Adam pulled into the yard and got out of the truck, wondering where he'd find Bill Dempsey.

"Mr. Adam!" He turned.

Rose burst out of the Dempsey's screen door and raced toward him. He held out his arms—an instinctive response—and she hurtled into them and buried her face in his neck. He felt hot tears on his shoulder.

"Hey, honey. What's the matter?"

"They were m-mean to me!" she sobbed. His immediate thought was to find out who'd been mean to Rose so he could find them and tear them limb from limb. "I hate 'em! I hate boys!"

"All boys?" He tried to cajole her out of her temper, but she wasn't having any of it.

"I *double-hate* boys!"

Just then Sheila Dempsey came out the door and approached, smiling. She didn't seem nearly as concerned as Adam thought she should be. "Rose is glad you're here," she began, then winked at him. "Ryan and Barnaby weren't quite as generous as they ought to have been with their new toys, I'm afraid. I've had a word with them."

"What happened?"

"Well, as you can imagine," she said, "the bows and arrows were a big hit. The kids lined up to take turns, and my boys said that all the boys had to get a turn before the girls—"

"And I stuck up my hand first!" Rose burst in indignantly. He wanted to smile at her tearstained expression but didn't dare. A child of his in this mood? That was asking for trouble. She was liable to take a poke at him.

A child of his. Where had that come from?

"She'll be fine," Sheila mouthed to him, pointing and smiling behind Rose's back, then added in a louder voice, "Rose, honey?"

"Mm?" Rose glanced over at her with interest, as though expecting the twins' mother to produce the coveted bows and arrows right then and there.

"You come back when there's not so many kids around," Sheila Dempsey whispered with a conspiratorial smile. "I know Ryan and Barnaby will be happy to share with you then. Okay?"

"Okay." Rose looked at Adam, and he could see her usual sunny mood returning. "We're gonna throw the ball through the hoop when we get home, aren't we, Mr. Adam? And *they* don't even got a basketball hoop!''

She relaxed her body and raised her arms slightly, which Adam interpreted as a request to get down. He lowered her carefully to the ground, and she ran to the passenger side of the truck, shouting goodbye and thanks to Sheila Dempsey. It was as though the storm of disappointment and outrage and injured feelings had never been.

"Kids," Sheila murmured to him, as he opened the driver's-side door. She gave him an eyebrows-up adult-to-adult look.

"Yeah," Adam said knowingly, wondering as he drove away what the hell she'd meant.

When they got back to the Double O, things didn't improve for Rose. Janie was feeling cranky from her illness earlier in the week and didn't want to play. She snapped at Rose and said she wanted to look at her comics by herself.

Rose wandered into the kitchen, silent tears rolling down her cheeks.

"There, there, sweetheart!" Mrs. T clucked. "Don't you mind our Janie. She's just having one of her times."

"Janie's mad at me, and Ryan and Barnaby wouldn't let me play with their new stuff, and Jennifer Myers had a nicer dress than me at the party and she didn't spill ice cream on it like I did."

Mrs. T smiled and continued putting away the groceries Adam had brought from town. What *was* it with women? Adam thought. They never seemed to take what kids said seriously.

"You'll see," his housekeeper told Rose, "Janie will be rarin' to play tomorrow. And we'll wash your dress and it'll be good as new."

Rose heaved a big sigh for someone her size. "I think I'm having a very bad day," she said in a small voice. She pulled out a chair from the table and climbed onto it. "I wish my mommy was here, that's what. I wish my daddy was here, too. Why did he have to go away to heaven like he did?"

"Poor lamb," Mrs. T murmured, and proceeded to stick her head in the refrigerator to rearrange the contents.

Adam felt helpless. He wanted to comfort Rose, but he couldn't. He wished he could tell her that he was here and that he was her true father and that he'd be happy to be her daddy, too, if everything worked out the way he wanted with her mommy. None of this was anything he could speak about, certainly not to a child.

"You hungry?" He couldn't imagine that she would be after the cake and ice cream and party treats he'd seen on the Dempsey kitchen counter when he'd delivered Rose, but he didn't know what else to say.

"Soup?" She gazed up at him with a tiny smile.

He grinned, feeling his chest swell to bursting. "I think I could lay my hands on some soup around here if I looked real hard."

"Chicken-*noodle* soup?"

He shrugged. "Maybe."

"Well...okay," she said, with a show of reluctance followed by another little smile that etched itself on his heart.

"*If* you find chicken noodle, then I *guess* I'll have some," she finished, then added sweetly, "Please."

"Coming right up," he said, and turned to reach for a can of soup from the cupboard. He started to open it, then felt a shiver race down his back as the can opener's steel edge bit into the tin. It was more than a shiver; it was a shower of ice pellets. What it was, was fear.

He was in love. Head over heels. With both of them.

I can't do it, he thought, panicking. *I can't keep the truth about Rose from Caroline.*

HER FLIGHT WAS DUE in at noon. Caroline sat at the window in the DC-10, glued to the sight below. Fabulous prairies rolled out forever in one direction; incredible snow-capped mountains thrust to the sky in the other; a green, brown and golden patchwork quilt of fields spread below her. And tucked into the hills between plains and mountains was the Double O. *Her new home.*

She could hardly wait. She had gifts for them all—a plush black-and-white orca for Rose, a silvery wind chime for Janie, specialty chocolates for Mrs. T, West Coast-motif playing cards for Curley, and for Adam? Caroline had felt shy buying a gift for Adam. What was appropriate? What was exactly right? She ended up with a small polished humidor containing a supply of fancy imported cheroots.

She wondered if he'd notice that she'd removed her wedding ring. She'd taken it off Wednesday night before she went to bed, after the meeting, the night she'd realized she was ready to make a commitment to another man.

She felt good about everything, including Beau. This morning, just after dawn, she'd driven out to the windswept cemetery overlooking Puget Sound and told Beau all about the changes she was making. She thanked him for bringing Adam and Maddie into her life. She knew many people would've thought she was crazy to be talking to a headstone, but she knew Beau would have loved the gesture. Besides, that early, there was no one else around.

Adam and Rose were waiting for her. She barely had time to glance at Adam before Rose practically strangled her in a big noisy welcome. She hugged Rose, thinking how small and fragile her daughter sometimes seemed. And how tough and wiry other times. So infinitely precious... Her life would not have been the same without this child.

Then, shyly, she stepped toward Adam and reached up to kiss his cheek. He wrapped his arms around her and held her for a few seconds, long enough to whisper how much he'd missed her. She knew her cheeks were pink when she stepped back and observed the highly interested look Rose was giving them both.

"Let's get my bags, Rosie," she said briskly. "You watch for my suitcase on the carousel."

That intrigued the girl enough to let Caroline stand back with Adam. "I have so much news," she whispered. "So much to tell you."

"Do you?" He smiled and took her hand. She felt him touch her ringless third finger, but he didn't look down. "Good news?"

"All of it," she said, finding it difficult not to blurt everything out right then and there. About Beau and how she felt about him, Adam—

But this was Rose's time. The adults could wait.

All the way home in the truck, Rose chattered, telling Caroline about the foal and the party and Janie's sickness and all the soup she'd had and how mad she was at the twins.... Caroline glanced at Adam over Rose's dark head. He seemed genuinely interested in hearing Rose's version of what had happened since her mother left, occasionally reminding her of some detail or adding one of his own.

"You've done something with your hair," he said once, about the only personal comment he made during the ninety-minute trip. Caroline thought he seemed somewhat reserved, but perhaps it was just in contrast to Rose's non-stop chatter and high spirits. After all, she had to remind herself, he was the same man he'd always been, proposal or no proposal. He'd always been reserved, even distant. That wouldn't change; nor would she want it to. That was Adam. If anyone's life had changed radically—or was about to—it was hers.

"Oh." She felt the ends of her hair, which now just swept her shoulders. "I got it cut."

"It looks terrific. Very, uh, big city," he said, smiling. She read the admiration and simmering desire in his eyes and felt a lot better. He wanted her; it was impossible for him to hide it.

They didn't have a chance to speak privately until well into the evening. The returning guests from the Tetlock Valley arrived just as they did, and there was the usual confusion of matching up luggage to guests and finalizing all the last details of their stay in Alberta. Some needed flight reservations confirmed, others required a stack of postcards supplied for last-minute dispatches.

Caroline loved every chaotic minute. Adam took her bags to her room and she changed into a more comfortable denim skirt and T-shirt, then went about making sure everything worked out for the guests. Janie and Rose played happily with their new toys. Janie seemed endlessly enthralled with the soft sound of the silver chimes, as Caroline had guessed. Mrs. T was delighted with the chocolates and said Angus would love the horn-handled penknife Caroline had bought for him.

She was dying to tell Adam the news about Beau. Finally—after all the guests had gone to their cabins for their last night at the Double O, after the dishes had been stacked in the dishwasher and Mrs. T and Janie had gone to their room, after Rose had happily fallen asleep with her new orca alongside her old toy, her much-loved, much-hugged whale—*finally* Caroline managed to slip away to look for Adam. She'd thought he was in his office on the main floor, but the room was empty.

She stepped onto the darkened veranda, her heartbeat tripling as she caught the characteristic scent of excellent tobacco. Adam had lit one of his new cheroots.

Caroline shivered and wrapped her arms around herself. The sky was clear and filled with a billion stars. It was cold, as though fall really was just around the corner.

"Come here." Caroline saw the cheroot's bright trajectory as Adam tossed it onto the gravel path and she went toward him, sure he could hear the pounding of her heart.

He hauled her into his arms and pressed her body along the length of his. "I missed you," he said, and lowered his mouth to hers.

Yessss! This was what she'd ached for; this was what she wanted. This was the man she wanted to wake up beside for the rest of her life. Adam kissed her with a deep intensity that seemed, somehow, to border on desperation, a feeling she could only attribute to the knowledge that his desire matched hers.

Eventually, Adam lifted his head and looked down at her for a long moment. Her heart fluttered and her knees felt like water. Her body ached for the satisfaction she knew so well he could bring her. "Tell me your news," he said quietly.

"Let's sit down," she suggested, going to the wooden love seat that formed part of the furniture grouping on the veranda.

"You sit. I prefer to stand," he said, his face hidden in the shadows.

"It's about Beau," she said, clearing her throat.

"About Beau?" He sounded surprised.

"Yes. Wonderful news. It turns out that his cousin, the one who told me Beau had stolen from the family company, had really taken the money himself. Beau found out and had tried to replace the money, temporarily, I guess, thinking he'd eventually get it out of Philip one way or another—"

''Beau didn't steal anything? He provided for you and Rose?''

''Not really. But in a way, yes. My lawyer is working out the details of a settlement for Rose and me. I don't care about the money, though. What's done is done, and everybody thinks Beau was crazy to do it in the first place.''

''Do what?''

''Crazy to try and cover up for his cousin. But you know how loyal he was and, well, maybe even a little naive about people.''

''He believed in people. He believed they'd do what they said they would.''

''Oh, Adam.'' She got up and came toward him. A tiny pulse of fear brought goose bumps to her arms, or perhaps it was the cool night air. Why did he seem so remote now that they were alone? Why didn't he put his arms around her? Why didn't he kiss her again? ''I feel so much better knowing Beau didn't really keep anything from me like I thought he had. You know, gambling or whatever. He just made a mistake, that's all, going to bat for his slimeball of a cousin who didn't deserve it. And then he died before he could make it good again.''

Why didn't Adam speak?

''So you're okay for money now, you and Rose?'' he said finally.

''We will be.'' She frowned. ''When everything gets straightened out.''

There was silence for a few moments. Caroline could hear the far-off yip-yip-yip of a coyote. The lonely sound made her shiver again.

''Cold?''

''A little.'' Caroline's heart hammered painfully. This wasn't what Adam had expected to hear from her. She'd

been so full of the news about Beau that she hadn't gotten
to the most important part—

"Want to go in?"

"No. Listen, Adam. I've thought about what you said to
me before I left."

She felt him tense in the darkness. "I've made up my
mind." She paused, then went on softly, "I said all my
news was good, and it is—"

"Caroline," he interrupted her harshly. "Don't say anything more."

Shocked, she hesitated. "What's wrong?" Horror struck.
"Have you changed your mind? Don't you want to marry
me now?"

"That's not it. That's not it at all. I've never wanted
anything more. The truth is, I've proposed to three women
in my life, and not one has mattered to me as much as you.
But there's something I have to tell you before you give
me your answer." He paused and Caroline held her breath.
Three women? "There's something you need to know."

Her voice nearly failed her. "*What? What* are you trying
to say, Adam? *What?*"

"I'm Rose's real father, Caroline. She's my biological
daughter."

The stars swam crazily in the black sky above. Caroline
felt her heart literally stop and her blood freeze to ice in
her veins. She grasped at the clammy dew-covered timber
upright of the porch. *"Your daughter?"*

"Yes. Mine."

"How—?" Caroline's mind felt thick and fuzzy. Somehow she couldn't grasp this concept. His *daughter?*

He gave her a sharp glance. "An accident. Isn't that what
they call it, when something like this happens? I'm not
proud of what I did. I offered to marry the mother when I
found out she was pregnant. She turned me down."

Adam had gotten another woman pregnant, some stranger, and this woman had given Rose up for adoption. And they—she and Beau—had adopted her. *Rose was Adam's child.…*

"Did Beau—did he know?" Was that agonized whisper hers? There was so much she didn't understand.…

"Beau knew I was Rose's father right from the start, but he swore he'd never tell anyone. Especially you."

"*Me?* Why not *me?*" Sudden rage at them both, at Adam and Beau, at what they'd kept from her, rose up and nearly blinded her. Her heart was pounding, frantic. "A dirty secret between the two of you, is that it? It's okay to tell your rodeo buddy—" she spit the words out "—but it's not okay to tell your wife?"

"Hold on, Caroline. He didn't want to hurt you. He said you didn't want to know about—"

"I didn't want to know who he'd rounded up as a sperm donor back when we were thinking of trying that approach. I was stupid enough to want to pretend it was my husband's baby I carried, not some stranger's." She held icy palms to her burning cheeks. Was there no dignity, no secrecy? No end to her humiliation? "I'm sure he told you all about that, too.…"

Adam and her husband had been best friends—Beau had been more than a brother to him.…

She stopped, shocked. "You. *You* were the donor he tried to get, weren't you? The one who said no."

Adam was silent. She stepped closer and grabbed the front of his shirt in both hands and tore at it. "You were the one—"

He nodded. "That's right. I was."

"*You* turned him down. My God…" Caroline felt her head begin to spin. The irony of it overwhelmed her. "I could have given birth to *your* baby," she said in an agonized whisper, the full ramifications coming painfully clear. "Rose could have been mine—*ours! Our baby.* I never would have known."

"None of that happened, dammit. I turned him down—"

"But if you hadn't—if you *hadn't.* Adam, don't you see what you've done to me, you and Beau? You've acted as though I didn't matter in any of this, as if this baby was just between you and him, some...some *product.*"

"He said you didn't want to know. All I know is what he told me."

"Who else knows?" she demanded.

"Nobody. Just the...the mother, I guess. And my lawyer in town."

"Why your lawyer? So you could try and get her back from me? You'll never get her back—do you hear me?" she whispered hotly, acutely aware that Mrs. T and Janie and Rose were sleeping in the house behind them. *"Never!"*

"It's nothing like that. He's a friend, that's all."

Caroline tried hard to hold back the tears. "And now...and now I've fallen in love with you and I made up my mind to marry you and for a while we were so happy and now you tell me this." Her voice broke and she let the tears flow, still clutching the fabric of his shirt. "How can I marry you now? No matter what I feel? I can't *trust* you."

"Caroline..." His voice was raw. "Sweetheart, don't do this to yourself." He put his arms around her. "We can work this out. If we care enough about each other—"

She wrenched herself free. *"Don't touch me!* It's not me you wanted, was it? It never was! You wanted *Rose.*"

With a cry of mingled rage and despair, she ran into the house.

CHAPTER TWENTY-TWO

THE NEXT MORNING Caroline made a list. She started with her obligations to Adam. She had told him she'd stay until the end of the season, and she would. That meant another week or so. One more batch of guests, and then the annual wrap-up party for the Tetlock Valley and Double O staff, scheduled for Labor Day. She also had bookkeeping entries to make, backed up from the time she'd been away. There was the final payroll to do. And bills to pay.

Then there was the question of keeping her own options open. Thanks to the forthcoming settlement from either Eunice or Philip Carter, the details of which were being worked out by Maddie, she no longer had the immediate worry of finding a job when she returned to Seattle. And she would wait until she found a place to live before registering Rose in kindergarten.

Plenty of time when they got settled to think about what to do with the rest of her life.

Caroline put down her pen and pressed her fingers to her weary eyes. *Adam was Rose's natural father.* That fact was seared into her mind. She couldn't stop thinking about it. Now that he'd told her, she could see resemblances between them. They weren't strong likenesses, but everything seemed to fit. She would never have jumped to any conclusions about their relationship—unlike romance novels she'd read where the secret baby always looked exactly like the father who hadn't known he'd fathered her. Well, wasn't this a twist! She tried to laugh, not very successfully. The tears were still too near the surface.

The hurt. The loss. The ache, knowing she'd lost any chance of happiness with Adam. How could she marry him when he'd sprung something like this on her? He'd said if they cared enough, they could work it out.

How could she work anything out with a man she didn't trust?

And three women! Good grief. He'd asked three women to marry him. She supposed Helen was the first. And look how that had turned out. She had to hand it to Adam—he'd never said a bad word about his ex. Had blamed himself for the failure of their marriage. But for a man who'd said he wasn't good at relationships, he'd certainly been involved in enough. He'd offered marriage to Rose's biological mother, too. Obviously the woman had had the sense to say no.

Not like her. She was fool enough to jump at his offer. *And still would...* No, she told herself firmly, she wouldn't trust her heart on this; she'd trust her head. Her heart had got her in enough trouble already.

What about Rose? Should she be told? Rose had always known that she'd been *chosen* by her parents; that was the term Caroline and Beau had used. She didn't think Rose had a really clear understanding of the adoption process; the child was too young. Caroline decided she'd try not to think about that for now, wait until Rose was older and then, if she had questions, she'd deal with them.

Would he want access to his daughter? Would she have the heart to deny him? These were questions that made Caroline shudder.

She turned back to her lists. There were the last rounds of visits for her and Rose to make. They'd say goodbye to the Dempseys and to Katie's family, and drive over to

Tumpville to say goodbye to Angus. And, of course, there'd be tearful farewells with Mrs. T and Janie. Curley, too. No question, this summer in Alberta had been wonderful, for Rose and for her.

Well, the summer was over, Caroline thought, putting down her pen. And the wonderful was over, too.

She was glad it was Saturday, the busiest day of the week. She did her best not to arouse suspicions at breakfast, but it was difficult when she was so clearly ignoring Adam. Janie and Rose were particularly annoying, looking at each other and giggling, as though on cue. Over and over again.

She met Adam's glance once or twice, defiantly, to be cut to the heart by the brooding pain she saw in his steady gaze. Had he slept as little as she had last night?

She was hypersensitive to each tiny interaction between Rose and Adam, each smile, each little joke. She remembered the feeling she'd had when she first met him, the threatening sense that this stranger was dangerous, that he could harm them. Was this, then, what she'd instinctively known and feared? *Adam was Rose's father. He had the power to take her away from him.*

And then the worst thought of all: *she* was the stranger, not Adam.

That thought horrified her so much that her first impulse was to pack up and run.

No, she wasn't doing that anymore. She wasn't running from anything. Including Adam. And, really, where did she get such an idea? Adam had said nothing about taking Rose from her. He'd said nothing at all except that he thought she should know the truth.

She and Beau had legally adopted the child at birth. There was nothing Adam could do about that even if he wanted to. The law was wholly on her side. And they were

both Americans—he was a Canadian. That was bound to
make any efforts on his behalf more difficult.

Still, what had he said about his lawyer knowing about
Rose?

How would she get through tomorrow, when Mrs. T and
Janie went home? Once the Tetlock Valley guests left after
breakfast, maybe she and Rose should go somewhere, too.
To a beach. To Calgary. She couldn't bear the thought of
lying sleepless in her bed under Adam's roof, knowing he
lay so near, perhaps sleepless, too. How could she stop
herself from seeking solace in his arms—the arms of the
enemy?

Early Sunday afternoon Adam came into the office where
she was putting finishing touches to the plans for the Labor
Day party.

He walked to the window without saying anything. She
fumbled at the keyboard, making mistakes she'd normally
never make. Finally she shut down the machine. He was
staring out the window, every line of his body taut.

"You wanted to see me?"

He turned. He looked grim. Grim and determined. Caroline clenched her hands on her skirt, feeling the perspiration on her palms. Her heart was jumping around like a
cornered rabbit.

"Yes," he said slowly. "I have one or two things I want
to say to you."

"I'm glad you caught me," she began resolutely. "Rose
and I were thinking of going somewhere this afternoon.
Maybe come back tomorrow. In another hour or so I'd have
left," she finished brightly, despising herself for her mundane attempt at chatter.

"That's not necessary," he said, frowning. "Look,
there's no need to run away from me, Caroline. I'd never
hurt you or Rose in any way or impose myself—"

"Oh, I wasn't worried about that," she broke in, aware that her voice still sounded impossibly horribly chirpy.

"Then what were you worried about?"

"Nothing. Nothing at all." What a liar she was. Did it show? She was scared to death, and all of it—everything—had to do with him. And loss. She feared losing Rose; she feared losing Adam and the life he had offered her.

"Never mind that," he said abruptly. He took a deep breath and met her eyes. Caroline ached at the look in his. "Listen, Caroline. Nothing's changed, not for me. I want to marry you. My offer's still on the table. I'm not offering marriage because you have nothing to go back to in Seattle, the way it might have seemed when I first asked you. Besides, now it looks like you've got plenty to go back to. I'm offering because I care about you and Rose."

"Of course you do! *She's your daughter,*" Caroline burst out, trembling.

Adam stared at her for a long moment, until Caroline thought she'd scream. "You're right. Of course I care about Rose," he said slowly. "She *is* my daughter. She's the child I never thought I'd see. Naturally I care about her. I can even say I love her. I think that's understandable."

"And that's why you want *me.*"

"It's *not* why, goddammit!" he said roughly. "*Listen to me.* I didn't want this to happen between us. You must know that. I fought it every single step of the way. You were my best friend's widow. You worked for me. You adopted my child, you and my best friend. No, I didn't *want* this to happen.

"But it's happened, dammit. It's happened. I've fallen in love with you. I want to share my life with you. I want to marry you. *You.* Rose is…Rose is just icing on the cake. I know that sounds crazy, but it's true. If you turn me down for good, well, fine. You walk away and Rose goes with you. And whether or not you ever want to tell Rose about me or whether you ever want to let me see her again, that's up to you. You're her mother. You deserve every credit, you and Beau. I deserve nothing.''

He turned back to the window and Caroline quickly dashed at a tear. Dear Lord in heaven, how could they get through this? How could they deal with this pain? How could people talk about these things?

"It's true. I abandoned her, more or less," he said quietly. "I thought it was best at the time. Her mother didn't want to marry me and I'm damn glad she didn't. She had more sense than I did. We had nothing in common but this…this accident." He paused, then turned to face her again. "I still think it was best, Caroline. I couldn't have given Rose half what you and Beau have given her."

He walked to the door. "That's what I wanted to say. It's what I meant to say the other night. As usual—" he shrugged slightly "—I messed up. You have nothing to fear from me regarding Rose. Do you understand?"

She nodded, almost against her will.

"And if I hadn't fallen in love with you and realized I couldn't marry you with something like that hanging over my head, without you knowing the truth, I never would have told you about Rose. Do you understand that, too? You'd have gone away from here knowing no more than you've ever known."

He reached for the door, then added, "What would have been the point?"

CAROLINE PUT HER HEAD down on her keyboard and wept. She wept until there were no more tears, then bolted up, panicked that she'd ruined the keyboard. She dried it off with her skirt and went to the window he'd stood at, wiping her eyes with the backs of her hands.

She saw Curley carrying a bucket, with Rose skipping along beside him, as she so often did. One of the dogs limped along behind Rose. Old Stormy. The sky was bright, bright blue, not a cloud in sight.

It was a perfect picture. Everything was perfect here— except her. Rose had never been so happy. Adam wanted to marry her; she could have the baby she'd always wanted. *He was Rose's father.* Who would ever have dreamed that such a thing could happen to her and Rose and Adam? That she'd fall in love, by complete chance, with the man who'd fathered her beloved adopted daughter? Couldn't she forgive Adam and put this behind her—for Rose's sake?

Caroline got up early the next day. At breakfast she casually asked Adam if he'd mind looking out for Rose, because she was planning a trip to town and wouldn't be back until after lunch. He said he would, and they both ignored Rose's yips of glee as they stared at each other. Was this an indication that she trusted Adam with her daughter, that she was giving him another chance? Caroline didn't know. All she knew was that she had to get away by herself and do some serious thinking. And Rose liked spending time with Adam. Could she deny her daughter that simple pleasure?

Caroline drove and drove. She took all the back roads and the narrow paved secondary highways. She eventually ended up on the road to Glory. In town she decided to stop and see Adam's friend and lawyer, Lucas Yellowfly. As it happened, he was just leaving his office when she arrived. She introduced herself quickly in the foyer, ignoring the curious gaze of the steel-haired receptionist. Yellowfly, a tall extremely handsome man, took her arm and, with a glance at the receptionist, gestured toward the door.

"Let's talk over a coffee," he said, then nodded at the

clearly disapproving older woman. "Back in an hour, Mrs. Rutgers."

"But Harvey Jessop is coming in at eleven-fifteen—"

"I'll see him when I get back," he said firmly, and closed the door behind them both.

He took her arm with a smile and led her to a coffee shop a few doors down the street.

"So you're Mrs. Caroline Carter," he said, with a smile when they'd settled themselves in a booth. "I've been looking forward to meeting you. Adam tell you that?"

"He never mentioned it."

"He wouldn't." Lucas waved to a waitress and put up two fingers. "Coffee okay?" She nodded. "And bring us a couple pieces of carrot cake," he added as the waitress came a little closer. He flashed her a smile, then returned his attention to Caroline. "Adam's been trying to keep you all to himself."

"I don't think that's true," she said doubtfully. Lucas was teasing her, she decided. She had a good feeling about him; she decided to cut right to the chase. "I have something I'd like your advice on—as a friend of Adam's."

"Shoot." Lucas leaned across the table, his attention completely focussed.

"Adam told me you know about Rose."

The lawyer looked startled, just for a second. "Adam told you about Rose?" he asked slowly. "Well, well." He whistled under his breath.

"Yes. I'm afraid I...I've been pretty upset ever since he mentioned it." Caroline took a deep breath and squared her shoulders. "Adam asked me to marry him—maybe he told you? And I just can't even think straight, now that I know about Rose. I can't help thinking that all he wants is to be part of Rose's life and...and..."

Lucas covered her hands with his. "Shh. This is a pretty small town." He winked. "Here comes the coffee."

Caroline was grateful for the interruption. She couldn't believe how she'd opened up to this man she'd never met before.

"So Adam wants to marry you?" Lucas continued when the waitress had gone.

"Yes. That's what he says, but I don't know if I can... believe him."

"Okay. Now listen to me." Lucas drew his coffee toward him and took a sip. "I've known Adam for a long time. Let's see...twenty, twenty-five years. If he asked you to marry him—and, no, he never said a word to me—it's because he wants to marry you. Period. It's got nothing to do with Rose being his daughter. Trust me. Adam's not like that."

"So you don't think he'd ask me to marry him just so he could be Rose's real father?" Caroline felt a tiny ray of hope in her heart. She hadn't realized until now how much it mattered.

"Never." Lucas shook his head and picked up his fork. "There isn't a sneaky or underhanded bone in Adam Garrick's body. And I know damn well that he had no intention whatsoever of getting married again." Lucas attacked his cake. "Not," he said, looking up again, "until he met you."

Caroline watched him eat, feeling the import of his words sink through her, like rain on parched soil.

Lucas smiled. "You should try the carrot cake. Best in town."

"What about Rose? Has Adam ever wanted to, I don't know, try and get custody or anything?"

"Sorry, sweetheart. Lawyer-client privilege. Can't tell

you. But I can tell you this, and it's one-hundred-percent cross-my-heart-and-hope-to-die...."

"What's that?" She smiled at the lawyer's use of the childhood expression.

He leaned toward her again. "He loves you. He's crazy about you. It might have happened once, maybe even twice, but it'd never happen again—Adam would never ever in a million years ask a woman to marry him if he wasn't head over heels in love. Now go ahead—try that cake."

Caroline had to agree she'd never had better.

Oddly Angus Tump clarified the situation for her, too, when she drove out to the Tump homestead at Cayley. Mrs. T wasn't home, but was expected shortly, so Caroline sat in the sun with Angus and Janie to wait. She didn't know why she'd come, really, just found herself gravitating toward the Tumps as she had with Lucas in Glory.

It was an odd way to spend half an hour, Caroline thought more than once as she hugged her knees on the top step of the porch. First, Angus Tump said very little. Nor did Janie. When Angus did speak, Janie would clap her pudgy hands together and repeat a few of his words. It was unsettling, and yet at the same time oddly satisfying. No one expected anything of her. Not in the way of conversation or insights or decisions. Nothing. The only distraction came from the occasional dog sighing occasionally or getting up to change position from where it dozed in a heap in the shade or sun. Or from the sudden loud slap of the fly swatter if Angus spotted an insect within arm's length, or the creak of his chair as he rocked.

"Well, now. Take a look at yon bee, miss."

"Bee!" Janie crowed, clapping her hands. She beamed at her father.

Caroline glanced in the direction the old man indicated.

A few bees investigated the clover in the patch of scraggly grass in front of the homestead.

"Now, does a bee jump thisaway and thataway a-looking for clover honey? Why, no, he don't. He takes his time. What's the hurry?"

It was true. The bees steadily worked their way across the patch, methodically moving from one blossom to another. Some they left almost immediately; some they rested on for several seconds. What in heaven's name was Angus Tump saying?

"If he don't find honey in one blossom—perhaps it's dried up or t'other bee's been there ahead of him—why, he goes on to the next one. He don't jump every which way, he takes his time. Takes up the clover honey where he finds it."

"Honey!" Janie sang out, and her father grinned proudly at her.

"When he spots it, yessirree, he *jumps* on it."

"*Jumps!*"

Caroline stared at the old man. He was grinning widely, pipe stem clamped in his teeth. He seemed to be waiting for her comment.

"I've never heard you talk so much, Angus," she said with a smile.

He rested mild blue eyes on her. "Ain't that I don't talk, miss, just that I don't use a lotta words, that's all." He happily tamped his pipe bowl with a stained and dirty thumb and ran a wooden match over the sole of his shoe. He sucked greedily at the flame, sending a cloud of fragrant smoke into the afternoon air.

Bees. What in heaven's name was Angus Tump going on about?

CHAPTER TWENTY-THREE

By THE TIME Caroline drove into the Double O yard, she'd been thinking about bees for twenty miles. She knew what Angus Tump had meant. Of course he couldn't possibly know the significance of what he'd said to her, but nevertheless... He was a strange man. She didn't discount anything he said.

Caroline parked and sat in the station wagon for a few minutes. She was later than she'd thought she'd be—it was near suppertime already—but she'd called Adam to let him know. He hadn't said much on the phone, except that he and Rose had had a good day together.

Those bees...

Maybe she should think about her own happiness. Maybe she should be like the bee that, as Angus had said, takes up the clover honey where he finds it.

Maybe she should do the same. Things would never be perfect. Her feelings for Adam and Rose and this place were about as perfect as it was possible to get. She was no naive teenager; she'd been around the block a time or two. With Beau. With his death. With the Carters. She'd had her share of grief, as well as real happiness. She was young. Maddie had told her she deserved happiness. Did she?

All Adam had done was ask for a second chance. He hadn't told her about Rose earlier because, as he said, what would have been the point? Wasn't that proof positive that he didn't have designs on her child? If things hadn't happened the way they had between her and Adam, she never would've known Adam had fathered Rose. Just as she'd most likely never know who the biological mother was unless she asked Adam and she didn't think she ever would.

All he wanted was a chance. Caroline felt like crying as she reached for the doorhandle, but she'd cried enough lately. It was in her power to give Adam that second chance. It was in her power to give Rose a father—to give them all a family. They could all use a second chance.

Caroline walked into the house. She didn't feel the way she had when she'd walked out that morning.

"Hi!" Rose was sitting at the kitchen table. Adam was standing at the stove, spatula in hand. He turned his head as she entered.

She stopped and leaned against the kitchen doorjamb. Rose had propped Raggy on pillows on a second chair beside her. There was a small bowl and spoon in front of the doll.

"My, this is a domestic scene," she teased, her voice not quite as steady as she'd hoped.

Adam's gaze caught hers. She read the hope there, hope she knew was reflected in her own eyes.

"We're having soup, me 'n' Raggy. Tomato, 'cause Mr. Adam can't find any more chicken-noodle. He says, guess you ate it all up, Rosie. That's just what he said, guess you ate it all up, Rosie. Want some?" she invited, gesturing toward a third chair at the table.

Caroline came a little farther into the kitchen.

"You can be my mommy," Rose went on. "I'm pretending he's my daddy and he's—" she pointed at Adam "—making supper for all of us. I'm the baby," she finished importantly, pointing to her own small chest, "and she's the baby, too. We're twins, her and me." She nodded at Raggy. "We're having grilled cheese."

Caroline could not have torn her eyes from Adam's if the house had fallen down around them. *I'll be the mommy, if you'll be the daddy....*

"Hey, what are you two smiling about so much?" Rose demanded, looking from her to Adam and back again. Adam moved toward her, spatula in hand. Caroline hoped he'd remembered to turn off the flame under the grilled cheese sandwiches.

"Hey! That's just what I was wishing for—mommies and daddies are *s'posed* to kiss like that. Janie said so. Yippee!" And Rose stood on her chair and laughed and clapped her hands.

Adam broke away long enough to sweep Rose into his arms and hold them both close. He was laughing, too. So was Caroline. And crying. She didn't know happiness could feel so good and hurt so much all at the same time.

The following June

IT HAD TAKEN Caroline a month to conceive. And that hadn't been for want of trying, Adam thought, as he jumped in his pickup and headed down the Double O lane toward the highway. Caroline had come into his bedroom the night after she'd said she'd marry him, dressed in some incredibly brief black lacy thing and said she didn't want any more surprises from him, just whether their second-born would be a girl or a boy.

He hoped he hadn't disappointed her. Adam touched the accelerator, glancing at the plume of dust in his rearview mirror. Another hot dry June afternoon, like the day he got the letter from her. This day was just as special.

The school bus would be at the lane in ten minutes, and Adam didn't want to be late. He had news for Rose.

He parked and got out and watched the bus approach, lights flashing red. He straightened from where he'd been leaning against the hood, arms crossed, as Rose hopped off the high bus step. He nodded at the bus driver, Charlie

Golightly, one of old Farley's distant cousins, whom he'd known all his life.

"Where's Janie?"

Rose thrust her book bag and lunch box at him. "She's coming. Hurry up, Janie!" she called. Then she turned back to him, eyes alight. "We goin' somewhere, Mr. Dad?"

Adam loved it when she called him that. Most times these days she called him Daddy, and he loved that, too. But "Mr. Dad" was special.

"Remember I told you I took your mommy to the hospital in Glory last night after you'd gone to bed?" He couldn't wipe the grin from his face.

"Yep. Oh—here comes Janie!" Rose jumped up and down and called to her friend, who was panting as she waddled toward them both, a big grin on her round face. She carried a lunch box, too, which she also thrust at Adam.

"Here!" she said, brushing her hands together briskly.

"Get in the truck, you two. I'm taking you both to visit somebody."

He tossed the lunch boxes and book bags into the back of the pickup while the two girls yelled and jostled with each other to get in. Rose ended up in the middle, Janie by the door. Adam reached across and locked it and made sure they both had their seat belts on.

"Remember how you wanted a baby sister or a brother someday, Rosie?"

"Uh-huh." She looked at Janie and they both turned to him, eyes wide.

"Well, you've got a baby brother, sweetheart, and he's damn near as good-looking as you are."

The cab filled with the girls' whoops, and Adam couldn't wipe the smile off his face all the way to Glory. He was a father—again.

If this was family life, Beau had been right. It was sure worth trying the second time round.

Three females under one roof…
How lucky can a guy get?

GETTIN' LUCKY
Kimberly Raye

1

FOR CABDRIVER Lucky Myers, the only thing worse than bursting into tears was doing it smack-dab in the middle of Houston's largest airport. On a busy Friday morning. And on a major PMS day.

"Yo, Lucky!" came the familiar male voice.

And in front of Buster would-you-look-at-the-hooters-on-that-one? Sinclair, fellow cabdriver and male chauvinist extraordinaire.

If it wasn't for bad luck, I'd have no luck at all. She swiped at her eyes and handed the passenger who got out of her cab a travel bag.

"Thanks so much for being understanding," said the woman, dressed in a cherry-red suit. "And for listening." She shoved her suitcases at a nearby baggage clerk. "I just knew I was going to miss my plane, but thanks to you I'll make it!"

A treacherous tear slid from the corner of Lucky's eye and she dashed it away, disgusted with herself. Geez, she could sympathize with the woman, but she didn't have to do it in front of hundreds of travelers. Besides, people had heart attacks every day. Just because the woman's father had suffered a severe one and was, at this moment, hanging on to life by little more than a thread didn't give Lucky any call to act like a blubbering idiot. She hardly knew her, much less the father.

But she knew how the woman felt. Lucky had lost her

own father last year. When the passenger had climbed into
the back of the cab and poured out her tearful story, Lucky
might very well have been hearing her own. Minus the
husband and daughter waiting at home in some little rinky-
dink Texas town, of course.

She sniffled, struggling for her composure as Buster
headed straight for her.

Black hair slicked back à la Elvis, he wore a neon-pink
flamingo-print shirt unbuttoned to midchest and a dozen
faux gold chains around his neck. Shirttails flapped in the
wind, giving an occasional glimpse of the overstuffed
waistline of his much-too-tight white jeans.

But the absolute worst thing about Buster, who looked
at anything with breasts, was the fact that he never even
spared Lucky a glance. Not that she wanted him to, mind
you. But it was the principle of the thing. All of her life,
male attention had passed her by in favor of better faces,
bigger breasts, more shapely rear ends. That bad-luck thing
again.

"Hiya, babe," he said, coming up to her. "You just drop
off the fare you picked up at the Four Seasons? I bet she
tipped out the wazoo. Stella said she was loaded."

Oh no! Lucky shot a watery gaze at her meter box. A
sick feeling churned in the pit of her stomach. Forget the
tip. The woman hadn't even paid her fare and Lucky had
been too worried about helping the poor, distraught thing
unload her luggage to notice.

She whirled, blinking furiously as she strained to see
through the crowd. She caught a glimpse of a red skirt, red
three-inch heels clattering behind a cart of speeding luggage.

"Hey!" she shouted. "Wait!" But the flash of color was
gone and so was Lucky's eighty-dollar cab fare.

Eighty dollars. The sick feeling graduated to full-blown nausea. More tears burned her eyes.

"So how much tip—whoa, do my eyes deceive me? Can this be tough-as-nails Lucky Myers *crying?*"

"I'm not crying. It's just allergies."

"You have allergies and moved to Texas? This is the pollen capital of the South..." The words faded when a blonde in a halter top swayed past them. "Wow. Would you look at the hoo—"

"Is that all you ever think of?" Lucky snapped.

"What can I say? I'm a romantic kind of guy." He waggled his bushy black eyebrows, the expression like two caterpillars doing a mating dance.

Lucky couldn't hold back a smile. Buster's outlook on women was so totally clueless, it was hard to keep a straight face, much less stay mad at the guy. "So you skipped all the way across the taxi lane to tell me what a Valentino you are?"

"Actually, no," he said, his hand going to his hip pocket. Due to the extraordinary tightness of his pants it took him a good thirty seconds before the envelope finally squirmed free. "When I checked in for my shift at the cab company, the mailman was there with this letter. Stella asked me to give it to you since I was headed your way. She thought it might be important."

Lucky took the envelope, her attention stuck on the return address: Marshall Nursing Home. She ripped open the seal and read the statement of account. The dread churning in her stomach settled into a hard lump by the time she reached the sum printed at the bottom. Oh no.

"Your grandma?"

"Yeah."

"She's okay, right?"

"She's fine." Lucky folded the letter and slipped it into

her pocket. "Everything's fine, as long as I win the lottery."

"That nursing home really eating up your cash?"

"Yeah, but it's worth it." Despite her mood, she managed a smile. "It's got this beautiful flower garden, with roses and daisies. That's why Daddy moved her down here from Chicago." Her eyes burned with a new bout of tears and she blinked. "He managed the expense when he was alive, and so will I. There's still three weeks until the payment is due. I've got nearly two thousand saved for school..." Suddenly the lump in her stomach felt like burning lead. If she drained her savings, she wouldn't be able to pay her tuition in the spring. At the rate she was going, she would never finish her teaching degree.

But her granny was the only family she had left now.

"I can do this," she said, more for herself than Buster. "With my savings and a few extra shifts on the weekends, I can make the three thousand."

"Whew!" Buster whistled. "Three thousand. I guess bowling with me and the guys is out tomorrow night then."

"I'm afraid so." Though that in itself was a blessing. Lucky wasn't in the mood for another Saturday night spent watching Buster and the guys guzzle beer and ogle women at the Bowl-A-Rama. She'd started Saturday night bowling in a desperate effort to beef up her nonexistent social life. How was she supposed to meet Mr. Perfect if she didn't get out and mingle? Unfortunately, Mr. Perfect, or even Mr. Almost Perfect, didn't hang out at the Bowl-A-Rama.

A good man. That's all she wanted out of life. That, her teaching degree and three thousand dollars. The last two she could earn, but the man was another story. How could she find herself a good one when even the not-so-good ones didn't give her the time of day?

"Geez, babe," Buster went on, "we're bowling against

the Fast Cab Kangaroos and we really need that arm of yours—'' He fell silent when he saw an attractive woman, bags in hand, standing near his abandoned cab. ''Later, babe. I think I'm in love.'' He made a beeline for his taxi.

''Lucky?'' came the female voice from the CB mounted on Lucky's dash. ''Are you finished at the airport yet? I've got a fare going from the Hyatt Regency to the convention center.''

''I'm on it, Stella,'' she said into the mike. Then she climbed into the back seat of her cab and bent to retrieve a gum wrapper. ''Holy Moses,'' Lucky breathed when she spotted a man's wallet stuffed with a wad of bills. Not fives, or tens, or even twenties, she quickly discovered. No, there were a few fifties, and the rest were hundreds. Hundreds!

The answer to Lucky's feverish prayers. No more overtime. No more double shifts...

Before she could drop to her knees and thank the powers above, the red-dressed woman's desperate words replayed in her head. *''One minute my poor daddy was fine, and the next, he was at Death's door. I just don't know what I'll do if I lose him.''*

The wallet had to belong to the woman. Lucky had a habit of checking the cab after every customer, and she knew it hadn't been there before the stop at the Four Seasons. Sympathy swept through Lucky like a heat wave through Houston. The woman had probably been in such a hurry, she hadn't bothered to transfer the money and credit cards to her own wallet. She'd simply grabbed her husband's and rushed off to be with her father. Now the poor thing had no money, no wallet, nothing. She was destitute. Unless...

Lucky could turn over the wallet to the police and let them make the return. But with her string of rotten luck, it would likely get stuck in a bunch of red tape. No, speed was important. The woman's father was dying. Death didn't wait for the mail, or even Federal Express.

Lucky opened the wallet, her gaze flicking over the dozens of credit cards peeking from the leather slots. Finally she found an ID card with a man's name—undoubtedly the husband's—and an address for their hometown. Locking up her cab, she rushed to a nearby pay phone and dialed Information.

"I'm sorry, but that number is unlisted," the operator said.

"But this is an emergency, a major emergency. You see, one of my customers left her husband's wallet in my cab, and I'm afraid she doesn't have any other money and she's off to see her father who's dying and—"

"Rules are rules. Would you like me to check another number for you?"

"No," Lucky replied. "Thanks, anyway." She slid the receiver into place and walked back to her cab.

She knew what she should do, but that would mean giving up an entire day's worth of work. The nursing-home bill burned through her pocket. *Remember me?* Remember Granny and the three-thousand-dollar flowers? On the other hand, her conscience wouldn't let her forget the woman's frantic voice. "He's dying. My poor daddy's dying."

"Okay," she finally said. She hauled open the door to her cab. "The Lucky Express to the rescue."

Reaching into her own pocket, Lucky counted out eighty dollars and slid the money into the fare box. She'd do the Good Samaritan thing, take the wallet back to the husband, then collect her eighty bucks from him. Better to cover the fare with her own money and wait an extra day than go back and tell Stella and the other cabbies she'd been stiffed.

That would be almost as bad as the crying—

She was *not* crying.

Lucky placed the wallet on the seat next to her, revved the engine and pulled into the flow of traffic. Grabbing the CB mike, she radioed Stella that she was taking the day off, much to the other woman's astonishment. A quick road trip and the wallet predicament would be solved. Then she could concentrate on making the nursing-home money, and go back to hunting for Mr. Perfect.

Of course, she'd have to try a new hunting ground. The Bowl-A-Rama was a complete bust. Maybe she could answer one of those singles ads. Or call one of those dating services. Yeah, those were possibilities. Okay, so maybe they were more like long shots, but a girl had to start somewhere.

HELL. She'd driven straight into the middle of hell.

Only hell could be this hot in October.

Just her luck, she thought, blowing a large bubble with her chewing gum. Lucky had never lived up to her name. Now, if she'd been called *Un*lucky Myers, well, that would have hit the nail right on the head. A flat tire, a broken air conditioner and at least a hundred extra miles she hadn't counted on—all in the past four hours. What a way to kill a Friday afternoon. So much for this trip being simple.

At least it couldn't get any worse, she thought as she blew another bubble. She hefted the tire she'd just changed into the trunk, then leaned against the bumper to catch her breath.

On second thought… The pressure built and she crossed her legs. Blast that six-pack of diet soda! She should have thrown every can back into the cooler when she'd stopped in Ulysses, the last resemblance to a town she'd seen since getting stuck in a maze of back roads. It seemed that Tyler Grant, the name written on the ID card, didn't actually live in Ulysses. The Grant spread was just "a spit and a throw past the Grant County limits,'' the waitress at Big Bubba's Diner had told her when she'd stopped to ask directions. If only Lucky knew exactly how far ''a spit and a throw'' was, she'd be in business.

Somebody upstairs was definitely out to get her. First the heat, and now acres and acres of land with no sign of civilization, much less a rest room. Right now, she'd settle for a tree. A quick glance around at the endless stretch of pastureland, and she realized that was about as likely as Brad Pitt beating down her door for a date—*Come on, Brad!* Her gaze fixed on a patch of trees in the distance.

She slammed the trunk closed. ''Sorry, baby, but you're on your own for the next few minutes.'' She stroked the Chevy's hood. Her father had loved this car with a vengeance, and Lucky had loved him, and while he might be gone, there was a part of him still with her. She smiled and patted the Chevy again. ''Don't go picking up any men without me.'' Then she grabbed a few tissues and headed for the white wooden fence lining the road.

Shade! her heated body screamed.

Relief! cried the six-pack yearning to be free.

She walked and sweated. And sweated and walked, until her cab disappeared behind her and perspiration drenched her T-shirt. Finally, after a good ten minutes dodging her way past cow patties, she reached the blessed shade. Not merely a few trees, she quickly realized, but a full-blown forest. She walked deeper before finding a spot to relieve the drought for a patch of thirsty grass.

Afterward, she turned to head back the way she'd come. Then turned again. And again. Lost. Great. Just *great.*

Her ears perked up when she heard a noise. *Clop-clop...* Desperate, she followed the sound through the maze of trees. Either she found a way out of here, or she'd melt. Like an ice-cream cone in a microwave oven.

Not that she was whining. Okay, so maybe a little. But even old Satan would be confessing his sins in this heat, *if* he found it bearable. Which he wouldn't. It wasn't hell, it was hotter than hell. Yep, the devil would have already bargained his soul and packed a bag for the Poconos.

Then again, she admitted several minutes later as she stared past the branches of an enormous tree, the Poconos were a little overrated. Her attention fixed on the very big, very dangerous-looking man who'd just galloped up to the river on one of the most beautiful horses Lucky had ever seen.

So the devil rode a horse. Well, she *was* in Texas.

TYLER GRANT REINED his mount to a halt, slid to the ground and unzipped his pants. Seconds later, he stood on the isolated riverbank completely naked, and mad as hell.

Damn that woman!

The past twenty-four hours rushed through his head with all the fury of a tornado. Hell, he felt as if he'd been hit by one.

He had. One in the form of an educated, attractive, reputable nanny, who'd turned out to be nothing more than a thieving con artist. He still couldn't believe it. He'd handpicked the woman from a dozen applications provided by the Dalton Agency, one of the most reputable employment agencies in the state, and checked each one of her impeccable references himself. It had all been a lie, he'd been scammed, and now he was in big trouble.

And he always came here when he was in trouble.

The water winked at him, its mirrorlike surface catching rays of sunlight that spilled through the branches of the towering trees sheltering the river. Memories pulled at him of long-ago summers: inner tubes tied to the surrounding trees, excited boys swinging out over the river, plunging into the water...

He stepped into the river. The water embraced his heated, tense body, pulled at his muscles to relax. Despite the past few hours, the never-ending demands of the ranch, the phone calls to the local sheriff about the thieving nanny, he smiled. The water was heaven. Home. God, it had been so long. Too long.

Guilt shot through Tyler and fired his resolve. He was home now, and he was staying, or so he hoped.

He had to find a new nanny, and fast.

His mother-in-law arrived tomorrow and she expected a governess for her granddaughter. If Helen Bell-Whitman didn't find one—one that met her high standards—he knew she'd cause such a ruckus they'd hear her all the way to the next county. His ears still rang from the moment he'd told Helen he was going home, and that was almost two months ago.

"You're going to go play nursemaid for a man who's had simple eye surgery? Hire someone to nurse him, Tyler. His condition is far from life threatening."

"It's not that simple," he'd told her. "Someone has to look after the ranch. Dad'll be out of circulation for at least a couple of months until his eyes heal from the surgery. He just purchased a new stud and somebody has to oversee the breeding."

"Breeding? Tyler, you're a partner in one of the largest private investment firms in the country, for heaven's sake! You run board meetings, not breeding sessions. Hire someone to handle that revolting work for you."

"He's my father, Helen." And I owe him, he added silently. For all those years I left him alone.

"There's no need to dirty your own hands over some

misguided sense of duty. You're an investment banker, not a rancher."

In another life, he thought. That part of him was dead and buried alongside his late wife. Nan had wanted him to be a banker, just as his own mother had wanted it. He'd given up the ranch for them, for a different world where he'd never fit in.

But this he was doing not only for his father, but also for his daughter, Bernadette. To show her another side of her heritage and see her smile again. And he *liked* getting his hands dirty. Working cattle involved dirt and sweat, calluses and aching muscles, and he'd never felt more alive.

Of course, Helen couldn't comprehend such a thing. And nothing would keep her from drawing battle lines and forcing Bernadette to choose, when—if—Helen found out what had happened with the nanny. Ulysses or Houston. Tyler or Helen.

Bennie would never have to make such a choice and suffer the consequences. Tyler would see to that. He closed his eyes and waded out deeper. Water lapped at his thighs. He would just have to find somebody, anybody, and soon. Helen flew in at Stoney's airstrip tomorrow afternoon for her first visit/checkup. Surely he could find somebody by then? He had connections. A few calls and he could have somebody here by late morning. She wouldn't be a Dalton woman, but he would just have to make do. Any nanny was better than no nanny at all.

OKAY, so he wasn't the devil, Lucky concluded after drinking in every incredible inch of his backside, from broad shoulders to narrow waist, to the most gorgeous rear end she'd ever seen. She'd only had a glimpse when he'd tossed off his clothes and headed for the water. But now that he stood in the shallow part of the river, she had a much better view. He was definitely just a man. A very *naked* man. *Oh, boy.*

He had buns that put Mel Gibson's to shame.

She blinked, but he didn't disappear. *They* didn't disappear.

Tight, tanned, muscular and curved just so...

And lethal to her sanity, she decided as she glanced down and saw that she'd stepped from the shelter of trees. She inched backward and took cover behind a thick tree trunk. Peering around the tree's edge, she directed her attention back to him.

To *them.*

She couldn't help wondering what kind of workout would yield such spectacular results. Undoubtedly a rigorous one, with a lot of flexing, pumping, grinding... A Flex Your Fanny video? A Terrific Tush workout seat? Probably some pumping and grinding of an entirely different nature.

Water rippled and she shrank back behind the tree just as the man stared over his shoulder. All she needed was to be caught trespassing. From what she'd seen of Ulysses, the county seat and home to the world's largest pecan, she'd be strung up to the nearest tree—

Her thoughts ground to a halt as her eyes riveted to his face. It wasn't so much that he was handsome. He was, in a Marlboro man sort of way. Rugged, tough... But more than anything, he was...male. There was nothing feminine about his strong jaw, firm lips, chiseled nose. And his eyes... She couldn't see the color, but somehow she could feel their heat. The heat when a man looks at a woman *that* way. The way Rhett looked at Scarlett. The way Romeo looked at Juliet. The way Buster looked at anything with breasts bigger than his. But Tight Tush wasn't looking at a woman, he was looking at *her,* and she felt that gaze head-on for the first time in her life.

Panic bolted through her and she even stopped chewing her gum for an endless moment. Surely he'd seen her. He looked as if he'd seen her. She felt as if he'd seen her.

Infinite seconds ticked by until his gaze passed the spot where she hid. Then he turned back around. Lucky resumed her chewing. Of course he hadn't been looking *at* her. He didn't even know she was there. Story of her life.

Reason kicked in and she inched backward. She had to get out of there before he really did catch a glimpse of her, not to mention that she had a wallet to return. Time was money. But then he scooped up several handfuls of water, doused them onto his body and she lost what little common sense she had.

The muscles in his arms rippled, catching gleaming rays of sunlight. Water streamed over his shoulders, down the curve of his back and those spectacular buns. She'd wind up dangling from the nearest tree for sure, but at least she'd die a happy woman. Lucky wiped at another trickle of sweat. Hot. Miserable. Thank God she'd brought an extra pack of chewing gum, otherwise her throat would be sand-paper—

Pop!

The bubble burst. Gum flattened against her face. And Tight Tush jerked around. Lucky ducked back behind the tree trunk, snatched the gum from her mouth and threw it away disgustedly. How could she have forgotten about it? Because she'd been chewing gum for ages, a habit that even hypnosis hadn't been able to cure. She was addicted. And stupid, she thought as she clamped her eyes shut and held her breath.

Water rippled, but otherwise, she heard no sound. Nothing, just her own breathing and the frantic beat of her heart. She kept her eyes closed, her back glued to the tree, out of his sight. Maybe she'd finally lucked out. Maybe he hadn't seen her. Lord knew she was due...

Her skin prickled with the strange awareness that someone was watching her and she changed her mind. She'd been caught in the act. A Peeping Tom. She could read the headlines now: Love-Starved Cabbie Resorts To Spying On Unsuspecting Men—

"Enjoying the view?" The slow drawl, rich and deep and slightly amused, slid into her ears.

Lucky's heart stalled, only to rev full speed ahead when she lifted one lid a fraction and saw a pair of large, tanned feet, the toes mere inches from the tips of her sneakers.

Her one eye opened farther and her gaze traveled up a pair of muscular legs encased in faded and slightly damp jeans. The material molded every muscle, showing off his lean calves, powerful thighs. Her gaze hit his zippered fly that was only half zipped, and stopped for a long moment. A wave of heat rushed to her cheeks and she forced her other eye open to get the full view. Not that she actually saw *it*, not that she wanted to, of course. Where the metal teeth parted, she saw only tanned skin and a funnel of dark, silky hair that swirled up over an incredibly tight abdomen. But the sight was enough to make her swallow. Hard.

"I guess you are." Tyler folded his arms across his chest and swept his gaze over the woman. At least he thought it was a woman. It was hard to tell, dressed as she was in faded baggy jeans— He did a double take. Make that unfastened jeans.

He stored that information for safekeeping and pushed his attention higher to the T-shirt plastered to her chest. The white material clung to her, outlining small but perfectly shaped breasts. Her nipples swelled, stretching the material to taut little points and he did some heavy-duty swallowing of his own. Okay, it wasn't that hard to tell. Definitely a woman.

"W-what?"

Her question forced his gaze to the final frontier. Her hair lay hidden beneath her cap, with the exception of a few dark tendrils collapsed against the slender curve of her neck. Her cheeks were flushed from the heat, her pink lips parted, her face damp with perspiration.

"I'm sorry," she went on. Wide eyes the color of warm cocoa collided with his. "I didn't hear you."

He smiled. "I asked if you were enjoying the view." But Tyler was doing a little enjoying of his own. Not so much from the sight of her, even though that was agreeable enough. No, it was the way she looked at him. Like a child eyeing the last cookie, the want plain and undisguised in her big brown eyes, and she didn't even know the size of his bank account. Of course, his money wasn't all women were interested in. He'd met some who just wanted a roll in the hay. But this one was different. Mixed in with that hungry light was an innocence he hadn't seen in a long time. And with all that hungry innocence directed at him, his jeans grew awful snug in certain strategic places.

"So are you?" he asked, shifting his stance to give a specific body part a little more room.

"Yeah—I mean no. I mean..." She shook her head. "Yes, the view was—is nice, but that's not why I'm standing here."

"Really? Then why are you standing here?"

"I had a flat tire on the dirt road back there." She turned and pointed, but couldn't quite make up her mind in which direction. "Some dirt road. Anyway, I'm not sure where it's at now. That's why I'm here. I'm lost."

"Lost? So that's why you were spying on me?"

"Exactly—no, not exactly. Look, I heard water and

thought I might find someone who could steer me in the right direction.''

''So why didn't you ask me for directions instead of hiding behind this tree?''

''I wasn't hiding.'' He raised his eyebrows and watched her face flush an even brighter crimson. ''Okay, so I was hiding.''

''Not a very effective way to get directions. I would have come right out and asked.''

''Oh, really? You'd ask a naked stranger for directions?''

''I would if the naked stranger were me.''

''But that doesn't make any sense. You can't be your own naked stranger.''

''Good point. Let's see, who could be my naked stranger?'' He stepped closer, one arm shooting out to lean against the tree. He gazed at the unfastened button on her jeans. ''Wait a second. *You* could be my naked stranger.''

''What are you talking—'' She glanced down. ''Uh-oh.''

''Planning on joining me in my nakedness?''

''Of course not.'' She closed her eyes and shook her head. ''Great. This is just great.''

''Not yet, but it could be.''

Her eyes snapped open. ''What?''

''This—you and me—two naked strangers.''

''I think one naked stranger is enough.'' She grabbed at her waistband with frantic fingers.

''Here. Let me.''

''No, that's all right. This always happens to me—'' His fingers brushed hers. Flesh met flesh and her hands stilled. Their gazes locked as they waited to see what he would do next.

Another breathless moment and Tyler slid the button into place. The action seemed to relax her. Relief eased her expression. "Do you always walk around with your pants undone?"

"My pants, my shoelaces, a few buttons on my shirt." She gave him a look that said she'd given the subject a great deal of thought. "I try, but it seems I'm always missing something."

"That must be quite a sight. A shame you're not from around here."

"No, it's fortunate." She blew out a long breath. "Geez, but it's hot here. Speaking of which, where is here?"

"Here is private property."

"Oh." As if she'd been caught with her hand in the cookie jar, instead of simply ogling the cookie, she added, "I'm sorry. If you'll point me in the right direction, I'll be going."

"I thought you didn't ask naked strangers for directions?"

"You're not naked. Not anymore."

He glanced down at his bare chest. "Almost."

"Well, almost isn't naked." She ducked under his arm and moved around him. "Is it?"

"No, but it's close enough." He turned toward her, closing the few inches of distance she'd opened between them.

"I could scream."

"You could, but what for? Because I'm a stranger, or because I'm almost naked?"

"Maybe both."

"But I'm not the stranger here. You are. Besides," he said, holding up his hands. "I never molest trespassers. Shoot them maybe. But never molest them." His words drew a smile from her. "So tell me, how did you get this far off the road?"

"I was looking for a tree. One tree." She laughed. "Now I'm surrounded by them."

"Well, to get unsurrounded, you head that way." He pointed to his left. "Straight through those trees about five minutes, then you'll be in open pasture. You'll see the road from there."

"Thanks."

"My pleasure."

"No," she said over her shoulder as she started off through the trees. "It was definitely my pleasure. You've got a great set of buns."

"I wish I could say the same." But her jeans were too baggy and he couldn't quite make out any curves. And that was the real shame, he thought as he watched her disappear between two towering oaks, because it had been quite a while since Tyler Grant had wanted to look. Really wanted to look. *Damn.*

If he'd had even half the wild child left in him, he'd have coaxed her out of those pants and seen for himself. But sixteen years away had tamed the hellion he'd once been. At thirty-two, he was exactly what his mother had always wanted him to be: a gentleman. Funny thing was, Tyler Grant had never regretted it until now.

2

WHEN LUCKY finally broke free from the trees, she saw her cab on the horizon. Breathless moments later, she vaulted over the fence and stared behind her. The pasture was empty, the grass swaying with the faint breeze. Not a sign of Tight Tush.

Unfortunately, her hormones whispered.

Thankfully, her brain corrected. As if he would have followed her in the first place. He'd been flirting. Just innocent flirting. She'd seen it time and time again.

But no one had ever directed any flirting at her and she was still a little shaken up over it. More so because she'd liked it. Yeah, she'd liked it a lot, she thought, climbing into the cab.

She definitely had to step up her manhunting efforts. Maybe if she smiled a little, invested in one of those push-up bras, she might persuade Buster— Wait a minute. Buster?

Yeah, Buster, her desperate hormones insisted. He was nice enough, maybe a little crass. He didn't do drugs, though she often wondered, considering how clueless he was when it came to the opposite sex. He was sweet at times. Funny. Obnoxious.

Available, her hormones chimed in. And gainfully employed, and that's all Lucky really needed.

That, and to find Tyler Grant, she thought as she shot a glance at the wallet sitting next to her on the seat.

She'd barely started the engine when she heard sirens. She glanced in her rearview mirror to see a cloud of dust on the horizon and a set of whirling red and blue lights. The sheriff's car pulled up behind her in a matter of seconds.

Lucky killed the engine when two uniform-clad officers climbed out of the car. One was a large man, intimidating in his starched beige uniform and wide-brimmed hat. Straight out of an old *Smokey and the Bandit* movie. She adjusted her rearview mirror to get a glimpse of his side-kick. He looked friendlier, his expression mildly curious as he licked an ice-cream cone.

"Can I see some ID, miss?" It was Smokey, leaning down, peering into the driver's window to capture her in the glare of his aviator sunglasses.

"You guys should have been here an hour ago," Lucky said, handing him her identification and proof of insurance. "I wouldn't have had to lug the spare out of the trunk myself."

"This is an Illinois license, miss, and it's expired."

"Oops. I forgot." One hand dived into the leather pouch hooked onto her radio knob. She rummaged through a mess of receipts, several sticks of chewing gum, a few tissues, until she finally found a crumpled slip of paper. "Here's the current license. I'm new here. Transplanted from Chicago." She gave him a wide smile.

His expression didn't even crack.

So much for southern hospitality.

Smokey scoured the papers, and Lucky had the sudden urge to check her speedometer. But she hadn't been speeding. The car hadn't even been moving. So why did she feel so guilty?

A glimpse of naked flesh and rippling muscles flashed in front of her and her face grew hot. Her gaze cut to Smokey.

Did he know? Had Tight Tush actually reported her for trespassing? He'd been so nice, so helpful, so...well, naked. She wiped a trickle of sweat from her temple. She hadn't seen a cellular phone. Actually, she hadn't seen much of anything besides—

"Long way from Houston," Smokey said.

"Just four hours. Is there something wrong, Officer?"

Silence stretched between them while Smokey handed her back her ID. "No," he started, his gaze sweeping the interior of the car. "We've had some trouble nearby so we're checking out all suspicious-looking vehicles—" The words stalled when those mirrored glasses came to rest on the wallet next to her.

"I think you'd better step out of the car. Now. We just caught you red-handed, missy."

Lucky closed her eyes at Smokey's words. How much time could she get for trespassing? Spying? Surely a fine was the most they could give her. "Look, this is all really just a big misunderstanding. I know I shouldn't have climbed the fence, but I had no choice. The diet soda just ran right through me."

"What the hell are you talking about?" Smokey demanded.

"Trespassing. That is why you're here, isn't it?"

"Hell, no, miss. We're here about a burglary. The perpetrator was last spotted headed down this road, out of town."

"*Burglary?*" Was Tight Tush really a burglar? An escapee from the local prison farm? "He didn't look like a dangerous criminal." Okay, maybe dangerous, she amended silently. Very dangerous, to her sanity, that is.

"You're under arrest."

"*Me?* But I just had to go to the rest room. And there he was. I couldn't help but look. Had I known he was a hardened criminal..." Her mouth went dry at the fitting vision the words conjured. "Er, that is, a criminal, I would have gone first thing to the cops. I swear—"

"Tell it to the judge." Smokey reached for handcuffs.

"But I didn't do anything wrong. You can't arrest me for unwilling spying. I did trespass, but it was an emergency and—"

"You're not under arrest for trespassing or spying, missy. You're under arrest for burglary." He motioned to the wallet his sidekick had picked up from the front seat.

"But I didn't steal that. I found it."

"Check for a weapon, Billy," Smokey told the sidekick.

"I don't have a gun!" she insisted. When he went to snap the handcuffs on her wrists, she tried to jerk free. "This is crazy! I was only taking a little leak, then a little peek, and I certainly didn't rob anyone! This is unlawful arrest!"

He snapped first one cuff on, then the other, before whirling her to face the cab. "Evidence doesn't lie. A wallet and several other items were reported stolen by Mr. Tyler Grant and we just found you in possession of that wallet." He started to pat her down and Lucky's face flamed hotter. He reached her sides and she erupted into a fit of giggles.

"Ahhhhhh! Please! Stop it," she begged, choking when tears started in her eyes. Another pat, another suppressed giggle and Smokey held up a pack of bubble gum. "I didn't know gum was considered dangerous in this state," she snorted, her eyes still watering, nerves still tingling.

"Quiet, missy. You find anything else besides the wallet?" he asked Billy. "Any of the other stuff?"

"A couple of packs of chewing gum, an air freshener, a flashlight. Back seat's clean."

"Maybe she hid the rest, or ditched some of it when she

saw us coming. Dammit, I told Tyler not to bring no city woman out here. Steal you blind if you ain't careful.''

"But I didn't steal that wallet. I was returning it!"

Smokey didn't acknowledge her frantic words. He slammed and locked the cab's doors, then shoved her keys into his pocket.

"I'm innocent! I was bringing the wallet back. *Back!*"

"Just calm down, ma'am," Billy said as he stepped forward, a puzzled look on his face. "Didn't Tyler say she hightailed it out of here in Mitchell Pike's old Chevy?" His gaze swept the cab. "This don't look like Pike's old rattletrap to me."

"Criminals ditch stolen cars all the time," Smokey said.

"You've been watching too many 'Adam-12' reruns," Billy told Smokey. "What criminal in their right mind would trade Pike's Chevy for a cab? Sort of conspicuous if you ask me."

"Nobody asked you," Smokey grumbled. He guided her into the back of the waiting patrol car. "If Tyler wanted someone to teach his daughter how to be a lady," Smokey went on, "he should've hired Merline over at the Piggly Wiggly. The woman's about as ladylike as you can get. Carries a linen handkerchief to church, and cooks the meanest fried chicken..."

Merline? The Piggly Wiggly? *Burglary?*

It wasn't hell she'd landed in. It was the Twilight Zone. A weird, twisted episode Texas style. She half expected to hear Rod Serling's deep voice, with the "Yellow Rose of Texas" playing in the background.

Not that even one moment of this nightmare actually surprised her, not with her never-ending string of rotten luck. But she was in Texas, of all places, and Texans were supposed to be nicer, weren't they?

More like kookier, from the looks of things. Way kooky.

"This is crazy," she said as the car sped down the road. "You can't arrest me when I haven't done anything."

"Maybe she's telling the truth," Billy said as he turned to Smokey. "Don't forget Pike's truck."

"We found her with the evidence, Billy. Tyler reported his wallet stolen by a woman, a *strange* woman, not from around here. Can't get any stranger than her."

"Have you looked in the mirror lately, fella?" Lucky's words earned her a quick glare.

"Could be like she said." Billy glanced at her. "Got kind of an honest face, don't you think? Honest eyes? And what burglar in her right mind would swipe a cab for a getaway car?" Billy shook his head. "Come on, Hank. The chief'll be some kind of mad if he has to postpone his fishing trip for nothing."

"Doggone it." Smokey shook his head. "Oh, all right. If it'll shut you up, I'll take her out to Tyler's first." The car nosed for the shoulder, then made a complete turn.

"Finally some justice," Lucky said. Tyler Grant could tell these bozos she wasn't the robber, she could return his wallet, ask for her eighty-dollar fare and get the hell out of Dodge. Or Ulysses. Or wherever she was.

They drove a good twenty minutes before she spotted the house, a sprawling one-story structure set at least a half mile back from the road. A lush green lawn surrounded the place. Several trees stood tall and proud, their large, lazy branches shielding the surrounding yard from the blinding sunlight.

It wasn't one of those fake mansion-style homes. No, this place looked lived in. It made you think of homemade apple pie and picnics. Just the sort of place that should have a bunch of kids racing back and forth across the grass. A few swings hanging from the trees. Bicycles on the huge porch out front. A cozy wicker love seat just the right size for Lucky and a certain naked stranger...

The car made a sharp turn, effectively killing the vision. They jerked to a stop outside the house. Smokey climbed from behind the wheel and stomped to the front door.

"Chicago," Billy started. "Why, I bet they got all kinds of ice-cream flavors, being a big city and all..."

Smokey disappeared inside the house and Lucky was left listening to Billy discuss the merits of wild raspberry delight versus chocolate fudge ecstasy.

"Here they come," Lucky said when Smokey appeared in the doorway. Lucky tried to stare past him to the man that followed, but she couldn't make out more than a tanned arm here and there, a jeans-clad thigh, scuffed boots.

"Seems you're off the hook, missy," Smokey grumbled as he yanked open the door, pulled Lucky from the seat and unlocked the cuffs. "Tyler here says you ain't the thief."

"At least someone around here has some sense—" The words died when she turned to find herself staring up at the delicious naked stranger with the unforgettable buns. "*You!* You didn't tell me *you* were Tyler Grant."

"I didn't know you were looking for him."

"Well, yes. I found his—your—wallet this morning."

"This reunion's sweet and all," Smokey cut in, "but Billy and I got a burglar to catch." He tipped his hat at Tyler and said, "Keep you posted."

"Wait a second." She whirled as the car doors slammed shut. "You guys have my keys—" The rest of her sentence drowned in the rev of an engine. The police car bolted down the driveway, gravel spewing from the rear tires.

"*I* have your keys," came the deep voice behind her. "And relax. I'll give you a ride back as soon as you tell me how you got my wallet."

"Like I told Smokey, I found it in the back of my cab."
She turned to find Tight Tush staring at her with his heated
eyes. Mesmerizing blue eyes as deep as the Caribbean. The
kind of blue you could wade waist-deep through and still
see your toes. She forced her gaze from his to look at the
rest of him. He was far from *au naturel* now, yet he looked
every bit as Marlboro-man masculine with his denim shirt,
faded jeans and worn cowboy boots. A far cry from Buster
and his bowling buddies.

"So you found my wallet?"

"In the back of my cab after I dropped off your wife."

"My *wife?*" Incredulity etched his features for a shocked
moment. "Well, how do you like that?" he finally said.
Then he burst out laughing. But it wasn't a happy sound.
Anger flashed in his eyes, turning them a deep, fathomless
turquoise. "Beautiful. Just friggin' beautiful."

"She was."

"Who?"

"Your wife."

"Honey, she wasn't my wife."

"But she was carrying your wallet and..." Her sentence
trailed off as Smokey's voice echoed in her mind...
burglary. "You mean she was—I've been carrying around
hot property?"

"Scorching, but the wallet wasn't the only thing she
ripped off. She took the entire contents of my safe. Nearly
fifty thousand dollars' worth of money and jewelry. Hightailed it out of here before daybreak."

"In Mitchell Pike's truck," Lucky added. "And she
headed straight for Houston where she probably ditched the
truck. Then I taxied her to the airport for a clean getaway.
To top it off, she stiffed me for an eighty-dollar cab fare.
I'm an idiot," she muttered, closing her eyes. "I can't be-

lieve I fell for the story like a big sap. A heart attack, of all things.''

''She had a heart attack?''

''No, her father did, or she said he did. She was racing to catch a plane so she could rush to his side and nurse him back to health like some Florence Nightingale. Why, the lying, conniving, sleazy little—''

''Daddy! Phone!''

Lucky's gaze darted to the open doorway behind him. *Daddy*. This mega babe was a dad?

''Daaadeee!'' The shrill voice stretched each syllable.

''I'll be right there.'' A frown creased his features. ''I would really like to ask you a few more questions, Miss...I'm afraid I don't know your name.''

''Lucky. Lucky Myers.''

''Lucky?''

''It's a nickname. Lucretia...Lucky.''

Another shrill ''Daddy!'' from inside and he said, ''Please. Come in a few minutes while I take this call, then we'll talk.''

He led her inside the house, into a large room. ''You can wait here in the library.''

Old movie posters were plastered on the dark-paneled walls. There was *Giant, East of Eden, Rebel Without a Cause, The Maltese Falcon, Casablanca, Key Largo* and at least a dozen others. They covered every spare inch not lined with bookshelves. An antique movie projector sat on top of the bookshelf nearest her.

''Wow,'' she breathed. ''Does that work?''

''Supposedly.''

''You don't know?''

''I've only been back a few months, and watching old movies hasn't been on the top of my list.''

''Where were you before?''

"Houston."

"Home?"

"No" he said a little too sharply and she glanced up to see a strange light in his ocean eyes. "This is home."

She smiled. "It feels like a home. Warm, cozy, though it's bigger than the entire first floor of my apartment building."

"And where is that?"

"Houston, too. But it's not much of a home. Not yet, anyway. But then six months isn't really enough time to get settled. I'm originally from Chicago, born and bred." She blinked at the sudden burning in her eyes and sought a distraction. Her gaze went to a glass cabinet sitting in one corner. Inside sat a cowboy hat and a pair of boots.

"A shrine to the great James Dean," he said as if reading her thoughts. "Rumor has it he wore those in the movie *Giant*."

"You're kidding?"

He shook his head. "My dad swears it." When her gaze went to the movie projector and the rows of old movie reels, he added, "Those are the real thing, too."

"This is great." She trailed her hand over the projector. "You like old movies?"

"Old, new. I like them all."

"A woman after my dad's heart."

A woman after your heart, she thought, then quickly discarded the notion. A lifetime and she hadn't managed to win anyone's heart. What could she possibly accomplish in the thirty or so minutes before she'd be on her way back to Houston? She was the invisible, flat-chested woman and he was *Playgirl*'s stud of the month. They were on opposite sides of the universe. There was no connection. Nothing.

He smiled, her heart shifted and she averted her gaze lest she salivate right then and there.

"So what about you?" she asked. "You like old movies?"

He shook his head. "I'm not much of a movie buff. In fact, I've been after Dad to do away with some of this stuff, but he's so stubborn."

"But it's great—"

"Daddy! Grandmother's on the phone!"

"Five minutes," he promised Lucky as he headed out of the room. The way her hormones were chanting, she knew they'd be the five longest minutes of her life.

3

"IT'S ABOUT TIME, Daddy." Bernadette Willemina Grant stood in Tyler's study, one hand planted on her hip, the telephone receiver clutched in her other. His twelve-year-old daughter wore a nearly threadbare T-shirt, faded jeans and large black rubber boots that crept halfway up her thighs. Helen would have his hide for sure.

He sat down at his desk and tried not to smile. "What happened to the dress Mabel put out for you this morning?"

"Daddy," she groaned, giving him a what-horse-just-walloped-you-in-the-head? look. "Jed's waiting for me. I'm helping him clean out Liz's stall."

"So you're all done with your schoolwork and piano lessons?"

"Of course not, Daddy."

"Well, shouldn't you be finishing it instead of cleaning out stalls? And honey, you really ought to put on a dress."

She rolled her eyes. "How am I supposed to concentrate, with Liz wallowing around in a stinky stall? And a dress—" she made a face "—I can't help Jed if I'm wearing a dress. Come on, Daddy. Mabel says it's okay if you say it's okay. I told her you would because you've always been a huge supporter of animal rights—"

"Go, but finish your lessons right after dinner, is that clear? And put on something nice when you're done in the barn."

"Thanks, Daddy." She gave him a quick kiss and bolted from the room. Her three-sizes-too-large boots slapped against the hardwood floor and Tyler couldn't help smiling.

"I was just getting ready to hang up," the woman's voice snapped the minute he said hello.

"Sorry you had to wait, but I was in a meeting—"

"That illustrates my point exactly, Tyler. Bernadette needs more attention. Do you know what she wants for a pet? Forget a nice French poodle or a cockapoo. She wants a lizard. Now, I don't have anything against reptiles. I have nearly ten alligator handbags. But my granddaughter wanting to nurture a live reptile causes me a bit of concern. When Nan was twelve, she was looking forward to her coming out. She'd roll over in her grave if she knew what you were allowing her daughter—"

"*Our* daughter, Helen. Nan and I made Bernadette together, and she isn't a Bell-Whitman. She's a Grant."

"My Nan's blood still runs through Bernadette's veins. Now, Tyler, you really should consider sending her back to Houston. Smithston's already agreed to let her start midsemester. They've got one of the best academic programs around and they offer dance lessons, etiquette, fashion coordination—everything Bernadette needs at her age."

"What makes you so sure she isn't already learning everything she needs to right here?"

Helen laughed. "Come now, Tyler. One top-notch governess in no way compares to an entire staff of highly qualified personnel, and Ulysses isn't exactly the social seat."

"There are plenty of social activities here. The Hickory Festival is in two weeks. Competitors come from all over Texas for the pecan pie competition. Then there's the beauty pageant."

Helen ignored him and plunged ahead, sugary sympathy disguising the ever-present steel in her voice. "You know

Merle and I understand you're not in Ulysses by choice.
We know you had no way of foreseeing your father's illness. But there's no reason to force Bernadette to stay there
and share in the misery. I'm sure once you take a look at
Smithston's fall schedule, you'll see what Bernadette's
missing and change your mind. I'll bring a copy this afternoon.''

"*This* afternoon? You mean tomorrow afternoon."

"Change of plans, dear. Merle's business meeting in San
Antonio has been moved to tomorrow morning at nine."
Before the news could sink in, she rushed on, "Merle and
I are flying in. We'll be there in a little over two hours. In
fact, he's waving me off the phone right now. Bye, dear. I
can't wait to meet that new Dalton governess you hired."

Two hours. He had all of two hours to find a governess.
Otherwise, he'd have a hell of a fight on his hands. Not
that Helen could do more than cause a stink, but what a
stink, and Bennie would be caught right in the middle.

He couldn't allow that. No, he wanted Bennie happy.
That meant keeping Helen happy and finding a governess.
Fast.

He glanced down at his stolen wallet, each bill accounted
for, tucked safely away along with his credit cards. His Visa
and American Express Gold Card were missing, but he
knew Lucky hadn't swiped them. The nanny had obviously
pocketed those for frequent use, which was fine by him.
He'd already reported the cards missing, and should she try
to use them, she would find herself behind bars.

Tyler closed the wallet and trailed his thumb along the
smooth leather edge as Lucky's image pushed into his
thoughts.

She had the most incredible eyes, so warm and brown,
framed by long, thick dark lashes. Though it wasn't her
eyes he really remembered. It was the way she'd looked at

him with those eyes. He could still feel her gaze on his bare back, sliding down, making his skin tingle...

Too bad he couldn't hire her. But it would never work. Those wide-eyed looks, all that innocence she oozed, were all part of a well-practiced act. Otherwise he wouldn't find himself so attracted to her, would he? And the last thing he needed was a seductress under his roof.

Then again, Ulysses was thirty minutes away. It would take him an hour to drive to town and back, which left only an hour to find some unknown somebody. The odds weren't in his favor. Ulysses had all of six hundred and eighty-two citizens, all fine upstanding people as nice as could be, but he was fairly certain none of them would be more qualified than Lucky, seductress or not.

Besides, she was intelligent. He'd seen that in her eyes amid all the hunger and innocence, and it was only for one evening. Come morning, Helen and Merle would be on their way to their business meeting.

Yes, he needed Lucky. In more ways than one, he thought.

That's why it would never work. This was business, purely business, and Tyler shouldn't be having these kinds of urges over a business acquaintance—a tomboyish, big-mouthed acquaintance. Besides, Helen wanted a fancy governess from a fancy agency, and she could smell an ordinary, working-class Joe quicker than a bloodhound could scent out a rabbit—

His daughter's high-pitched squeal cut into his thoughts, brought him up out of the chair and over to the window. He stared across the yard to the huge red and white barn where Bennie stood out front wielding a water hose.

"I can nail you with one shot, mister!" She smiled and turned the spray on Jed, a wiry old man who'd been at the ranch as long as Tyler could remember. Jed returned fire and Bennie squealed, water soaking her from head to booted foot until she looked like a wet puppy, all scrawny and vulnerable, and happy. Yes, she looked happy, and Tyler felt as if someone had landed a boot up against his backside.

A few seconds later, he headed out back to tell Bennie about Helen's change of plans. Then he'd make Miss Lucky Myers the offer of a lifetime.

For Bennie, he reminded himself again.

AFTER DEVOURING the titles on all the old movie reels, Lucky moved on to the numerous bookshelves.

Breeding Cattle. How to Make a Winner. So Mr. Big Bucks was in the cattle-prostitution business. Obviously it paid better than most escort services if this spread was any indication—

"Bennie!" The shout brought Lucky over to a huge bay window overlooking the back of the house in time to see Tyler Grant face off with a young girl, no more than twelve or thirteen. The Terminator with a water hose.

She aimed her weapon, but Tyler was too quick. The spray barely soaked the back of his shirt before he moved, hefting her over his shoulder in a head-on tackle. She shrieked, squirming in a fit of laughter as he attacked her with tickling fingers.

Lucky smiled, despite the pang of longing that shot through her for a naked stranger who looked really great in a wet shirt—

"Hold it right there, snake woman!"

The book she'd been holding sailed to the floor. Lucky whirled, to find herself staring down the barrel of a very lethal-looking shotgun.

"Now hold on a minute." Her gaze flew to the old man

brandishing the gun. Snow-white hair covered his head, the same color as the beard that hid half his face.

Colonel Sanders. She was being attacked by Colonel Sanders.

For a shocking moment, her gaze riveted on the bandages covering both his eyes.

Make that a *blind* Colonel Sanders.

Panic bolted through her and she forced a calming breath. If he couldn't see, he couldn't aim, and that meant she had a chance. "Just calm down, mister. You—you've got the wrong person."

"Shut your lyin' mouth! You might've put one over on my boy, but I knew you was rotten from the get go, missy."

The tip of the barrel wavered, and Lucky inched sideways several feet. Her thigh came up hard against the glass case holding the James Dean boots and hat. Wood creaked and the man swung around. The barrel streaked through the space between them and crashed into the shelf holding the old movie projector.

Wood splintered, the projector hit the floor, metal pieces clanged and rolled, and the man let loose a string of violent curses.

"Dadblame it, sonofa—"

"Dad! Put that gun down!" Tyler strode through the doorway, his hair a tangled, dripping mess. He had a white towel draped around his neck, his shirt and trousers soaked and streaked with mud.

She sniffed, wrinkling her nose. It smelled more like fertilizer or horse doo—

"Good Lord," breathed the short pudgy woman with gray hair and wide gray eyes who rushed in after Tyler.

Tyler's eyes flashed anger and outrage as he reached the old man. His hands went to the wayward shotgun and the gnarled fingers gripping the handle. *"What the hell are you doing?"*

"Trying to give this yellow-bellied thief what she deserves." The old man resisted, playing tug-of-war with his larger, obviously stronger son. "She thought she could put one over on us, boy. But I ain't letting her get away with it."

"Give up the gun right now," Tyler ordered, the words soft, yet steely. "I mean it."

"Aw, go on and take the blasted thing." The old man released the weapon and let Tyler steer him to a chair. "Tried to warn you, boy. You cain't trust no woman who calls a fourteen-point buck *precious*. It just ain't natural."

"Give me the keys to the gun cabinet, Dad."

"Didn't get it from no gun cabinet." The old man crossed his arms, his mouth set in a pout that resembled a stubborn child's. "That there's my own personal protection. Keep it under my bed for just such emergencies."

"You could've caused one hell of an emergency if you'd pulled the trigger." When the old man held his stance, Tyler added, "Give them to me." The man looked ready to refuse, but after a long, tense moment, he dropped the keys into Tyler's outstretched hand. Something dangerously close to regret flashed in Tyler's eyes before he smiled. "Keep him out of trouble, Mabel," he told the pudgy woman.

"Come on, Ulysses. I just made up a batch of stew."

"Now that's the best thing I heard all day." Ulysses grasped the woman's hand and pulled to his feet, a smile creasing his face. "You wouldn't happen to have some fresh-baked biscuits to go with it?"

"And fresh buttermilk to drink."

"Hot damn, Mabel! My eyes might be shot, but my taste buds are in their prime." The old man's excitement fled as he cast a frown over his shoulder. "Don't turn your back on her. And keep her away from my Jimmy Dean hat and boots." Then he shook his head. "Precious. Of all the blasted things…"

"Don't mind him." Mabel ushered the man out the door. "He's cranky because one of the cable channels is running a twenty-four-hour Clark Gable marathon and he's gonna miss it."

"Oh, well, that explains it then," Lucky said, still dazed from the past few minutes.

"Aw, who cares about those old shows," the man grumbled.

"You do, you stubborn old coot," Mabel said. "Now come on."

"Are you all right?" Tyler's hand went to her arm, his thorough gaze combing her from head to toe.

"I—I think so." She shook her head. "Who was that?"

"That was Tyler Ulysses Grant the first, founder of this ranch and one pigheaded old man. He had double eye surgery a few months ago to correct a retina impairment. When the police car rolled up earlier, everybody here thought Hank had nabbed the thief. My father's a little hottempered and I guess he thought he'd get a jump on the justice system. He only meant to scare you."

"Mission accomplished," she mumbled, pulling in a deep breath. "But I think my heart is beating again." Not beating. Pounding. A frenzied rhythm that had started the moment Tyler's long lean fingers had touched her to check for injuries.

Fingers that were still touching her.

"I'll be all right," she said, expecting him to let go. He didn't for a long, drawn-out second. Something simmered in his eyes. That unreadable something she'd seen earlier.

"Why are you staring at me like that?"

"Like what?"

"Like you're ready to swallow me whole."

A grin lifted the corners of his mouth. "Now there's a thought. Though, I have to admit, I usually like to take my time, savor each bite…" His voice trailed off as he studied her with those damnable eyes of his. A drop of water slid down his temple, his strong jaw, and Lucky had the inexplicable urge to reach out and catch the drop. Taste it. Taste him…

He wiped his face with the edge of his towel and Lucky cleared her throat.

"I'm sorry about you getting ripped off and everything. If you'll give me the eighty bucks your nanny stiffed me for, I'll be on my way. I've got a lot of work waiting."

He gave her the once–over, from the top of her baseball cap-covered head, to the ends of her sneakers, before leveling a stare at her. "So how about working for me this evening?"

Before her hormones could start harmonizing "Hallelujah," she blurted out, "I don't think there's a big need for taxi drivers out here in Timbuktu."

"Ulysses," he corrected. "And I don't need a driver. I need a nanny for my twelve-year-old daughter."

She couldn't stop the chuckle that bubbled on her lips. "Do I look like a nanny to you?"

"Not now, but with a little work you could pass. Besides, it's just for a few hours. One evening. The woman you picked up in your cab was my governess, or was supposed to be. She was here all of two days before she cleaned out my safe and took off. Now I need a temporary replacement."

"Aren't you afraid I might warp your daughter or something? I mean, I know I won't, but you don't. You just met me."

"You returned a wallet full of credit cards and money, without even deducting your cab fare. That says a lot." Frustration darkened his eyes to arctic blue. "Look, Lucky. Here's my situation. My in-laws are arriving today. If they find out about what happened with the real nanny, I'll never hear the end of it. All I need is someone to pose as a nanny tonight while they're here. Just a warm body."

"No." Not that her body wasn't warm at the moment. It was. Dangerously warm. "I'm sorry about what happened and I wish I could help you out, but I can't. Why don't you call a service or take out an ad or something?"

"No time. I need someone now. Someone I can trust." He raised desperate eyes to her. "I'm willing to pay, Lucky. Just one evening. I'll teach you enough to get you through a few hours of conversation, my mother-in-law will be happy and I'll be off the hook."

"How much?"

"Five hundred dollars," he said.

"Make it a thousand."

"I thought you didn't want to do this."

"I didn't say that. If the price is right, I'll do anything— within reason, of course. This seems reasonable. A little kooky, but hey, you're the one with the thousand bucks and I'm neck-deep in debt."

"What kind of debt?" He looked suspicious. "It isn't anything illegal—"

"Nursing-home payments. I have a granny—my dad died last year and I don't have any other family left—and she's at this really expensive nursing home in Houston. Anyhow, they've been letting me slide on the payments since my dad passed away, but now I have to bring the account current. So it's a thousand bucks, or no deal."

"Okay," he said after a long moment. "A thousand bucks. One evening. You eat dinner, pretend to be the nanny, spend the night and say goodbye to my in-laws at breakfast. That's it.''

"What about my cab fare?"

"A thousand dollars, plus the cab fare."

"And I want half my money up front."

"For someone desperate, you sure make a lot of demands." He nodded. "I'll have to go to the bank." He glanced at his watch. "You can ride to town with me, and I'll drop you by Earline's beauty shop. She can get you fixed up while I take care of things at the bank."

"What about your wife? Since I'm playing this little role for your in-laws, don't you think she might want to give me a look-over before you hire me?"

"She certainly would," he replied. "But she passed away a couple of years ago. A car accident."

Yes!

Yes? What kind of morbid person was she? He'd just admitted a tragedy to her. Granted, a tragedy that made him unattached, but still a tragedy.

"I'm sorry. I didn't mean to pry."

"You didn't. Now, first things first, we need to get you out of those clothes."

Whoa, baby. Was this guy a mind reader or what? She took a deep breath, tried to calm her raging hormones and fished a stick of gum from her pocket.

"No gum chewing." He plucked the gum from her hand and motioned to her pocket. "Give it up."

The money. She handed over the gum and tried not to stare longingly. Just think about the money.

"Do you need to get in touch with your boss and tell him where you'll be?" Tyler asked, drawing her attention.

"I don't have a boss. I'm an independent driver for Speedy Cab. Which means I work when I want to, pay a flat fee from each fare to the cab company and don't work when I don't want to.''

"Won't someone be worried about you if you're gone all night? Your family? Husband?"

"No," she retorted, wishing his words didn't bring the familiar ache to the pit of her stomach. "There's just my granny. No other family. No husband." *Hint. Hint.*

"Good—I mean, it's good that we won't be inconveniencing anybody with our little charade." He smiled, that slow, lazy, naked-stranger smile that made her heart beat faster and her body go from warm to blazing hot.

Of course, his smiles didn't mean anything, she told herself a few minutes later as she followed him down the hall toward the guest room. The faded denim of his jeans pulled and tugged at all the right places as he walked and Lucky tried to fix her gaze at a point just above his shoulder. She had no doubt that he flirted with every woman. Some men were like that. They oozed sex appeal.

Not that anyone had done any oozing in her direction, mind you. Which was all the more reason for her to take the job. Lucky had quite a few things to learn in the manwoman department if she ever wanted to find that special someone, settle down and have herself an honest-to-goodness family. She intended to finish school first, but meanwhile, she could polish her manhunting skills.

Since Tyler Grant seemed pretty good at attracting the opposite sex, maybe she could learn a thing or two from him while she played nanny to his daughter. How to flirt, at least. He was a master at that, and once she returned to the real world, a push-up bra could only do so much.

FIFTEEN MINUTES LATER, after Tyler had showered and changed, he stood in the guest-room doorway and stared at the woman standing near the brass bed. A knock-'em-dead *woman*.

The baseball cap lay discarded atop one frilly Victorian-lace pillow. Jeans, sneakers and T-shirt lay in a heap near the floor-length mirror.

His gaze fixed on the creamy expanse of skin at her ankle, up one sweetly curved calf, then knee, before the image disappeared beneath the hemline of a straight black skirt that hugged every inch of thigh and hip to perfection.

"You can't really mean to make me wear this?" She fingered the extravagant lace cuff of the cream silk blouse she wore, her gaze going to the plunging vee, before sweeping down to the very fitted skirt. "I feel like an overstuffed sausage."

"The other nanny left those behind. She was a little smaller than you."

"Obviously, Sherlock."

His gaze swept her up and down. "I'll go get Mabel. A few safety pins and a seam ripper, and she can fix whatever ails you. Once she's done, you'll look like quite a lady."

She planted stiff fingers on her hips, her narrowed brown eyes pinning him to the door frame. "Meaning I don't look very feminine now?"

"Hold on there, I didn't say you didn't look feminine." He strode over to her. She was definitely tall, coming well past his shoulders. Still, she had to tilt her head to look at him, giving him a full view of her long, slender neck. "You look feminine, all right. No doubt about that."

"And feminine is not ladylike?"

"Not in your case."

"And why is that? Because I don't look like the type of girl you'd take home to Mother?"

"You," he said, trailing a finger down the tempting slope of her neck, "look like the type of gal I'd take home to bed.'' No sooner had the words left his mouth than he regretted them. *Great, Tyler. Real businesslike.* Why don't you just rip her clothes off, do it on the floor and get it over with?

Shock swept her features, then anger, and Tyler knew he was in for it. But when she opened her mouth, the only thing in her voice was undisguised curiosity.

''Really? Why?''

He had to laugh at that one. ''Are you kidding?''

''No. So what is it about the way I look now as opposed to thirty minutes ago that made you say that?''

Okay, so she was serious. ''You look...'' His gaze started at her ankles, and moved upward. He couldn't believe they were having this conversation. All of the women in his past had had plenty of self-confidence when it came to looks. Too much. But this woman... She's got it, too, buddy. She's just good at hiding it. At punching your buttons. *It's an act, Sherlock.* A well-played act. Still, when she stared at him so...expectantly, he couldn't seem to keep his mouth shut.

''Curvy,'' he finally said. ''Very curvy. The skirt shows off your legs, your hips.'' His attention slid higher. ''And the blouse... It shows off everything above the waist. Yes, lots of curves. Subtle curves. Just right for a man's hands.''

''Curves? Where?''

For an irrational instant, he wanted to eat up the few inches of distance left between them and touch his lips to all the ''wheres.'' But she was his employee for the next twelve hours. His daughter's nanny all of fifteen minutes. And completely off-limits. Great. Now comes the attack of the straitlaced businessman. *Damn.*

''Well?'' Impatience edged the word.

''There,'' he managed to say, his voice gruff as he pointed to the slope of her calves. ''All along there.'' He indicated her legs, long shapely legs. His attention slid higher. "And, of course, there." His jabbed a space in the air to indicate where his attention had finally landed, and a pleased smile lit her face.

"Really? These clothes really make you want to touch me here?" Her hands went to the objects of discussion and he swallowed hard. *Damn. Damn.*

"Geez, and all because of a little blouse," she said. "Forget the push-up bra." Her incredulous voice drew his gaze.

Sexual energy. Potent. Stronger than anything Tyler had ever felt before passed between them. *Damn. Damn. Damn.*

He shook his head as if he could shake away the strange feeling. The strange truth—that he was reacting like a hormone-enraged teenager in the back seat of his daddy's car, and all because of a woman named Lucky, who wore baseball caps, chewed gum and spied on unsuspecting men.

The notion was ridiculous. He was out of his mind, not only to have hired her in the first place, but to actually be lusting after her as though he'd never seen a woman in a tight skirt before.

He'd never seen *this* woman in a tight skirt before, or a silk blouse, for that matter. And she was good, he told himself. It was positively ingenious how she thought to play the innocent virgin. What man could resist such a challenge?

He could. It wasn't as if she had anything that other women didn't, and he didn't have time for games. Lucky was his nanny and Helen was coming.

"We'd better go. We've got a lot to do."

"Yeah," she said, glancing at the mirror one last time before slanting an irresistible grin at him. "You know, I could get used to this."

So could I, his rebellious libido whispered as he left her to go in search of Mabel. *So could I.*

And that was the damned trouble of it all.

4

"WE'RE ALMOST DONE with your hair, sugar. Just hold your head up straight."

Lucky's head bobbed and something bumped her forehead.

"Sorry 'bout that, sugar."

Lucky glanced up as Earline, the owner of Ulysses's only beauty salon, parted bright pink lips and smiled. "They're a work hazard." *They* referred to a pair of double *D*'s squashed beneath a pink knit top. "There," Earline declared, plopping her comb and scissors down to reach for a bottle of styling spritz.

"I don't usually put anything in my hair," Lucky said.

Earline gave her a serious look. "We need height, sugar. To frame your face and bring out those beautiful eyes of yours."

Beautiful eyes. Lucky gave the idea some thought, then smiled. "I've never had height before."

Or breadth, for that matter, she added silently when one of Earline's work hazards bopped her upside the head again.

Ah, breasts... Pointy pyramids to liven up her flat-as-an-Arizona-desert landscape. Breast men would come from all over the world to view in hushed awe. They'd snap pictures to display alongside photos of all the great wonders of the world—the Eiffel Tower, the Taj Mahal... She'd be a universal sex symbol. Yeah, right.

Earline leaned in, her chest bumping the back of Lucky's head again. "Oops, there I go again. Like I said, job hazard."

"Yeah, when it's really cold," came a slightly amused southern drawl, "Earline can put out an eye with one of those." Doris, Earline's assistant, stood squeezing perm solution on a fifty-something-year-old customer.

Earline glared at the younger woman then turned back to Lucky. "Are you married, sugar?"

"No, but I intend to work on that when I get back to Houston."

"Well, remember one thing when you start hunting for a man. The eyes are everything. My Roger wasn't the best-looking boy back in high school, but he sure knew how to look at a woman. Why, I nearly passed out the first time he looked at me."

"The whole town nearly passed out the first time you looked back," Doris offered. "You were Miss Hickory Honey, for heaven's sake, and he was the class geek."

"Hickory Honey?" Lucky asked.

"The town's yearly beauty pageant. It's the kickoff for the pecan festival that starts in two weeks." Doris pointed to a neon pink flier taped on the wall. "Despite all the ranch land around here, we've got acres and acres of pecan trees. We're the hickory capital of Texas."

Earline sighed. "Being Miss Hickory Honey was the second biggest thrill of my life."

"What was the first?" Lucky asked.

"The first time Roger and I... Well, you know, sugar."

No, she didn't know. That was the trouble.

After Earline had blown and spritzed and brushed until Lucky felt dizzy, the woman reached for what looked like a tackle box.

"Now on to the makeup," she declared. "We'll just

widen your eyes a little.'' She leaned in, wielding a mascara brush the way a Samurai did his sword.

"I think my eyes are wide enough," Lucky said, blinking frantically as the brush came at her.

"Nonsense. Wide eyes are sexy, sugar. Now hold 'em open."

After five unsuccessful attempts, Lucky finally managed not to blink. The mascara went on, then a light dusting of powder and blush. Earline finished with a little lipstick, then stood back to survey her work.

"Ready, sugar?"

For all Lucky's excitement, she couldn't squash the sudden apprehension. She'd never been in a full-service beauty salon before. Most of her haircuts had been at Jake's Barbershop back in Chicago. No spray spritz or blow-dryers. And forget the makeup. Of course, that alone probably accounted for her nonexistent love life.

The chair swung around and Lucky found herself staring at a complete stranger. Soft layers of short brown hair framed the stranger's face. Mascara accented obscenely long eyelashes and gave deep cocoa brown eyes an exotic look.

Exotic. The word echoed through her head and Lucky reached up, her fingers trailing over the soft curls accenting her cheekbones. Her cheekbones. Not some stranger's. This was really her face. Her hair. Her exotic eyes.

"You like it, sugar?"

"Yes," she whispered, her throat closing around the word. "You're a genius, Earline."

"I wouldn't go that far. Oh, hell, maybe I would." The bell on the front door tinkled. "But now comes the real test."

Lucky turned to see Tyler walk through the door. He

stopped dead in his tracks, an unreadable expression on his face.

"Well?" she asked. She sat up straighter, her chest pushing up and out a fraction, as if he would notice. But a girl had to try. "What do you think, um, er...Mr. Grant?"

Her words seemed to penetrate his frozen exterior. He blinked and a serious expression passed over his features. He glanced at his watch. "I think we'd better hurry. We've got forty-five minutes and you still have to meet Bennie."

While Lucky stifled her disappointment and climbed from the chair, Tyler paid the bill. He gave Earline a sizable tip and Doris a smile that would have melted every snowflake during Chicago's worst blizzard.

Not that it bothered Lucky. She knew Tyler Grant was one of *those* men, the experienced kind who flirted with every woman, otherwise he would never have turned all that charm on her.

Experienced. Exactly the sort of man to teach her a thing or two. She focused on that possibility and ignored the strange tightening in her stomach. Experienced was good. Just what she wanted. She only wished he wasn't beefing up his résumé right in front of her.

"HERE'S YOUR MONEY." Tyler handed her an envelope once they'd climbed into Jed's battered Ford pickup that had a giant *R* emblazoned on the side. He keyed the ignition. The engine grumbled and knocked and he cursed.

"I told Jed to replace the battery in this thing."

"If it was the battery, it would be more like a grinding noise." She demonstrated. "See? That's nothing like the knocking. It's probably just being a little temperamental. These '79 Fords sometimes do that." When he raised questioning eyebrows to her, she rushed on, "I'm sort of into cars and trucks—anything on four wheels. Trust me on this.

Count to five, give it just a little gas and turn the key nice and slow.''

He did as she said. The engine purred to life and Lucky shrugged. "What can I say? It's a gift."

"Thanks." He pulled out onto the main strip through town.

"Thank you." She counted the bills, then shot a glance in the side mirror at her reflection. "So what do you think?"

"You look…different."

"Different?" She stared into the side mirror again. "Different in a bad way, or different in a good way?"

"Different in an…appropriate way."

"Oh," Lucky murmured, stifling another pang of disappointment.

Appropriate. It wasn't a "Gee, Lucky, you're drop-dead gorgeous," but it would have to do. At least he hadn't said *in*appropriate.

One thousand dollars, she told herself when her stomach did the all-too-familiar churning thing again. She could do this. She would do this. She would dance naked on top of the Empire State Building for a thousand dollars.

Okay, maybe not *naked*, but scantily clad. Bra and panties, max. Maybe she'd even throw modesty aside and use a pair of those skimpy bikini panties—

"Let's review." He braked for a stop sign. "Who are you?"

"Lucky Myers, nanny extraordinaire." When he shot her a frown, she amended, "My name is Lucretia Myers. I've been with the Dalton Agency for five years. My most recent assignment was with a low-profile but filthy-rich oilman from Houston, separated from his wife with temporary custody of two teenage girls. He and the girls spent most of their time at a vacation home in Scotland.'' She frowned. ''A *Texas* oilman in Scotland? Did you make this up?''

''Yes. And?''

''Sounds a little far-fetched, if you ask me, but you're the boss.'' She took a deep breath and recited the spiel she'd memorized during the thirty-minute trip to town. ''I've been in Scotland for the past five years—''

''Which is why you seem slightly out of touch.''

''That gets me off the hook on any Texas questions, but what about Scotland? The closest I've been to Scotland is sitting front row through *Braveheart*. It was pretty informational, but I only saw it seven times and—''

''Seven? That's all?''

''I was going for eight, but then my dad died and I moved down here. I've been pulling extra shifts at the cab company to hold my own. That doesn't leave much time for movies.''

''You could always buy the video.''

''And miss seeing Mel up close and personal?'' She shook her head, a smile playing at her lips. ''That would definitely kill the fantasy. Maybe if I had one of those big-screen TVs, but it would have to be really big to give the same theater effect.''

''So size is important to you?''

Her heart hit a speed bump that turned out to be a major pothole when she looked over at him. He was just so beautiful sitting there, gripping the steering wheel, staring straight ahead as if he'd asked her about something as mundane as the weather. Size, girl. Definitely a flirty comment if she'd ever heard one.

She chose her words carefully. ''If you're talking TV screens.''

''And if we're not?''

"Then it depends on what we're talking about." She swallowed. "So what are we talking about?"

He grinned. "What do you think we're talking about?"

"That's not fair. You can't answer my question with a question. I asked first. Are we talking screens or…?"

"Or what?" He shot her a smoldering glance, his lips hinting at a grin.

"Men." There, she'd said it.

He nodded. "Actors."

"Actors?" She tried not to sound depressed.

"What else?"

"Actors," she said firmly. "Yeah, actors." She stared through the windshield and searched for a vision of her favorite actor. Instead of seeing a wily Scotsman, she kept picturing a cowboy. A very naked cowboy, with water streaming down his skin and the sunlight playing off his muscles and his… "Definitely a big-screen man," she murmured. "Really big."

"Who?"

"Uh, Mel." She stiffened in her seat. "Yeah, big-screen all the way. Definitely."

"Yeah," he grumbled, and Lucky had the strangest sensation that she'd just disappointed him somehow.

"So back to your mother-in-law. What should I talk about?"

"You don't talk. I'll do all the talking."

"What if she asks me questions about Scotland?"

"She won't. Helen was there once and spent the entire two weeks sick in her hotel room. Allergies, though she'd die before she ever admitted it. Scotland is the one place she doesn't like, so I doubt she'll drill you on the subject."

"I don't know about this." She shook her head, doubts creeping through her, her mouth watering for a piece of gum.

His hand reached across the seat to close over hers. "You can do it, Lucky. Just relax and remember everything I told you."

"Yeah, relax." She took a deep breath and suppressed the disappointment when he returned his hand to the wheel. "I can do this," she said more for herself than him. "It's not as if I'm totally clueless when it comes to educating a child."

"It's just one night," he reminded her. "You won't be educating anyone."

"I do have some college under my belt," she went on as if he'd never said a word. "Liberal arts with a minor in education."

"You're not going to be a real nanny."

"I've had child psychology and all the basics. That's something." She glanced at him. "Isn't it?"

He nodded and smiled. "Let me guess, underneath that rough exterior lurks the heart of a kindergarten teacher."

"More like an auto-shop teacher. I've always liked cars and kids."

"So why are you driving a cab in Houston instead of teaching mechanics to some rowdy kids back in Chicago?"

She shrugged. "My granny. She was originally from Texas, and when she got sick with Alzheimer's, Dad moved her here from Chicago. He wanted to come himself, but I was going to college and working part-time as a mechanic, and he didn't want to leave me. Then he died, the nursing-home payments fell to me, and so did his cab." She blinked away the sudden moisture in her eyes. "Granny is my number-one priority right now. I'll finish school eventually."

"What about a student loan?"

"Do you know how much shop teachers make? I make more driving my cab. I couldn't swing a new career, nursing-home payments *and* loan payments. It's better to pay as I go, even if it takes a while." She turned on him then. "Would you stop looking at me like that?"

"Like what?"

"Like you feel sorry for me."

"I do feel sorry for you."

She stiffened. "Don't. I don't need your pity."

He grinned. "Oh yes you do. You, sweetheart, are about to meet my mother-in-law. I guarantee, fifteen minutes into it, and you'll be begging for my pity."

"Gee, you're doing wonders for my confidence."

His grin disappeared. "Tell me the story again."

She banged her head against the window. "*Ugh.* Not again."

"Again."

She took a deep breath and tried to focus her thoughts. "Okay, I've been in Scotland. The oilman got a divorce, his wife got the kids, which ended my assignment. Then the agency sent me here."

"Exactly. And remember, whatever you do, don't encourage any questions. Just give the barest answers, and I'll pick up any slack in the conversation. Dinner will fill up some of the time, then you can pretend a headache and escape to your room. After that, we'll have tomorrow morning to get through, which shouldn't be too difficult. Merle, that's my father-in-law, is expected at a nine o'clock meeting in San Antonio, which means they'll be in a hurry. Thirty minutes for breakfast, then I'm off the hook and you're on your way back to Houston."

Simple. Then why did she have the unconscious urge to start chewing even though the nearest piece of gum was in the glove compartment of her cab?

Geez, her cab. "Where's my Chevy?"

"It's hidden away in the garage near the barn. I sent Jed and one of my part-time hands to pick it up."

"But no one drives my cab but me," she blurted out before she could think about how silly it sounded.

"I thought men were the only ones territorial about their cars."

"I'm not territorial. Not exactly." She took a deep breath. "Okay, maybe a little, but that cab is all I have." All I have left of my father.

"I'm sorry," he said as if he sensed her sudden melancholy. "I should have asked your permission first, but I'm sure Jed didn't hurt it. If so, we'll take him out back and have him whipped." He flashed her that all-too familiar naked-stranger smile, and she couldn't help but grin.

Great buns and a sense of humor. Lord help her.

"So what does the initial stand for?" she asked as they turned into the driveway and passed the gate where an *R* had been fashioned in black iron.

"Reata."

"You're kidding, right?"

He stiffened and shook his head. A strange expression crossed his face and Lucky got the feeling she was prodding old wounds instead of making small talk. "So your father has a thing for the movie *Giant?*"

He nodded.

"Is it the movie in particular, or the fact that James Dean was in it?"

"Both." Everything about the way he sat there, fingers gripping the steering wheel, gaze riveted straight ahead, told her to shut up. To mind her own business.

"Any particular reason why he picked a name from that movie and not some other James Dean flick?" she heard herself asking.

"It had...special significance."

"Oh." Silence fell around them as he braked to a stop and killed the engine.

"Come on. Jed's picking up Helen and Merle right now. You've got just enough time to meet Bernadette before showtime."

Lucky climbed from the truck, teetering dangerously when her heel sank an inch or so into the dirt. Tyler caught her a moment before she pitched forward.

"Maybe I could wear my own shoes tonight."

"Tennis shoes don't go with the outfit. Don't stand up any more than necessary and just relax."

Taking a deep breath, she concentrated on each step. She could do this. For a thousand dollars, for Granny, she could wear the shoes, the hair, the clothes, and do it all without a piece of gum.

"Where's Dad?" Tyler asked Mabel when they entered the house.

"In his room, but he's as grumpy as an old mule since I told him about Helen. Threatened to go after her with his shotgun whenever he manages to find it."

"You have an awfully violent family," Lucky told him.

Tyler shook his head. "Dad's just temperamental." He reached out and trailed a fingertip along Lucky's cheek. "He wouldn't have hurt you."

Her body tingled, and from only the barest touch of his finger. If she ever felt more... A full hand, for instance, an arm locked around her, his lips on hers... She'd be a goner for sure.

As if he'd just realized what he was doing, his hand dropped away. "Hold tight, I'll be right back," he said and left.

Lucky closed her eyes and fervently prayed he would be.

"DAD?" Tyler called out as he walked into his father's bedroom. He came up short in the doorway as he caught sight of Ulysses sitting in his rocking chair, a bowlful of ice cream on the tray in front of him, and a bottle of Maalox in his hand. *"Dad!"*

The old man's head snapped around, his bandaged eyes directed at Tyler for a split second before passing him by. He tipped the bottle.

"Put that down!" Tyler reached him in two strides and snatched the bottle out of his hands.

"But I cain't eat no dadblasted ice cream without syrup."

"That's not syrup."

"Sure it is. Mabel put my syrup here on the left and my stomach medicine on the right. Said to take a spoonful right after dinner so's the fried potatoes don't get to me." He groped for the bottle on his right, his fingers skimming over the handle and the sticky strawberry spout. He touched a fingertip to his lips. "Hell, boy, you know my stomach medicine tastes just like Mabel's homemade syrup?"

"That *is* Mabel's syrup."

Ulysses frowned. "Are you telling me I cain't tell the difference between my stomach medicine and my syrup?"

"Exactly."

"Hell, boy. I'm blind. I ain't deaf. Syrup on the left, stomach medicine on the right. I know what I heard."

"You have to be careful." It's a good thing Tyler was here. A damned good thing, otherwise Mabel would be rushing his father to the nearest emergency room to have his stomach pumped, or whatever they did for a Maalox overdose. "Dad," he said gently, "maybe you heard wrong, or maybe Mabel got her left and right mixed up—"

"Damned straight she did."

"Either way, you have to take it slow and easy and be careful about what you put in your mouth." His father could down a bottle of the rat poison Mabel kept in the bottom kitchen cupboard, or take one too many pain pills, or turn his electric blanket on too high and bake himself to death or…a dozen scenarios raced through Tyler's mind. All bad. He shook away the panic. Nothing so tragic was going to happen. He was here to look out for his dad now and things were going to be A-okay.

"My dadburned eyes." Ulysses stared moodily at his bowl. "I'll never see a dadblasted thing ever again."

Tyler hunkered down beside him. "The bandages will be off tomorrow, and the doctor said there's a ninety-eight percent chance your vision will be back to normal within a week or two."

"What about the other two percent? Pretty flimsy success rate if you ask me." He snorted. "Damn city doctors. Cain't trust a one of 'em. Just after the insurance money. That fancy-schmancy surgeon's probably lying on some beach in some foreign country, sipping one of those fruity drinks with the little umbrellas, while I'm sitting here blind, and with a ranch falling apart around me."

"I'm taking care of the ranch."

His dad's frown vanished and a smile eased the lines around his eyes. "And doing a hell of a job, son. I don't know what I'd do without you." He patted Tyler's hand, then the smile gave way to another frown. "Now, if that old busybody mother-in-law of yours would keep her nose out of our business, things would settle down just right." He grabbed his spoon to jab at his ice cream. "But no, she has to come running out here to mess things up." He shoved a spoonful of ice cream into his mouth and swallowed. "And damn near dinnertime, too." He waved the spoon at Tyler. "She'll be sitting at my table, crowding my space. Why, I got just the right amount of elbow room as it is."

Tyler swallowed. "I think you're going to have even less."

"How's that?"

"Well, it's like this, Dad." Tyler launched into a quick explanation of the turn of events and Lucky's new role as nanny. He ended with an optimistic "It's just for one night."

"One night too many," his dad grumbled. "Forget the fried potatoes. Pass me the Maalox, son. I think I need a shot now."

WHILE TYLER talked to his dad, Lucky spent fifteen minutes waiting and debating whether to sit or stand. She alternated between both, then the urge hit her. She'd had two more sodas at Earline's and her kidneys were working overtime.

After a quick bathroom trip, she made her way back down the hallway. Passing the library, she spotted the shattered projector, the pieces still scattered across the hardwood floor.

Before she could stop herself, she walked inside. There was just something about mechanical parts that said come and get me, baby. She preferred car engines, but other things—appliances, TVs, even old movie projectors—held the same appeal. The challenge. Lucky could fix anything. Almost anything, she thought, spying the pieces. This might prove more difficult.

Not that she had the time to fix the projector, she amended. She wouldn't be here long enough to really sink her teeth into the project. She was a temporary nanny. A one-night stand.

Ah, well, a girl had to start somewhere.

A quick glance at the clock and she slipped off her shoes, hiked up her skirt and got on her hands and knees. Grabbing a nearby ashtray, she started gathering parts.

Five minutes later, she was ready to call it quits, when

she spotted the camera lens. Setting the ashtray aside, she climbed under the desk and reached for it.

"What are you doing?"

Tyler's voice froze her hand a fraction shy of her goal. Her head shot up, slamming into solid wood, and she screeched.

"Are you all right?" He knelt beside her, so close she backed into him when she tried to scoot out. Her bottom touched one hard thigh and heat shot through her, effectively refocusing her thoughts from her throbbing head to her throbbing hormones.

"I'm fine," she managed to say, dragging in a deep breath before she scooted a few more inches out and away from him. "These parts were just lying here and it seemed a shame... Geez, you scared the daylights out of me." She turned an accusing gaze on him. "Is this a trait that runs in your family?"

"What?"

"Sneaking up on innocent, unsuspecting guests."

"Innocent, huh?" One eyebrow lifted and his gaze darkened to a deep blue as he stared at her stocking-clad legs. The skirt had slid a few inches higher and the hem straddled her upper thighs. "You don't look so innocent to me."

"Really?" She smiled, catching and holding his gaze, drinking in the feeling those eyes gave her when they stared at her the way he was staring at her now. She felt power. She felt desirable. She felt like a wom—

"Tyler? Bernadette?" The slam of the front door punctuated the woman's voice. "We're here!"

"Damn!" Tyler growled. "They're early." He climbed to his feet and pulled Lucky up beside him.

"Come on," he said, yanking her along after him.

"But my skirt..." She pulled away from him and jerked at the hem. Tyler turned, and in one smooth motion swept the fabric down her thighs, leaving a sizzling path where his fingers had grazed her.

"Tyler!" The voice moved closer and panic swamped Lucky. "Where in the world...?"

One thousand dollars, she recited to herself. If she just concentrated on the words, she could do this. *One...*

"Your shoes," Tyler said.

She whirled, scrambling for one pump while he reached for the other.

thousand...

"Tyler Grant!" came the voice, slightly irritated and dangerously closer.

"Here." He shoved one shoe on her foot, helped her on with the other, then hauled her out into the hallway just as a woman rounded the corner.

dollars. But it wasn't enough, she realized as she stared at the older woman, into eyes as cold and assessing as the principal's who'd nearly expelled her for chewing gum in the third grade. Then Tyler stepped up behind her.

"You look different," he whispered, his voice deep and steady and soothing, "in a good way."

And Lucky managed a wobbly step forward.

5

"HI, I'M LUCK—retia Myers." Lucky thrust out her hand. "It's a pleasure to meet you."

"I'm Helen Bell-Whitman. I take it you're the governess Tyler has been telling me about?"

"Yes, ma'am."

Cold black eyes swept Lucky from head to toe before shifting their attention to Tyler. "The first time I arrive for a visit, and no one has the decency to meet me at the door."

"You're ten minutes early," he replied smoothly, obviously not the least bit intimidated by her Big Bad Mother-in-law stare.

"The flight in was smooth," Helen went on. "We made excellent time."

"Where's Merle?" Tyler asked.

"Still out in the car. An important business call came just as we arrived. I'm sure he'll be along shortly. So this is Reata." Her disapproving gaze swept the paneled interior of the hallway. "This can't be much larger than our guest house."

"This house is over five thousand square feet with six bedrooms," Tyler told her.

"Atrociously small," she sniffed with disdain.

"Can we at least wait until after dinner before we start arguing?"

"I never argue, dear. I was simply pointing out that Bernadette would be much better off back home—"

"This is her home, Helen. Speaking of Bernadette, Miss Myers was just going to fetch her."

"I was?" Lucky asked, then Tyler gave her a discreet nudge. "Oh, yes, yes. I was."

Which way? Lucky's brain screamed as she cast desperate glances in either direction.

As if Tyler had tuned in to her frequency, he touched her arm, just the slightest pressure that indicated she should turn and go the opposite way down the hall.

"Yes, I'll just go see about Bernadette." She retreated, leaving Tyler to deal with his mother-in-law while she fixed every ounce of mental energy on keeping her balance and finding Bernadette's room.

Neither proved very easy, but finally, after a few directions from Mabel and an occasional wobble, Lucky found the pink wallpapered room. The feminine decor went no farther than the walls, however. A double bed draped with a thick orange and white quilt dominated the room and Lucky wished she'd thought to grab sunglasses out of the cab. Maybe she could charge Tight Tush extra for eyestrain.

The thought stayed with her as she scanned the rest of the room. A pair of huge black rubber boots flanked one side of the closet, the soles caked in dried mud. A desk occupied another corner. Schoolbooks lay scattered across the top. Lucky thought she saw beige carpet beneath the mess of clothes on the floor. Overall, the entire room looked as if a tornado had whipped through.

Or the very sulky-looking girl who sprawled on a lime-green beanbag chair, her eyes glued to a handheld Nintendo game. She had dark hair the exact shade as her father's, but hers was slightly longer and pulled into a haphazard ponytail. A bleep sounded and she frowned, her expression exactly the same as one Tyler would have worn. Her features were softer, more delicate, her complexion several shades lighter than her father's, but otherwise the resemblance was eerie.

"Bernadette?"

The girl didn't spare her a glance.

"I'm Luck—retia. Did your father mention me?"

The girl let out a heavy sigh. "The name's Bennie. B-E-N-N-I-E," she spelled. "And you're another one of the agency nannies. A fill-in until the permanent nanny arrives to replace Miss Walker who left unexpectedly. Though I'm not supposed to mention any of that to my grandmother. As far as she's concerned, you're the permanent nanny. Grandmother would have a fit if she thought I'd scared another one away."

So Bennie didn't know about the con-artist nanny. That would make things harder, because she expected Lucky to act like a real nanny. To *be* the nanny.

Lucky cleared her throat and did her best Fran Drescher imitation. "Well, your grandmother's here and your dad wants us front and center."

Bennie shook her head. "You can report for duty. I'm not going anywhere."

"But your grandmother came a long way to see you." Lucky pushed aside some of the clothes covering the bed and sat down. Sighing, she slid her feet free of the heels. Her toes launched into a chorus of "Born Free." "Don't you want to see her?"

"Sure I do, but like I told Dad and Mabel, I'm not wearing that." Bennie stuck her nose up at a white lace dress that lay several feet away.

"That…that's something, all right." It really was a beautiful dress, and that was the trouble. It was too pretty. A hands-off dress, the kind you wore for really special occasions, not the sort of dress you could really breathe in. Lucky was getting claustrophobic just looking at it.

"I want to wear jeans and I don't see why I can't."

"But tonight isn't just any night. Your dad's trying to make a good impression on your grandmother."

Bennie rolled her eyes. "But I look awful in that and it's itchy and Grandmother would have a fit if I started scratching myself at the dinner table. One time I burped and she almost had a heart attack."

Lucky caught a giggle with her hand and pretended to cough. "Well, can't you just scratch discreetly?" Bennie seemed to give the idea some thought. "I'll make you a deal," Lucky went on, trying to tip the scales in her favor. "When you start to itch, you just wink at me. I'll distract your grandmother and let you get in a few good scratches. She'll never know." When Bennie stayed silent, Lucky added, "Your dad's trying real hard to impress her and he wants us to help him. I'll let you in on a little secret, I haven't gotten all dressed up like this in a long time, myself." Try never. Oh, well, she was fibbing for a good cause. Surely that counted for something.

Bennie gave her a thorough once-over. "You should do it more often. Your hair looks real nice. The clothes, too." Another quick glance and she started to giggle. "But I can tell you aren't used to wearing heels."

Lucky glanced down at her throbbing feet. "Does it really show that much?"

Bennie nodded, suddenly all serious sympathy, and got up to place a hand atop Lucky's. "If you help me scratch, I'll distract Grandmother whenever you have to stand up."

Lucky smiled. "You've got yourself a deal."

WHILE LUCKY WHEELED and dealed with Bennie, Tyler listened to Helen drone on about her newest charity project and kept a watchful eye on the door. Where the hell were they?

"…we're planning a special theme for the event, grand-mothers and granddaughters, and it's sure to be one of the biggest galas this season."

"Wonderful," he murmured as Mabel walked in with a tray of canapés.

Helen surveyed the hors d'oeuvres. "My Clara uses ar-tichokes instead of mushrooms."

"Artichokes overwhelm the taste," Mabel declared, de-spite the warning look Tyler gave her. "Mushrooms bring out the spices used in the bottom layer of homemade rel-ish."

Helen shook her head. "Perhaps that's the way things are prepared out here, but in Houston we do things a little differently. My chef, Clara, trained at La Dubois in Paris. Did you know that, Tyler?"

"Don't think I've ever heard of it." Tyler didn't miss the flush of anger creeping into Mabel's face. Uh-oh.

"Come now," Helen said, and laughed. "La Dubois is one of the best restaurants in the world. Five-plus stars. Now, now," she added when Mabel's face looked ready to explode. "No one expects five-star cuisine way out here, dear. I'm sure your mushrooms are very…tasty."

"I like mushrooms," Tyler piped in, but it didn't ease the harsh lines around Mabel's mouth. He gave Mabel his biggest smile. "So what's for dinner?"

"Your head on a platter," Mabel whispered as she whisked past him with the platter of canapés.

"I'm afraid I didn't hear her." Helen cast a curious gaze on him. "What did she say?"

"It's a surprise." Tyler poured himself a glass of Scotch and downed it in one quick gulp. "Mabel loves surprises."

"You really shouldn't drink so quickly. It looks posi-tively uncivilized. Speaking of which, where is your fa-ther?"

"He had an upset stomach. He'll be having dinner in his room."

"Did he have some of Mabel's canapés?"

"Afraid not. He saved them all for you." Okay, as much as he wanted to please Helen, he had his limits.

"He shouldn't have bothered, but what a...lovely gesture, I suppose. Such a sweet old thing. Do give him my regrets. I was looking forward to seeing the poor man again."

"Rest assured, he's equally heartbroken." Or he would be heartbroken, if he had to sit and listen to Helen all evening. She was too much a reminder of Tyler's mother, and her presence never failed to cause a bout of depression in Ulysses, and an insatiable craving for Maalox.

He motioned to Helen. "Let's go into the dining room."

"Merle's still not here." She glanced at the diamond Rolex circling her wrist. "If it's a business dinner, he's early, but tack on the word *social,* and he'll be late every time. I should have taken his cellular phone away before I got out of the car. By the way, where is Bernadette?"

"Right here, Grandmother." Bennie appeared in the doorway.

Tyler's gaze moved to the lace-scalloped white dress Bennie wore, the matching quarter-inch pumps. He blinked. His Bennie? Wearing a dress and smiling at the same time?

"Darling!" Helen cried, opening her arms wide. Dutifully, Bennie walked into her grandmother's embrace.

"You got her to put on a dress," Tyler said, sidling up beside Lucky who stood in the doorway, one hand braced on the doorjamb. "I'm impressed."

"Piece of cake." She smiled at Helen who smiled at Bennie, obviously pleased with her granddaughter's wardrobe choice.

"Do you remember the drill?" he asked.

"Wealthy oilman, kids, Scotland...piece of cake."

"Miss Myers," Helen started, but the clatter of dishes from the dining room effectively drowned out the rest of her sentence. Every gaze turned toward the archway.

"Dinner is served," Mabel announced, her face pinched into a frown directed solely at Helen.

"I don't suppose we're having a nice big piece of Bubble Yum?" Lucky whispered, her eyes hopeful as Tyler steered her forward, all the while conscious of Helen's intense gaze.

"Remember the story and I'll buy you an entire case of the stuff," he promised in a low voice. His grip tightened ever so lightly when Lucky snagged her heel on the plush carpet and started to pitch forward.

"What do you think of my dress, Grandmother?" Bennie piped up, effectively distracting Helen while Lucky caught her balance.

"Lovely, dear. Just lovely." Helen followed Bennie, who twirled toward the dining room. "Wait until you see the outfit I brought for you. It's simply divine."

"What did you do to my daughter?" he whispered to Lucky.

"We have an agreement. She scratches my back and I scratch hers. So to speak." A warm giggle passed her lips.

The sound filtered through Tyler's head, skimming his nerve endings like champagne bubbles tickling his nose. A strange warmth flooded him.

Think cool thoughts, he told himself. Searching for a lost calf during the dead of winter. Plunging into an ice-cold creek after hours of herding cattle.

Try as he might, though, he couldn't summon any goose bumps, or push away the enticing image of Lucky underneath him, soft and warm and open. Especially with her so close.

She was good, all right. A woman who knew how to rope, hog-tie and brand a man without him ever knowing what happened.

"Here." He thrust her into a chair so fast she had to catch the edge of the table to keep from tipping over. He skipped a chair and sat down, ignoring her raised eyebrow. Bennie took her seat opposite Tyler, and Helen sat down beside her.

"Well, it's about time," Helen declared, her gaze darting to the dining-room doorway. "We were about to start dinner without you."

Tyler turned to see his father-in-law, a large man with gray hair and matching eyes, looking impeccable in a charcoal suit.

"Good to see you, Tyler," Merle said, clapping Tyler on the shoulder and giving him a quick handshake before rounding the table to hug his granddaughter and sit on her free side.

"Whatever took you so long—" Helen's sentence drowned in a high-pitched buzz.

"Hold that thought, dear." Merle reached into his coat and pulled out a cellular phone. "Whitman here," he barked into the phone, before mumbling, "Excuse me, I have to take this call."

"So," Helen said as a scowling Mabel started ladling soup into everyone's bowl. "Tell me about yourself, Miss Myers. You're from the Dalton Agency, correct?"

"Yes, she is," Tyler interjected. "She's one of their best. She's been living in Scotland the past few years, caring for the children of a rich Texas oilman."

"Why, I know nearly every oil family in the state. What's his name?"

"Uh, Mel," Lucky stammered, shooting Tyler a panicked look. "I mean, er, Dale. Dale...Stinson. Yes, Dale Stinson."

"Dale Stinson?" Helen asked. "You say he's in oil?"

"Among other things."

"Well, I can't say as I've ever heard of him. Merle—" she turned to her husband "—do you know any Stinsons?"

"Tell him no," Merle grumbled into the phone before throwing Helen a distracted glance. "What, dear?"

"Stinsons. Do you know any Stinsons?" He shook his head and Helen went on, "The name certainly strikes a familiar chord. Tyler, are you acquainted with this Mr. Stinson?"

"Not personally, but I've heard of him. Mr. Stinson is very busy overseas. Scotland is practically his first home."

Helen stared expectantly at Lucky. "What part of Scotland?"

"Glasgow," Tyler fired off before Lucky could open her mouth. "That reminds me, isn't there a display of Scottish armament at the Museum of Fine Arts? Speaking of museums, I'm sure Bennie would love to hear about the new addition to the children's museum."

"Oh, yes. The new wing will be splendid. And with me as chairwoman for the fund-raising gala, it's sure to be *the* event of the season..." Her voice droned on as Lucky turned her attention to the silverware surrounding the bowl of soup in front of her.

Tyler reached for the appropriate utensil and felt Lucky's anxious gaze on him. She followed his every move as he silently coached her through the soup and salad. To her credit, she carried off everything as if she'd been born to it. Tyler actually started to relax. By the time they reached the chicken entrée, he was even enjoying himself. There were worse things than being stared at by an attractive woman. Then the evening took a sharp turn toward Disaster City.

Bernadette, a fidgety audience for her grandmother who talked nonstop about the upcoming fund-raiser, shifted in her chair. Her expression went from attentive to uncomfortable, to desperate. She stared at Lucky. Their gazes met for all of three seconds, then Lucky's fork clattered to the table.

"Those Scottish," Lucky declared in a loud voice that made even Merle pause, cellular phone in hand. "Talk about ingenious. You know, I never knew that mooning was a historical part of battle."

Tyler's jaws locked around a bite of chicken.

"Then there it was on the big screen, Mel Gibson flashing his assets for the entire English army. I realized then why the Scottish really wear those kilts. Definitely a distraction if there's five hundred guys waiting to slice you into mincemeat."

Helen looked horrified.

Tyler swallowed and bolted out of his chair. "If you'll excuse us. I think Miss Myers is having one of her spells."

"Spells?" Lucky asked.

"Hot spells. Where you get dizzy, disoriented, *stupid.*" He muttered the last word for her ears only.

"Oh, yes, yes. One of my spells." She fanned her face dramatically and let him usher her out of her chair.

"You look like you're the one having the spell," Lucky said in a hushed whisper. "You're all red."

"That's because my butt is in the hot seat," he hissed, steering her toward the door. "And you just put me there."

"Oh no," she replied as he whisked her out into the hallway. "I would never do that to you or your butt," she said, her voice filled with conviction. "*Especially* your butt."

6

"LEAVE MY BUTT out of this." Tyler whirled on her.

"You were the one who brought it up. And since you did, I've been meaning to tell you. It's quite impressive."

"What are you? A butt connoisseur?"

"Some women like muscular arms, some like hands, some like chests, I like butts. What's wrong with that?"

"Nothing, except you don't have to go pointing it out to my mother-in-law, who, by the way, is supposed to think you're a high-society nanny."

"So nannies can't like butts?"

"You're insane." His frustrated whisper echoed off the paneled walls. "I say, 'Don't talk. Don't invite questions.' Do you listen? Of course not. Hell, you not only talk, you go ninety to noth...g about men showing off their butts and their—"

"Keep your voice down or they'll hear you." Lucky motioned to the partially open door leading to the dining room. The heel of his boot shot out, the door slammed shut and Lucky jumped.

"You deliberately drew attention to yourself when I had her distracted," he hissed, "talking about her fund-raiser."

"You had her looking at Bennie with every other word."

"So?"

"Soooo," she exaggerated the word. "Being a lady isn't all it's cracked up to be. Take me for instance. I'm all decked out in this blouse and skirt, stockings, slip—the

whole package, and I look very ladylike, but as for comfort...'' She slid her feet free of the killer heels. "These
shoes are straight out of an episode of Torture Devices of
the Strange and Deranged.''

"What do your shoes have to do with the hot topic of
butts?''

"Nothing. They're just an example of what we women
endure to make you men happy. Which brings me to my
point. You wanted Bennie in a dress. She agreed, but there
were conditions.''

"What conditions?''

"That I would sort of help her out if she needed to
scratch. You see, all that lace is very uncomfortable. I know
because there was this time in the fifth grade when I got
picked to be the fairy princess in the Christmas pageant.
Not that I wanted to be the fairy princess. I wanted to be
the troll that lived under the bridge. He got to wear a beard
and boots and carry this leather scabbard, not that it was
real, but it looked real and... Anyway, I was too tall for
the troll, so I wound up in lace tights and fairy wings, and
I was still too tall. The tights were too small, and every
time I moved they slipped lower and the lace rubbed my
skin raw.''

"Let me get this straight, you launched into a discussion
about Mel Gibson's butt and screwed things up with Helen,
just so Bernadette could *scratch* herself?''

She nodded and watched him digest the information, his
face solemn, his eyes as hard as turquoise chips. Just when
the tension was thick enough to smother her, he burst out
laughing.

"You're not mad?'' she blurted out.

"Why would I be mad?''

"Well, scratching's not very ladylike, and I didn't exactly keep my end of the bargain, but I had to talk fast, and I was nervous.'' She gave Tyler a wide-eyed look. "What do we do now?''

"*We* don't do anything. I'll head back in there and see if I can patch up any mess you made. And you,'' he said, glancing at his watch, "are off the hook for now. Dinner is practically finished. I'll just tell Helen the spell got worse and you called it a night.''

She took a deep breath. "So it's over.''

"*Almost* over,'' he corrected. "After another quick performance at breakfast, you'll be finished, Helen will be out of here and I'll be off the hook.'' He passed a hand over his face and she noticed how tired he suddenly looked.

Her heart gave a painful thud.

"I'm really sorry if I messed things up.''

"At least it was for a good cause.'' His fingertips brushed her jaw, straightening the silk collar that had somehow turned up. "But under no circumstances bring up the subject again.''

"Deal,'' she said, hoping her voice sounded even while her senses were spinning. Bouncing. Doing a very fast, furious version of the macarena.

"Thanks for helping Bennie,'' he said.

"Thank you,'' she breathed.

"For what?''

For making me feel like Dorothy spinning away into the unknown. For making my heart pound so fast I feel as if I'm having cardiac arrest. For making me feel things I haven't ever felt before. "For not being mad,'' she finally said. "And for having *the* best pair of buns I've ever seen.''

An odd glimmer lit his eyes. "I'm not going near the buns comment, but I'm certainly not angry.'' He touched her shoulder and trailed his fingertips down her arm. "Though I'm not so sure about mad.''

Before she could question him, he pulled his hand away, his fingers skimming the side of one breast in the process.

"Sleep tight." He turned to stride back into the dining room while she stood there, barely breathing, trying to figure out what had just happened between them.

He'd touched her. Not just touched, but *caressed*. Her nipple stood at attention beneath the cream silk blouse and a wave of heat flooded her face.

Not that his touch meant anything. Tyler Grant was a flirt, a lady-killer, a wildcatter, wielding charm and sex appeal like Rambo with an Uzi. A girl had to be careful. She could enjoy the attention, the flirting, the whole seduction game, but she couldn't forget whom she was playing with, no matter how her traitorous hormones tried to claim amnesia.

It was just a game, and Tyler Grant was one smooth player. And for the first time, Lucky was off the bench and smack-dab in the middle of the action.

"CHECKMATE!" Helen cried after the shortest chess game in the history of the world. "Didn't you see me coming, Tyler? Why, even a child wouldn't have made that last move. It played right into my hands." The implications were there, but Helen was too pleased at winning against Tyler, who never lost a chess match, to see it as anything more than a well-deserved victory.

"You must be feeling a little under the weather, son," Merle said, sparing a glance at the chessboard before he resumed his pacing. His steps paused periodically as he dictated into a microcassette recorder.

"Actually, there must be something going around." Tyler patted his middle. "I'm feeling a little queasy. I think I'll look in on Bennie then call it a night."

"But it's only a little after nine," Helen cried. "I was

hoping we would have a chance to discuss Bernadette's enrollment at Smithston. I've brought the brochures and an application—"

Tyler interrupted with an exaggerated moan. "Cramp," he croaked in explanation, clutching his middle.

"This isn't one of those spells your nanny had, is it?" Her words dripped sarcasm and Merle patted her shoulder.

"Now, now, dear. The woman couldn't help herself. You heard Tyler. It hits her suddenly. That's understandable with her being so accustomed to the cool Scottish weather. This must be quite a change for her, though I can't say as I've ever heard of a heat allergy."

"I'm sure my cramp had nothing to do with an allergy," Tyler assured them. "Probably something I ate."

"I bet it's the mushrooms," he heard Helen tell Merle after he'd bid them both good-night and started for the hall-way. "They're dangerous. Not fit for civilized taste buds."

"You're allergic to mushrooms," Merle said.

"I am not. I have an iron constitution. The Bells don't have allergies, dear. We're all as healthy as horses."

Their voices faded as Tyler headed down the hall, past the kitchen and library. He turned a corner toward Bennie's room.

"I tell you, Ulysses." Mabel's voice carried from his father's partially open bedroom door. "That woman is downright rude. Imagine her criticizing my food. Why, I've won the annual pie competition for the past five years in a row. That woman wouldn't know a frying pan if it jumped out of the cupboard and bit her on the rump. And it wouldn't have a lick of trouble finding its target…"

Tyler rubbed his tired eyes. *It's almost over.* The thought gave him the energy to push open the door to Bennie's room.

She sprawled across the bed on her stomach, her chin

propped on one hand as she scanned the pages of *Texas Horse and Trainer*. The package Helen had brought her lay on the floor several feet away.

"Hi, Daddy." She smiled up at him.

"Did you like your new outfit?"

"Ugh, are you kidding? It's white with roses all over it."

"I'm sure it's pretty. Why don't you try it, honey? You might like getting dressed up once in a while."

She gave a heavy sigh. "Okay, maybe I'll try it."

"That's my girl. Lights out in five minutes."

Her mouth dropped open. Before she could get in a word edgewise, he turned and pulled the door closed. Bennie would argue until doomsday if Tyler gave her the chance. And he tried never to do that, especially since she was so effective at wearing him down. When she turned a smile on him, he was a goner. Thankfully, she hadn't figured that out yet. The day she did, he'd be in deep trouble. But he was already in deep trouble, a voice reminded him when he heard a door open, then walked smack-dab into Lucky.

"Oops, I'm sorry," she mumbled, her hands splayed against his chest as she caught herself. "I didn't hear you out here."

"Obviously." His gaze scanned her rumpled T-shirt and bare legs. Legs that went on forever. Long and tanned and...

Tyler swallowed and forced his attention back to her face. "Do you always walk around half-dressed?"

"I'm not half-dressed. Girls at the beach show ten times more than I'm showing, and I didn't think it would matter what I was wearing in the privacy of my room."

"You aren't in the privacy of your room. You're out in the hallway." His gaze lowered of its own accord, and he saw the goose bumps rise on her tanned skin. His fingers itched to reach out and ease her sudden chill.

Chill? How could she be cold? He was burning up. Hot, and getting hotter by the millisecond.

"I was just going to tiptoe to Bennie's room and say good-night," she told him. "I didn't expect to find you lurking in the hallway."

"I wasn't lurking. I was saying good-night myself."

"Good night then," she said, but before she could dart past him, he felt himself leaning toward her.

"Yes, it is a good night. A very good night..." He pressed against her, his chest brushing the tips of her breasts. A subtle touch, but it was still enough to send a jagged bolt of lightning down his spine, straight to his groin.

She looked startled for a quick moment, then her gaze brightened with wonder. It was the cookie look all over again, and the realization sent another jolt through him.

"I...I know this is harmless flirting and all," she stammered. "But I don't think this is really safe..."

He watched her form the words, warn him about Helen and why their current stance was too provocative. But what she was saying didn't really register. The only thing that stuck was the way she moved her lips. Full, soft lips he wanted so much to taste, needed to taste.

"I really want to kiss you," he told her.

"Me? Really—"

Then his mouth covered hers. He tasted her, nibbled the fullness of her bottom lip while she stood stiff as a board. Then she opened her lips on a sigh and her moment of surprise passed. His tongue tangled with hers, stroking, coaxing, and sensation skimmed down his spine, clear to his toes.

It was unlike anything he'd ever felt before, anything he

should feel with this woman. There was nothing particularly special about her. Sure she was attractive, and she tasted really good... To hell with good. She was intoxicating, mesmerizing. *Of course, Sherlock.* She knew exactly what she was doing. She'd probably practiced this innocent-hungry thing on some other poor sap who'd fallen hook, line and sinker. But not Tyler. He wasn't some gullible, hot-for-anything-in-a-skirt guy. No way. Not him.

He deepened the kiss, drinking in her sweetness, and she melted against him. She was just so...innocent. So... hungry. And she wasn't even wearing a skirt. Right. Tell that to the judge, sucker.

From far away he heard the slam of a door, the low murmur of voices and he forced himself away from her.

"Wow," she said, her eyes closed, her head resting against the wall as if she didn't have the energy to hold it up. "That was something."

Something, all right. But what?

Nothing, he told himself as he spun on his heel and walked away from her. It was just chemistry between them. She was a mistress of seduction with all that wide-eyed charm, and he was just a lowly guy. A starving dog in the face of a juicy T-bone.

Only for a little while. Thankfully, she would be gone tomorrow. He focused on that thought and strode outside to the barn. Some neighboring kids had been out joyriding on their daddy's tractor and had plowed down a stretch of fence in the north pasture earlier that day. The last thing he wanted was to be out fixing fences, but he knew he didn't stand a chance of sleeping and with cattle grazing that pastureland he had to get the barbed wire back up.

Fifteen minutes later, Tyler urged his horse forward, across the dark pasture. He reached the broken fence and went to work stretching the loose wire and stapling it tight.

Even with the ranch smaller than Tyler remembered, there was always work to do.

Guilt shot through him. At one time this ranch had rivaled its namesake from the movie *Giant*, the half-million-acre spread dominated by Rock Hudson and Elizabeth Taylor. But no more. The ranch had dwindled, a parcel of land sold here and there, until his father's Reata was just a shadow of what it had once been, the herd nearly sold off.

Tyler was doing his damnedest to change that. In less than two months since his return, he'd managed to track down several of the people who'd bought a piece of his father's land. He'd purchased every last acre back, all except for a few acres here and there. He was so very close to seeing Reata exactly the way it had been before he'd left sixteen years ago. Before he'd broken his father's heart by walking away.

But past regrets were just that. Past. He was home, he was making up for lost time, reclaiming Reata and increasing the size of the herd. Things were falling into place. Now if he could just send Helen packing, her mind at ease that her granddaughter was becoming every bit the lady her daughter had been, he'd be sitting pretty.

CAFFEINE. She needed caffeine.

Lucky stumbled toward the kitchen the next morning, her eyes blurry, her neck stiff and her legs wobbly from a restless night in an unfamiliar bed. And let's not forget the dreams. The sort that made your cheeks burn and your body crave a cold shower.

But of course, the shower hadn't helped a bit. Ah, but the caffeine. A little coffee, a diet soda, a piece of chocolate cake—the desperate woman's cure-all.

She adjusted the too-tight waistband of the black slacks

she'd found in the guest room and promised herself she'd start a diet the minute she got home. Exercise, her conscience screamed, but she stifled the voice before it could summon any guilt. Lucky had long ago convinced herself that the walk to the refrigerator counted as exercise.

She peeked into the kitchen to make sure the coast was clear. Although she was dressed like Nanny of the Year, she was in no hurry to run into anyone. She couldn't think, talk, even smile until she'd revved up her system.

"Bad night?" Tyler's voice sounded behind her and she jumped.

"Geez, don't do that. You scared me."

"*I* scared *you?*" His critical gaze fixed on her and he fingered a wayward strand of hair that had slipped loose from the hairband she'd borrowed from Bennie. "I take it you're not a morning person?"

"I'm fine in the mornings," she grumpily replied. "It's the middle of the night I have trouble with."

"It's 6:00 a.m."

"My point exactly. It's still dark out. Morning doesn't really start for at least another two hours."

"For you. Here we're up at five."

"Ugh," she said, slumping against the wall, wishing he wasn't standing so close and her head wasn't pounding so hard. Or was that her heart? It couldn't be her heart. Not this early. Not without a shot of caffeine.

"Go on back to your room and finish getting dressed," he said. "I'll have Mabel bring you a cup of coffee."

"I am finished," she said defensively, tucking the traitorous strand of hair behind one ear.

"Not your hair. Your shirt is on backward."

"It is not." She glanced down at the simple crew-neck pullover she'd found hanging in the closet. "How can you tell? It looks exactly the same from both sides."

"They don't put tags on both sides," he said, fingering the white flag peeking up at her collar. One fingertip brushed the pulse beat at the base of her neck and her breath caught.

"Uh-oh." She lifted her hand to shove the stubborn tag back beneath the neckline. "I could have sworn I had it right."

"These things can be tricky." He watched her fidget with the tag. She shoved it down, and it found its way back up again.

"Blast it," she muttered.

"Blast what?" came a woman's voice.

Lucky's gaze swiveled back toward the kitchen to see Mabel standing in the doorway, a basket of fresh eggs in her hands.

"Nothing," Tyler said, grabbing the tag and tearing it free.

"Thank you," Lucky breathed. The smile he gave her warmed her insides better than hot cocoa on the coldest morning.

"What are we blasting?" A jug of milk in her hands, Bennie followed Mabel inside, pausing to wipe her feet when the older woman frowned at her.

"I don't want any traces of that barn on my clean floor."

"Yes, ma'am," Bennie said. "Look, Daddy. We milked Betty Lou. Mabel's going to make pancakes and sausage for breakfast and fresh whipped cream from this milk." Bennie set the pitcher down on the counter. Picking up a half-empty glass of juice, she took a huge gulp.

"Shouldn't you be wearing something else?" Tyler asked her, his gaze going from her plain blue T-shirt, down past her blue jeans and sneakers, then back up again. "Like a dress."

"But Daddy—"

"You know your grandmother will be upset if she sees you like that. Put on that outfit she brought you last night, the one with the pink flower things on it." When Bennie turned a horrified expression on him, he added, "Please, honey. You'll look really pretty."

"Of course she will," Helen declared, walking into the kitchen. She wore an apricot-colored silk blouse and slacks, her makeup and hair perfect, as if she'd just walked out of a salon. Her cool eyes zeroed in on Lucky who busied herself drinking orange juice. "You look positively wretched."

The juice stuck in Lucky's throat. Wretched? Tired, maybe, out of sorts, even under the weather, but *wretched?* Definitely too harsh a word, even for somebody who'd put on her shirt backward. "Actually, I'm feeling much better."

Helen's eyes narrowed slightly. "Good, then you can join me. We didn't get much of a chance to chat last night."

"I'm sure Miss Myers would rather retire to her room. She's still a little ill." Tyler's gaze riveted on her. "Aren't you?"

"Come now, Tyler. If the girl says she's feeling better, then I'm sure she's feeling better, no matter how she looks." Helen sat down at the breakfast table and patted the seat next to her. "Come and have a seat, Miss Myers. I won't bite you."

Lucky started to ask Helen if she would be willing to put that in writing, but instead of her own voice, she heard Tyler's.

"I'm sure Miss Myers would love to visit, but she needs to rest. I want her in top form for Bernadette."

At the mention of her granddaughter, Helen gave Lucky

another thorough once-over. "She does look a little pale. And those clothes..."

"I'm feeling fine," Lucky heard herself say a second before she felt Tyler's hand on her arm.

"The medicine," he declared, his grip warning her not to say any more. "I think she took a little too much for her heat allergy and now everything's a little disorganized upstairs."

"I haven't taken anything—" His fingers tightened and the words stalled in her throat. "Actually, I could lie down a few minutes. Oh, my pounding head," she added for good measure.

"Medicine." Helen looked thoughtful. "Well, it's a relief to know she doesn't behave this way on a regular basis. I would hate to think this is the sort of woman you hired to teach my granddaughter how to conduct herself like a proper young lady."

"I don't need anyone to teach me anything," Bennie chimed in, only to have Tyler cut her off.

"Rest assured, Miss Myers is the epitome of grace and elegance. This is simply a bad day for her."

"And is this one of your bad days, as well?" Helen gave him a pointed stare. "You look dreadful, Tyler. In fact, I don't think I've ever seen you quite so *rough*-looking." She sniffed. "And that smell. What have you been doing?"

"It's called work," he replied, his voice calm and even, though Lucky could feel the tension in his body, his fingers still firm on her arm. "Why don't you visit with Bernadette while I help Miss Myers back to her room and get cleaned up?"

"A lovely idea," Helen said. "Miss Myers and I can chat later when she's feeling better. A long chat, after breakfast."

"Not enough time, I'm afraid." Tyler did his best to look

regretful, but Lucky could see the relief dancing in his eyes. "If you and Merle are going to make San Antonio by nine, you'll have to hit the road in the next half hour."

"There's been a change of plans. Merle had urgent pre-meeting business." Helen stared pointedly at the pitcher of juice, then at Mabel who looked as if she'd rather eat nails than pour the woman a drop. "He left an hour ago."

"*Left?* But y-you're still here."

"Of course I am, Tyler. One evening is so little time. I thought I would just stay and get reacquainted while Merle went on without me. I'm staying two weeks." She smiled and clasped Bennie's hand. "Two wonderful weeks to visit with my granddaughter and—" she shifted her attention to Lucky "—get to know the woman you've hired to care for her."

Lucky forced a swallow and turned her gaze to the man with the iron grip on her elbow.

And for the first time since she'd met him, Lucky saw Tyler Grant completely and utterly speechless.

7

"YOU'RE NOT GOING to throw up, are you?" Lucky watched Tyler pace the length of the library, a strange expression on his face.

"*Staying*," he muttered. "She's staying." He raked tense fingers through his hair. "For two weeks. *Two* weeks." He shot her an incredulous glance and kept pacing, his complexion visibly paler. He was upset, really upset, and she had the insane urge to cross the room and wrap her arms around him.

It was definitely too early in the morning.

"I'll just go back to my room and pack," she told him. "That way, if you really want to toss your cookies, you don't have to worry about being unmacho in front of me. I was hoping to make it home before the lunch-hour traffic. It's really heavy near the airport on Saturday—"

"You can't leave." He turned in her direction. "She's staying for two weeks."

"I understand that." He'd gone off the deep end. She could see the desperation in his eyes and it did funny things to her. She could feel the sympathy churning inside her, spreading, swamping her common sense.

"No," she blurted out as he advanced.

"No what?"

"No to whatever you're thinking."

"You can't leave. Please, Lucky. It's just two weeks."

"I can't abandon my life for two weeks."

"Not abandon. Just take a little vacation. You don't have a husband waiting at home, no kids."

"But I've got my granny. I visit every Monday. What will she say when I don't show up?"

"I don't know. What?"

She opened her mouth, but the words stalled on her lips. What would Granny say? Probably nothing. With Alzheimer's, half the time she didn't recognize Lucky. She simply sat out in the garden, picking flowers. She loved the nursing-home flowers.

The thousand-dollar-a-month nursing home that Lucky could barely afford. Forget afford. She was two months behind, her tuition money hanging in the balance, and she was desperate. As desperate as Tight Tush staring at her with his deep blue eyes.

"You really think we can pull this off for two weeks?"

"I'll help you, teach you everything you need to know. It won't be easy, but you can do it."

You can do it. For those few moments as he stared at her, she actually did feel like she could. Funny how blind faith could pump up your ego and make you contemplate the impossible.

She shook her head. "I know you're in a tough situation, but I can't lose two weeks of work."

"I'll pay you," he said. "Another thousand. That makes two thousand dollars for two weeks of your time."

She shook her head. "I'm already getting a thousand for last night, so technically it would only be one thousand dollars for two weeks of my time. I want two thousand for two weeks, plus last night's money."

"*Three* thousand dollars? For pretending to be my nanny? I could get a real one for less than that."

"Yes, but I'm already here, and you're asking a lot. You

want me to risk my life way out here for peanuts? No way.''

"Risk your life?"

"Your father nearly shot me yesterday."

"I took his gun away, so there's no risk. Two thousand," he insisted. "Total. That's my offer. Take it or leave it."

"You must not be a morning person, either."

"What does that mean?"

"You're not thinking clearly, otherwise, you would realize what a terrible mistake you're making. Helen already thinks I'm the governess, and you would have a lot of explaining to do if I up and left and you had to call the agency again."

He sighed. "Now I do feel like throwing up."

She smiled. "Agree to my terms and the urge will pass."

"Three thousand dollars." He ran a hand over his tired face. "I must be out of my mind."

"Three thousand, plus the eighty-dollar cab fare your nanny stiffed me for. *And* you promise to get rid of any and all firearms in the house."

He nodded. "All right, three thousand and eighty dollars, and the guns are history." His gaze zeroed in on her again. "But remember. You do everything I say, when I say it, and overall, do your best to avoid Helen. Got it?"

"I'll try." Doubt crept in and took a few bites out of Lucky's ego. "Do you really think I can pull this off?"

"You have to. Now stay in your room while I shower and change. I'll meet you back here in half an hour, after I have a sit-down with Bennie and tell her your post is going to take a little longer to fill, so you'll be staying for a few weeks."

"She's really great," Lucky said.

For a split second, his harsh expression eased and a smile tugged at his lips. "I know, that's why I can't let this little setback mess everything up. Bennie is the one thing I've done right in my life.''

"Oh, I'd be willing to bet you've done more than just one, Tyler Grant.'' That kiss, for instance. *Ooo, boy.*

She turned and left, her heart pounding double time. Mabel must have put something in the orange juice because Lucky was usually comatose until 8:00 a.m.

WHAT THE HELL was he doing?

The thought flashed in his mind as he watched her leave the room, her hips molded beneath the clinging black slacks.

Control, he told himself. She was his employee, he was her employer, and despite the sparks between them, she wasn't his type. When, *if* he ever settled down again, it would have to be with someone like Nan. Someone sophisticated, wealthy, refined. Helen's idea of an appropriate wife.

Lucky was completely off limits. He would coach her and pass her off as the best nanny this side of the Rio Grande. Nothing more. Period.

"Lucky's staying?" Bennie said when Tyler told her the news. Where he'd expected his daughter to turn sulky, accusing eyes on him, she actually smiled.

"It's Miss Myers to you, and it's only for two weeks," Tyler told her. "Until the agency can send a capable replacement."

"Until Grandmother leaves," Bennie chimed in.

"Pure coincidence." Tyler averted his gaze. He couldn't fill Bennie in on the details about the theft and Lucky's true identity. She might slip up and spill the news to Helen. "Miss Myers is very kind to have agreed to stay and help us, so I want you to cooperate and be nice, is that clear?"

"Since when am I not nice, Daddy?"

Tyler gave her a knowing look. "You want the full list?"

Bennie turned red and shook her head. "I'll behave. I'll act like the perfect lady." She gave him a kiss and left.

Lucky joined him in the library a little while later. She'd turned her shirt around, the material molding to her perfect breasts the way the slacks clung to her hips. The clothes were a little too small to look elegant. Inviting, yes. Elegant?

Forget inviting. He needed elegant.

"If you're going to pull this off for two weeks, then we have to prepare. There are certain things Helen will expect you to know. Proper etiquette, culture, who's who in Houston—things like that. We'll start tonight."

"Start what?"

"Lessons," he said, pulling a few leather volumes from the shelves. "Here," he said, handing her the books. "Start reading these."

"*Wine-tasting Made Easy* and *What Not to Say at the Dinner Table*. You're kidding, right?"

He shook his head. "The Dalton Agency doesn't peddle your average nanny/baby-sitter. We're talking educated, sophisticated women. Dalton nannies are trained for the wealthiest families."

"Obviously." Her gaze dropped to the books in her hands. "Gifts from your mother-in-law?"

"Actually, they were my mother's," he said, wondering why he didn't just keep his trap shut. Her gaze lifted, connected with his. That's why. She had eyes that begged him to talk, to pour out his soul. Damn, she was good.

"Trying to better herself?" Lucky asked.

"Trying to better the rest of us," he replied.

"So she didn't go for the rugged-cowboy type?"

He shook his head. "She liked the three-piece suit,

pocket-full-of-money type that doesn't sweat or get his
hands dirty.''

She smiled, her eyes crinkling at the corners, sparkling
with honesty and something else. ''Well, there's nothing
wrong with a little dirt and sweat. It builds character, or
that's what my daddy always said. So where is your mother
now?''

''She and my dad divorced when I was sixteen. She left
and I went to live with her.''

''You two must have been close.''

Tyler sighed. ''There was no being close to my mother,
though I tried. I went to the right schools, had the right
friends, wore the right clothes, even married the right
woman according to my mother's standards. Nannette, Bennie's mom, was as blue-blooded as they come. She was
perfect. Beautiful, smart, a product of good breeding and
heir to one of the oldest fortunes in Houston.''

''Did you love her?''

''You cut right to the chase, don't you?''

She smiled. ''I've always been very straightforward. So
answer the question. Did you?''

''We weren't *in* love, if that's what you mean. I loved
the idea that my mother was so taken with her, and she
liked the idea of dating someone her parents didn't approve
of.''

''You? But you're smart and handsome and—''

''I'm the son of a lowly rancher,'' he corrected, unable
to stifle a surge of pleasure at her quick defense. ''My father is self-made. His father was a sharecropper. Peasant
stock compared to royalty.''

''Nonsense, people are people. We all put our pants on
one leg at a time. So you do it in a fifty-room mansion in
River Oaks, while I'm in a one-room efficiency on the
south side. We're still doing the same thing.''

It sounded so simple—too simple to someone who'd spent his life trying to measure up, and too close to the truth. He pulled another volume from the shelf and handed it to her.

She smiled and clasped the books to her chest. "I'm not making any promises. I'm about as peasant as they come, but I'll do my best."

"Fair enough. Just read as much as you can, as fast as you can today, and tonight you and I will meet for a crash course in the fine art of being a Dalton nanny."

Meanwhile, Tyler was going to see what he could do to keep Helen preoccupied for the next two weeks. Right after he tortured himself with another cold shower and gave his libido a good lecture on how to control itself. And his heart. Definitely his heart, he decided when she turned another smile on him. Two weeks.

What the hell had he done?

"DON'T YOU WORRY about a thing. Between me, Buster and the boys, we got your granny covered."

"And tell everybody I'm sorry I have to miss Saturday's game. We're bowling the Quickie Cab Iguanas and I know the guys are nervous."

"About bowling against a bunch of lizards? They'll be fine without you and I'll give 'em your apologies personally."

"Thanks, Stella. You're a lifesaver."

"No need to thank me. Just take care of yourself, and make sure this guy's on the up-and-up."

"Oh, he's legitimate, all right. He gave me part of the money as a down payment, and he seems like a decent guy."

"Don't let him fool you. He's still a man," Stella declared, ''and they're all predators, every last one of them. They'll eat you alive at the first sign of weakness.''

''I should be so lucky. Of all the things I've ever been afraid of, being eaten alive by a good-looking cowboy has never been one of them.''

''Men don't care about looks. As long as you're breathing and you've got double X chromosomes, you're fair prey.''

Lucky wasn't in total agreement. Experience had taught her that it took a little more than simply being the correct sex to attract a man, any man, and to catch a guy like Tyler... The task was so daunting she didn't even want to think about it.

For a good-looking man of means like Tyler, a woman would have to have the entire thing going on: great body, great face, an abundance of feminine assets and a mind. One who could read several books in a single afternoon and look dynamite doing it.

Lucky had the mind, but it was all wrapped up in the wrong package. No pretty-colored paper or great big bow. She was more the plain brown wrapping-paper type, with plenty of strapping tape and a warning that read Tampering With Mail Is A Federal Offense. Violators Will Be Prosecuted.

''Don't underestimate him just because he's nice,'' Stella cautioned. ''You're a good girl, easy pickings for a lonely man out there in the middle of nowhere.''

Don't I wish, Lucky added silently. ''He's definitely not interested, but thanks for the advice.''

They talked a minute more while Lucky promised to take care and guard her innocence. Then she hung up and sat down at Tyler's desk to cram for a few more minutes before he arrived for their first nightly lesson.

She tried to concentrate, but talking with Stella had

stirred Tyler's image. And sitting in his chair, the scent of leather and male surrounding her, didn't help matters.

Bolting to her feet, she walked over to the broken movie projector. She busied herself putting the pieces that didn't require a screwdriver back together. Still, the task wasn't distracting enough.

Her nerves tingled as she remembered Tyler's soft but firm touch against her breast. Okay, so he was interested, despite what she'd told Stella. But only because Lucky was the only available female for miles.

She was practice. A convenient substitute for some gorgeous, well-endowed socialite. One who didn't put on her shirt backward and could tap-dance ''Yankee Doodle'' in four-inch stiletto heels without missing a step.

The realization gave her an ill feeling inside, but she forced it away. Forget the whys. Tyler was directing some attention toward her and she was determined to make the most of it. To flirt back and sharpen her own skills so when she returned to Houston, she could do some serious man-hunting, she reminded herself.

''That projector is a lost cause,'' Tyler said, leaning against the doorjamb.

''Nothing is a lost cause.'' She fit another piece into place then rubbed her hands together. ''You haven't seen me with a screwdriver and a wrench.''

''You'll have to settle for a fork and a knife.'' He motioned her to follow him. ''Let's go.''

''What do you mean and where are we going?''

''Helen's taking a bubble bath, so we're taking advantage of the time. Nanny lesson number one, you can't stare at me all through dinner.'' He led her into the dining room where she found two complete plate settings with enough silver to kill a dozen werewolves. ''There's a reason and a purpose for every fork, knife and spoon,'' he said.

"But I've been reading all day about wine-tasting."

"That'll come later. This is the most urgent. This and your appearance." His gaze traveled over her face. "Didn't Earline show you any makeup techniques?"

"I like the natural look." Liar. She'd tried for half an hour to duplicate Earline's eye-makeup technique, and had wound up looking like a circus clown. "I think I might need an extra lesson. I've never really been into makeup. It's hard work."

"Mabel can help you. But first things first." He indicated the lavishly laid table.

They started with napkins—the hows, whens and wheres of using them. Then Tyler went through a detailed description of each piece of silverware, and an hour later, Lucky had the headache of her life.

"You're not paying me enough for this." She stifled a yawn. "It's after ten on a Saturday night. I should be getting double-time."

"Think of this as a bonus, not work. You'll be wiser, more socially acceptable. Don't you want to improve yourself? Be a more well-rounded woman?"

Woman. He certainly had a way with words. And gazes. Hungry gazes. Yes, he had the hunger part down pat.

And as for well-rounded... Well, she really wouldn't mind a certain duo being better rounded.

"Okay, so maybe it isn't so bad that I'm learning this stuff." She chewed her bottom lip, a habit she'd picked up over the past twenty-four hours while she was on a gum fast, and studied the place setting. Carefully, she picked up each utensil and repeated what he'd told her. "And bottom line," she finished, "you start at the outside and work your way in."

"Good." The smile he gave her was more than good. It

was great, and worth the heavy-metal drum solo beating inside her head. Definitely worth it.

"You know, I've been meaning to ask you," Lucky began.

"Yes?"

"How did you learn to kiss so good? I mean, I'd like to learn, and if there's a school that produces great kissers, I'd be really interested in enrolling."

He stared at her incredulously. "You want to learn how to kiss? You have to be kidding? That kiss..." He shook his head. "I think you've got kissing down pat."

"Me? Really?" She brightened. "You think I'm a good kisser? Why? What was it I did? I need specifics."

"Are you serious? You're serious." He shook his head. "Look, Lucky." He took a deep breath and she saw the muscles in his arms tighten. "That kiss last night... It shouldn't have happened. You and I have to work together. I'm your boss and you're my nanny. Besides that, we're worlds apart and I don't have room in my life for a woman. I've got my daughter to think of, and this ranch and my father... Aw, hell." He leaned forward and captured her lips with his.

Before Lucky knew what was happening, she was in his arms, sitting on his lap, caught in a deep, urgent kiss that sent her senses reeling. Geez, he had great lips. Ah, and a wonderful tongue. He stroked and coaxed and took her breath away, and though she'd promised herself to stay alert and note every nuance for future reference, she couldn't think, much less document Tyler's incredible technique.

He swept her away with his mouth, his hands. His fingers stroked the length of her spine, fitting her against him. Soft female curves to hard male muscle. He felt wonderful. Strong. Hard...

"Tyler, boy, is that you?"

Lucky and Tyler jerked apart at the sound of Ulysses's voice. Lucky scrambled from Tyler's lap, wiping at her lips, her gaze fixed on tall, dark and gorgeous Tyler Grant. He looked stunned, shocked at what had just happened.

"Son?" Tyler's father stood in the doorway, wearing his bathrobe. The bandages were off now, both eyes red and nearly swollen shut. "I can't see a dadblasted thing." Ulysses groped his way into the room and sank into a chair. "Those damn city doctors."

Lucky took deep breaths and tried not to look at Tyler. Not with his father right there.

"Dad, the doctor said to relax. It'll take a few more days for the swelling to subside and for your eyes to adjust to the light. Then, hopefully, your vision will start to return to normal."

"Normal? Hell, I'd be happy with shapes, a few splotches of bright light—somethin' to show me the dad-burned surgery actually worked!" He waved his hands in front of him. "You don't know what it's like, boy. A man like me's used to fendin' for himself. It ain't natural for me to be stumblin' around." He felt on the table next to him and grabbed a bowl of potpourri. "So this is where I left my popcorn." Ulysses scooped a handful and prepared to shove it into his mouth.

"Dad!" Tyler grabbed his father's hand.

"What? Now I can't have popcorn? You been talkin' to that doctor about my dadburned cholesterol level again?"

"Dad, this isn't popcorn."

"'Course it is." He tugged at the bowl, but Tyler was stronger. He placed the bowl out of Ulysses's reach.

"Come on, Dad. It's late. Let me help you back to bed."

"I've been in that bed for hours, boy. My back's aching.

'Sides, I could use a little snack. What in blue blazes are you doing?''

"Having a...um, a talk with Miss Myers. She'll be re-placing—''

"That dadburned thief! Hot damn, boy, didn't you learn your lesson? You can't trust women like her.''

"Ulysses, here you are.'' Mabel came up behind Tyler's father. "I've been looking all over for you. Come on out to the kitchen and I'll fix you a sandwich.''

The old man patted Mabel's hand. "With the little pick-les?''

"A whole jar of them,'' she assured him.

"Lock up your personals, son,'' Ulysses muttered as he let Mabel help him up and usher him toward the door. "And watch your back.''

Lucky shook her head as Ulysses and Mabel made their way down the hall. "Your father doesn't exactly like me.''

"It isn't you. It's your type.''

"He doesn't like cabdrivers?''

"No, he doesn't like the type of woman he thinks you are—a fortune hunter, just like the nanny who ripped me off. Dad doesn't take too kindly to women only interested in a man's money, whether she wants to marry him or rip him off, or both. Give him a few days and I'm sure he'll mellow.''

"And if he doesn't?''

Tyler smiled. "I'll give Hank a call and we'll borrow his bulletproof vest.''

8

"I SEE YOU'RE FEELING better today." Helen's gaze roved over Lucky when she arrived for breakfast the following morning.

"A good night's sleep will do wonders." Tyler followed her, looking refreshed and sexy and too damned wide-awake in a red plaid shirt and faded jeans, his damp hair looking deliciously messy.

"Actually, I do feel better." Lucky ignored the urge to touch one damp tendril near his freshly shaven jaw. Instead, she slid into the seat next to Bennie.

"I thought," Tyler said to Helen as he poured syrup onto his pancakes, "we'd take a little look around the ranch after breakfast. Jed is covering for me this morning, so I've got a few hours. How does that sound?"

"Stimulating, dear, but I'm afraid I have other plans." Her gaze locked with Lucky's. "Miss Myers and I have a date to get to know each other better. Did you know that Bernadette will be the fifth-generation Bell to attend Smithston?"

"That little filly isn't a Bell, she's a Grant," Tyler's father said as he felt his way, with Mabel's assistance, to his seat. "And she's staying right here. This is her home."

"*Your* home." Helen turned to Bennie who was busy slathering her pancakes in butter-pecan syrup. "Dear, that's terrible for your heart and your hips."

"I don't have any hips."

"Keep eating this figure-poisoning food and you'll have more than one pair, I guarantee it. Isn't that right, Miss Myers?"

"Not necessarily," Lucky replied. "It's all a matter of metabolism."

"Nonsense." Helen placed the syrup out of Bennie's reach.

"It's a proven scientific fact. I picked up this doctor once—er, met this doctor once, a friend of Mr. Stinson's...a Scottish friend. Anyhow, he'd done a huge amount of research on the subject. Metabolism is everything."

"Perhaps that's true," Helen said, "but there's no way for Bernadette to know what sort of metabolism she has without eating like a horse and seeing where the pounds do or do not accumulate. And if they do accumulate somewhere, primarily the hips, darling, because Merle's family is definitely a hip family, then it's virtually too late to do anything about it." She patted Bennie's hand. "You don't want to be a fat debutante, dear."

"If Grandfather comes from a big-hip family, what do you come from?" Bennie asked around a syrup-drenched pancake.

"A big-mouth family," Ulysses piped in. Tyler nearly choked on his pancakes. Bernadette giggled and Lucky fought to keep from smiling.

"I see you're feeling better, too," Helen told Ulysses.

"Never felt better in my life...er, that is, if my dad-burned eyes weren't giving me so much trouble." He blinked the dadburned eyes in question, still red and swollen to little more than slits. "It's a good thing Tyler came home. I'd be lost without the boy."

"I'm sure you could make do just fine with a hired hand."

Ulysses poured syrup over his pancakes. "I could make do just fine if you minded your own business."

"Well, I never..."

"Ain't that the truth," Ulysses grumbled.

"Why, you...you insulting old goat! You make it impossible to carry on a civil conversation."

"Ain't nothin' civil about a stuck-up city gal buttin' into my business."

"Neanderthal," Helen huffed.

"Fund-raisin' fruitcake."

"Stubborn peasant."

"Rich bi—"

"Enough!" Tyler took a deep breath and glared at Ulysses. "Dad, you promised to be nice and this isn't the sort of conversation Bernadette needs to hear." He turned to his mother-in-law. "This...petty name-calling is beneath you, Helen."

Helen, as graceful as ever, sniffed and adjusted her napkin. "Of course, dear, it's just that he...he's so infuriating."

"And she sticks in my craw, boy."

"I don't stick anywhere on your person, least of all your craw. Whatever that is."

"What's a craw, Granddaddy?" Bennie stared hopefully at Ulysses.

"Well, darlin', you see, it's—"

"Not a fit topic for a young lady to be discussing at Sunday morning breakfast," Tyler cut in. "Can we eat, please?"

Ulysses shrugged. "Ask her. She's the one from the big-mouth family."

"That's big hip, Granddaddy," Bennie corrected.

"That's Merle's family." Helen frowned. "And for everyone's information, there are absolutely no ill traits in my family. The Bells are a result of good, pure breeding for over six generations, clear back to English royalty.''

''I don't know, Helen.'' Ulysses wiped a dribble of syrup at the corner of his mouth. ''Last I remember, you had a little extra baggage hangin' around them hips of yours.''

''Where's my butter knife?'' Helen growled. ''I'll show you extra baggage, you—''

Ulysses threw down his napkin and staggered to his feet. ''Get my shotgun, boy, and let's put the old girl out of her misery!''

''Old girl?'' Helen was on her feet, hands on hips, glaring.

''Call 'em like I see 'em.''

''And you can't see an inch in front of your face.''

''This round's over,'' Tyler announced. ''Everyone back to their corners.'' Helen sat down, and Ulysses excused himself and let Mabel help him back to his room.

Lucky couldn't help staring. Angry and frustrated, Tyler still looked good. So tall and muscular and delicious she was ready to chuck the pancakes and have him for breakfast, or lunch, or dinner.

He was every bit the cowboy this morning, with faded jeans that had been washed so many times they looked nearly white. They molded to the lean length of his legs. Scuffed brown boots peeked from the frayed hem. His shirt hugged his shoulders, the sleeves rolled up to reveal tanned forearms sprinkled with dark hair. He wasn't wearing his faded cowboy hat, but Lucky could picture it on his head, shielding his blue eyes and shadowed jaw.

She sighed, her lips still tingling from last night's kiss.

''Are you feeling okay?'' Tyler's voice penetrated her thoughts and she sat up straighter. ''I know all this carrying on so early is upsetting.''

''I'm fine.''

"Because you look a little...peaked," he finally said, his eyes assessing her flaming cheeks.

"I feel great." She ate another forkful of pancakes and Tyler turned to Helen.

"Are you sure you wouldn't like to see the rest of Reata?"

"And miss my talk with Miss Myers? Not on your life, Tyler. You run along and do whatever it is you do around here."

"Math right after breakfast," Tyler told Bennie.

"But it's Sunday—"

"And you still haven't finished your lesson from Friday."

"But I want Grandmother to teach me how to fight like she did with Granddaddy."

"Bennie, honey, fighting's not very ladylike," Tyler said.

"That's right." Helen patted her granddaughter's hand. "Ladies disagree, they don't fight."

"Then can I learn how to disagree?" She cast hopeful eyes at Tyler.

"Math," he said, but despite his I-ain't-taking-no-bull expression, there was a softness in his eyes. "Then practice your piano." Bennie made a face and Tyler winked before striding out of the dining room. A few minutes later, Bennie ate the last of her pancakes, and Lucky was left to face the Big Bad Mother-in-law on her own.

"So," Helen declared. "What do you say we find someplace more comfortable and have our little talk?"

"I—"

"Excuse me," Mabel said, appearing in the doorway. She gestured toward Helen. "You've got a phone call. They said something about the Ritz-Carlton withdrawing their offer for your fund-raiser or something like that."

"Oh no." Helen jumped up and rushed out before Lucky could swallow the last of her food.

Mabel moved forward and started clearing away the breakfast dishes. "My advice is to get while the getting is good."

"I'm out of here." Lucky got to her feet, hightailed it through the kitchen and out the back door. Outside was better. Plenty of places to hide from Helen if the need arose.

"You're still in one piece. I guess Helen didn't get much of a chance to talk." Tyler's voice drew her around the side of the house. He stood in front of the barn, saddling the beautiful black horse she'd seen him riding down by the river. "Let me guess, she's on the phone about her gala."

"Good guess."

He gave her a slow smile and Lucky knew there was no guessing involved. Somehow he was behind the sudden fund-raiser upset. Good-looking and clever. She was in deep trouble.

"It could take a while," he went on. "Once she starts in with her high-society friends, she can talk for hours, and this latest setback should keep her busy for a long time." He fastened a strap, gripped the saddle horn and swung himself onto the horse.

"Where are you going?"

"I've got work to do."

"But you can't just leave me here to twiddle my thumbs. What am I supposed to do for the next few hours?"

"Sneak back into your room and read the books I gave you."

"Are we having a pop quiz tonight?"

He grinned. "Maybe."

"With a bonus like the one last night?"

He frowned. "About last night..."

"It was a mistake. I'm your employee. You're my boss."

"Exactly. It shouldn't have happened."

"You keep saying that, but then you keep kissing me."

"Only twice."

She grinned. "Third time's a charm."

"There won't be a third time. Come on, Lucky. Have a heart. I don't need this...you and me and this...thing between us. I've got responsibilities."

Her grin turned to full-blown smile. "We have a *thing* between us?"

"Damn, you're good."

"At what?"

He shook his head. "You're good, but I'm not falling for it, sweetheart. I can't. If you've got any smarts in that pretty head of yours, you'll leave well enough alone, stop trying to play me and concentrate on collecting your money."

"I'm playing you? How?"

He growled. "Study." Then he steered the horse around.

She watched him gallop away a few seconds later, her gaze straying from his broad shoulders to his tush sitting in the saddle, to the muscular thighs gripping the horse.

It wasn't a sight for the faint of heart, or the sexually deprived, and she had to literally force her gaze away.

Strangely enough, it wasn't the sight of him riding the horse that stayed in her mind. She kept picturing him by the breakfast table, that warm smile on his face as he stared down at his daughter.

The Texas heat, she told herself. She was getting punchy again, because who in their right mind would trade such a great image of buns for a scene out of "Father Knows Best"?

Not her, not with him. Tyler Grant wasn't viable husband

material. But playing him... Now there was an intriguing thought.

With a smile on her face, Lucky started toward the house. She came to a jarring halt when she spotted Ulysses. He'd taken up residence in a rocker on the back porch. His cane sat across his knees, his hands gripping the chair arms.

Relax, she told herself. The man is as blind as Tyler is gorgeous. Just put one foot in front of the other and sneak by him. Easy. She took a deep breath and forced her legs to move, slowly, cautiously. She stepped onto the porch and headed for the doorway. Ulysses rocked back and forth a few feet to the right, mindless of her presence. She smiled. Piece of cake. Like taking candy from a baby—

Ulysses smacked his cane down to block her path. Lucky stumbled. "Got you!" he declared.

"Hey, what's the big idea?" Lucky grabbed at a porch post to regain her balance.

"Hush up and listen good." He pointed his cane at her. "I know your type, girlie, and don't you forget it."

"You know the unsophisticated, grease-monkey, Chicago-born-and-bred taxi-driver type?"

"Gold digger," Ulysses muttered. "Come runnin' out here to my ranch, flauntin' yourself to catch my boy and get your hands on his money, but I see right through them man-killer ways of yours, gal. A cab-driving nanny... Hah! A front, I tell you, and a damned poor one. But you mark my words, my boy sees right through you. He's known a lot of women like you, all tried to catch him, but not a one of 'em ever did. Married himself a gal with her own money. Lots of it." Ulysses poked at her with his cane. "That's it, ain't it? That's what brought you out here, ain't it? Now he's got double the money, so's you're thinkin' to really cash in. Admit it, gal!"

Ulysses shoved the cane at her again, and Lucky barely

resisted the urge to crack the blasted wood over his head. He was old and blind and obviously clueless. She was fairly sure God wouldn't let someone into heaven after she'd beat up on an old, helpless, blind man, no matter how provoking.

"Look, Mr. Grant. You're wrong. I'm not after Tyler's money. Well, okay, maybe a little of his money, but I'm earning that."

"Yeah, I just bet you are."

"I am. Oh no. I don't mean that kind of earning. I'm talking honest-to-goodness earn, as in work."

"You think you can work yourself right into his wallet, reel him in like some bigmouth bass and he won't resist 'cause you know just how to ring his bells. Is that it, girlie? You huntin' my boy?"

"I'm not hunting anyone, especially your boy. I don't know the first thing about reeling in men or ringing their bells, though I was hoping to remedy that when I got back to Houston."

"Sure you was, and I'm performin' brain surgery at noon today." He tapped his cane on the ground. "You mark my words. You let my boy alone and use those feminine wiles of yours on some other man."

Wiles? She smiled. She had wiles?

"I'm watchin' you," Ulysses warned. "You ain't gettin' your hands on my boy or his money. He's stayin' right here where he belongs." He sat back in his chair. "Damn city slicker. A vamp, that's what you are. Well, you ain't vampin' my boy. Not no, but hell no…"

Ulysses's grumbling followed Lucky into the house and down the hallway. *A vamp.* She smiled wider. Vamp was good. Of course, sultry sexpot would have been better, but at least she'd moved up from flat-as-a-pancake Lucky.

She should have gone straight to her room the way Tyler

had said. But the lure of the library and all those projector pieces distorted her rational thinking. All that machinery and nobody to put it back together.

Lucky went into the library and started sorting pieces. After fifteen minutes of careful scrutiny, she decided the thing was fixable. She begged a Phillips screwdriver, a flathead, and a wrench off of Mabel and went to work. Lucky was halfway into reconstructing the machine when a high-pitched scream shattered her concentration.

She bolted down the hall and followed Mabel and Bennie, who were already racing toward the living room. The three of them came to a staggering halt in the doorway, their gazes riveted on Helen, who sat in a mauve armchair, a cordless phone on her lap and a green lizard perched in her perfect silver coiffure.

"There's a *thing* on my head!" she shrieked, waving her arms excitedly. "Get it off! Get it off!"

Bennie dashed into the room and snatched the lizard from her grandmother's head.

"I—I was just sitting there on the phone and it just flew at me." Her frantic gaze went to Bernadette. "Don't panic, dear. Put it down slowly and Mabel can stomp it with her shoe—"

"Grandmother! That's murder!" Bennie stared down at the lizard. "And as for you, I've been worried sick about you."

"You...you..." Helen gasped and jumped to her feet, rubbing her arms as if a dozen creepy-crawlers swarmed over her. Her breaths came in short, ragged gasps. "You—you know this...this *lizard?*"

"Of course," Bennie said and shock gripped Helen's features. "And he didn't fly at you. Marlon doesn't fly, he crawls. He probably dropped from overhead."

"Marlon?"

"Yeah, he's my—"

"—nanny's pet," Lucky said, taking the lizard from Bennie. "Bad boy," she scolded. "Didn't Mommy Myers tell you to stay in your jar?" *Mommy Myers?* Okay, so she didn't think fast on her feet. But hey, she was trying.

"So it's your lizard." A momentary flicker of relief passed Helen's features as she realized Lucky was the happy owner and not her granddaughter. Then the relief gave way to outrage and more harsh gasps. "My Bernadette's nanny is keeping a lizard!"

"Why, he's been in the family for years," Lucky exclaimed. "Used to belong to my granny, then my dad, and now me." Great. She was the proud owner of a hand-me-down lizard. "Are you all right? Marlon didn't hurt you, did he?"

"I think I'm…hyper…ventilating…need…to lie…down." Helen staggered toward the hallway. "Mabel, please…if you have a…paper bag."

"To put over your head?" Mabel beamed. "My pleasure, Helen. You just come with me."

"Sorry Marlon surprised you," Lucky called after Helen. "He just loves company."

"Thank you, thank you, thank you," Bennie said once she and Lucky were alone. "I owe you one."

"Ugh." Lucky handed the lizard over to Bennie. "How did he get out?"

"I sort of let him out."

"Why?"

"I hate the thought of him being cooped up in the terrarium. He deserves freedom like everyone else."

"Then let him loose in the backyard."

"So Jed's cat can have him? No way. Besides, Marlon's one of my best friends. Isn't that right, buddy?" Marlon blinked in answer and Bennie smiled. "Anyhow, I usually let him crawl around my room in the mornings. Marlon loves exercise.'' The exercise-lover in question curled up in Bennie's palm like a wet green noodle, his eyes closed.

"Yeah, I can see that," Lucky said. "He's a regular aerobics king."

"Thanks again." Bennie's gaze dropped to the lizard. "Come on, Marlon. It's back to the torture chamber for us. Too bad you're not a math wizard instead of a lizard."

Chuckling, Bennie disappeared down the hallway and Lucky went back to the library. She scooped up the half-assembled projector and the rest of the parts and toted them back to her room. She could finish the job later, once she'd retrieved her toolbox from the trunk of the Chevy.

But now...

No more mothers-in-law, or flying lizards, or cranky old men wielding canes. Lucky was going to do what she should have done right after breakfast—hide in her room.

TWO HOURS LATER, Lucky stifled a yawn and willed her eyes open to the page in front of her. So much for reading to kill time. The words blurred and she slammed the book shut. She needed some fresh air or she'd wind up sleeping the day away—the longest Sunday of her entire life—and she couldn't, in good conscience, accept money for lazing around.

She was headed down the hall when she heard Bennie's voice.

"I *hate* this."

Lucky ducked her head into Bennie's room and saw the girl sitting at her desk wearing the dress Helen had brought her. "What's wrong?"

"Me," Bennie fumed. "I'm what's wrong. I'm not good at anything, least of all this stupid math. Mabel explained the percentage formula to me at least a dozen times this morning, but I still don't know what twenty percent of eighty-nine is and I don't care. I hate percentages, I hate math and I hate trying to do something I really hate, especially wearing this awful outfit. If I have to sit here a second longer, I'm liable to go blind.'' She rubbed her eyes, then covered her ears. "Or deaf. My head is just pounding and pounding and—''

"I know the feeling.'' Lucky walked into the room and stared at the textbook spread open on Bennie's cluttered desk. A blur of math problems glared back at her. "Maybe you need a break.''

She shook her head. "Daddy'll have my hide if I don't finish this stuff. Then there's the piano... Ugh, I hate Beethoven.''

"Forget Beethoven for a little while. You need sunshine and fresh air. Your dad seems like a pretty humane guy. I'm sure he doesn't want you to go blind or deaf.''

Bennie seemed to think about that for a long moment. "Well, fresh air does give you a new outlook sometimes. Besides, you're my nanny.'' She gave Lucky a smile. "I know Daddy wants me on my best and most cooperative behavior, and that means doing what I'm told, and that means taking a break if you say so.''

"So where are we going?'' Lucky asked once they were outside.

"To the barn. You like horses?''

"Mr. Ed was pretty cool.''

"Mr. Who?''

"Never mind,'' Lucky said as Bennie dragged her toward the barn.

"This is Liz.'' Bennie introduced Lucky to a shiny brown horse with a white splotch on her face. "She's named after Elizabeth Taylor, Granddad's favorite actress.''

"Your family's really into this old-movie stuff.''

"Granddad loves movies, but Dad doesn't seem to like them much. Not the old ones, anyway, but he did take me to see *The Santa Clause* last year." She stroked the horse. "Liz is the best birthday present ever. Granddaddy gave her to me last month when I turned twelve."

"And you're already doing percentages? Isn't that illegal?"

"It should be." She fed Liz a sugar cube and pouted.

"Can I feed him?" Lucky took a sugar cube, held it out to the horse and said, "How many sugar cubes do you suppose an animal this large usually eats?"

"She can eat as many as ten."

"Let me see," Lucky glanced into the bucket and counted. "It looks like you've got about fifty percent of that. You might need to get some more."

Bennie frowned. "Oh no. I'm sure five is enough. I don't want to spoil her appetite for lunch."

"That's it," Lucky said with a smile.

"That's what?"

"You just told me what fifty percent of ten is. It's five."

"I did?" Bennie's eyes lit with excitement. "I did!"

"And it wasn't so bad. You didn't go blind or deaf or feel a second of pain."

"It was easy. I mean, fifty percent is half of something, and half of ten is five."

"What are you two doing?" Tyler's voice drew them both around to the barn door. Clothes streaked with dirt, he stood with a saddle balanced over one shoulder, work gloves on his hands and a frown on his face.

"I solved a percentage problem," Bennie declared.

"That's great, honey," he said, swiping at the sweat lining his forehead. "Why don't you run on inside and see what Mabel's got for lunch? I'm starved."

"You're not so bad, for a nanny," Bennie told Lucky

before leaving the barn. She paused to give Tyler a smack on the cheek and an enthusiastic, "I did it!"

Tyler's gaze followed his daughter until she disappeared. Then he turned to Lucky.

She expected him to lay into her, to tell her how angry he was that she'd lured Bennie away from her studies. Instead, he smiled, that disarming smile that melted her defenses like hot popcorn melts butter.

"I've never seen her so excited over percentages before. Mabel isn't just my housekeeper and cook, she's a retired teacher who fills in as Bennie's tutor whenever we're between nannies. She's been trying to teach Bennie for weeks what you just did in a few minutes."

"Percentages are tough." Lucky grinned. "I ought to know, I had the very same thing explained to me a long time ago, only it involved spark plugs and lug nuts."

"You really love cars, don't you?"

"All kinds," she whispered. "But don't tell my Chevy. I wouldn't want her getting jealous."

"What about me?" The words came out so low, she almost didn't hear them. She wished she hadn't heard them. Then she wouldn't have to think about what they meant. Not that they really meant anything at all, she reminded herself. Tyler Grant didn't mean anything with all his teasing, his heated looks, his hungry gazes.

Wait a second. Hungry?

She did a double take, but the look in his eyes had faded. Deep, unreadable blue pools stared back at her.

Okay, forget hungry. Her imagination. Too much syrup on the pancakes this morning. Her brain was suffering from sugar rot. Nix the hunger idea and move on to something safe. "Why isn't Bennie going to school like every other kid?"

"Because Helen would come unglued if I put her in public school. She thinks Bennie is far above the average education system.''

"And what do you think?''

"I think she would do just fine in school with other kids her own age. *In*appropriate kids, as far as Helen's concerned.''

"You sure do pay a lot of attention to Helen's concerns.''

He shrugged. "I don't have a choice. She's my daughter's grandmother, and I don't want Bennie to ever feel caught in any disagreement between me and Helen. I want Bennie to have all the advantages. If she likes ranch life, fine. But if she ever has a craving for more, for Helen's world of ladyhood and tea parties and opera, I want her to feel comfortable with that, too. I want her to see all life has to offer and realize she can have everything. It isn't this life or that. She can fit in both worlds.''

"Like you?''

"Not like me.'' He shook his head. "I couldn't have it both ways, but Bennie can. She will.'' He lifted the edge of his shirt and wiped at his sweaty forehead again. When he finally spoke, his voice was considerably softer. "You're doing a good job with her. I really appreciate it.''

"Good, because I've got a proposition for you.'' She faced him. "I'm supposed to be Bennie's temporary nanny, so why don't I actually *be* the nanny?'' When he looked doubtful, she rushed on, "I can't stand sitting around doing nothing and getting paid for it. I want to earn the money you're forking over. I'm not prep-school polished, but I'm educated enough to be a darn good tutor. Besides, Helen is sure to be suspicious if she sees Mabel tutoring Bennie. That's the nanny's job.''

"All right,'' he said after weighing the idea for a few seconds. "You can help with her schoolwork and oversee her piano and French lessons, but I still want you to stay as far away from Helen as possible.''

"No problem. Consider me invisible." Which wasn't so far from the truth, at least for her chest. "I'm going to earn every penny of that money, you'll see."

"Oh, I plan on seeing, all right. Two weeks is a long time. You'll only be able to hide from Helen for so long before she gets ahold of you. Then it'll be showtime.''

"Meaning?"

"We're still on for our nightly lessons. You're fine in the academic department, but we need to work on your social skills." He shrugged. "And since we'll be working so closely together, we need to get something straight."

"No kissing."

"No kissing, no questions about kissing, or any other related topic. Strictly business.''

"Whatever you say, boss. But you're the one who keeps kissing me.''

"Don't remind me."

"Speaking of which, if you want a business relationship, why do you keep doing that—''

"Cut it out. I'm serious. No more questions. And don't look at me like that.''

"Like what?"

"Like that." He gestured toward her. "With your eyes so wide, your lips parted like that and that expression.''

"What expression—''

He growled and spun on his heel, and though Lucky had no firsthand experience, she had the inexplicable feeling that she'd just seen her first sexually frustrated man. And that she'd been the responsible party.

About time!

LUCKY SPENT the next several evenings with Tyler, and though she broached the subject of their kisses many times, he never failed to cut her off, and he was careful to keep his distance. Drat the man. How was she supposed to get this man-woman stuff down if he insisted on being so stubborn? And grouchy?

"You could smile once in a while. Your face won't break," she told him Wednesday.

"Remember all this stuff I'm teaching you and I'll smile."

"You drive a hard bargain." Lucky fidgeted in her chair.

"Just concentrate. You don't have to memorize every word. I just want you to have a general view of Helen's world and what she expects. Now, everyone who's anyone lives in River Oaks."

"I know the area like the back of my hand." Lucky launched into a description of streets and landmarks and Tyler frowned.

"Forget potholes and stop signs. You need to be familiar with some of the prominent families, such as..."

The list of Houston's elite seemed endless, but Lucky memorized every name, trivia about the families, Helen's charity contacts, and of course, Smithston. Not that Tyler had to tell Lucky anything about the elite school. It was all Helen talked about at dinner every night.

"Smithston is simply divine," Helen declared over pot roast on Thursday. "All three of Louise's daughters graduated from Smithston, and all of them married very well, I might add."

"That wouldn't be Louise Cromwell, would it?" Lucky stared across the table at Helen, watching her eyes widen in surprise. It was now or never. Either she shared some of her new knowledge or her brain was bound to explode from overload.

"Why, yes, it would. Don't tell me you know Louise?"

"Not personally, mind you. But she did a wonderful job

with that fund-raiser for the Houston Ballet last season.''
Lucky smiled and Helen frowned.

''But I thought you were in Scotland last season?''

So much for showing off. ''Well, uh, yes, but good news
travels fast, and it was such a worthy cause.''

Helen stared at Lucky for a long moment, those dark
eyes assessing. Finally she smiled. In the nick of time, too.
Lucky could feel the sweat beads about to pop out on her
forehead.

''Louise is a genius, and one of my dearest friends. Perhaps she could help me with all this trouble I'm having
with the museum fund-raiser. I simply have to find a new
location. I've been on the phone every day, all day, and
each place I call is already booked.''

''Guthrie's Barbecue. They do fund-raisers,'' Ulysses declared. ''Hosted the Texas Cattlemen Association's annual
cook-off last year. Got the best ribs this side of the Rio
Grande.''

''Barbecue? Really, Ulysses. I need a ballroom, a concert
hall, something appropriate for the affair.''

''Affair, my behind.''

''Now that is uncalled for,'' Helen huffed. ''Do you have
to be so vulgar every time you open your mouth?''

''No, I can eat, too. But it's more fun ribbin' you. You
know, you got a vein the size of Texas that pokes out on
your forehead when you're mad—''

''Dad!'' Tyler cut in.

''Uh, not that I can see it, mind you.'' Ulysses groped
for his water glass, his swollen red eyes fixed on the air in
front of him. ''My old sight still hasn't come back. But I
remember clear as day how it did look.''

''Rude,'' Helen said scornfully. ''That's what you are.''

''Snooty. That's what you are.''

''Buzzard.''

"Old fuddy-duddy."

And the insults went on and on with Tyler playing referee, Bennie smiling and Lucky doing her best not to laugh. As stressful as this nanny business was, it was the most fun Lucky had had in a long time, which spoke volumes for her lousy social life. But no more. In just over a week she returned home, richer and wiser, and she was going to nab the first available good-looking man she found.

Hurry! Hurry! her hormones chanted. If only her heart were half as enthusiastic.

WHILE LUCKY'S NIGHTS were filled with facts and headaches, her days were spent with Bernadette. Helen, thank goodness, was preoccupied with getting her gala back on track. The moment her plans fell into place, something happened to upset them and she was back on the phone. First, it was the location. Then she spent hours looking for a florist. Then the band cancelled. She stayed so busy she spared Lucky only a few harried glances. Thanks to Tyler.

He'd told Lucky he was a well-connected investment banker, a very successful one, but that image of him never quite fit with the rugged cowboy she saw day after day. As much trouble as Helen was having, however, Lucky had no doubt that Tyler had friends in very high places.

Helen's preoccupation gave Lucky and Bernadette some time to themselves, to study and do other things Lucky deemed were ladylike endeavors.

"I don't see why we have to do this," Bennie said one day. "I hate high heels and you hate high heels and I'm never going to wear them and you shouldn't, either, otherwise you'll wind up with bunions and calluses and all kinds of gross stuff like that."

"We're not learning this because we have to, Bennie.

We're doing it because we want to. For your dad. All this is really important to him.''

Bennie gave a heavy sigh and nodded. ''Oh, all right. For Daddy.'' She balanced the book on her head, stepped into the inch-high shoes and wobbled across the room. She also started wearing a dress every evening to dinner, and putting in extra time at the piano. Score one for Lucky the nanny.

Now, if Lucky the woman had been half as successful. Tyler—damn his stubborn, professional hide—had gone from flirty and fun to stuffy and preoccupied, and Lucky was back to fantasizing about Buster and push-up bras.

''STELLA, how's my granny?'' Lucky asked Friday evening when she phoned the cab company.

''Fine—''

''It's been a full week and I'm going crazy without you,'' Buster declared, ripping the phone from Stella's hand.

''Really?'' She smiled. ''You miss me?''

''Hell, yes! The Kangaroos creamed us. Stella's game stinks worse than Georgie Petrie's bowling shoes.''

''Stella?''

''She filled in for you. We had to have another person or the league would've disqualified us. When are you coming back? Because I lost a load of money, not to mention there's this new girl at the shoe counter that I want to impress, and losing isn't exactly impressive...''

''You missed my *bowling?*'' Her smile dissolved and she had the sudden vision of herself bowling a perfect strike with Buster's face as the tenth pin. ''Rest assured, I'll be back soon,'' she vowed with tight lips. ''How's my granny?''

''Fine. I ain't had my visit yet, my turn's tomorrow, but between all of us, somebody's looked in on her every day.''

''Tell everybody thanks for me.''

''Talk is cheap. If you're really thankful, get your carcass back here. We play the Munson Cab Magpies tomorrow night and...''

Buster went on about the new shoe girl and the whopping fifty bucks he had riding on the next game.

Forget Buster, she told herself once she managed to hang up a few minutes later. Who cared if he missed her? She didn't.

And she certainly didn't care one way or another if Tyler Grant kissed her again, the jerk. She would just get some practice somewhere else. Tyler wasn't the only man in the world.

At least that's what her hormones—those vocal devils— kept saying. If only the rest of her could agree.

9

"LUCKY, I'm in deep trouble!" Bernadette stood in the doorway of Lucky's bedroom Saturday morning. "Grandmother saw Marlon in my room. I told her I was babysitting him for you and I think she bought it, but anyway, she got this funny look in her eyes. I think she wants to take him back to Houston and have him made into shoes!"

"He's a three-inch lizard." Lucky put aside her screwdriver and stared at the antique projector, fully intact and operational once again. "What's she going to make? Barbie shoes?"

"Please," Bernadette pleaded. "He needs a new mommy."

At the distraught look on her face, Lucky nodded and found herself quickly cradling the limp lizard. "I'm not really the nurturing type. I've got a houseful of dead plants, small children cry and hit me with candy and... Oh Geez, I think he's really dead this time." Yuck. She was holding a dead lizard. Okay, so dead might be good in this case. A quick flush down the toilet and her mommy days would be over.

"He's just tired." Bernadette peered at Marlon, then poked him with a finger. "He sleeps a lot."

"I don't know," she said, then Marlon promptly blinked, killing the toilet fantasy. "Okay, so he's not dead, but I still don't know about this mommy business—"

"Bernadette! I'm choosing flowers for the centerpieces and I would like your opinion."

"Quick," Bennie said, yanking Lucky to her feet. "Get out of here and take Marlon to safety."

"Don't you think you're overreacting?"

"Grandmother loves to wear dead animals. She has an entire closetful of them. I won't let her add Marlon to the list."

"Okay." Lucky let Bennie pull her out the door and shove her down the hallway. "But you owe me, big time."

"Anything you want."

"Tea lessons. All refined ladies drink tea. I found a great book about it in your dad's library, complete with a video demonstrating appropriate tea behavior."

Helen's footsteps sounded closer and Bennie nodded frantically. "Anything, just take a hike for a little while and if Grandmother asks, you never even saw Marlon."

"Don't I wish," Lucky said once Bennie had disappeared. "But I guess we're stuck with each other." She slid Marlon into her pocket and headed out to the barn to kill some time.

"Dadblasted hired hands. If you want something done right, you got to do it yourself."

She turned to see Ulysses standing in an empty horse stall, a shovel in one hand.

Uh-oh. She started to back out, but Ulysses turned his angry red eyes in her direction.

"Hold it right there, girlie. You spyin' on me?"

"Uh, no. I was just taking a walk."

"Likely story." He turned back to shovel a pile of manure. "Well, hell's bells," he grumbled over his shoulder. "Stop spyin' and come on over here and give me a hand. This barn needs to be cleaned out from top to bottom."

"Should you be doing all of this in your condition?"

"I'm as fit as a fiddle, missy."

"But your eyes..."

"I worked this ranch my entire life and I'll be damned if I'm going to stop now. Jed and Tyler are overworked as it is. Hands are scarce. Here—" he motioned her toward a water hose "—make yours useful. That concrete aisle needs hosing."

"But—"

"Ain't afraid of a little work, are you, city gal?"

"Work, no. Lunatic old men with shovels, yes."

He glared at her for a long, silent moment, and Lucky barely resisted the urge to turn and run. She should. He had a shovel and he hated her. He could bop her on the head and bury her and no one would be the wiser.

Except maybe Bennie. Yeah, the little girl was sure to miss Marlon who'd be six feet under since he was tucked away in Lucky's pocket. She stiffened and held Ulysses's stare. Just let the old guy try to bop her. She'd shatter his precious projector all over again. Then he could put it back together himself.

After what seemed like eternity, he chuckled. Okay, so maybe the old geezer wasn't so bad and, of course, she could never destroy something she'd put hours into restoring.

He directed Lucky to hose down the concrete walkway that ran between the stalls, then set about shoveling more manure from the dirt floor of the stall. They worked for the next fifteen minutes in companionable silence and Lucky actually started to enjoy herself. Other than the smell—*and what smell!*—she rather liked having something to do besides the lady lessons she'd been torturing Bennie and herself with. She sprayed her way toward the end of the aisle, then turned to work her way back up.

"What's going on in here?"

Her head jerked up and she saw the unmistakable shadow of Tyler Grant in the barn doorway. She heard Ulysses's shovel hit the dirt a second before he walked out of the stall and straight into her line of fire. The spray hit him full force and he stumbled backward.

She let go of the handle and the water dwindled. "Oh, Geez, are you all right—"

"Help, boy, she's killing me!"

What?

Tyler sent her a murderous look, rushed to Ulysses's side and helped the man who stumbled and groped along the aisle as if he couldn't see two inches in front of his face. "Dad, what the devil is going on?"

"I heard a ruckus and I come out here to find this city gal makin' a mess out of my barn. I tried to stop her, son, but you saw what happened. Little filly's got a temper and I couldn't get within two feet of her."

He was lying. The man was lying, and Tyler believed him!

"Never ever wander out of the house again without somebody with you, Dad." Tyler helped Ulysses toward the barn door.

"What's all the ruckus?" Mabel met them just inside the doorway. "Ulysses? Are you all right?"

"Thanks to my boy here. You saved me, son. I don't know what an old man like me would do without you." Ulysses put on his most pathetic pout for Mabel. "Honey, my backside aches something fierce and I sure am hungry."

Tyler handed Ulysses over to Mabel and turned on Lucky, a frown carving his face.

"You didn't believe that, did you?" she demanded. "Why, I never heard a bigger bunch of..." Her words dwindled when Ulysses motioned frantically to her from just behind Tyler, and suddenly the situation became crystal clear. An act. A poor helpless act, and a pretty pitiful one. And Tyler believed it.

"Go on," Tyler growled at Lucky. "You were saying?"

"I never heard a bigger... Oh, all right. You caught me." *Sucker,* her conscience chided. Okay, so she was. A lizard-sitting sucker who had a heart.

Ulysses smiled and disappeared with Mabel, leaving Lucky to face Tyler on her own. Showdown at the OK Corral.

"Are you crazy?" he bellowed. "You could have killed my dad with that damned water hose! I know you don't like him, but—"

"Listen, buddy." She planted her hands on her hips. Suckers had their limits like everybody else. "It was an accident. Here I was trying to help out and he walked into my line of fire." She gripped the handle and aimed the hose at him. "Just like you're doing right now."

"You wouldn't dare."

"Oh, wouldn't I?"

"Dammit to hell!" he sputtered, arms raised to ward off the sudden spray of water.

Lucky soaked him good from head to boots before her courage faded and her lust took over. The hose went limp in her hands.

Water slid down Tyler's tanned face, the strong column of his throat. His drenched T-shirt molded to the hard muscles of his torso. Geez, he looked good wet. Too good. Too mad. He shoved dripping hair from his face and stalked toward her.

He reached her in three strides, gripped her upper arms and Lucky clamped her eyes shut. She couldn't stand the sight of blood, especially her own, and Tyler had murder on his mind.

He kissed her full on the mouth.

His lips were hard, insistent, not that they had to be. She softened immediately, her lips parting for the searching heat of his tongue. He devoured her for one fast and furious moment before he broke the contact to stare down at her, an unreadable expression in his eyes.

"I'm crazy," he muttered. Then he released her and stalked out of the barn, leaving Lucky dazed and confused and on fire.

She took a deep breath, turned the hose on herself and let the water fly.

OF ALL THE CABDRIVERS in Houston, Tyler had to wind up with Lucky. And she thought she was the unlucky one?

His tomboyish ugly duckling had turned into a swan. An intelligent, compassionate swan who got along with his daughter, which wasn't the problem in itself.

He was the problem. The way his heart did that funny double thump when she smiled at him, and the way he caught himself smiling back when he'd already decided not to, the way he leaned closer when she passed by him, the way his palms itched to reach out, to touch her. Hell, the way he had touched her, kissed her.

It was her fault. She was an expert at seducing men. She had to be or he wouldn't be falling so hard, so damned fast.

Or *getting* hard so damned fast, he thought later that evening when Lucky met him in the library for their lesson. Just the sight of her in cutoff blue-jean shorts and a white T-shirt pumped his blood faster. He tore his gaze from her and concentrated on uncorking two wine bottles.

"What's this?" She plopped down in the chair while he perched on the edge of the desk. "I thought you just wanted me to have a general knowledge of wines, in case the subject came up. I didn't know there was going to be an actual quiz."

"One week down, but we've still got a full seven days to go. I thought if you wowed Helen by choosing a bottle of wine, it would win you a few brownie points. Now," he said, indicating one of the bottles, "this is a white chardonnay."

"Chicken or seafood," she said with a pleased smile.

"Not bad, but we need details." He poured the pale liquid into a glass and held it up to the lamp for a quick study. "Light in color, almost like a sauvignon blanc." He held the rim to his nose. "Green apples and vanilla." He took a sip and savored the subtle burst of flavor. "Soft and fragrant..." He smiled at her. "Overall, a very well-balanced wine." He poured her a glass. "Your turn."

She took a tentative sip and went through the spiel.

"Good. Now, this chardonnay will be served with the salad and soup. After that," he said, reaching for the next bottle, "It's on to the main course and this 1991 Beringer Private Reserve cabernet sauvignon." He recited more tasting notes then handed her a glass. "Try it."

Taking a deep breath, she sipped the wine. She didn't miss a word or a gesture, the recitation ending on a huge hiccup. "Oops, sorry." Another hiccup. "I guess my system's not really used to this. I'll try not to do that tomorrow night."

She smiled, and for once the library's paneled walls didn't seem so gloomy, or the old movie paraphernalia a painful reminder. Not with Lucky across from him.

She sat cross-legged in her chair, her bare feet curled beneath her, her face free and clear of makeup, her hair pulled back in a simple hairband. Her eyes were warm chocolate, her cheeks glowing from the wine she'd consumed, and Tyler knew he'd never seen a woman look more beautiful.

She hiccuped again and took another drink. "This isn't bad."

"It shouldn't be at sixty dollars a bottle."

She choked on her next mouthful. "Sixty dollars?"

"Don't look so shocked. A first-growth Château Margeaux or Château Latour Bordeaux can go for two hundred dollars."

"It is good," she admitted, taking another sip. She stared at him for a long moment. "You know, I'm trying really hard to picture you in an expensive suit, forking over two hundred dollars for a bottle of wine, but I can't. You seem more like the beer-drinking, hell-raising type."

"I am. I just tried to pretend for a while that I wasn't."

"Well, if it's any consolation, I like the hell-raising type, though I don't know much about the beer part. I've never tried beer." She sipped her wine, hiccuped and smiled. "But this stuff is pretty good."

It was all he could do to keep from leaning forward and tasting her wine-wet lips. Just a leisurely trail of his tongue across her full bottom lip... Today, he'd been too worked up to take it slow. And he wanted it slow.

Hell, he wanted it fast, too.

Slow, fast, any way he could get it with her. *Her.* The realization hit him like a lightning bolt straight to his groin. As if that wasn't enough to fry his control, she decided to make matters worse.

"Why don't you kiss me?" Before he could answer, she stood and leaned into him. "Never mind. I'll kiss you." Her lips were soft and warm and full.

"Why did you do that?" he asked when she pulled away.

"I've been wanting to kiss you all day since the barn, then you didn't kiss me, so I kissed you and—"

"I meant stop. Why did you stop?" Before she could answer, he captured her lips again. She tasted of wine and woman and desire and he couldn't help himself. He moved her around, tipped her back over the desk and followed her down. He pressed into the cradle of her thighs. His tongue tangled with hers in a long breathless kiss that ended on a hiccup.

"Sorry," she breathed, "but you're making my head spin."

He grinned. "That's the wine."

"No," she said in all seriousness. "It's you." And the way she stared at him with all that wide-eyed innocence while her fingers traced naughty circles over the bulge in his jeans, it was all he could do not to embarrass himself.

"Ah, that feels so good," she said, her eyes closed, her lips curved into a smile.

"You feel good." He trailed a fingertip along her cheek, then dipped his head to follow the path with soft kisses. "You taste good, too."

"You've got great hands, Tyler." She wiggled underneath him. "Stop that," she said hoarsely. "No, don't stop. I love it."

Him kissing her cheek? She'd go crazy with a little ear nibbling. He leaned down and ran the tip of his tongue along the delicate shell.

She moaned, "Ahhhhhhhh," and caught her bottom lip, her eyes closed, her body arching. "Ooooooooooo."

He dipped his tongue into her ear and she came off the desk.

"I can't take it. Stop… Don't stop… I can't breathe." She gasped and he pulled away to stare at her face. "I said not to stop," she said, her eyes still closed, her lips curving. "That tickles. Oh, ah, not there…" She giggled and squirmed. "Keep going. Yeah, touch me just like that. Right there…"

"Lucky, I'm not touching you."

"Of course you are. I can feel you. Ooooooo, yes. Yes!"

"I'm not touching you!"

Her eyes snapped open and her smile faded. He leaned away from her and they both stared down the length separating them.

"Ah-ha! There you are, you bad boy!" She sat up and scooped Marlon off the inside of her thigh. "Mommy Myers was worried about you." She glanced up at Tyler. "I, uh, this is my recent adoptee."

"It's Bennie's lizard."

"She gave him to me. She's afraid Helen will make shoes out of him."

"I feel like making shoes out of him." He glared at Marlon before letting out a deep breath. "I'm insane. I'm envious of a damned lizard."

"Lizard envy," she said. "Is that anything like—"

"Close." He kissed her again, long and hard and desperate. "He got to third base and I'm still stuck in the batting cage."

"But you're up to bat now." She sat Marlon on a nearby chair and faced Tyler. "And if you swing as good as Marlon," she grinned, "I'd say you'll make it to third base."

"What about a home run?"

A dream, Lucky thought the moment the words sang through her head. This had to be a dream because no way in her ordinary, boring life would a tall, dark and dangerous cowboy be telling her he wanted to…

"I want you, Lucky. Now."

Way. She swallowed and tried to keep her heart from jumping right out of her chest. "This isn't like the last time, where you kiss me then change your mind—"

He touched two fingertips to her lips. "Now," he whispered again, kissing her hungrily. He swept her into his arms and strode through the darkened house. When they reached his bedroom, he slid her to her feet.

"We can't, not with everyone just down the hall—"

Another kiss silenced her. "I just need to get something." He disappeared inside while she shifted nervously in the hallway and did her best to keep from shouting hallelujah! It was really going to happen. Him and her. Together!

He came up behind her, a blanket in one arm, his shirt pocket stuffed full of foil packets. Condoms.

"Are we going to use all of those?"

He grinned. "We're going to give it one hell of a shot. Come on." He grabbed her hand and they headed outside. Behind the barn, they mounted a staircase that led to the second floor and a single doorway. Tyler paused to kiss her before he unlocked the door and led Lucky inside.

"What is this place?"

"The ranch foreman's office." He tossed the blanket on a nearby desk, slammed and locked the door behind them, then turned to the sofa. In seconds he'd folded it out into a bed that took up nearly the entire room.

"What if he comes back?"

He reached for her. "I'm the ranch foreman."

"Oh." She smiled up at him and his mouth touched hers.

Tyler's kiss was better this time, deeper, hungrier, more urgent, and much more frightening. But the urgency and fear were nothing compared to the desperate heat swirling through her body. Her nipples throbbed, her legs quivered, her insides ached.

Before she knew what was happening, he lifted her onto the desk, swept a stack of ledgers, a coffee mug and several pictures onto the floor, then pressed her onto her back. Large, strong hands worked at the buttons of her fly. He swept denim and panties off in one smooth motion, then parted her legs. Settling himself between them, he pulled her full against him.

She felt his hard length beneath his jeans. He rubbed against her, rough denim brushing sensitive flesh, and the friction made her gasp. He caught the sound with his mouth. His tongue tangled with hers to coax small, eager whimpers from her throat. He nibbled a path down her jaw, the slope of her neck.

She glanced down just in time to see him push up her T-shirt and free her breasts. A lifetime of insecurity kicked in and she struggled to cover herself. She didn't want to ruin things this time with an attack of the invisible, flat-chested woman.

"Don't," she said, shoving the shirt down.

He pushed the fabric back up and stared while Lucky's heart literally stopped beating. "I wonder," he murmured after an endless moment, "if they taste as good as they look."

Before she could even think of a reply, he dipped his head, drew one swollen nipple into his mouth, and shot Lucky's notions about men and chest preferences clear to the moon.

"Do they?" she asked breathlessly when he pulled away to scorch a path up the curve of her neck to her pulse beat.

"Do they what?"

"Taste as good?"

He lifted his head and smiled down at her, that all-too-familiar naked-stranger smile that made her nerves tingle. "Better," he said. "But I'm not through tasting." His weight shifted and his body slid lower. Then his mouth touched the inside of one bare thigh. "Eat your heart out, Marlon."

Tyler loved her with his mouth, his tongue, touching and tasting and heating her body. Then she exploded, crying out his name as a sweet river of sensation flooded over her, through her.

"I want to taste every inch of you." He trailed his fingers over the moist heat between her legs. "Feel you." His voice was ragged. "I'm damn near ready to burst just thinking about it."

"Then stop thinking and start doing."

"Impatient," he murmured. "I like that."

"Desperate," she said, "and I don't like it. *Do* something."

He grinned and caught her mouth in a hungry kiss. Then he scooped her into his arms and eased her down onto the mattress. He pulled the T-shirt over her head then stood back to unbutton his shirt. It slid away from his chest, down his arms and hit the floor. His boots followed. A zipper hissed and his jeans and briefs joined the pile of clothing.

She'd never seen a man naked before. Okay, well, she'd seen *Tyler* naked before—in the river. But no one else. Not in person, and, well, movies didn't come close to this. To *him*. Dark hair sprinkled his chest, swirling to an enticing line that headed for his navel, then lower…

She swallowed. He grinned. Then he grabbed a foil packet, slid on a condom and lowered his body to hers.

Panic swamped her all of five seconds as the tip of his hardness probed her throbbing heat. He brushed soft kisses on her lips, her eyelids, murmured explicit words of exactly what he wanted to do to her, and her initial fear passed.

"Oh, Lucky, you're so tight," he whispered a moment before he braced himself and plunged into her. "Oh no. Oh *no*. A *virgin?*" He stilled his movements, but it was too late.

Pain splintered through her and she clamped her eyes shut. "Just—just a formality," she mumbled as a scalding tear squeezed past her lashes to burn down her cheek.

"You're crying." He caught the drop with his tongue.

"I am not," she whispered back after a few heartbeats, "I—I never cry. Ever." Thankfully the tears dissolved as quickly as the pain. She moved her hips and relished the rush of sensation that shimmied through her.

"If you don't stop that, you'll make me lose control."

"Good. I don't want you in control. I want you totally out of control, and completely inside me." She lifted her pelvis, drew him deeper and he let out a low moan.

"Demanding," he said as he started to move inside her. His face eased into a grin. "I like that, too."

Then there were no more words, only a flood of sensation as he drove into her, slow at first, then faster, deeper, until she couldn't take any more.

She cried out. Her body burst into a thousand colorful specks while her hormones finally let loose that hallelujah victory cry and joined Tyler's fierce groan as he followed her into the land of the sexually satisfied.

Seconds later, he leaned away from her. "What did you say? It sounded like hal—"

"Nothing." She shook her head. *Everything.* She'd done it. And with him. And it had been great—

"I'm a jerk."

"You," she declared, "were wonderful.'

"And you," he said, leaning up on one elbow to stare down at her, "were a virgin. Hell, I never even thought..."

"I didn't exactly have 'virgin' tattooed on my forehead."

"No, but the way you looked, all that wide-eyed innocence. I thought it was an act, that you were used to seducing men."

"Me?" She smiled and pushed him onto his back to straddle him. "A seductress? Really?" He nodded and her smile widened, then her gaze shot to the pile of condoms. "One down and a few dozen to go."

"Damn, woman. A guy can only do so much."

She shrugged and pretended indifference. "Well, if you can't keep up...keep *it* up..." She started to move away, but an iron hand gripped her arm.

"*It* doesn't want you to go. I think you've made a new best friend."

"Just how friendly can I be?" She touched him gently, and grinned at his indrawn breath. "What about something a little...friendlier?" She mounted him, sliding down his length until he was full and throbbing inside her. "How about that?"

He nodded, his face severe, the muscles in his neck bulging. "Yeah, friendly's good." He gritted his teeth.

"Just good?" She moved, and flames licked at her senses.

"Great," he growled. "Greater than great." His hands cupped her buttocks and rocked her in a slow, gentle motion.

Then she lost herself in the wonderful feeling of loving Tyler Grant.

THE SLAM OF A DOOR jerked Lucky awake. "Tyler, wake up," she whispered. A heavy footfall on the steps below punctuated her words. "Tyler, come on. There's someone downstairs!"

His eyes snapped open. "Dammit," he breathed, his gaze darting to the windows where sunlight blazed just outside. Then he was on his feet, pulling on his jeans.

"I overslept." He worked at his zipper. "It's morning," he growled. "*Morning.*"

"I knew we shouldn't have done this with so many people nearby." Lucky wrung her hands as the footsteps moved closer, climbing the stairs outside. Her gaze riveted on the door. "What are we going to do? Everybody will know. Helen will know," she said in a rush of words. "And your father, and he warned me not to ring your bells and now he'll think I'm loose and easy, the wicked city girl come to claim his baby boy—"

"Shh." He peered past the drapes.

"Easy for you to say. You men have it so easy. You get a pat on the back while we women..."

We women. The words struck her like a lightning bolt from the femininity gods. A woman. A fully initiated, red-blooded, sexually active goddess extraordinaire!

"It's just Jed," Tyler told her. "He's probably looking for me. We've got a huge cattle shipment coming in today and I should have been up hours ago." He shrugged on his shirt and grabbed his boots. "I'll head him off at the pass. Wait ten minutes, then get dressed and go back to the house. And remember everything we went over about the wine. You're going solo with Helen tonight. I've already lost several hours of work. There's no way I'll make it back in time for dinner. Lucky?" He frowned. "Did you hear me?"

She nodded. "Wine, Helen." A woman. A real woman.

"And behave yourself." His gaze narrowed. "Are you okay?"

"Never better," she mumbled, waving him off just as Jed reached the top step outside.

Tyler stared at her, his face serious, contemplating for the space of two heartbeats. He strode over to give her a quick, hungry kiss. Then he was gone, the door closing behind him.

Once the voices outside faded, she crawled out of bed and floated into the small office bathroom. Her body tingled, her insides ached.

A woman!

She looked the same, she thought as she gazed into the mirror, yet she didn't. There was something about her eyes—a knowing that lit up the dark depths. And her mouth—pink and swollen from a night of passionate kisses. And her cheeks—full and rosy. She looked...like a woman.

"Eat your heart out, Marlon. You've been replaced."

10

OKAY, so maybe Lucky had fibbed when she'd promised to behave. But everybody knew you didn't let a car sit for days on end without letting the engine run a few minutes, and it had been so long since she'd been behind the wheel of her cab. Besides, with Helen still busy trying to line up a new band for her gala—the first *three* had miraculously cancelled—and Bernadette tasting practice pies for Mabel's entry in the annual Hickory pie competition, the coast was clear. And Lucky needed something, anything, to keep her mind off last night.

She still couldn't believe it. She'd floated through most of the morning, happy and dazed. Then she'd encountered Tyler out by the barn, getting ready to ride out, and reality had set in. She'd given him a brilliant smile and he'd barely tipped his hat. His face had been a stoic mask, his eyes shuttered with regret. A mistake, his look told her. We made a mistake.

So maybe they had in terms of their situation, but Lucky refused to let that fact color her happiness. This was her moment of triumph. Victory. She'd lost her virginity and she'd loved every moment. She refused to feel ashamed or regretful for something so wonderful, so…right, whether he wanted to admit it or not.

She forced Tyler from her thoughts and climbed into her cab. The engine purred to life. Ahhh. Her Chevy she could count on. Men would come and go, but this car would always be there. No matter what she looked like, how small her breasts, how long her legs. The engine missed, sputtered, and her happiness dissolved.

"Et tu, Brute?"

She had the sleeves of her navy silk blouse rolled up, her toolbox out of the trunk and the hood popped in that next instant. Relief swept through her. Just a bad plug.

"Hey there, Miss Lucky."

"Billy?" Panic swept through her as she stared at the pudgy officer outlined in the open garage door. "What are you doing here?"

"Me and Hank came out to talk to Tyler, but he ain't here."

"Um, Billy, you didn't happen to see Tyler's mother-in-law, did you?" The last thing she needed was Billy and Hank blowing her cover.

"Cain't say that I had that pleasure. Mabel said she was taking a nap, something about a headache over some fundraiser."

Thank heavens, Lucky thought.

"Hank's in the kitchen saying hello to Ulysses," Billy went on. "But he'll be along any minute. Haven't seen much of Ulysses since his surgery. We miss him at bingo. Nice old guy—"

"Billy!" Hank came barreling around the side of the house. "What the hell did you do to the patrol car?"

"I turned it off."

"Well, the engine won't start."

"Hi, Mr. Hank," Lucky said.

He spared her a quick glance and said, "Howdy, little lady," then did a fast double take. *"You're* the city gal Ulysses was talking about?"

"Yep," Billy chimed in. "She's Tyler's temporary nanny."

"How temporary?" Hank asked.

"Two weeks. One down. One to go."

"Good," he grumbled, turning toward Billy. "The blasted battery's dead or somethin'."

"Does it make any sound?" Lucky asked.

"Not a peep," Hank replied, his comment directed at Billy.

"Then it's probably not the battery," Lucky said. "Unless it's old."

"Battery's brand new," he said over his shoulder.

"What about the connectors?"

"They're fine, too. Now, Billy, I want you to go call Jess and tell him I need him out here—"

"Are you sure?" Lucky cut in. "Because if the engine's not turning over, it's obviously not getting any juice. And if the battery's new, then it has to be the connectors."

Hank glared. "And what do you know about connectors?"

Lucky rubbed her hands together. "Can I take a look?"

Billy nodded, Hank grumbled, and Lucky grabbed her toolbox and headed for the patrol car sitting out front. She popped the hood, took one look at the battery and smiled. "It's your connectors, all right. They're corroded. You have to keep them clean. If you don't get a good solid connection to your battery, it can be dangerous." She spent the next half hour cleaning and replacing the connectors. The engine purred to life.

"Thanks," Hank muttered grudgingly, shoving his hand out for a shake.

Lucky accepted the gesture, knowing it was probably harder for him than passing a kidney stone. "Any time."

"When is Tyler going to be back?" Hank asked, once he and Billy had climbed into the car.

"Late tonight."

"I already told Ulysses, but he was busy eating some of Mabel's pie and I don't know if he heard everything. We've got pictures being faxed to us from an airport in New York. Seems that thieving city woman tried to sell Tyler's watch. A surveillance camera got her on tape. We need Tyler to identify her. Tell him to drive into town as soon as he can."

"Did they catch her?"

"Dadblamed woman got away, but the police up there have a few leads. She purchased a plane ticket for Canada. They radioed the authorities there, and she'll have quite a surprise waiting for her, if it is her. That's what we need Tyler for. Ulysses never got a good look at her, what with his eyes and all, and Mabel says she thinks she can identify her, but she'd hate to be wrong, so that leaves Tyler."

"I'll be sure to tell him."

"Thanks again, Miss Lucky," Billy said.

"Yeah," Hank agreed, and Lucky couldn't help but smile.

An expression that dissolved the minute she turned and saw Helen standing in the library's huge bay window, watching her.

She swallowed the sudden lump in her throat and waved.

Not that it did any good, she realized when she noted the grease covering her hands, the open toolbox at her feet.

As she packed up her tools, she contemplated climbing into her cab and making a run for it. Tyler was going to be mad as hell if Helen told him.

If Helen had even seen anything. Maybe she'd just glanced out the window at that moment. Maybe she was nearsighted and had glimpsed nothing more than a few blobs of color. Maybe lightning would strike Lucky and she'd be spared having to explain anything to Tyler once he returned.

But then, Lucky Myers had never been very lucky.

Night fell crisp and clear, no lightning bolts in sight. Not even a little thunder. Helen, as it turned out, had twenty-twenty eyesight, and had seen the entire car-fixing episode. Lucky's ad-lib about the Scottish chauffeur showing her a bit of mechanical repair met with raised eyebrows. And even the wine-tasting notes Lucky recited that evening didn't keep Helen from meeting Tyler at the kitchen door when he walked in a little after midnight.

"SHE WAS *WHAT?*" Tyler rubbed his tired eyes and tried to concentrate on what Helen was saying.

"Up to her elbows in grease. She was fixing the sheriff's car. I saw it with my own two eyes. She's not setting an acceptable example for Bernadette. And you know what? Louise Cromwell has never even heard of a wealthy oilman named Dale Stinson. I tell you, Tyler, something doesn't add up with Miss Myers. And tonight..." She rolled her eyes. "Do you know what she wore to the table? White shoes. Not winter white, or cream or eggshell, but *white,* and it's long past Labor Day."

"By all means, let's cut off her head."

"I'm serious. This is not the sort of woman who should be instructing my granddaughter. You really should send Bernadette back to Houston with me. She's dying to go home—"

"She said that?"

"Not in so many words, but she did say she missed going to the theater with me and playing tennis and shopping, and I don't blame her one bit. You're always off doing whatever, rounding up God knows what while she sits in this house, isolated with a woman who doesn't know her white from her eggshell—"

"I'll talk to Miss Myers." When Helen didn't look satisfied, he added, "And I'll think about Smithston."

"That's all I'm asking."

If only she knew how much she was really asking. Tyler would sooner go head-to-head with an angry bull than see Bernadette caught between two people she loved. Had his daughter really missed theater and tennis and shopping?

Granted, she'd been behaving more like Helen and less like her old self for the past few days, but he'd thought it was her contribution to their charade. An act. But maybe...

God knew he'd been dead wrong before. Last night, for example.

A *virgin*, and all along he'd thought Lucky's wide eyes, pouty lips and perfect body—so damned awkward and sexy at the same time—had all been a facade, her I've-never-been-kissed behavior a well-rehearsed act. But there was nothing rehearsed about Lucky, and that was the trouble. She was all too real. No fronts, no airs put on just for his benefit. She felt the chemistry between them and she didn't hide her reaction to him and her. The two of them. Together.

Whoa, son. Back up. There was no together. So they'd had sex? Sex was just sex, even if it was with a virgin. Especially since it was with *this* virgin.

Used-to-be-virgin. He shook off the guilt. She'd made her choice, and he'd made her no promises. He hadn't even hinted at the C-word. Hell, he hadn't thought past the lust clouding his brain. He'd needed to touch her, taste her, smell her, and then he had and it had felt so...right.

What the hell was he thinking?

What happened between them was completely, totally, irrevocably *wrong*. She was a tough-talking, gum-chewing cabdriver from Houston. Not the sort of woman who should be raising his daughter.

Hey—who said anything about raising Bennie? Lucky was temporary. One more week and she'd be gone. One week... His libido sent a wave of images to taunt him. Boy, what he could do with her in one week—

Last night was a mistake he wouldn't repeat no matter how much he wanted to. There was no future beyond her pretend nannyship. No happily-ever-after, with Helen breathing down his neck and the ranch weighing on his shoulders. He had too many problems and no answers. And Lucky definitely fit into the first category.

He needed a shower, a cup of coffee and a good kick in the butt, in no particular order.

"Daddy?" Bennie walked into the kitchen wearing a pink nightgown.

He did a double take. "A nightgown? What happened to your Simpsons T-shirt?"

"That's old news, Daddy. Grandmother brought me this. You like it?"

"It's..." Pink. "Pretty. Real pretty, honey."

Bennie smiled. "I knew you'd like it. Grandmother said Mama used to wear one just like it when she was my age." Her hair was tousled, her features pale. She yawned and rubbed her eyes. "Are you okay?"

"Fine, honey." He rolled his head on his shoulders and sat down in a kitchen chair. She crawled into his lap and he rested his head on top of her soft hair. The smell of powder, soap and little girl sent a wave of affection through him and he hugged her. "I'm just tired."

"Me, too." She stifled another yawn.

"Late night?"

She nodded. "I was picking out my clothes for tomorrow. Grandmother and I are having brunch. Everybody who's anybody has brunch. Anyway, it was a toss-up between the yellow lace or the peach silk. The yellow's fine, but the peach brings out my complexion, don't you think?" Without waiting for a reply, she kissed his cheek and climbed from his lap. ''Get some sleep, Daddy.'' Then she padded back to her room.

Picking out clothes? His I'd-rather-be-wearing-yesterday's-jeans daughter? And *brunch?*

He pinched his leg to make sure he wasn't having a nightmare. Ouch! So much for wishful thinking. He was stuck in reality with frilly pink nightgowns and peach silk brunch clothes and a mother-in-law who made Cinderella's wicked stepmom look like Parent of the Year. And worst of all, he was stuck with a woman—yes, a woman now—he couldn't have.

Forget reality. He was in hell.

TYLER FOUND Lucky bright and early the next morning near the garage, leaning under the hood of a '64 pink El Dorado Cadillac, Earline's pride and joy.

''I'm sorry to put you out like this, Lucky,'' the beautician drawled, ''but that no good Jess Mangrum is as drunk as a skunk and I'm afraid this thing is gonna up and quit on me if I don't find out what all that noise is about. Billy said you sure were handy under the hood, so I thought what the hell?''

''No problem.'' Lucky emerged from under the hood, a black fan belt dangling from her hands. ''You need a new belt. I'll tighten this one as best I can until you can get a new one.''

''You're a honey, that's what you are. Tyler's lucky he found you. I hope he plans to keep you around for a while.''

''Not at this rate,'' Tyler said as he came up beside Earline.

Lucky jumped. ''Geez, you scared me.''

''Apparently not enough.'' He narrowed his gaze. ''What are you doing out here?''

"Just finishing up." She slammed the hood shut and wiped her hands. "It's all yours, Earline. It should last you at least a couple of days, enough time to get a new one."

"Thanks so much. You're wonderful. She's wonderful," Earline added, turning to Tyler. "A real—"

"—honey, I know," he finished for her.

"I thought I told you to behave," Tyler said once Earline and her pink Cadillac had left. "You call playing town mechanic when you're supposed to be a refined nanny behaving?"

"Helen saw me," Lucky declared, guilt in her eyes.

He nodded and watched her chew on her bottom lip. The sight did nothing to feed his anger and everything to stoke the fire spreading to certain parts of his body.

"I was afraid of that," she said.

"Dammit, Lucky, why didn't you let Hank fix his own car?"

"Because he couldn't. Not all men are mechanically inclined, you know. Gender doesn't predispose you to certain interests. The battery connectors were corroded and I cleaned them. I was just being nice."

He reached out and wiped a smudge of oil from her cheek. "Don't be so nice next time. I need you to look and act like a lady for the next few days. Just until Saturday. Then Helen leaves."

"I didn't get a speck of dirt on my blouse," she quickly told him, motioning to the spotless cream silk she now wore.

He smiled, drinking in her impeccable appearance. "I have to hand it to you. No one would be able to tell you'd just been fixing someone's fan belt—" The words stalled in his throat as he glanced down at her shoes, one black and one navy.

"Geez," she said, her gaze following the direction of

his. "I could have sworn those shoes were both the same color. Must've been the bad lighting."

"Bad lighting?"

"I already told you I'm not much of a morning person. I can't see clearly before 8:00 a.m. and I've been up since seven. So shoot me."

"Don't tempt me." He turned to stalk toward the Jeep. "Helen came at me last night with her guns blazing, so don't give her any more ammo."

"Wait—" She followed and grabbed his arm before he could climb into the Jeep.

"I've got fences to fix," he said.

"But I need to talk to you."

Here it comes, he thought. She wants to talk about the other night. To get into his head, pick his brain on everything from his feelings, to what china pattern he'd like. Damn, couldn't women get it through their heads that sex was just sex sometimes? Did they always have to talk everything to death?

"Hank had some news about your runaway nanny."

Whew, that was close.

"Thanks for telling me," he said after she repeated everything Smokey had told her. "I'll go into town later today and ID the pictures."

"Good." She started to turn away. "Happy fence-fixing."

"Lucky, wait. I... About the other night." *Hey, who was that?* Oh, God, it was him. He shook his head. Stop that. "You have to understand that it was just..."

"A mistake?"

"I was thinking temporary insanity, but mistake works, too."

"That's what I thought you'd say."

"And you agree?"

She smiled. "Fat chance, Tyler Grant. I've been waiting my whole adult life for what happened the other night, and I won't let your guilt mess this up for me. I'm basking."

"Basking?"

"And glowing, so stop feeling guilty."

"I took your virginity. How am I supposed to feel?"

"You didn't *take* anything. I gave it to you, buddy. My choice. You don't owe me anything. So stop worrying about me slipping a noose around your neck."

And just what did she have against slipping a noose around his neck? He was an attractive guy. A good catch. Only he didn't want to be caught. He was already caught between a rock and a hard place with Helen and the ranch and life in general.

"Stop beating yourself up," she told him. "Just forget it."

"I don't want to forget it. I *have* to. Can you understand that? No, I guess you can't. You were close to your dad. But me..." He shook his head. "I could kick myself now for tagging along after my mother and leaving my father. I try to picture how I'd feel if Bennie up and left me for Helen. It would kill me."

"You were just a kid then and Bennie would never do that."

"No, because I won't see her backed into a corner. I want to stay here with my dad, and that means keeping Helen happy, and that means giving Bennie every opportunity to be the lady her mother was. She can have that right here in Ulysses. She *can*."

She touched his arm, her fingers warm and soothing. "She does. She's learning tons of stuff, and I think she's even starting to like it. I don't have to nag to get her to put on a dress or do her studies, and she hasn't burped or snorted tea through her nose not once. She's even mastered

Beethoven's Fifth on the piano, and she's a whiz at conjugating French verbs.''

He gave her an incredulous look. "French? *Bennie?*"

"*Mais oui, mon cher.* Bennie taught me. I can say it in Italian, too. Want to hear?''

But he'd heard enough. *My beloved.*

He smiled. Then frowned. Then he kissed her.

11

___

IT WAS A KISS straight out of a steamy romance novel. Lots of clutching and grasping. Plenty of panting and moaning. Heaving chests and racing hearts. And then it was over.

"I—I guess that was a mistake, too," she said, gasping for a breath as Tyler staggered backward a few feet.

"Yes." His eyes were dark and desperate, riveted on her parted lips. "No... Hell, I don't know."

"We could try it again. Then maybe you could make up your mind."

He stared at her long and hard before he grinned. "I don't think that would be a good idea."

"Why's that?"

"Because I'd have you spread-eagle on the front of this Jeep, making an even bigger mistake than a kiss."

Speaking of bigger... Her gaze dropped to the prominent bulge in his jeans and her eyes widened. "Did I...do that?"

"Damn, woman," he growled, his gaze going to the sky. "What did I do to deserve this? Kick a cat in a past life?"

Her eyes narrowed. "I just asked a simple question. You don't have to fly off the handle."

"Simple? *Simple?*" He glared at her. "Do you know what those simple questions, those simple, wide-eyed, innocent questions do to me? They turn me on, that's what. Hell, Lucky. I'm only human."

"I really turn you on?"

He threw up his hands. "I give up. I'd better go before…"

"Before…" Her gaze went to the front of the Jeep and her cheeks heated.

"Before," he growled, sliding behind the wheel.

"YOUR RADIATOR'S busted," Lucky declared the next day as she stared through a thick layer of steam at Doris, Earline's assistant. "I can patch it up, but you'll have to replace it."

"Can't you replace it?"

Lucky smiled. "I'm fresh out of radiators, but any gas station should be able to order one."

"There's only one station in town, and that's Jess Mangrum's place. The man's three sheets to the wind most of the time. That's why, when Earline said what a great mechanic you were, I raced right out here."

Lucky patched the radiator while Bennie stood lookout. Tyler's new shipment of cattle had kept him away from the house most of the day, and Helen had moved on from hiring a band to redesigning the promotional materials to reflect the changes she'd been forced to make. At the moment she was poring over typestyles and various layouts, but Lucky wasn't taking any chances.

Guilt shot through her and she forced it aside. It wasn't as if she was breaking her promise to Tyler. Of the cars she'd fixed, not one of them had had a faulty belt.

"Thanks so much," Doris said, handing Lucky a box of homemade pralines. "Just a token of my appreciation."

"Can you teach me how to fix a car?" Bennie asked later as she and Lucky munched on warm pralines.

"Your daddy would have my hide. Fixing cars isn't very ladylike."

"What about fixing tractors?" Bennie asked when they walked around to the front of the house.

Lucky came up short, her gaze fixed on the green monster sitting in the driveway, a very frantic-looking teenager perched in the driver's seat. The teenager turned out to be Johnny Simmons, the oldest son of a neighboring rancher. "It's hard to steer and the lift doesn't work," he told her.

"This is way out of my league. It's a *tractor*."

"Come on, Miss Lucky. Earline told Charlotte Webster who told Billy Jenkins, whose little brother is in 4-H with my kid brother, that you fixed her Cadillac. *And* Bud Shiney's Buick and Ray Michaels's Impala and..."

"But I don't know beans about tractors."

"They're just like cars," Bennie said, surveying the tractor. "That's what Jed says."

Lucky peered inside. "Well, it's got a steering wheel, but there's no gas pedal. That's not like a car."

"You don't have to drive it," Johnny said. "Just fix it. Please, Miss Lucky." He sounded so desperate, and Lucky was a sucker for desperate.

Ten minutes later, they'd pushed the tractor behind the garage. Lucky went to work under the hood while a nervous Johnny went inside for a piece of Mabel's pie.

It wasn't too far off from a normal car engine, but it had a hydraulics system unlike anything Lucky had ever seen. She spent a good half hour studying Jed's tractor for comparison.

"I think the hydraulic lines were crossed," she finally determined. "It looks like the lift line was going to the steering, and vice versa." For the next hour, she unfastened the connectors and reran the lines.

"Let's try it out," Bennie said once Lucky had finished.

"No." Lucky wiped her hands on a rag.

"Come on, Lucky." A mischievous light glittered in

Bennie's eye. "How will you know it works if you don't start her up?"

Lucky shook her head and walked over to her cab. "Johnny can do it." She leaned into the trunk. "Bennie, can you hand me that wrench—" Her words drowned in the roar of a tractor.

She jerked up, her head banging the trunk lid. "Ouch—" The word caught as she swiveled around and saw Bennie sitting in the driver's seat of the tractor. "Bennie, get down from there."

"Let's take a little ride. Come on, Lucky." She gunned the engine. "It'll be fun—oops!" Bennie's foot slid off the clutch and the tractor lurched forward.

"Bennie!" The tractor jerked and launched across the backyard, headed out to pasture. Lucky bolted after it. She ran beside the tractor, grabbed the edge of the seat and tried to pull herself up. "Turn it off!"

"I can't. I—" Bennie wrestled with the steering wheel. The tractor made a sharp right and nearly took Lucky's arm out of its socket. "Lucky! Help me. I can't stop it!"

The back door burst open and Mabel rushed through. "What the sweet Jesus is going on? Oh no! Bennie, Lucky! Hold on. I'll get some help."

Hold on. Was she kidding? Lucky fought for a grip and barely managed to pull herself onto the seat of the speeding tractor. "Over," she shouted above the engine's roar as she grabbed hold of the steering wheel.

"Let up on the gas!" Bennie screamed from the seat beside her. "Hurry eeeeeeeeee!" Bennie jerked at Lucky's sleeve. "Watch where you're going—" They rolled over a stretch of barbed-wire fence, across the pasture toward a small duck pond.

"Come back here, dadblasted city gal!" Lucky twisted

to see Ulysses dart off the back porch in hot pursuit *without* his shotgun. There was a God—

"Lucky, watch it!" Bennie screamed and Lucky swung back in time to see the edge of the duck pond. She swerved, and found out that big bulky tractors didn't actually swerve. She fumbled with the brakes, and lurched to a stop just as the tractor plunged into the water. She and Bennie pitched forward, straight over the nose of the machine, into the murky pond.

"You gals all right?" Ulysses asked when he and Mabel reached the pond.

Lucky spit out a mouthful of water and gasped for air as she struggled to her feet. *Ugh.* She plucked a lily pad from her dripping hair and trudged around the submerged tractor, her pumps sinking two inches with each step.

"That was great!" Bennie followed her, not the least bit upset that she was soaking wet and covered with some kind of slimy green weed. "Mega cool, wasn't it, Lucky?"

"Cool?" Lucky took a deep breath and tried to calm her pounding heart. Water trickled down her face and she wiped her stinging eyes with the edge of her sleeve. "You almost got us *killed,* Bennie. I could be duck food right now—"

"You're responsible for this, Bernadette?"

Lucky's eyes snapped open to find Helen in front of them.

"I didn't mean to—"

"To get caught on the tractor with me," Lucky cut in. "But I needed her to show me how to start this baby up." She patted the tractor's rear bumper. "Then my foot slipped and off we went."

"You." Helen turned her narrowed gaze away from her granddaughter and the look of relief on Bennie's face was almost enough to ease the dread churning in Lucky's stom-

ach. If only Helen hadn't been steaming as bad as the half-submerged tractor.

"Now, now," Ulysses said. "Let the girl be."

Wait a second. Ulysses taking up for her? Maybe she'd hit her head during the dive into the pond. Maybe she was even dead.

"It was an accident," he went on and Lucky pinched herself. Pain radiated up to her head. Definitely alive. Unfortunately. "It's over. No harm done."

"An accident? You call my granddaughter trapped on a runaway tractor and thrown into a nasty swamp an *accident?* It's a disaster, a travesty. A shameful display of adult supervision. You can bet Tyler's going to hear about this, and you, Miss Myers, will be looking for a new job."

And Lucky had no doubt that it was true. Driving a tractor into a pond was sure to classify as a breach of her promise to Tyler. Even though she was fairly certain the tractor didn't even have a fan belt.

IT WASN'T HELEN who met Tyler at the door when he returned that evening. It was his father.

"Is Helen mad?" Tyler asked after he'd heard the story.

"Are you kidding, boy? She'd be waiting here right now, 'cept Mabel gave her something for her migraine. A little of Jed's moonshine. Told her it was medicinal tea." He chuckled. "Best medicine around. She's been sleepin' like a baby for the past hour, and she's sure to be out all night. Look, boy, I know this puts you in a bind, but don't be too hard on Lucky."

"She was fixing cars and tractors when I told her not to."

"She was helpin' folks out, and the tractor wreck was an accident." When Tyler shot him a look, Ulysses cleared his throat. "Uh, not that I seen it, mind, but Mabel relayed every detail."

"Do you mind telling me what brought on all the sympathy for Lucky? I thought you didn't like her."

"Never said that."

"Not in so many words, but you nearly shot her the first day, and you've been griping about her ever since."

"She ain't so bad."

"She's got a big mouth," Tyler said.

"The gal speaks her mind. Cain't fault her for that."

"She's stubborn."

"Just standin' up for herself. 'Sides, she's mighty handy with her toolbox." He chuckled. "She even fixed my old projector." When Tyler's gaze narrowed again, Ulysses added, "Not that I'll be watching any movies in the near future, not with my dadburned eyes being out of commission. Still, it's the thought that counts. Nice gal."

Later, as Tyler showered and changed, he thought over his father's sudden about-face. His father had always been a fair man, but since the breakup with Tyler's mother, he hadn't taken kindly to outsiders, especially females. He'd been hostile to all of Bernadette's nannies because he feared one of them would steal his son away. But Tyler wasn't going anywhere. He was staying until Ulysses made a complete recovery, and so was Bernadette, and Lucky was going to behave herself. Or else.

A HALF HOUR LATER, Tyler found her sitting on the front seat of her cab, her toolbox beside her.

"My dad gave me this for my sixteenth birthday." She touched the worn red metal. "I really miss him."

Something softened inside him, and he stiffened. He was mad, he reminded himself. Mad and out for blood. "Is that why you put a tractor in the duck pond? A tractor you shouldn't have been fixing in the first place?''

"Okay, get it over with," she said, closing her eyes.

"You promised me, Lucky."

"I know, and I broke my promise, though I didn't really break it, not technically. I didn't fix any fan belts. But I did work on a few cars, though Helen didn't see me. She only saw the tractor, so did your dad and Mabel. I figured he'd be getting the rope ready for Helen to string me up.''

"Dad's stubborn and can be mean when he wants to be, but you fixed his projector. That old thing means a lot to him. He would have staged a standoff with the whole damned town on your behalf.''

"He did seem excited when I showed it to him." She grinned. "He actually opened the glass case and let me touch the esteemed cowboy hat and boots. Boy, your father really liked James Dean.''

"My father *was* James Dean. That was the trouble. My mother wanted a Rock Hudson and she got James Dean. A Jett Rink instead of a Bick Benedict. My parents met for the first time at the premiere of *Giant* at the Austin Palladium. My father had just finished working his way through Texas A&M, as an agricultural science major, and my mother had just returned from a boarding school in London. They met during intermission.

"She had romantic notions about huge cattle ranches and lots of money," he went on. "My father had a ranch, all right, but only a few acres and a small shack right here where this house is. He'd just bought the land and was barely starting out. The reality of ranch life didn't quite meet her expectations, and neither did my father, but it was too late by then. They were already married, and she was already pregnant with me, and divorce wasn't an option as far as her parents were concerned." He shook his head. "It didn't work. My mother was used to lots of money, servants, city life. My father worked hard for her, built this place up, but it wasn't enough. Her parents died in a car accident, she inherited the family money and left when I was sixteen, and I went with her.''

''But why? You seem like you love it here.''

''I do. I did. But I also loved my mother and I wanted her to love me. I thought if I acted the way she wanted, became the man she'd wanted my father to be, it would make a difference.'' He shook his head. ''The only thing it did was break my father's heart. He lost his faith when we left, sold off pieces of the ranch and let the herd dwindle.'' Determination swept his features. ''But I'm changing all that.'' He felt her hand on his arm and warmth spread through him.

''No wonder you don't share your father's love for those old movies.''

''They're all reminders, *Giant* in particular, of a time in my life I'd rather forget. I remember my parents fighting. My mom would retreat to her bedroom and my dad would hole up in the library, watching his movies, wishing for a happy ending like the one on screen. It always made me sad to see him like that.''

''Where is your mother now?''

''Living in Connecticut, recently remarried to some Wall Street wizard. She's happy, I suppose. We don't talk much.''

''Her loss,'' Lucky said, and pleasure spiked through him. ''I'm sorry I messed things up. Was Helen really mad?''

''I don't know yet. She's sleeping. I expect she'll be fit to be tied.''

She sat there for a long moment, her gaze fixed straight

ahead. "She thinks she's better than me," Lucky finally said.

"She thinks she's better than everyone."

Lucky shook her head. "I grew up in a small place, went to public school. My clothes were clean, but worn." She continued to stare off into the distance. "But I never felt second best. I had my parents and I knew they loved me. You know," she went on, "my happiest memory is of one Thanksgiving we spent in my father's cab. He had to work, otherwise we weren't going to eat that month, and instead of sulking at home, my mother packed up the turkey and the dressing, bundled me up, and we ate dinner in the parking lot of O'Hare Airport." She smiled. "It was cold and cramped, but I've never felt as warm in my entire life."

"You're a lot luckier than you think, Lucky Myers." He lifted his hand, his fingertips going to her mouth. Her lips were soft. They parted beneath the slight pressure of his touch. Soft, and warm, and so damned tempting. *No!* If he kissed her once, he would want to do it again, and again, and then...

"Are you up for a little sight-seeing?" he asked.

"Are you kidding? I'm going stir-crazy. Give me five minutes."

When they met back outside near Tyler's Jeep, Lucky had traded in her worn tennis shoes for a pair of shiny red boots.

"Where in the world did you get those?"

She looked pleased. "From my fix-it stash. I've got a box of homemade pecan pralines, a recipe book and a coupon for a free manicure at Earline's."

"It seems you're getting pretty popular around here." He climbed in next to her and gunned the engine. He caught her sideways glance and saw the grin tugging at her lips.

"What can I say? I give great transmission."

"THIS IS LIKE a bad episode of 'Hee-Haw.'" She stared at the smoke-filled interior of Billy Ray's, Grant County's only and most notorious honky-tonk.

"I know it's a bit down to earth…" A crowd of people filled the place, despite the fact that it was only Tuesday night. Longnecks in hand, they whooped and hollered, a fast country two-step blaring from the sound system.

"It's not that. I don't feel above it." She drank in the dozens of women wearing western shirts, jeans and belt buckles big enough to eat dinner off of. "I just feel different," she added. Her gaze collided with his. "Out of place."

He reached for the hem of her T-shirt and knotted it at her waist. His knuckles skimmed her midriff and electricity sizzled across her skin. "You look casual and country. Perfect."

"Tyler!" They both turned to see Hank. "Got some news on your nanny. Even with the ID you made on her, she slipped past them New York cops and made it into Canada where she scammed a wealthy Canadian. Now they're as hot to catch her as we are."

"Keep me posted," Tyler said after turning down Smokey's offer of a beer.

"Lucky! Hey, Lucky!" Earline's excited voice carried from a table set up near the entrance.

"What are you doing?" Lucky asked, her gaze taking in the stack of applications and mountain of neon pink fliers.

"Signing up Hickory Honey wannabes for this year's pageant. It's Friday, you know. You will be at the festival, won't you?" Earline poked a finger at Tyler. "She can't miss the festival. I'm crowning this year's Honeys."

"She'll be there," Tyler promised. The next song started and he tugged her toward the dance floor. "Let's dance."

"Okay, but if I step on your toes, it's your own fault."

"I'm liable to be the one stepping on your toes. I haven't done this in a long time. Too long," he added in a regretful voice and Lucky squeezed his hand and gave him a dazzling smile.

He swung her into his arms, and then she was laughing and smiling and doing her best to follow his lead. She missed a few steps, but even that was fun. There was the encouragement of all the couples that sailed past, and by the time Lucky collapsed on her seat, she could hardly breathe, her face hurt from smiling, and warmth bubbled inside her.

"I think you're a hit," he said. "You must have been busy the past few days. How many cars did you fix?"

"Altogether about ten." She shot him a worried glance. "I already said I was sorry."

"Say it tomorrow. I'm not mad tonight."

She smiled and sipped the soda he'd ordered for her. "Then I'll take advantage of your good mood."

"Now that sounds interesting."

"I wish it would get interesting," she whispered to herself, her heart beating faster. "Much more interesting."

AN HOUR LATER, they left Billy Ray's, hand in hand, and headed for the ranch. A quiet silence engulfed them as he parked the Jeep out back and they simply sat there, staring up at the stars.

"It's always like this out here," he told her. "I used to walk out onto the balcony of my apartment in Houston, but even on the clearest night, you couldn't see this many stars."

"It's beautiful."

"Yes," he said, but he wasn't looking above them. He was looking at her. "You really have a great mouth."

"Nobody's ever said that to me before. I've heard I have a big mouth, a smart mouth, a loud mouth, but—"

Warm fingertips pressed against her lips. "All of the above, too. But I was talking more about the shape of your mouth. Perfect for kissing." His lips closed over hers for a long, delicious moment.

"You did it again," she said when their lips finally parted. "You said you weren't going to kiss me and here you are—"

"I'm not." He pulled her closer. "I can't."

"I know. It would never work." She slid her arms around his neck. "Never."

"Ever," he added, then he kissed her again, his mouth fierce and desperate now, as if he'd been away from her far too long.

Eager hands slipped under the hem of her T-shirt to caress her bare skin. Electricity danced along her nerve endings, sending sparks to her nipples, her thighs. Then his mouth left hers to kiss a wicked path down her neck, and lower, until his hot breath warmed the fabric covering her nipple.

"You're not wearing a bra." His voice was ragged.

"No one usually notices."

"I noticed."

She opened her mouth, but the only sound that escaped was a loud gasp as his wet mouth closed over the stiff peak. She clutched at his shoulders, pulling him closer, closer—

"Hell's bells, Tyler! Do you know what time it is?"

Ulysses's voice echoed in her ears and they both jerked upright, like two teenagers caught in the back seat of a car. Or the front seat of a wide-open Jeep. The spell was broken.

"Saved by the bell," Tyler muttered.

Bell? Damn but these Grant men had an obsession with bells.

12

"SHE ENDANGERED Bernadette's life," Helen exclaimed the next morning. "That sort of behavior is intolerable."

"It was an accident," Tyler said.

"She's supposed to be teaching Bernadette how to be a lady, Tyler. Not how to change spark plugs or fix transmissions. That's why the world has mechanics."

"So Miss Myers has a few eccentric hobbies. You enjoy needlepoint and playing bridge."

"I hardly see a comparison."

Neither did he, but he was desperate, and he hadn't become the Grant in Landry, Preston and Grant Investments by letting someone outwit or outtalk him. He could play hardball with the best, and Helen ranked up there in the top ten.

"Of course there's a comparison," he went on. "You're good at needlepoint and bridge. Extremely good," he added, watching Helen's face soften. "Which is one reason you enjoy both activities. Miss Myers happens to be more mechanically inclined, and so her leisurely pursuits are geared more in that direction—"

"Sorry to interrupt you, son, but there's a phone call for Helen." Ulysses appeared in the doorway, cordless phone in hand. "You two-timing Merle, woman?"

"I'm sure it's Julius Morrow, the photographer for the *Houston Star*. They've agreed to do a cover promotion for the museum benefit and they want to come out here to get a few preliminary photos. This isn't exactly the sort of image I had in mind, but Julius assured me that the rustic look is in right now. He'll be here Friday morning." She took the phone. "Julius, dear, how are you?"

Tyler didn't wait for her to finish her call. He had work to do, and while Helen wasn't completely satisfied, she was busy and that would keep her focused on her own affairs rather than on Lucky for a little while longer.

Long enough for this entire fiasco to be finished. Four days, Tyler told himself. She'd already fixed a number of cars and waterlogged a runaway tractor. What else could happen?

"YOU WANT ME to *what?*"

"Enter the Hickory Honey competition with me," Bennie said. "Come on, Lucky. I'll be in the junior division, and you'll be in the senior. We'll prove to Grandmother that we're real ladies. She loves pageants. She's a huge supporter of Miss Picasso and Miss Merlot, oh, and Miss Delphi, too."

"Run those by me again."

"Miss Picasso—the most talented new female artist in Texas. And there's Miss Merlot, the best female wine connoisseur. Miss Delphi is the title for the most cultured debutante in Houston."

"I think this is a little different, honey." Visions of Earine ran through Lucky's head. Boobs out to there, big Texas hair up to here, blue eye shadow bright enough to land an airplane in a thick fog. "Don't you think the Hickory Honey competition is a little more…down-to-earth than your grandmother's used to?"

"Granddaddy said it's the fanciest shindig this side of Dallas." Great. A shindig to impress Helen. Not!

"It's perfect," Bennie said enthusiastically. "You have

to do this with me, Lucky. I'd be too embarrassed by my-self, but with you, I know I could work up the nerve. We'll get all dressed up and walk around in high heels. Grand-mother will love it. She'll forget all about the tractor thing.'' She grabbed Lucky's hand. ''Please, please, *please.*''

No. It was there on the tip of her tongue. Just say no.

''Please,'' Bennie added, and Lucky nodded. *Wimp.*

''This is great.'' Bennie jumped around. ''You're great. Just wait until Grandmother sees us. She'll be speechless.''

Helen speechless? This might not be so bad after all.

''STELLA, it's me. How's my granny?''

''Fine. The boys have taken a real liking to her. Can't say as I blame them. She's so sweet.''

A warmth spread through Lucky. ''If she asks, tell her I'll be home soon. So how did we do against the Munson Cab Magpies?''

''We forfeited, and I never was so glad. I thought bowl-ing would be fun, but I can't seem to get into the game.''

''They had to forfeit because you didn't want to play?''

''Oh, no. The guys had other plans.''

''What could be more important than bowling and beer?''

''Your granny invited everybody to her bingo game. It was great. I won fifty bucks, and Buster won a hundred. He even met a new girl. The bingo caller. Gladys, I think her name was.''

Granny was fine, the guys weren't mad and Buster had a new babe. All was right with the world. Now if only Lucky could see things turn out as good right here in Ulys-ses. Fat chance. She was headed for blue eye shadow and teased hair, and the worst night of her life. Just her luck.

"I NEED A FAVOR," Lucky told Tyler Thursday morning when she finally managed to work up enough nerve to talk to him about the beauty pageant. Sort of.

"Me, too." Bennie waltzed in on Lucky's heels. "It's very, very important, and you absolutely *have* to do it, otherwise, our plan will be ruined and Grandmother will stay mad and—"

"Okay," Tyler agreed before she could go on. "As long as it's not painful or illegal."

"It's not illegal," Lucky assured him. "But I'm not so sure about the painful part." He shot her a questioning gaze, and she added, "We want you to keep Helen busy tomorrow while Bennie and I go into town for the day. We'll meet you and Helen at the high school tomorrow night for the festival kickoff."

"All day?"

She grinned. "So it's painful. You're a strong guy."

"Please, Daddy." Bennie threw her arms around his waist.

Tyler smiled, then the expression faded into a sniff. "Bernadette, are you wearing perfume?"

Bennie smiled up at him. "Grandmother gave it to me. Smells good, huh? It was Mom's favorite."

"And what's on your cheeks?"

Bennie beamed. "Pale Pink Parfait. Grandmother said Mom wore perfume and blush when she was my age, and lip gloss, too, but I keep chewing that off. So what do you think?"

"It's…nice, honey. Though you might lighten up a little." He shot a glance at Lucky that said, *Is she old enough for this stuff?*

Lucky shrugged. *Look who you're asking.*

"So promise you'll help us surprise Grandmother?" Bennie said.

"What's the surprise?"

"If I told you, it wouldn't be a surprise. Just have Grandmother there by seven."

"I'll try, but I don't think she'll go." He looked into his daughter's face, so full of hope, and sighed. "Helen's going to have a fit if you're not here tomorrow. Some photographer is driving in from Houston to take publicity photos for her fund-raiser."

"That's even more perfect," Bennie declared. "You have to get her to the festival, Daddy. It'll be a prime photo opportunity. Please, please, *please.*"

Oh no. Bennie was doing the please thing again. Maybe Tyler wouldn't be as marshmallow soft as she was. Maybe he would put a stop to things before... The big sucker.

"Thank you, Daddy. Thank you, thank you, *thank you.*" Bennie gave him another hug then darted out of the library.

"Hey," he said when Lucky started to follow. "Aren't you going to thank me, too?"

"For signing my death certificate?"

He frowned and motioned her into a chair in front of him. "What are you talking about?"

She sank into soft leather and shook her head. "Nothing. Listen, thanks. This means a lot to Bennie."

"Yeah." He slumped on the corner of the desk and Lucky had the overwhelming urge to reach up and touch his shadowed jaw. He was so beautiful and brooding and... celibate.

Not that it wasn't his own fault. She was ready and willing and able and...in love.

As if that mattered. She was in love with a man she couldn't have. One who wouldn't have her. Forget unlucky. She was cursed. What next? A swarm of locusts?

"She's growing up so fast, I can't keep up. Perfume, of all things. And that Peppermint Pink Popsicle stuff."

"That's Pale Pink Parfait."

"Yeah, that, too." He shook his head. "She's nearly a teenager and I'm clueless as to what to do with her. For her. About her."

Lucky gripped the arms of the chair. She wasn't going to touch him. Not for all the croissants in France. All the mufflers at Muffler Mania. No way. Uh-uh.

Hair-sprinkled muscle met the warmth of her palm. "Just love her, Tyler." She stroked his forearm. "That's all she really needs from you. Just love." *Bad hand.* Down, girl. Down. She managed to pry her hand away from him.

Okay, distance was better. No touching. She glared at her hand. You got that? Do that again and your history, sister.

"I wish things were that simple." He shook his head. "Bennie needs more, things I can't give her. She needs a woman to show her all this pink pickle stuff."

"You're off by an entire food group," Lucky muttered. "It's *parfait,* not pickle. One's dairy and the other's vegetable, and whoever heard of a pink pickle anyway?"

"See?" He threw up his hands. "I'm totally clueless. Nan did all the woman things with Bennie. When she died, I thought I could step in. Bennie had always been so much like me—wild and unruly. Since she was knee-high, she loved to wrestle and watch sports. She could spit farther than any toddler I'd ever seen."

"You must have been proud."

He beamed. "I'm always proud of her." His face fell. "But now I don't know what to do. She's growing up and she's turning into a woman." He stared at Lucky. "She needs a woman."

"I think you're the one who needs a woman." *Who said that?* Okay, so she had, but it wasn't as if she could help herself. He was standing right there in front of her, his denim-clad family jewels at eye level, about to pop a zip-per. So she'd looked, and she'd commented. Big deal? At least she hadn't touched.

Why hadn't she touched?

"I do," he growled. "And I'm in a helluva mess because of it." He stalked behind the desk, his *big deal* disappearing behind several inches of thick mahogany.

"Because why?"

"Because I want you."

"Me? You really want—"

"Don't even start. I have enough to worry about right now. Let's just try to make it through the next couple of days without touching or kissing, or doing anything really stupid. Okay?"

So kissing her was stupid? Yes. It was because it wouldn't stop there and it had to because there was no future for them. She knew that, yet it didn't ease the knot in her chest or dispel the urge to slap his handsome, stupid face.

"And you think your father's the blind one?" She bolted to her feet and glared at him. "You know something, Ty-ler? You are clueless. You're the most clueless man I've ever met. You give new meaning to the word." She turned and left him staring after her. *And the only really stupid thing I ever did was fall in love with you.*

LOVE WAS A BITCH. Lucky spent Thursday night tossing and turning, plotting ways to kill Tyler. Painful ways. Of course, she would always stop just short of actually doing him in, but the moments leading up to her change of heart were pretty good. Lots of crying and begging on his part. Still, her wimping out prevented any real satisfaction and she awoke grouchy and puffy and thoroughly unhappy.

As luck would have it, Lucky didn't even have the satisfaction of wallowing in her own misery. Bennie hauled her out of bed before the crack of dawn to get an early start into town. Mabel drove them in Jed's pickup, the bed full of her cooking entries: pecan pie, pecan cake, butter-pecan syrup, pecan pralines, pecan divinity and candied pecans.

"Lucky!" Earline squealed, intercepting her as she climbed out of the truck outside the high-school gymnasium where the festival was being held. Hooking her arm through Lucky's, Earline steered her two pageant hopefuls toward her pink Cadillac.

"We've got a ton of things to do before—oh, no, sugar." Earline frowned as she studied Lucky's face. "You're full of water. Oh, well," she brightened and started the ignition. "No need to worry. I know a surefire trick. We'll wrap you in cling wrap and sit you out in the sun for a few hours."

"Isn't that dangerous?"

"Only if you stay out too long. But we'll bring you in and unwrap you well before you dehydrate. You don't have a thing to worry about. I swear you won't end up like Sara Mae Mulberry."

"She dehydrated?"

Earline nodded. "And suffered sunstroke. She was so out of it, she stood up at the annual church picnic and did a striptease when the choir sang 'Beulah Land.'" At Lucky's horrified expression, the woman added, "But that was before I perfected the wrap." She patted Lucky's arm. "No need to worry. You're in good hands, sugar, and the choir's not even doing 'Beulah Land' tonight."

"WE'RE HERE," Earline declared late that afternoon when they reached the gym. She cast a pride-filled glance at Lucky and Bennie. "I'm telling you, it's in the bag."

Lucky took a deep breath, glanced down at the dress

Earline had spent most of the afternoon altering, a red se-
quined number that hugged every minute curve, minus the
excess water, of course. It was a bit more revealing than
she was used to. Used to? Okay, so she had underwear that
left more to the imagination than Earline's *lucky* dress, as
the woman had called it.

But Lucky needed some luck. Especially tonight.

Bennie, on the other hand, had an angel sitting on her
shoulder. Beautiful in a pink dress and pink pumps and a
matching shade of pale pink lipstick, she was a shoe-in to
win. Lucky smiled. Maybe this would work.

"WHAT IN HEAVEN'S NAME is going on?" Helen followed
Tyler into the crowded gymnasium, all the while voicing
the same complaint she'd made not five minutes ago in the
truck, then before that on the way to town, then back at the
house. "We're wasting Julius's time traipsing all over the
place, chasing after Bernadette. All we need are some simple shots."

"You'll get them," Tyler promised. "Now, let's find a
seat."

"In here?" Her gaze swept the already overflowing rows
of bleachers. "You have to be kidding. There's no back to
these chairs. Everyone is all crammed together. Dreadful,"
she huffed. "Simply dreadful."

"Positively," Julius, long blond hair pulled back in a
chic ponytail, quickly agreed. "And the lighting is hid-
eous."

"Oh, hush up, the two of you," Ulysses grumbled. "I
cain't concentrate with all that cackling."

"For your information," Helen said, bristling, "I don't
cackle."

"Cackle, cackle," Ulysses grumbled.

"Oh, shut up, you heathen."

"Uptight old biddy—"

"Hey, Tyler!" Hank called to him from a few rows away, effectively drowning out Ulysses's insult. "Good news. We got her! Canadian government nabbed her before she caught a plane to France. Recovered a load of stuff, too, you lucky son of a gun!"

"What is that man bellowing about?" Helen demanded, squeezing after Tyler down a crowded bleacher.

"Nothing."

"It didn't seem like nothing. Who was nabbed?"

"Yes, who?" Julius asked. "It sounds positively scandalous."

"Mind your own business," Ulysses said. "A man cain't even have a moment's peace with the two of you yacking."

"I don't yack."

"Yack, yack—"

"Quiet," Tyler said, sliding into a vacant spot and pulling Helen after him. "It's showtime."

"GOOD EVENING, folks! Welcome to the fourteenth annual Hickory Honey competition. I'm your hostess with the mostess, Earline Butterworth, and here's our first contestant."

Five contestants trailed by before Earline's assistant grabbed Lucky's elbow and herded her up to her mark.

"You're next," Doris said. "When Earline says your name, start walking."

Lucky nodded and rubbed her damp palms together. *You can do this.* For Bennie. You can walk through fire, dance over hot coals, bake in cling wrap like a leftover piece of chicken...

"Our next contestant is new to Ulysses... Let's give a great big welcome to Lucky Myers!"

Lucky took a deep breath, stared straight ahead and

strolled onto the walkway. Strolled, not stumbled, even though she was wearing three-inch heels. All those lessons had paid off. She smiled. This wasn't so bad. Just a few more feet, a little turn, and she'd be finished.

She hit the end of the runway and paused. Helen stared back from the second row, her eyes filled with shock. Panic bolted through Lucky and she stumbled. Then she saw Tyler. The way he looked at her, his blue eyes filled with so much—wonder, appreciation, hunger.

She caught her balance, pushed her shoulders back and smiled even wider. She turned, slowly and gracefully, hips swaying. *Eat your heart out, Tyler Grant,* and sashayed back up the runway to a round of cheers and applause.

"One down," she said, rushing backstage to stand next to Bennie who hugged her excitedly.

"You looked great! Did Grandmother see you? Oh, she must have died. I bet she apologizes for every mean thing she's ever said to you. Oh, this is great!"

"Come on, Bennie." Doris motioned the girl forward.

"Knock 'em dead," Lucky said, crossing her fingers. Helen in particular.

"And in our junior division, we have Ulysses's own Miss Bernadette Grant..."

Bernadette walked out onto the runway, her steps practiced and careful, and pride surged through Lucky. Bennie looked so beautiful. So ladylike. So sweet—

"Whoa!" Bennie squealed, arms flailing as she caught her heel on her hem and fell backward. She landed on her rump and slid out onto the runway, like a lacy pink bowling ball aiming for the center pin.

"What in heaven's name—" Helen's shout echoed above the background music. She gestured wildly toward the stage, then to the man next to her who clicked picture after picture with an expensive-looking camera. Uh-oh.

Lucky winced as Helen grabbed the camera and yanked the man around like a French poodle on a leash. Take that, Jacques. And that. And that, you camera-snapping, pony-tail-wearing Frenchie.

It was too painful. She couldn't watch. Her gaze shifted to Tyler who'd bolted to his feet to plow over the first two rows of people to get to his daughter. But Bennie was already scrambling to her feet. She dusted herself off and tossed a grin at her father. Tyler stopped, one leg hooked over the seat.

"Now for my next trick," she declared. "A quadruple backward flip." She kicked off her pumps and made her way back up the stage in a perfect succession of flips.

The audience went wild. Lucky joined in, applauding and cheering before her gaze found Tyler again. Her hands went limp.

He was still straddling the seats, to the dismay of the people in front of him. Not that he cared. He had this silly, dreamy look on his face, a smile tilting his lips, pride brightening his eyes. Something twisted in Lucky's gut and she all but melted into a red-sequined puddle.

Geez, she had it bad.

And that wasn't good.

"I was terrible." Bennie giggled, then moaned and threw herself into Lucky's arms.

"You were wonderful!"

"I fell and Grandmother had a coronary." Breathlessly, Bennie peered around the stage curtains. "She's still having a coronary." Bennie frowned and caught her lip between her teeth as she surveyed Helen and Frenchie. "I guess I really messed things up this time." Her head drooped and she stared at her now-shoeless feet. "I'm sorry, Lucky."

"Don't be sorry! This whole thing was a great idea, and it would've worked. It still might…"

Bennie shook her head. "You don't have to make me feel better. This is a disaster. This never would have happened to my mama. She was so pretty and graceful. She did everything right, said the right things, wore the right clothes." The girl turned eyes bright with tears on Lucky. "But me... I'll never be half as good as she was, and Daddy will never love me half as much."

"Oh, Bennie." Lucky hugged the girl tight. "That's not true. Your father loves you."

"Not enough," Bennie cried into Lucky's shoulder. "I'm not enough. I've read all the right books and watched those instructional videos you found in Dad's library. I want to be a lady like my mama. More than I've ever wanted anything."

"It's all right," Lucky crooned. "Come on, baby. They're about to announce the winners. Let's go get you some tissues."

TYLER WATCHED as Lucky hustled Bennie toward the ladies' room. His daughter's voice echoed in his ears. *I want to be a lady...*

So it hadn't been an act. The interest in clothes, Beethoven's Fifth, all those French verbs... She really did want to learn all that stuff, to be the lady her mother had been.

And she didn't stand a chance of doing it stuck way out here in Ulysses, with books and videos. To be like Nan, she needed the same opportunities—Smithston and Houston and Helen. *Damn.*

"There you are!" *Speak of the devil.* Tyler turned to face Helen. "This is all your fault," his mother-in-law said. "Julius is headed for the nearest FedEx office right now to overnight those horrible pictures back to Houston for tomorrow's society column."

"I'm sorry."

"I know you're dead set on staying here in this god-awful place," she said. "But I really wish you would open your eyes and smell the cappuccino, Tyler— What did you say?"

"I said I'm sorry." He raked a hand through his hair. "For bringing you and Julius here tonight. It was a mistake. Bringing Bennie to Ulysses was a mistake."

"Of course it was. This dreadful place is completely and totally unacceptable. Houston is her home. For heaven's sake, Tyler, she should be with other young ladies her age, not out risking her life on runaway tractors and pageant runways, and with that...that nanny."

"I know."

"You should fire that woman immediately— What did you say?"

"Dammit, Helen. Don't make this any harder on me. I said you were right. Houston is her home. I... Dammit."

"Are you saying you're letting me take her back?"

"I'm saying I'm taking her back."

"Thank God." Helen threw her hands up in the air. "You've finally come to your senses." She beamed. "Things will be absolutely perfect. Ulysses is all wrong for you, Tyler. You don't belong here."

But he did, he thought as he watched Helen disappear back into the gymnasium and found himself caught up amid a crowd of well-wishers backstage.

"Great kid you got there, Tyler. A regular chip off the old block. It's so good to have you back. You planning on joining the singles group over at the church? We'd love to have you come in and talk to the 4-H group at the school. I hear you're planning on increasing the herd? Bet your daddy's real happy about that. Proud, too."

This was the one and only place he'd ever really belonged, and sixteen years ago he'd walked away of his own free will and made the worst mistake of his life. He couldn't do it again, yet he couldn't say goodbye to his daughter. He wouldn't do that. He and Bennie belonged together, and they would stay together, even if it meant giving up the ranch for Houston. He'd walk through hell for her and challenge the devil to a fistfight.

And he'd break an old man's heart. Again.

Yep, he'd definitely done something terrible in a past life. Forget kicking the cat. He'd probably run over the damned thing.

"GIVE ME that blasted gun, girlie. I've got a snooty battle-ax of a mother-in-law to get rid of." Ulysses grabbed the gun, aimed at the colored balloons and started firing.

Pop. Pop-pop. Pop. Pop-pop-pop-pop-pop—

"Dad!" Tyler walked up to the balloon booth and yanked the imitation Uzi out of his father's hands. "What are you doing?"

"Killin' me a woman, son."

"He's won two purple stuffed teddy bears and a polka-dot alligator." The girl at the booth stacked Ulysses's prizes on the counter.

"Damn straight. How many till I get that hot-pink turtle?"

"Five in a row."

"Take that, Smellin' Helen." Ulysses grabbed another gun from the counter and started firing again.

"Dad."

"Don't bother me now, boy. I'm concentratin'." *Pop. Pop.*

"Your aim's really good."

"Thank you, boy. Now quiet." *Pop-pop. Pop-pop-pop.*

"Especially considering you're blind."

Pop! The gun went limp in Ulysses's hands and he threw

his arms up in the air. "It's a miracle, son. I've been healed. Praise be!"

"Dad." Tyler tapped him on the shoulder.

"Don't bother me now, son. I'm givin' thanks to the Lord."

"You've been able to see since the bandages came off, haven't you?"

"I know I'm a sinner, Lord. But now I aim to change my ways. Thank you for smilin' on me and givin' me my eyes back."

"You've been lying to me."

"And forgive my boy here for doubtin' your blessings."

"That time in the barn with Lucky. You walked in front of her on purpose and she covered for you. She knew, too, right?"

"I'll be in church every Sunday mornin' from here till the day I meet my maker."

"Mabel was in on it, too. And Jed."

Ulysses turned two angry red eyes on Tyler. "Don't be taintin' Mabel's name like that. She's a good woman."

"So you fooled her, too?"

"Shame on you for doubtin' the Lord's work." Ulysses turned his arms up at the sky again. "I won't be slippin' any more quarters out of the offerin' ever again."

"Shame on you, Dad."

"Aw, hell, boy." Ulysses let his arms drop.

"Why, Dad?"

"You came home, boy, and I wanted you and Bennie to stay permanently. I thought if you thought I needed you—"

"That we'd stay."

Ulysses nodded. "I know it was a low trick—and Mabel had no part of it, mind you. The woman's a saint. But I did what I had to. I didn't want to let you go again."

"I'm sorry, Dad. Sorry I left, sorry I hurt you, sorry the ranch suffered because of it."

"Now, that's the last thing you ought to be sorry for. The ranch is just land."

"But you worked hard for it."

"Not for *it,* boy, for your ma. For you. All I ever wanted was a little piece of land, a few head of cattle. I'm a simple man, Tyler. Always have been. Your ma didn't understand that. I built this place up for her. When she left, it lost its meaning." He shook his head. "Now I ain't blamin' things on her. She's a good woman, she's just different from me, is all. She wanted different things out of life. I loved her and wanted her happy, so I let her go. I let you go, too, because I wanted you to be happy. And I'll let you go now if it's what you want."

"I want Bennie to be happy."

"Then do what you have to, boy. Your old daddy understands."

It was as if a weight had been lifted. Tyler took a deep breath and for the first time he didn't feel the tightness in his chest. The guilt. "Thanks, Dad."

"Don't worry none about me," Ulysses went on. "I'll be fine. Why, my hearing's nearly shot, but it ought to last a good six months more. And if I decide to have that surgery on my old arthritic knees, why, I'm sure I won't be laid up more 'n a few months. Three or four at the most. Mabel and Jed can run things, even if the ranch is a good size larger thanks to you. But don't go frettin' over us. We'll manage—"

"Dad."

"Oh, go on." Ulysses waved him away. "I've got a hot-pink turtle to win for my grandbaby. A going-away present." He slapped a twenty on the counter. "Maybe I'll even get something for Lucky." He picked up the Uzi and aimed. ''Take that Yellin' Helen, you old nosy, highfalutin, pain-in-the-ass, hemorroid-causin' nanny goat...''

The words faded in a string of *pops* as Tyler headed back inside the gym. He still had a loose end to tie up, one that belonged to a beautiful and lethal-to-his-sanity cabdriver.

And for the first time since he'd decided to return to Houston, Tyler actually smiled.

13

"CONGRATULATIONS, Lucky! You deserve it, darlin'! Glad to have you here in Ulysses, sugar! Hey, Lucky, I've got this knocking in my engine…"

The praises and well-wishes surrounded Lucky as she shook hands, accepted hugs and smiled so much her cheeks felt ready to explode. This beauty-pageant business was tough stuff, especially since Lucky had never in her wildest dreams expected to win. She'd hadn't even wanted to win. But winning felt kind of nice, especially for the invisible flat-chested woman.

"I knew you could do it!" Earline hugged Lucky. "This lucky dress has never let me down. It was made for a winner!"

If only Lucky's prize were a hunky cowboy instead of a new saddle and a year's supply of hoof-and-nail cream. But, as usual, Lady Luck wasn't shining on her, she realized when Bennie rushed up to her and told her she'd just talked to Ulysses who said he'd just talked to Tyler who'd said he'd just talked to Helen. Bennie and Tyler were going back to Houston.

"It's all my fault!" Bennie started to cry again. "I fell and now Grandmother is mad, and so is Daddy, and this is my punishment for entering the stupid beauty pageant in the first place. How could I have had such a crazy idea?"

"You didn't. I did."

Bennie shook her head. "You can't take the blame again. And it won't matter anyway. It's settled. We're going back and that means you're not going to be my nanny anymore, and I was really hoping you would end up staying and—"

"That's not in the cards, baby." Lucky wiped the moisture from Bennie's cheek. "I was only temporary. You know that."

"This isn't fair," Bennie wailed. "It's not supposed to turn out like this. We're friends."

"And we'll always be friends, no matter how far apart we are, or if your father hires a dozen more nannies. You'll always be special to me and I'm really going to miss you." Bennie threw her arms around her and the tears Lucky had been fighting spilled over. "You're really special," Lucky whispered. "Always remember that. You're special and beautiful and…" *I love you, and I love your dad, and I love it here.* But she couldn't say any of those things. It would only make leaving more difficult. "I—I'm going to catch a ride with Earline," Lucky said instead, putting Bennie away from her. She dashed the wetness away and tried to gather her control.

"Don't cry," Bennie said.

"I'm not. I—I just have something in my eye." Lucky hurried away as fast as three-inch heels and a skintight straight dress allowed. She was going to save Tyler the trouble of firing her and leave tonight.

She already had a portion of her money. She could leave Tyler a note with an address where to send the rest. He would make good on his deal, she knew that, though she wouldn't blame him if he changed his mind, especially when he realized Lucky was responsible for tonight. Her letter would spell everything out. My idea. I'm the uncultured ditz. The harebrained schemer. No way would she let Bennie take the rap. Lucky could still see the shock on Helen's face that brief moment when they'd made eye contact. There'd be hell to pay for tonight.

She pushed her way through the crowd backstage in search of Earline.

Chicken, a voice whispered.

So? Better to be a chicken and leave before she made a fool of herself and cried in front of Tyler Grant.

Tough-as-nails Lucky Myers didn't cry. Crying was for sissies. Or babies. Or lonely women hopelessly in love for the first time in their life.

And Lucky didn't qualify, she told herself. She didn't.

SHE WAS LEAVING.

He'd known it when he'd found her missing from the festival. But somehow it hadn't seemed quite real. Now, as he stood at the open garage door and watched her fumble with her car keys, reality hit him like a fist in the gut.

"Darn it." She tried unsuccessfully to unlock the door of her cab.

"Sneaking off without saying goodbye?"

"Saving you the hassle of firing me." She tried the key again and missed by a good inch. "Just for the record, I didn't try to mess things up on purpose. I really thought Helen would be pleased when she saw Bennie looking so pretty and ladylike." She sniffled.

"Are you crying?"

She shook her head and swiped at her nose with a raggedy tissue. "Of course not."

"You are." He stepped forward, the knowledge drawing

him, touching something deep inside him that he'd tried so hard to bury. "You're crying."

"You must have been by the homemade-wine booth." She sniffled again. "You're imagining things. I never cry." She yanked open the car door.

"We need to talk, Lucky."

"Look, I didn't mean to make things worse for you," she said. "I wanted to make up for the tractor incident. I had no idea Helen would go ballistic when she saw Bennie—"

"Not about tonight. About you. Me…us."

"*Us?* Since when is there an us?"

"Since…since I took your—accepted your virginity. Now there's an us. A me. A you… By the way, you looked great tonight. You deserved to win."

"Thanks to you. You taught me that getting dressed up can be fun. But it's not me, Tyler. Some pretty clothes and a lot of makeup can't change who I am."

"Please don't cry."

"I'm *not* crying."

"It's okay. It's healthy. Women cry all the time."

"Look," she said, turning wide, bright eyes on him. The first of the festival's fireworks sizzled across the night sky in brilliant jags of blue and purple and red. Shadows played across her damp face, making her look vulnerable, despite her murderous gaze. "For the record, crying has nothing to do with being a woman. I can belch, cuss and spit with the best of them, you included, Tyler Grant, and don't you forget it." She climbed in and moved to close her door, but his hand blocked the way. "Now move it or lose it, buddy. I've got things to do."

"We're not through. We—"

"There is no we. You said yourself it would never work between us. I'm a tough-talking, gum-chewing cabdriver from the wrong side of the tracks. Hardly your type."

"Dammit, woman, you don't know what my type is."

"So tell me." Lucky gave him a pointed stare. A burst of green stars overhead revealed the wetness on her cheeks.

"You," he said truthfully. "You. A woman who's real. One who isn't afraid to butt heads with me. One who tells the truth and makes my daughter laugh. A woman who turns me inside out, and turns me on."

"*Used* to turn you on. The novelty wore off right after I gave and you accepted." The flood of multicolored Roman candle dazzle spilled past the open garage door. "You went slumming for a little while, and now it's back to country-club living—women with legs up to here, breasts out to there, designer clothes and a family name you can trace clear back to the prehistoric era—your type, buddy. Face it, Tyler. You want everything I'm not."

He laughed, a harsh, angry sound that stirred his blood as fiercely as her words. "With the way I'm feeling now, I'd definitely argue that. And for the record, your legs are pretty damned long. And pretty damned *pretty*." He grabbed her arm and in two strides pulled her to the door of the garage. Then he hauled her flush against him. "And I want you, Lucky. I miss you." Before she knew what was happening, he lifted her onto the trunk of the Chevy and pushed her dress clear up to her thighs.

"This doesn't solve anything," she murmured as his lips ate at hers. "I mean, it does solve one thing, but not the important things." She tugged at his shirt while he worked the zipper of her dress. "Not that you, uh, your...well, you know, isn't important. It is, and I want you and I—"

"Damn, but you talk too much, woman."

"Did you say woman?"

"Uh-huh."

She smiled. "That's what I thought you said." Then she met his lips in a bone-melting kiss that ended with her flat on her back, sprawled on the Chevy's trunk, fireworks bursting overhead. "I'm still not your type."

"Yeah, yeah. No breasts out to here." He pushed down the bodice of her dress and closed his hungry mouth over one nipple. He nibbled and suckled while she gasped and panted. "Or legs up to there." His hand traveled her leg, pushing material up until his fingers reached the silk-covered heat between her thighs.

"And the name," she murmured. "Don't forget the name."

He pulled away from her, staring deep into her eyes as he slid panties and panty hose down her legs and pulled them free. "*Lucky*. Your name is Lucky. I don't care about tracing it, or impressing people with it. I'm the only one that needs to be impressed." He glanced down at his straining denim. "And I'm pretty damned impressed right now." He ripped his shirt up and off, then worked at his jeans. The deft slide of fingers, the hiss of a zipper and he was ready. "You do this to me, Lucky."

"Any woman would do that. You're a normal, hot-blooded male. You automatically get aroused. I could be anyone." Even as she said the words, she heard the challenge in them. The eagerness for him to prove her wrong, to make her feel special. To make her feel like a desirable woman, for once in her life. Okay, so make that twice.

"No one makes me this crazy." He stroked his rigid length and desire spiraled through her. "No one makes me

ache this much, burn this hot. Just you.'' She heard the
conviction in his voice, saw the sincerity in his eyes, and
warmth filled her.

A warmth that had nothing to do with the sexual tension
gripping her body and everything to do with the undeniable
fact that she loved this man. She *loved* him.

''You really want me that much—'' He silenced the
question with an urgent kiss.

''Don't even think about doing that right now,'' he said
when he ended the kiss. ''I'm ready to explode, and if you
start all those innocent, breathy questions, I'm liable to explode right here and now, and I thought we'd go for someplace a little more private.''

But the thought of him pulling away from her for even
a few seconds was unbearable. She needed to touch him.
To feel him. Her hands skimmed his shoulders, clutched at
his muscles. ''This is private.''

''We're on top of a car.'' He kissed her long and hard.

''But everyone's still at the festival.''

''This is true.''

''And I really need you right now.''

''But we're outside.''

''You're outside.'' She sucked in a ragged breath.
''That's the problem. I need you inside. Now. *Please.*''

''You're the boss, honey.'' He pulled her to the edge of
the car and plunged into her with one deft stroke.

She sighed and he groaned, his forehead against hers,
eyes closed for a long moment. ''I've needed this for so
long,'' he murmured. ''I've needed you for so long. I've
been such a jerk.''

''I'll say.''

''I'm sorry, Lucky. I really am. Do you forgive me?''

He stared down at her, so desperate and unsure and her heart went out to him.

She smiled. And gasped. "Move it or lose it, buddy. It's not nice to keep a lady waiting."

"Yes, ma'am." He kissed her long and slow and deep, while his erection throbbed inside her. Anticipation skittered along her nerve endings, priming them, readying them for the devastating assault of feeling that was sure to follow.

He didn't disappoint her. He cupped her buttocks, rocked her against him. Slow at first. Then his fingers flexed, muscles bunched and he urged her closer, himself deeper. He moved her faster, his hips bucking, hers rocking. Faster and harder. Deeper and more desperate. Then it came. The heavens opened up, trumpets blared and the angels sang.

Heat flooded her, washing through, melting her until she collapsed against Tyler's sweat-slick, heaving chest. He drove deep one last time, groaned and clutched her fiercely. As they held each other, hearts beating a frenzy, breaths shallow and fierce, the sky faded to a serene black.

"The fireworks are over," she finally said, the statement true in more ways than one. Everyone would be home soon. Reality check. "We'd better get dressed."

He lifted his head to stare at her. "I don't care whose type you think you are. You...me...we'll make this work out for us."

Joy rushed through her, his words capturing her heart the way his strong arms captured her body. He wanted her with him, despite who she was, because of who she was.

"Will you marry me?"

"I think that's my line," he said.

"Then I accept."

"I'm not asking." He shook his head and moved away from her. "Dammit, Lucky. I can't. I want to, I would in a heartbeat, but I can't."

A sad smile lifted her mouth. "That's what I thought you'd say." She righted her dress, retrieved her panties and started to pull them on. Tyler fastened his jeans and reached for his shirt.

"We'll hook up in Houston," he said. "And I'll set you up in an apartment close by me. A nice high-rise or something."

She blinked back the sudden tears and tried to keep her voice steady. "I'm sorry, Tyler. It's all or nothing." What the hell was she saying? She loved him, she wanted him. So it wasn't marriage? It was the best offer anyone had made her in a long time. Try ever. So maybe he thought it wouldn't work now. The closer they became, the more hopelessly in love he fell, he'd start to see things her way. All she had to do was say yes.

"No. This would never work between us. I want what my parents had. Love. Endless, boundless, I'll-love-you-till-doomsday-and-beyond love."

Shrugging away, she started toward her cab. He caught her by the shoulders and forced her to face him. "I do love you."

"Not enough." She pulled away and surprisingly, he let her.

"Please, Lucky. Don't... I'll take care of your grandmother." He said the words as if he was negotiating a business deal instead of the rest of her life. Gone was the sexy cowboy who smiled and flirted and made her feel good inside. In his place was a cold, calculating businessman who didn't take no for an answer. Suddenly she realized how different they were.

It had nothing to do with looks or money or sophistication. They were different because they valued different things.

Tyler valued money and what it could buy him.

And Lucky valued her self-respect.

"You won't ever have to worry about another nursing-home payment." He ticked off the advantages. "I'll take care of both of you. You can quit your cab driving and finish your degree at the University of Houston. I'm offering you money and stability, Lucky. Everything." *Nothing.*

She didn't say a word. There was nothing to say. She walked toward her cab, praying with each step that her pride would hold together what was left of her heart before she turned and raced back to his arms. She was crazy. She should be jumping for joy, thanking the heavens. *He loved her!*

"Dammit, Lucky!"

She slid behind the steering wheel and slammed the door.

"I want to give you more," he said, following her. He leaned into the window. "I do."

A sad smile curved her lips as she stared up at him. "You're going to miss me, Tyler Grant." And then she kissed him, a slow, savoring kiss that ripped at her heart. "I—I have to go," she said as a car turned into the other side of the double driveway. Headlights blazed, illuminating Tyler's dark, troubled face.

His gaze darkened as he touched her cheek, his thumb catching a trickle of wetness.

"Yes," she admitted softly. "I'm crying." Then she

shoved the cab into reverse and left Tyler Grant staring after her.

"THAT WAS LUCKY," Mabel said, half a dozen blue ribbons pinned across the front of her blouse.

"She's really gone," Bennie whispered.

"It's about time," Helen added.

"Oh, pooh-pooh," Julius exclaimed. "I wanted more pictures."

"You all right, son?" Ulysses asked.

"No." He turned to stride out to the barn. He was lonely, heartbroken and mad as hell at himself. Good Lord, he'd offered to *buy* her. What had he been thinking?

He hadn't been thinking, he'd been feeling. Desperation had closed in on him and he'd reacted the only way he knew how when it came to the people he loved.

He'd tried to buy his mother's acceptance by marrying into enough old money to put a sizable dent in the national deficit. He'd tried to buy his father's forgiveness by putting Reata back together. And he'd tried to buy Lucky's love by offering to care for her and her grandmother.

All last-ditch efforts. All failures.

Lucky couldn't be bought. Or changed. Or compromised.

He'd tried to do all three, but the funny thing was, he loved her even more because she'd refused him. She was Lucky.

And she'd left him.

"YOU MADE HER LEAVE!"

Bennie's angry voice drew Tyler down the darkened hallway to the library. He started to open the door, then he heard Helen.

"She shouldn't have been here in the first place, Bernadette. She's hardly qualified to care for you."

"She's more than qualified. She was my friend, Grandmother. My *friend*. How could you make Daddy fire her?"

"I didn't make your father do anything. He agrees with me and wants what's best for you. And I don't appreciate your tone of voice, Bernadette Willemina Bell."

"I'm a *Grant*," Bennie said. "I'm not a Bell. I never wanted to be one. I love you, but I won't ever be what you and Daddy want me to be. I'm different, and so is Lucky. But there's nothing wrong with that."

"I see the sooner you return to Houston, the better."

"I don't want to go," Bennie said, her chin rising a notch. "I like it here."

"But Smithston..."

"I never wanted to go to Smithston. I want to go to school in Ulysses." Her voice broke. "I know I'm not all the things you want me to be," Bennie went on. "But can't you love me anyway? I try to like the same things as you. That's why I entered the beauty pageant. I wanted to please you and Daddy, to make you both proud of me." Bennie was crying full force.

Tyler didn't blame her. He felt like crying himself.

I won't ever be what you and Daddy want me to be. You and Daddy... *Daddy*. He pushed open the door and walked inside just as Helen wrapped her arms around Bennie.

"Oh, sweetheart, I am proud of you," Helen said, and for the first time, Tyler saw a tear roll down his mother-in-law's cheek. It stopped him dead in his tracks. "I don't mean to make you feel awkward, dear," she went on. "I simply want the best for you. Your father and I both do, that's why we're all going back to Houston—"

"We're not going," Tyler cut in. "We're staying right here." He faced his daughter. "You did all of this for me, didn't you? The piano lessons, the French, the dresses... You really have no interest in those things, do you?"

She stared guiltily at her feet and wiped her eyes. "You're always telling me, 'Wear a dress, Bennie. Act like a lady.' I thought you wanted me to like all those things, to be like Mama."

"Oh, baby." He pulled her into his arms. "Your mother was your mother, and you're you. I don't care what you like as long as you're happy. That's all I ever wanted. I don't want you to feel torn between me and Helen, between our different ways of life. I want you to have everything you want."

"But I already do." She stared up at him through glistening eyes. "I have you and Granddaddy, Grandfather and Grandmother." Her gaze went to Helen. "I love you, Grandmother, but I also love jeans and ratty sneakers and pet lizards. Maybe I won't like those things when I grow up. Maybe I'll like tea and museums and opera. Maybe not. But I want you to love me anyway." Her gaze lifted to Tyler's. "I want you to love me."

"I couldn't love you more, sweetheart."

"Then bring Lucky back. I love her, and so do you."

"What?" Helen's shocked voice drew both their gazes.

Tyler smiled down at his daughter and gave her a wink. "Can you excuse us, honey?" Bennie nodded and left the room, and Tyler turned to Helen. "Bennie and I are staying here. No more nannies, and Bernadette goes to school in town. You can fight me if you want to, but I'm asking you not to. For Bennie's sake."

"If I do, I'll lose her, won't I?"

"Yes, and I don't want that. You're her grandmother, Helen. You should be a part of her life."

For the first time, Tyler saw Helen's shoulders actually slump. She looked...vulnerable. He did a double take. Yeah, vulnerable. Who would've figured?

"I'm very headstrong, Tyler," she went on in a defeated voice. "I know that, it's just that I've always had to be. My father expected it of me and I couldn't let him down. My father was strict with me, he pushed me hard, always afraid I wouldn't fit in, that someone would realize a Bell wasn't so perfect."

"No child is perfect."

"His would have been. That's why I had to be. No one could know that the great Samuel Bell couldn't father a child." She stared up at him, a sad look on her face. "I'm adopted, Tyler. I know that doesn't make up for my pushiness, but perhaps it helps you understand a little better why I am the way I am. I had to live up to the Bell name, so no one would ever doubt that I was Samuel Bell's daughter, so he wouldn't doubt it."

"Nan never told me."

"She never knew. No one does. Just my parents and Merle, and now you." She wiped at a tear. A melancholy smile lit her eyes. "Nan always said I was a snob, and she was right." She closed her eyes. "I miss her so much." Her expression grew serious. "Do you really love this Lucky person?"

He nodded. "More than you can imagine."

"Well, then." She took a deep breath and wiped at her ears. "You do what you have to do. Be happy, Tyler," she said, patting his shoulder. "And keep Bernadette happy. And this old snob will take herself home and butt out of your business.''

''Praise be, it's about time.'' Ulysses stood in the doorway and munched a bowl of ice cream. ''Two miracles in one night. That must be some kinda record, eh, son?''

''Dad,'' Tyler said in warning.

''Don't trouble yourself, Tyler,'' Helen said. ''I can handle *that*.'' She jabbed a finger in Ulysses's direction and fire lit her eyes. ''It'll be a pleasure to leave you behind. No, no, I take that back. It would be a pleasure to leave you six feet under.''

Ulysses waggled his eyebrows. ''Gettin' spunky on me, huh, Helen?''

''I am not and have never been spunky. Bold, yes. Self-assured, of course—''

''Stuck-up, and how!''

''Hateful man,'' she huffed.

''Ugly woman.''

''Old billy goat.''

''Snooty know-it-all.''

''You two should get a room,'' Tyler said. His father hooted, Helen bristled, and Mabel appeared in the doorway with a broom. He left the three of them to their bickering and headed down the hall to pack. Now to set things right.

14

"LUCKY?" Stella's concerned voice came over the CB radio as Lucky sat, her engine idling, in the cabbie lane outside of Houston's Intercontinental Airport.

"I'm here, Stella. What do you need?"

"Just checking on you. Me and the boys have been worried about you the past two days since you got back. You have to snap out of this. How about bowling this weekend? We're playing the Burnin' Rubber Bald Eagles and they've got a new guy on their team. Young, single, cute. And I heard from Marge, the dispatcher at Burnin' Rubber, he's in the market for a wife. Perfect for you."

For the old Lucky. But she was different now. She'd given up her manhunting aspirations. She'd already found a man, caught him and turned him loose. She stunk at hunting.

"I'm really not up to meeting anyone right now."

"Come on, Lucky. You have to pick yourself up and get on with your life."

"I will," she promised. "Soon." But at the rate she was going, she'd be too heavy to pick herself up.

Yesterday alone, she'd consumed an entire quart of ice cream, half a dozen doughnuts and a chocolate-fudge cake Buster had brought over to the nursing home for her granny. While two days wasn't enough time to gain any real weight, she'd be fat and miserable in no time.

Right now she was just miserable.

All or nothing…

If only nothing didn't feel like…well, nothing.

The back door of her cab opened, shattering Lucky's thoughts. Thankfully. "Where to, mister?"

"An all-night wedding chapel."

"Excuse me?" Lucky pushed up the brim on her baseball cap and stared into her rearview mirror. A sly, devilish grin stared back at her and her heart kick-started before racing forward.

"I said, an all-night wedding chapel. I'm getting married. At least, I think I am." Tyler's voice was deep, rich and music to her ears. "I want you with me at Reata, as my wife. You can finish school, teach, fix cars, wreck tractors, do whatever you want, as long as you do it with me." He sat the familiar green lizard on the back of the seat between them. "And Marlon."

Her heart slammed against her ribs, threatening to burst free. Calm, girl. Make sure he's for real. She took a deep breath and stroked Marlon with her fingertip. His huge eyes closed and he sat there, lazy as ever. "What about Helen?"

"She's not marrying you. I am. At least, I hope I am."

"I mean, won't she have something to say about it?"

"Yeah. Congratulations." At her raised eyebrow, he added, "Okay, she'll say it grudgingly, but I don't care."

"I'm not a prime example of ladyhood. What about Bennie?"

"Bennie loves you, and she isn't the least bit interested in being a lady. It was all an act."

"I could have told you that."

"So why didn't you?"

"Would you have believed me?"

"Maybe." When she raised her eyebrow again, he added, "Okay, probably not. I told you, I'm only human. I've got faults. I'm stubborn and headstrong."

"And domineering and blind and infuriating and—"

"I get the picture. I'm all those things, and more. And I want you to marry me anyway. I know you covered for Bennie—the tractor thing, the beauty pageant—they were all her ideas. She told me. That took a lot of guts to take Helen's wrath. I appreciate it, and I'm sorry."

"You're welcome, and don't be. I love Bennie."

"Then marry me and you can spend the rest of your life loving her." His voice took on a quiet note. "I want you, Lucky. More than I've ever wanted anything before. Marry me."

"I don't know." She chewed a fingernail and eyed him in the rearview mirror. "You're not exactly my type."

"And what is your type?"

You. But she wouldn't say that, not yet. Not after the pain, and extra calories he'd put her through.

"Well…" She turned on him, her knees on the front seat as she stared at him, dressed in faded jeans and a faded denim shirt. She quickly noted the dark shadow covering his jaw, the exhaustion carving his perfect features. Good. He looked every bit as bad as she felt. "Well, you're not exactly the kind of guy I'd take home to my granny."

He gave her a wicked grin. "Not enough of a gentleman?"

"Too much of a gentleman for someone like me. I don't know the first thing about what's in season or who the hottest designers are. My idea of a social event is an evening of bingo at the senior citizens' home. I don't know fine wine from Kool-Aid or a Monet from a Picasso. I wear white after Labor Day and I've never vacationed in the Hamptons or been mentioned in the society pages or—''

Two strong, warm fingers touched her lips, cutting her off. ''I don't care about any of those things. I never did, I just got so caught up in making Helen happy I forgot that for a little while. It's not what's on the outside that counts—your clothes, your friends, your bank account. It's what's on the inside—a good heart, a kind and giving nature. I know what a real lady is, Lucky. Hell, I've always known. It's you.'' The words were quiet, *desperate,* and she couldn't refuse.

She dived over the back seat, straight into his arms, his life, this cowboy who made her feel wanted and wicked and every bit a lady for the first time in her life.

His lips captured hers and Lucky closed her eyes to the wonderful feeling. Heat skirted her senses, coaxing them to life. She felt the tickling on the inside of her thigh.

''Not now, Marlon.'' She giggled and squirmed. ''Tyler's liable to get jealous...'' She opened her eyes to see the lizard staring at her from his perch on the back of the seat.

''It's not Marlon this time.'' Tyler moved his fingers for emphasis. ''It's me.''

She gasped and smiled. ''He's been giving you lessons.''

''I've been giving him lessons. So tell me,'' he said, his lips hovering near hers, so close she felt the warm rush of his breath. ''Are we going to get lucky tonight?''

''You, cowboy, are going to get Lucky *every* night, and Marlon can find his own date.''

Harlequin Romance®

Delightful
Affectionate
Romantic
Emotional

Tender
Original

Daring
Riveting
Enchanting
Adventurous
Moving

Harlequin Romance®—
capturing the world you dream of...

HARLEQUIN®
Makes any time special ®

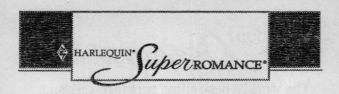

...there's more to the story!

Superromance.
A *big* satisfying read about unforgettable characters. Each month we offer *six* very different stories that range from family drama to adventure and mystery, from highly emotional stories to romantic comedies—and much more! Stories about people you'll believe in and care about. Stories too compelling to put down....

Our authors are among today's *best* romance writers. You'll find familiar names and talented newcomers. Many of them are award winners—and you'll see why!

If you want the biggest and best in romance fiction, you'll get it from Superromance!

Emotional, Exciting, Unexpected...

HARLEQUIN®
Makes any time special®

Visit us at www.eHarlequin.com

HSDIR1

HARLEQUIN *Presents*

The world's bestselling romance series...
The series that brings you your favorite authors,
month after month:

Helen Bianchin...Emma Darcy

Lynne Graham...Penny Jordan

Miranda Lee...Sandra Marton

Anne Mather...Carole Mortimer

Susan Napier...Michelle Reid

and many more uniquely talented authors!

Wealthy, powerful, gorgeous men...
Women who have feelings just like your own...
The stories you love, set in exotic, glamorous locations...

HARLEQUIN *Presents*

Seduction and passion guaranteed!

HPDIR1

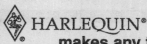